Reclaiming Ter Chadain

by

C. S. Yelle

The Protector of Ter Chadain
Book One

Argus Enterprises International, Inc.
North Carolina***New Jersey

For Alli,
I hope you enjoy the adventure.
CS Yelle

Reclaiming Er Chadain © 2011
All rights reserved by Craig Yelle

No part of this book may be reproduced or transmitted in any form or by any means, graphic, electronic, or mechanical, including photocopying, recording, taping, or by any informational storage retrieval system without prior permission in writing from the publisher.

A-Argus Better Book Publishers, LLC

For information:
A-Argus Better Book Publishers, LLC
9001 Ridge Hill Street
Kernersville, North Carolina 27285
www.a-argusbooks.com

ISBN: 978-0-9846348-1-1
ISBN: 0-9846348-1-9

Book Cover designed by Dubya

Printed in the United States of America

DEDICATION

For my wife Jenny who gave me the courage to dream again. For my boys, Karsen, Baxter, and Kasey who always believed. For my daughter Amy, who doubted. For my reader, Mike and his wife Kathy, whose encouragement, insight, and patience kept me hoping. For Steve and Yvonne who are always in my corner. For Jane and her rock solid voice of reason. And for my nephew Ben and his excitement for writing.

Chapter 1

Leaves rustled overhead. Sweat glistened on Logan's chest and arms as he threw another log into the woodpile. Perspiration dripped from the end of his nose. His long, dark hair clung to his face and neck as he worked.

"Logan, that's enough."

Logan turned. His father walked up to him, reached for the boy's shirt hanging on a broken branch of a nearby tree, and tossed it to him.

Slipping it on, Logan smiled.

"Your mother wanted you home early today for your lessons."

Logan nodded. "We're learning about court in the royal palace and how the Zele Magus and Viri Magus always struggle for control of the ruler's favor." His voice trembled, excited, as he buttoned his shirt.

"She always did have a good handle on the inner workings of those kinds of things when she was at court. I had no time for that."

"Is that why you left when you got married?"

"Your mother was a lady in the royal court. A soldier has no need for royal court, my wants were simple: defend Ter Chadain from threats within as well as from invading forces. I wanted a different life for my family."

"But you caught mother's eye anyway?" Logan smiled knowingly.

"Don't you ever get tired of that story?"

Logan shook his head.

"It will have to wait. Your mother is expecting you and we can hear that story again by the fire tonight." The man turned and headed off towards his ax leaning against a tree.

"Aren't you coming?" Logan asked after him.

"There is one more tree I want to take down today, I'll be in shortly."

"I'll help you and go in later." Logan followed after him.

"And risk your mother getting upset with me for keeping you away from your lessons?" He chuckled. "I don't think so. Get going and I'll be in after a while."

Logan turned back to the cart filled with wood to take it home. A loud hiss came from his right and then a thud.

Logan ducked.

Arrows.

Twigs and leaves crunched on the forest floor. Logan turned in the direction of his father. A crack echoed not far off, but Logan saw only shadows and trees.

Logan ran.

He crashed through bramble, shoving away limbs and leaves. He looked right, left, and then lunged around an old trunk. He saw the boot first. The foot turned at a sharp angle.

His father lay in the mud.

Logan knelt, carefully rolling him onto his back. An arrow rose up out of his chest like a beacon. Logan quickly felt for a pulse.

It was faint.

Another hissing rushed to his ears as an arrow lodged in a tree nearby, the shaft vibrating. Logan dropped to the sticks and leaves, the dirt and decaying matter stirring as his breathing came in short bursts.

Feeling a soft touch at his side he turned. Pain rippled within his father's deep blue orbs. "Run," he gasped. And then his eyes lost their focus, staring past Logan.

"Father," the young man cried softly, but his father didn't hear.

Another arrow flying overhead sent Logan into motion.

Logan burst to full speed, moving from side to side, making himself as difficult a target as possible. Several arrows struck trees around him as he ran, their vibrations singing a demented tune.

Just then, a horrible thought sent him stumbling.

Home!

Logan pushed himself, darting around obstacles with the experience of many years in these woods. Rounding the large oak at the corner of the house, something felt terribly wrong.

The doors to both the barn and house stood open with no signs of his sisters or mother in the yard.

He rushed into the house, shouldering the door, slamming it against the wall. The echo bounced off the interior as he came to a sliding halt. His mother lay on the kitchen floor. A large pool of crimson blood flowered around her, her own kitchen knives protruding from her stomach. Her eyes clenched tight against her attacker.

Logan knelt, pausing only to bow his head, and then sped to the rear of the house and out the back door in search of his sisters. Almost immediately he halted, holding back bile.

Senia slumped over the side of the well. Blood ran down her legs, pooling at her feet. Touching her shoulder caused her head to loll to one side, revealing the long, deep slit in her throat. Her hazel eyes stared off, her mouth opened wide in her last scream.

Hairs rose on the back of his neck, nausea flowing over him.

The blood dripped, dripped, dripped into the water below.

Logan stumbled frantically over the tufts of grass in the yard, tears blurring his vision as he raced to the barn.

He staggered inside, falling on his hands and knees, scrambling urgently to his feet. Moving slower, his eyes adjusting to the darkness within, he crept from one stall to another, wincing at each opening at the prospect of what he might discover.

Reaching the far end of the barn, he heard a soft weeping coming from above.

"Teah?" he whispered.

"Logan?" his sister asked.

"Hurry, we have to get out of here."

"What about Mother and Senia?"

"I'm sorry, Teah. It's too late."

"No! They can't be dead. Father, what about Father?"

"Teah, we have to get out of here. Now! They're still around and I think right behind me. We need to go."

The girl's wavy blond locks peeked over the edge of the hayloft; the tears welled up in her big blue eyes. "Just you and me?"

"Come on," he urged, holding up his arms. Sliding lightly into his large hands, she fell into his embrace. He kissed her forehead.

A too familiar hissing reached his ears. He flung them to the ground, arrows sinking into an overhead beam, quivering where his head was moments before.

"Get them," the order came from outside the barn.

They scrambled to their feet and ran out the back door, squinting as they burst into the field behind the barn. Logan and Teah ran between the tall stalks of corn, changing directions often and putting as much distance between them and the farm.

The stalks caught at their shoulders, twisting their torsos violently from one side to the other as they frantically pushed through the rows.

The sound of pursuit headed away and they cautiously slowed their pace.

Teah leaned heavily against Logan. The sun touched the horizon, sending burst of reds and oranges into the sky in sweeping expanses. It would be dark soon and the clear sky meant it would be cold tonight. Both wore only light summer clothing. Logan's brown trousers were ripped; Teah held her muddied cotton dress up from ground. Goosebumps dotted both of their arms. Dropping back, Teah wrapped her arms around herself, rubbing her shoulders.

Logan looked back at his sister as they moved along. He slowed enough to walk by her side, placing a comforting arm across her shoulder.

Teah stumbled, fell, and lay motionless with her face to the earth.

Logan reached down, but she pulled her arm free from his hand, spinning on him.

"Who were those men? Why would they want to hurt us? What have we ever done to make them want to do that to us?" Her body shook as tears ran down her cheeks. The fierceness in her eyes caused Logan to draw back.

"I don't know. I didn't get a chance to see them. They killed Father and chased me back to the farm."

"I saw them." Teah whispered as if afraid they would appear. "They were all in red uniforms silver markings on the chest and silver helmets. Like the ones mother told us about in our lessons."

"That doesn't make any sense," Logan admitted. "Why would royal soldiers be out here trying to kill us? What are we to them?"

He looked across the fields. "We have to get to Tumbleweed on the other side of the Latrel Plains. Father made me promise that if trouble ever arose, we would go find Grinwald. He made me promise not to talk to anyone else. Just find Grinwald."

"He never mentioned anything to me," Teah said, "Certainly not anything about this Grinwald." She shrugged. "We don't have much choice, do we?" Getting to her feet, she stood motionless.

"Are you tired?" he asked, taking her hand. Their eyes met again as the anger washed from her.

"I guess I'm past tired," she said hollowly. "Why?"

"I don't think we should stop, but it doesn't look like you can go much longer. Do you think you can go for a while?"

She shrugged again, stepping up next to him, her head hanging down.

"We should be there by morning." He turned and began walking, Teah keeping pace silently.

The setting sun blazed in the sky as they came to a rise. It beckoned them to walk into it, to start over without looking back to the past. But Logan did stop, looking back to the farm as his sister turned with him. An ominous glow haloed the dwelling as fire destroyed the last remnants of the homestead, forcing them to move forward into whatever might lay ahead.

No home to go back to now, he thought. He turned, angrily wiping tears from his eyes. "Whoever is responsible for this will suffer a very painful death. This I swear." He turned back to the west setting his jaw defiantly and pushing on.

Teah walked by his side, often stumbling on the uneven matted prairie grass. Each time she picked herself up slowly and started off again as Logan watched and waited patiently. An hour later, she collapsed in a heap forcing Logan to pick her up in his arms and carry her.

Logan had carried his sister for a long while before he looked down. She was looking back at him.

"You can put me down now."

"That's all right. I can carry you for a while longer."

"No it isn't. You need to conserve your strength if we are to reach Tumbleweed. I know I can't carry you." She pushed against his arms, forcing him to set her down or drop her clumsily.

"I guess you're right." He stretched his arms and back. "I am kind of tired. We have to keep moving in case they pick up our tracks."

"Agreed," Teah said, striding steadily ahead of him.

The sun rose at their backs the next morning. Logan walked with his head down plodding along. Walking by his side, Teah placed her hand on his arm as a settlement came into view. He raised his head, Tumbleweed sat before him at the western edge of the Latrel Plain. A discouraged moan escaped his lips. There were many houses in the settlement.

"How are we going to find Grinwald with so many people?" Teah asked.

"I don't know," Logan puzzled. "Hopefully we can find someone who knows of him here."

"Father told you not to talk to anyone else." Teah gave a sigh and her eyes glistened with tears.

Logan wearily reached around and squeezed her as tightly as he had the strength to. "I miss them, too. We better keep going." He turned and began to walk, his shoulders slumped heavily and his arms hanging limply by his sides. Teah trudged alongside.

The land rolled up and down for the last mile, each rise a mountain that strained their endurance. Their thighs burned, their lips cracked. The long green prairie grass ripped at their legs, holding each step back as the dead dry mass of built-up growth crunched under their feet. They pushed the tall blades away from their faces, infuriating a bevy of insects from their hiding places to wait out the day's heat. They neared the outskirts of town when Logan fell to his knees. He wobbled there for a moment and fell to the ground with a cloud of dust.

It was as if he were inside a dream as the ground rushed towards him, overwhelming him with darkness.

Chapter 2

Logan smelled the familiar earthy odor of the forest floor as he slowly opened his eyes, expecting to see the cold staring eyes of his father. Instead he lay on a soft bed in an earthen house filled with bright candle and firelight.

Logan pressed his eyes closed, trying to clear his mind. He sat up with a start, looking wide-eyed around the room for his sister.

Teah turned from her place in front of the hearth. "Logan!" She sprang to her feet, moving over to hug him tightly.

"Where are we?" he asked, keeping her close.

"We're at the town healer's house. When you collapsed people watching us came out to help. They brought us here and he has been taking care of you."

"How long have we been here?"

"All day; you were exhausted."

"Where is the healer now?" he asked, looking around the small dwelling and seeing no one else.

"I' m right here, young man," a man said, coming through the door.

He was about his father's age with a trimmed grey beard, short salt-and-pepper hair, and glasses that sat at the end of his nose precariously, threatening to topple off at any instant. He was of slight build and about a head taller than Teah.

The healer came forward, feeling Logan's head gently.

"Seem to be doing much better now. Are you hungry? I was out getting some dinner." He held up a freshly killed rabbit.

Teah and Logan nodded and the man smiled widely, moving over to a counter in the kitchen and beginning to prepare the rabbit for dinner.

"You are Logan and Teah Saolto. Your sister explained a little bit about your ordeal when they brought you here, but I was wondering if you could fill in a couple of gaps in her story for me."

The man looked over his shoulder; Logan nodded.

"You were attacked and forced to flee?"

Again Logan nodded.

"Did you get a good look at the men who attacked your?" the man asked, walking over to him.

"I was too busy running for my life to get a good look at them." Regret hardened his voice.

"I saw them," Teah added. The healer and Logan turned to her. Her face burned. "They wore all red with silver breast plates that had a large tree on it. Each had a helmet of silver with a large red feather on top, like the ones Mother told us the royal army wears." Teah looked to Logan, pain etched on her face.

"What happened to you and your father?" The healer asked as Logan turned slowly back to him. "Your sister said you were out cutting wood in the forest."

"I had just finished stacking wood on the cart when I heard a strange sound. When I ran to where I last saw my father, he was lying on the ground with an arrow in his chest."

Teah gasped. Her face went pale white and her lips turned a dull blue. Logan gripped her hand.

"I ran home and found Mother in the kitchen and then Senia by the well." He chose his words carefully not to cause more pain for his sister.

"I heard Mother greet someone riding up when I was in the barn," Teah added, staring off at something in the unseen distance. "I was about to come out and see who had arrived when she and Senia began to scream. Mother's screams stopped suddenly."

Teah took a long breath and let it out slowly. "Then I saw Senia running. She tried to get to the barn, but two men grabbed her and held her until two other men and a woman came out of the house to the well."

"They all wore the red and silver as you described?" The man leaned in closer.

"No," Teah shook her head. The woman wore a deep red cloak with a hood. The hood was thrown back, so I saw her long blonde hair and blue eyes. Even so far away her eyes scared me as she questioned Senia."

Teah shivered and Logan placed a comforting arm around her.

"The woman asked Senia her name, but she was too frightened to speak at first. The woman slapped her, asking her again. When she said it was Senia, the woman gave the men a nod, and they began to grab at her, laughing."

Tears began running down Teah's cheeks, which she swiped

futilely. "The woman stopped the men. She asked where Logan and father were. When Senia didn't respond the woman slapped her so hard her head snapped backwards. Senia said you were chopping wood in the forest."

Teah looked up at Logan as he held her. Her mouth and face contorted with pain. "The woman turned away saying, 'No time for play, men, finish her quickly and move to the forest,' and kept walking."

Teah shook and sobbed, pressing her head into Logan's shoulder. The next words came in shaking gasps. "Senia screamed. One man stabbed her in the stomach, while another took her by the hair and slit her throat, then flung her against the well. I ran to the loft until Logan came."

Logan held Teah tightly with one arm, wiping away tears of rage and disgust. He cleared his throat, glancing at the old man. "After I reached Teah in the barn, we ran into the field and lost our pursuers in the corn."

The healer sat silently, frowning with his hand stroking his chin.

"What is it?" Logan finally asked.

"How old are you now, boy?" The man asked.

Scowling, Logan ran a hand through his hair. "What does that matter, our family has just been killed by what sounds like the King's army?"

"We will be sixteen in a few hours," Teah spoke up, glancing at her brother, her voice soft yet firm.

Logan turned to her with a start. "I've been asleep that long?"

"Just as I suspected," the man shook his head.

"Suspected what?" Logan asked.

"They were hoping to kill you before you reached the age. They know of the prophecy, and once you reached sixteen years old, it would be nearly impossible to do so. They will still be searching and eventually come here for you. We can only hope that Caldora is looking elsewhere."

"Caldora? The woman who was at our home?" Teah asked.

"She is much more than just a woman. She is the Zele Magus advisor for King Englewood. It is believed she is the most magically powerful Zele Magus in Ter Chadain." The man stood and began to pace.

Teah's eyes widened. "You mean she's one of those sorceresses that mother told us about, one of those women that live in the Zele Citadel in Ceait?"

"Your mother spoke to you of such things?" The healer stopped before her, mouth open.

"She taught us about all the things she encountered while at court in Cordlain during our daily lessons," Logan told him. "Why would they want to kill us?"

"Not Teah, just you."

"Why would they want to kill me?" Logan pressed. "And how do you know all this?"

"I believe your father may have mentioned me." He turned with a muted smile.

"You're Grinwald?" Logan's eyebrows rose.

"I'm Grinwald. We've been waiting thirteen years for you. You are the protector."

Logan shook his head. "I'm no protector." He raised his hands high. "I am definitely not the legendary hero mother told us about," he added sternly looking to his sister. "We had lessons about the protector, and how one would appear when a queen from the Lassain lineage was not on the throne. We are Saolto. Our father was a soldier in the Ter Chadain army and our mother was a lady in the royal court."

Grinwald shook his head, his eyes softening. He dropped to one knee, bowing his head and sweeping out his hands. "Of Lassain lineage you both are." He raised his eyes to Teah before dropping them again. "And you, my young lady, are the next Queen of Ter Chadain."

Teah and Logan stared at one another.

"I know this is very confusing," Grinwald said.

Teah pressed her fingers into Logan's palm. His grip tightened, drawing her closer. Their lips thinned, and Logan's eyes narrowed at this old man beseeching them. Teah shivered. Logan slowly ran his hands through his hair, drawing a deep breath through clenched teeth. Teah looked nervously to him, placing a calming hand upon his arm, and then back to the man kneeling before them.

"I'm at both your service," Grinwald said. "I've been preparing for this day for thirteen years. That was when I delivered you to the house on the edge of Treebridge Forest and came to live here. We all knew in order for you to survive, you needed to get away from civilization. Your real parents, Queen Gianna

Lassain and Gaston were killed a few years after you and Teah were born. The powers laying claim to the throne of Ter Chadain knew if they killed the entire royal line at once, they would rule forever. I was given the charge of protecting the two of you if the royal family came under attack. We fled the palace when the attack came, waiting here in Tumbleweed until I could be certain of what happened. When word reached me your parents were indeed dead, I proceeded with my plan to hide you."

"Why you?" Logan asked.

"Because, my dear boy, I was your parent's Viri Magus Advisor."

"You're a Viri Magus?" Teah gaped. "You're a wizard?"

He stood and gave a flourishing bow. "Lucias Grinwald, High Viri Magus of Ter Chadain at you service, Your Majesty."

He noted their frightened expressions and gave a light chuckle.

"Yes, you might call me a wizard, but surely you know there is nothing untoward or unnatural about our practice. The Magus embraces the world of magic all around. Taking the natural magic and bending it to our will. Some people might refer to us as wizards or sorceresses, but I am a well-trained member of a society who takes the teaching of magic very seriously."

Teah examined Logan from the corner of her eye. His back was rigid—as was hers.

The wizard beckoned with his hand. "How much do you know of us—or of the Zele Magus? I imagine your foster parents were thorough in their instruction."

Teah said nothing, refraining from even biting her lip. Logan drew in a breath silently, which sent a vibration through Teah's hand. Yes, they knew of the orders. The Viri Magus—the male order; the Zele Magus—the female order. Long ago, Zele Magus and Viri Magus used their powers together to accomplish feats for the queen and the country, but that art became lost over the centuries when the dangers were exposed. Many inexperienced Viri and Zele Magus lost their lives trying to master the blending of powers in order to create the wonders the unified magic had done in the past. Their bodies were left like burnt out husks, the magic scorching them from the inside, or they would simply explode. The entire city of Tourist was leveled by the unskilled attempt at the blending, so it was now forbidden.

Logan reacted first. "We are schooled in some basic information about the Viri Magus and the Zele Magus." He stroked Teah's hair, creating an opportunity for her to look at him. He stared hard into her eyes. Slowly, she nodded—they would not divulge how much they knew. Teah breathed in and softened her expression, turning to Grinwald and nodding with a small smile.

"So I have royal blood and Teah is going to be the queen," Logan said. "That would make me a prince, wouldn't it?"

Grinwald nodded.

"I don't understand. Why would that make me the protector?"

"Under normal circumstances you would just be a prince, but every five hundred years or so, a defender is needed—a man of royal blood and of mythical proportions."

"Mythical proportions, what does that mean?"

"It means you have been given the ability, by the powers that be, to safeguard your beloved sister like no one else can. That means you have been given the powers of the protector."

"I don't have any of those powers," Logan reasoned, looking to Teah.

"On the contrary, you will get your powers when you turn sixteen. It is very exact. It is as if you are given a wealth of knowledge and abilities from all generations of protectors who have come before you. So I have read."

"So you've read?" Logan asked, turning to share Teah's incredulous look.

"I haven't met a protector before you. Lift up your night shirt," Grinwald urged, moving off to a small desk in the corner. "It begins at sunset on the eve of your sixteenth birthday." He came back carrying a large book.

Logan reluctantly lifted up his bed clothing.

The healer pointed at the boy's chest with a crooked finger.

Teah's and Logan's eyes followed. Teah gasped, Logan's eyes widened. Over his left breast glimmered two silver swords crossed above a crown.

"Where did that come from?" Logan exclaimed, covering the mark with his hands. His hands pulled away as if the image was on fire. "It's cold, like metal."

"It's been there all your life, waiting for this time to become known. It has been this way over the centuries."

Grinwald held up the large tan book, showing a matching image to Logan's tattoo on the cover. The words below read:

"The Protector's Prophecy." He then propped the book against his waist, opened it, and read: "If the true bloodline does not rule Ter Chadain, the Protector shall appear and reclaim the throne for the rightful Queen."

The book quivered against his gut.

"You are that protector." He looked at Logan. "It is always a blood relation because that makes the bond stronger between queen and protector." He then looked at Teah. "The bond between you and your brother will be even stronger since you are twins and, in the history of the protectors, siblings always make the connection that much more powerful."

When neither Teah nor Logan responded, Grinwald sighed, forcing a smile.

"You see, over two thousand years ago Tera Lassain came to Ter Chadain from Caltoria across the sea with a group of 'magicals.' Tera is said to be the most powerful sorceress who has ever lived."

"And since Tera and the other magicals were escaped slaves from Caltoria, the Caltorians attempted to invade Ter Chadain to recapture what they saw was rightfully theirs. Tera was the emperor's personal slave and he vowed to take every magical back to Caltoria and make them pay for their defiance," Teah added.

"That's correct. The emperor was so angry with Tera for uniting the smaller duchies of Ter Chadain against him, he swore to take any magicals he could from Ter Chadain no matter if they were descendants from the escaped slaves or not," Grinwald said.

Teah stood up, holding her head high, pushing out her chest a bit, and giving Grinwald a confident smirk as the man stared at her blankly. "The Caltorian's persistence made it necessary for Tera to create a spell that kept the invaders from landing on Ter Chadain shores. As long as a queen of Lassain lineage sat upon the throne, Ter Chadain was safe from Caltorian aggression. It is said that this was the greatest magical creation anyone has ever perpetrated."

Grinwald smiled shaking his head then raised a finger to Teah who placed her hands on her hips. "As time passed, many tried to bring down the ruling Lassains and finally someone succeeded. It was during the time of exile and war between Ter Chadain and Caltoria, that Tera created a spell to aid her in reclaiming the throne. It is that spell coursing through your veins that drives you in the direction you must now proceed. It is that magic which allows for the creation of a protector when a Lassain is not on the throne of Ter Chadain. It is that magic that will allow you to reclaim Ter Chadain and expel the invaders from Caltoria. And that spell is arguably the greatest magical accomplishment of all time."

Logan spoke, still holding his hand against the image on his chest. "It has to be nearly four hundred years since a protector has been in Ter Chadain."

"Five hundred years," the Viri Magus corrected, opening the book to another page and showing Logan first and then Teah. Grinwald traced the family tree depicted on the pages. "First there was Queen Tera and Bastion Lassain. The Lassain line then continued in power unbroken until Queen Lonavette was deposed three hundred years later and her Uncle, Stalwart Lassain, became her protector. All was peaceful for over six hundred years when Queen Caderal was overthrown and her cousin Falcone Lassain became not only her protector, but her husband as well. Another protector was needed some five hundred years later."

"When Queen Jennavia was dethroned by King Englewood's ancestors." Teah interrupted.

The Viri Magus turned to her with a start nearly dropping the book causing the pages to turn. "Yes, that is also correct."

"Queen Jennavia's brother Galiven became protector and they reclaimed the throne once more. Mother told us we needed to know this, she insisted upon it." Teah said and then moved over next to Grinwald to look at the page it was open to.

"Mother gave more and more lessons these past few months and they concentrated on the history of the protectors and their queens. Do you suppose she was making sure we understood because she knew this would happen?" Logan asked, sharing a look with Teah.

"Your foster mother knew this day would come and she took her duty very seriously, preparing you the best she could," Grinwald agreed.

Teah, looking into the book, began to read the page:

"The Prophecy of the Protector warns that if a protector…"

Grinwald slammed the book shut. It caught some of Teah's hairs and pulled them out.

"Ouch. What was that for?" Teah protested.

"This book is for the trained eyes of the Viri Magus and is not meant for children," he said, placing the book back on the table. "We must be prepared to help Logan accept his abilities as a protector."

Logan stared off at nothing as he traced the swords upon his breast.

"Your sister was also waiting for you to reach your sixteenth birthday. She has royal blood in her and must now accept her role in putting a rightful queen on the throne again."

She looked back at him, smiling widely, wrapping her arms around him holding him tightly. "Don't worry brother, I'm still the Teah you've always known, but I'm scared," she whispered in his ear.

He hugged her back. "I'm glad I still have you," he said softly.

Teah pulled away suddenly, her eyes wide with shock.

"What is it?" Logan asked. "What's wrong?"

"If you are the protector and we are both of the Lassain lineage, that would make me a …"

"A queen," Logan sighed. "We have already established that."

"But that would also make me a Zele Magus," she said in a whisper.

Logan tilted his head to one side as he stared at his sister. All Lassain queens were, indeed, Zele Magus. Gently, he stroked her cheek. "Mother did say that."

Teah sat staring at Logan, unable to respond. The siblings looked to Grinwald as he glanced from one to the other.

With a curt nod, he confirmed their reasoning and spun around.

"I'd better get this meal prepared," the Viri Magus said as he walked back to the counter.

"So King Englewood had Gianna and Duvalle, our birth parents, killed to take over the rule of Ter Chadain," Logan turned to Teah as she sat next to him on his bed.

"That is why you will become a protector. If our parents still ruled and you lived in the palace in Cordlain, you would never become a protector since there would be no need." Teah softly rubbed his back.

"The magic of the protectors lies dormant until it is needed to free Ter Chadain from another's rule," Grinwald agreed.

Logan whispered to Teah as Grinwald turned to his rabbit, "Is this really happening? Our real parents were royalty and killed so another family could rule Ter Chadain. Not only has King Englewood killed our biological family, but he also murdered the only family we knew as well."

"Was Senia our real sister?" Teah asked, turning to Grinwald.

"She was your adoptive parent's child," Grinwald replied solemnly.

"For both families we have lost," Logan leaned close to Teah with his teeth clenched, "I will avenge their deaths. If becoming the protector will give me the ability to do that, I will embrace it."

Teah bit her lower lip, her eyes filling with concern.

Logan and Teah sat in silence, staring into the fire, deep in their own thoughts until supper was ready.

Grinwald placed the rabbit stew on the table and motioned them to come over. The three had some stew, silently absorbing the revelations of the evening. Logan often brought his spoon to his mouth, only to forget to eat and lower it once more. Teah carefully finished her stew, but the tears started midway through the meal, silent and unceasing.

The Viri Magus stood, stretching. "We should all get some rest. Tomorrow will be a very busy day. We need to leave at first light to avoid being discovered by the ones who tried to kill you at the farmstead. The men would surely have found your trail by now and be in pursuit. We need to be on our way as soon as we can.

"Take the other bed, my dear." Grinwald pointed to the bed across from Logan's. "I will sleep on the floor." He placed some blankets on the floor and crawled between them, turning his back to the siblings.

Teah climbed into bed as Logan slipped between his covers. Sharing one last look of mixed concern and determination, Teah rolled her back to Logan.

Logan lay staring at the sod ceiling as the past day's events replayed through his mind. The rhythmic, constant breathing of Grinwald and his sister indicated their sleep as he waited for sleep to take him. Finally, he too closed his eyes and let the day pass into the next.

Chapter 3

Logan woke around midnight. His heart raced as if he were running for his life again. His mind sped from one thought to another, but the thoughts were not his own, coming at him with a violence he couldn't defend against. Visions wracked his mind and his body, hitting him, one after another, with pulses of excruciating pain. His back arched, a final vision cascaded through his limbs. Arrows struck him. Men's heads flew off. A blade reared and then fell.

And then, suddenly, the pain stopped.

Men leaped before him in the throes of battle, locked in struggles for their lives. Looking down, he found a body not his own, but that of someone much taller.

He tried to raise his hand, but he had no control over this body. Instead, the body moved of its own volition. He leapt into the fray, taking down adversaries at every stroke of his curved blades. Death screams filled Logan's ears as the blood sprayed in all directions. Logan battled against his body. When it roared, he shrieked with terror. His arms rose to cleave a body in two.

Just as suddenly, silence killed the screams. A bright flash of light blinded him and he now sat in a small tavern, enjoying a mug of ale. A large man approached. Logan glanced over at him. Quickly the man drew his blade.

Logan wanted to scream, but he was nothing more than a passenger. Long blonde hair fell over his face as he somersaulted backwards. He came upright with the same two curved blades crossed in front of him.

First one arm of the man, and then the other, landed on the floor in a bloody mess.

With a jolt, the setting changed.

He stood in a grand hall. On a large throne, a lovely woman gazed down on him.

Slowly, he bent to kiss her outstretched hand. He once again looked into her eyes filled with love.

The doors to the hall flew open. Her eyes grew large. His hand dropped away. A mob rushed in, pressing ahead, although the guards battled to stop the advancing threat. Logan's arms moved with lightning speed. The now familiar blades were crossed before him.

Seeing him, the mob slowed.

Standing before the lady, he waited as the intruders decided what to do next. Then a piercing scream erupted. A man jumped out of the crowd and leveled a spear at the woman.

Spinning, Logan swept the spear aside, sending it splintering onto the floor. Rage swelled within him. He sped into the hostile crowd so quickly that many were dead without a sound. Soon the crowd ran for the great hall's doors. None of them made it. Each was cut down by the whirling blades.

The flash of light appeared once more and Logan was in a much calmer setting allowing him to catch his breath as he handed out food to some young children in a small village. He could feel the warmth of his gesture spread through him in comforting bliss.

Logan was suddenly hurled onto the ground face first as he could feel several men holding him down.

They pulled something free from his back and then secured his hands behind him. Lifted to his feel, Logan stared into the loathing eyes of a man with a long scar across his left cheek. The man held two swords with their scabbards, waving them menacing.

"Remember this, Protector?" the man scowled, pointing to the deep purple mark. "Now it is my turn to do some carving on you."

This vision cut short and violently jumped to another, and then another. Only this time Logan understood. The lives of the previous protectors filled him.

The protectors' memories washed over him, drowning him, enraging him, catapulting him into stories too horrible for a mere child to bear.

Chapter 4

The clock on the wall struck twelve as King Englewood sat on his throne, violet robes covering his muscled chest, his long black hair spotted with gray. Chin in hand, he listened to the chimes ring of his fate.

"Where is she?" He turned to a page dressed in red and silver.

"She should be here any minute, Your Majesty. The sentries sent word she was spotted outside the gates of Cordlain just moments ago." The boy bowed and exited the room.

A moment later, a figure draped in a deep red cloak strode into the throne room, paused and bowed slightly. "I have returned as you commanded, my King."

"So it is done? The boy is dead and the girl is our captive?"

"Both have eluded capture."

The King slammed his fist down on the arm of his throne, the sound echoing off the stone walls of the large room. "Are you so incompetent that even a task as simple as this is too much for you? If the prophecy is true, then the boy this very night turns into what we have feared, a protector. Has there ever been a protector who has not succeeded in putting a Lassain queen back upon the throne?"

"No, Highness there hasn't, but there is still hope to capture the girl and use her as leverage against him. We can still place her on the throne for the protection she will provide us from the Caltorians."

The King looked around quickly, wringing his hands. "Quiet, do you want our plans to be found out? If you fail me in this I will personally hand you over to the Empress to be her magical slave. She has already requested it to be so. Are you sure, absolutely sure, the spell works like that?" he whispered.

"As I have told you before," she moved closer and spoke in hushed tones, "placing her on the throne, even as a mere figurehead with no authority will enable the spell to keep further Caltorians from entering Ter Chadain territory. That will not help us, however, with the Caltorians already here and imbedded within our armies."

"I know, I know. It was the only way I could keep them from removing me from the throne. I had to allow them to bring troops over to 'supplement' our armies. I fought their generals taking over completely, but all my attempts were in vain and now only my palace guards are faithful to me alone."

"And now you have the Protector to worry about as well," Caldora added.

"Thank you for pointing that out," he hissed. "Take some Shankan, kill the boy, and get me the girl."

Disgust filled her features. "I would prefer my own men," she said. "Shankan are so undisciplined and vile."

Bred assassins, the Shankan were raised from birth to kill without remorse or reason. They were loyal only to those who paid the best, or whom they feared the most.

"Take the Shankan," King Englewood ordered. "They fear your powers. Warn them if they harm a hair on the girl's head, their head will part company with their necks. Now go, we don't have time to waste."

"And about the boys we have collected in case the Protector survives?"

"Send them out on their mission as well. We can't be too careful. If the Protector does get to some of the dukes and duchesses, it will be a good insurance policy."

Caldora bowed and left the hall.

King Englewood stood from his throne with his hand upon his lower back, stretching backwards. He then walked slowly down the corridor behind the throne to the bed chambers he shared with his wife, Queen Eliza.

He paused outside the door leading to Aston's bed chamber. "I do this for you, my son. To ensure your future and rid ourselves of the horrid Caltorians."

He turned and entered his bed chambers, closing the door quietly.

*****

Caldora stormed from the hall. She entered an office just off the corridor where a large man sat at an oak desk. His thick, greasy, black hair was slicked back and remnants of his last meal flecked his twisted black beard and red and silver tunic. He tipped over his chair in surprise at her appearance.

"Zele Caldora," the man said, righting his chair, and then standing beside it.

"I need a regiment of men to travel with me to Ceait, Captain. I also need a 'murder' of Shankan." The last request was filled with loathing.

"It will take me a day or two to get the regiment together, but the murder of Shankan you can take with you now. They are housed in a small farmstead just outside of town. My men wouldn't room anywhere near those animals. Where would you like to meet the regiment?"

"Have them gather outside Wilderton and wait. It shouldn't take me long to use the Shankan to rid myself of the problem, and then I can use the regiment to provide safe passage back to Cordlain with my prize. Are they all faithful to our cause?" She asked with a raised eyebrow.

"If you are asking if my men are loyal to the King, they are. If you are asking if the Caltorian generals have control over them, no, they don't. My men protect the castle and must be loyal to the King. It is one of the last grips we have on our military and we will hold it in a clenched fist. The Caltorian scum will need to pry it from our dead hands."

"Well, Captain. I am impressed by your conviction, but try to keep it under better restraint; else you might lose your head if you have such a loose tongue in the wrong company."

"Thank you, Zele Caldora." The captain bowed nervously.

"I best be on my way," she sighed. "I am not anxious about having the Shankan in my company. How many Shankan are in a murder?"

"Twenty, my lady," he said, and then his hand flew up. "Oh, before I forget. Rongren took two Shankan as you instructed and left the day your message arrived from Treebridge. He should be reaching Tumbleweed any day now."

"Very good, he might make my life easier very soon." She smiled and strode out of the room.

Chapter 5

Teah and Grinwald flew to Logan as soon as his scream filled the cabin. His eyes were open, but stared straight ahead, his features contorted.

Teah shook Logan, but he didn't respond. She whirled on Grinwald. "What's wrong with him? I've lost everything in the last two days and I'm not going to lose Logan, too."

Grinwald gently brought her hands away from Logan's arms. "It's the Infusion of the Protectorship. I have studied and read many documents regarding this. He is being transformed from your brother to the Protector of the Throne and the enforcer of your ancestor's laws. He'll still be Logan down deep, but his abilities will be those of the protectors who have come before him. He's now the most powerful weapon in all the land. There'll be no warrior who can equal him."

She stilled and looked at her hands. "What about me? Do I somehow become the Queen like he is becoming the protector?"

"You have always been the Queen. You have the inborn ability needed to rule Ter Chadain as the Lassain you are."

"I don't think I can do this," Teah said, tears welling up. "I'm afraid, Grinwald."

"It is understandable to be afraid, my Queen," the man said moving over to comfort her. "It is your royal bloodline which will allow you to overcome the fear to rule Ter Chadain as a true heir to the throne."

She laid her head upon Grinwald's shoulder. Together, they watched Logan. Logan still looked off at something in the distance as sweat streamed from every pore on his body.

Without warning, Teah felt a strange tingling in her extremities and a sudden pain over her left breast. She tried not to flinch, but the pain caught her unaware and she cried out softly.

"What is it, my dear?"

"Nothing, I'm fine," she said, moving back to her cot.

As Grinwald concentrated on Logan once more, she pulled her nightshift away slightly, looking down the neck. There was little light in the hut, so she leaned towards the fire, her back to the Viri Magus. As the firelight shone down her neckline, silver flashed from her left breast. Reaching under her clothing she felt the cold metallic smoothness of a tattoo. She waited for the trance to take her, but it never came.

"Has there ever been a female protector?" she asked softly.

"What? No, the spell cast by Queen Tera was specific to the male," Grinwald replied, not looking at her.

"Is there a symbol that the queen gets like the tattoo Logan has?"

"As I said before, you are the Queen because you were born that way. There is no transformation, no tattoo. You are and have always been the Queen."

Teah lay back on her cot, looking to her brother. "What's happening to me?" she whispered, not taking her eyes off Logan as she traced the hardened tattoo through her nightshift.

*****

The visions left as abruptly as they began. Logan collapsed and slept deeply until he was violently shaken awake, Grinwald staring down at him with a worried look.

"Good. We need to get out of here if we are to avoid your pursuers. Get up and eat something. I'll be back shortly. I have some things to gather for our journey." He turned and hurried from the hut.

Logan stretched stiffly. Turning to Teah at the table, he caught her stare. She quickly turned away.

"What's wrong with you?" he said softly.

"Nothing," she replied, avoiding his eye.

"Did you see?" he asked.

"See what?"

"What happened to me last night."

"Yeah, it was kind of scary. Grinwald said you would be the same Logan, but you now have all the experiences of the dead protectors who lived before you."

"I did see a lot of strange things. It was as if I did all of it in one night. I don't feel any different, though."

"You don't?"

"No. Maybe he was wrong about me getting powers. Maybe it is all about the knowledge. Grinwald admitted he never met a protector before. What if the information he read was wrong? Do I look any different to you?" He stood up, rotating in place with his arms held wide, his palms facing the ceiling.

She looked him up and down as he spun slowly. "No."

She turned to look at him more closely. Her knee hit the table leg and she knocked a pitcher of goat's milk off the table. Before she knew what happened, Logan stood next to the table holding the pitcher. They stared wide-eyed to each other and then at the floor. Not a drop of milk spilt.

Logan had moved from the bed to the table six feet away, catching the pitcher before it hit the floor.

"Did you see that?" he asked in a whisper.

"Yes," she shook her head. "Well, no. You moved so quickly. One second you were by the bed, and the next you were here, holding the pitcher." She gasped. "I wonder?"

She swept her hand out suddenly, pushing a tray with fresh fruit off the edge of the table.

Logan jumped, but she caught the tray and set it back on the table before he could finger it.

They stared at each other in disbelief as Grinwald walked in.

"What's the matter with you two? You're both as white as corpses."

"Logan caught the pitcher of milk before it broke on the floor," Teah said softly.

"That's good, isn't it?"

"I moved from the bed to the table and caught it before it hit the floor," Logan explained.

"I repeat. This is good, right?"

"There was no way I should have been able to move so quickly. I just reacted and I was there."

"You are seeing some of the transformations that happened last night," Grinwald said with a wave of his hand. "You'll surely see more this day. Now we must hurry and eat. They've been in town asking about you. We need to be off as soon as possible."

"But Teah..." Logan began.

"Needs some privacy to change before we leave," his sister cut him off.

"Hurry up then, we don't have much time." Grinwald strode to the cabinets.

Logan peered at his sister as she pressed her index finger to her lips, shaking her head slightly. Logan frowned, but said nothing.

As Logan packed food alongside Grinwald, Teah went behind a sheet hung in a corner of the small hut. She took off the nightshift. The newly formed mark on her left breast shone softly in the dim light against her pale white skin. She touched it cautiously, flinching at the cold metallic feeling. The swords crossed over a crown were the same as Logan's markings. She could hear Grinwald hurrying Logan to dress, so she quickly put on her clothes, stepping back into view.

*****

Since Logan and his sister didn't bring anything with them, Grinwald organized a pack for each with supplies.

"Where are we going?" Logan asked as Grinwald closed the door behind them.

"To gather support for the revolution," Grinwald told him. But, first, we must collect some artifacts to complete your transformation into the protector."

He moved past the boy, heading down the street of the small settlement, leaving Logan standing there. Teah shrugged, raising eyebrows at her brother, and followed the Viri Magus. Logan had little choice but to fall in behind his sister.

The street bore worn dirt ruts from wagons. Small buildings similar to the healer's hut lined the thoroughfare. Made from turf found readily around the settlement, grass growing on the roofs.

Making a sharp turn they were out of the village in seconds.

Only a few hundred feet from the last dwelling the prairie opened up before them and the breeze rolled unhindered across the grassland, blowing their hair around their faces, lifting their clothing with the gusts.

They fell in line as they picked up their pace, heads held high.

"Stop where you are." A call came from behind them.

The voice, eerily familiar, stopped them in midstride. They turned slowly. At least ten men in red uniforms stood across the path in formation, their silver helms matching the silver emblem emblazoned upon their breasts. A large red feather jutted out from each of the silver helms.

Some stood at the ready with swords in hand, but most had bows drawn, arrows aimed at them. No. Not at them, at Logan.

"We don't need you healer," one of the men shouted. "Just hand over the girl and step aside."

The Viri Magus moved toward the men, easing Teah behind him and stepping between Logan and the archers. "What about the boy?" he called out.

Logan began to protest, but stopped when Grinwald passed him a sharp look.

"Don't concern yourself about the boy. He will be taken care of quickly and cleanly if you would step out of the way."

Logan stepped up; Grinwald grasped his arm. Teah took a step back, then another. She glanced at the high brush a few feet away.

"Stay where you are, girl," the man said, pointing at Teah.

Teah stopped, biting her bottom lip as she looked between the archers and her brother.

"What do you want from these two?" Grinwald stalled.

"It's not your concern. The King of Ter Chadain has decreed the girl be brought to him and the boy be executed on sight. Now, out of the way," The man growled.

Grinwald chuckled. "What would he want with two settlers from this isolated village? Is he getting bored with kidnapping and torturing his citizens in the large cities? Now he has to stretch his murdering clutches to the people who have tried to find peace away from his tyranny?"

The commander pointed at Grinwald as the archers all turned to train their arrows on the Viri Magus. "That is treason, old man. You will join the boy in this execution." He looked back at his men. "Fire!" he ordered.

Grinwald said something softly, arms waving in front of him. Teah gasped, staring at his hands. As the arrows flew, fire burst from the Viri Magus's fingertips.

Red light flowed from Grinwald's hands in streaming ribbons. Those ribbons turned to fire upon reaching the arrows, incinerating the projectiles mid air, the ashes floating harmlessly to the ground. He then coiled his arms and struck again, sending a huge rush of fire into the men.

They burned to ash where they stood.

Grinwald turned, took a step, and then collapsed into Logan's arms.

Logan lowered to the ground, cradling the Viri Magus. Teah ran to them, kneeling at Grinwald's head as he slowly opened his eyes. His brown eyes looked wearily into hers.

"I guess I overexerted myself, Your Highness."

"What do we need to do for you, Grinwald?" Logan asked.

"I just need a few moments to regain my strength. I don't think there are any more soldiers in the area. I believe we have time."

Logan looked up, quickly scanning their surroundings.

"Take all the time you need," Teah said softly, brushing the man's hair from his face. "You saved Logan and me. I didn't know Viri Magus could do that."

"Not all Viri Magus can. But a Viri Magus who has reached the rank of Master can, however it takes a great deal of strength and I haven't used so much magic in a long time. The more I use the magic, the stronger I become. Since I've been in hiding I didn't want to take the risk of being discovered, so I didn't use my magic for nearly thirteen years. I guess I'm a bit rusty." His voice was weary, and he struggled to keep his eyes open as he spoke.

"Not too rusty to save us," Logan smiled.

They sat there as long as they dared, then Logan lifted the man in his arms.

"Put me down, boy," Grinwald protested. "I am not an invalid."

"We can't wait any longer. Someone will come and discover us with the ashes of those men and figure out you're a Viri Magus. We need to go and you can't walk yet, so I will have to carry you. Besides, you're light," Logan said, lifting Grinwald up and down.

Grinwald's glasses nearly fell off with Logan's jostling display. He grimaced as he grabbed the frames.

"I'm only light due to the powers you received last night. If you were still the boy who came to our village a few days ago, you would not be able to carry me very far."

"It's a good thing I've changed then. Isn't it?"

"Are you two done?" Teah asked, grabbing her brother's arm and pulling them after her. "Which direction do we need to go, Grinwald?"

"Keep heading east."

"East?" Logan said stopping, "Back towards Treebridge?"

"There is something very important in that forest and we need to retrieve it before we gather support for our mission. All the King's troops who came to your farm will be long gone by now. It will be as safe a place as any right now."

"Those were the troops at our home," Teah said softly. Logan nodded. "I will never forget that man's voice as long as I live. I'm glad he is dead."

"That settles it then. Back to Treebridge," Grinwald declared.

Logan didn't know if he ever wanted to return there.

Of course you don't want to return. You want to go and kill that vile Englewood.

The voice burst forth inside his head. Logan nearly dropped Grinwald.

"Watch it, boy," Grinwald growled. "I will break if you drop me."

"Sorry." Logan said absently. He recognized the voice as Protector Bastion from his visions.

Is that really you?

Who do you think it is, Galiven? Bastion shot back.

Bastion, you should leave Galiven alone, Stalwart spoke up.

Don't stick your nose into this, Stalwart.

Why do you bicker so much? We are here to guide this young lad along his way and, if you insist on bickering about our past lives, then we cannot help him with his journey. I am sorry, Logan, that they are like this. Falcone weighed in. *Follow the Viri Magus and you should be alright.*

Alright? Stalwart shot. *Why did he keep your sister from reading from the Book of Prophecy? What is he hiding from you?*

You need to go to Cordlain and kill King Englewood, Bastion shouted again.

I think he needs to follow the Viri Magus and then help put his sister on the throne. Killing Englewood should come after freeing Ter Chadain from Caltorian control, Galiven spoke gravely.

Stop, Logan screamed in his head.

The only sounds were the twigs and leaves cracking underfoot.

I can't think with all of you shouting at once. Please, let me be, so I can think. With all of you in my head, I will go crazy and help no one if you don't stay quiet until you are needed. Agreed?

Bastion, Stalwart, Falcone, and Galiven all reluctantly agreed and went silent, but not before Bastion stated again:

Go kill the King.

Anger surged through Logan's blood. It rushed through his veins, clouded his eyes, overwhelming him. All he could think about were the dead staring eyes of his father as he passed from this world only inches from him. ***They would pay for what they had done. There was no place they could hide from him now that he commanded the powers of the protector.***

Chapter 6

Logan carried Grinwald for over an hour.

"Put me down now," the Viri Magus said.

"Are you sure you can walk?" Teah asked.

"I'll be fine. We need to keep moving until night. It's too dangerous to walk out here in the dark, so we will make camp at sunset."

Logan set him down allowing the Viri Magus to take the lead and then fell into line behind Teah.

"What makes the Lassains so different from the rest of the people in Ter Chadain?" Logan asked.

"It's the magic that runs through your veins. The same magic that has run through the Lassain veins for over two thousand years. You and Teah have magic that most of us only dream of having."

"But I can't feel any magic," Teah said.

"It's not always a visible magic, but a magic that makes up who you are. Some of your ancestors had little usable magic, but the magic was still there. Others, like Queen Tera, had vast amounts of magic that gave her the power to create the protector's spell."

"Why would Stalwart Lassain not trust the Viri Magus?" Logan asked.

Grinwald and Teah stopped and spun around.

"What do you know about Stalwart and the Viri Magus?" Grinwald asked sharply.

"Just what mother told us," Logan said, staring hard at Teah and giving a slight twist and nod of his head.

Teah nodded her understanding. "Why did Stalwart distrust the Viri Magus so much?" she added.

Grinwald stood with his mouth agape. Clearing his throat, he motioned for them to continue walking ahead of him so they could hear him as he spoke. Once they were walking along the path again, Grinwald began. "Stalwart was the second protector and the Uncle to Queen Lonavette. When the Queen first came to power, the Viri Magus held the coveted position of head council to the Queen.

"Zincar Tollen was the Viri Magus responsible for guiding Queen Lonavette and Ter Chadain with respect to magic. Zincar was a very arrogant man and believed that Ter Chadain should be under the control of the Viri Magus and not the Queen. Rumor has it, rumor mind you, that Zincar was behind the overthrow of Lonavette. It is said that the Lassain males were eliminated at the same time Lonavette lost her throne. Reason has it that the Viri Magus was the only authority in Ter Chadain at the time with the power to eliminate them all."

"To remove the possible creation of the protector," Teah said with her eyes wide.

"To remove the chance of the Lassains reclaiming the throne," Grinwald agreed. "They thought they had all the Lassain men disposed of, but they forgot about Stalwart Lassain living in a remote area of Brandermain Duchy as a farmer. No one had heard from Stalwart for years and he was believed dead. While Lonavette was imprisoned at Cordlain, Stalwart was transformed into the protector."

I didn't even know that Lonavette was deposed, Stalwart told Logan, *when suddenly, I became the protector one night in my farmhouse. The Zele Magus Lionella came to me and instructed me on how to proceed. The Viri Magus fought us at every turn.*

What about me, I was there with you, Bastion chided.

Oh yes, Bastion was in my head, meddling at every turn, but he did manage to help us a little. Stalwart chuckled.

"The Viri Magus controlled the court in Cordlain with a new king in place. For years they struggled with the Zele Magus aiding Stalwart. Lonavette, of course, was eventually returned to the throne. The Zele Magus then took over the position of head advisor."

"You said you were Viri Magus to the Queen, our mother," Teah said. "How did the Viri Magus regain the head council position?"

"We paid the price for many, many years, but we finally proved our loyalty once again, and I was just the latest in many Viri Magus who have held that position. It often changes from Viri Magus to Zele Magus," Grinwald angrily replied, "depending on the personal choice of the Queen of Ter Chadain."

He strode to the front of the group once more and kept walking without looking back.

Teah turned to Logan. "How did you know about that? Mother never spoke of Stalwart or Lonavette?"

"It just came to me," he shrugged and kept walking.

He cannot be trusted, Stalwart echoed in Logan's head.

"Did you see Grinwald's hands back there?" Teah asked quietly.

"What about them?" Logan questioned.

"They were glowing red, and when he killed those guards, the air was filled with red lines that pulsed into them."

"I couldn't see that." Logan told her. "Maybe you saw it because you are the Queen. Maybe only a queen can see that."

"Do you suppose that was the magic I saw?"

"It could be," Logan agreed.

"Don't say anything," Teah urged. "I don't know why Grinwald isn't telling us more about what I saw in the book, and maybe it would be bad for him to know I can see his magic."

Logan nodded his agreement, and then added, "I don't know why he won't tell us more, but he has helped us—and put his own life in danger. I think we can trust him for what he says—just understand he may not be sharing everything he knows."

"You're right," Teah agreed.

They stopped as it grew dark and made camp, pressing down the grass until there was a large enough area to sit in a circle comfortably.

"I'm sure the soldiers back at the settlement won't be the last ones looking for us. We need to rest and be on our way at dawn." Grinwald said, handing out dried meat and bread.

"How many people do you think are searching?" Teah asked.

"King Englewood is sending as many men he feels are necessary. Since he sent Caldora to your home, he isn't leaving anything to chance. As you could tell from the soldiers who tried to stop us, they want Logan dead and you alive."

"I can see why they want me dead," Logan said stoically, "but why do they want Teah?"

"If he has a Lassain to put on the throne and manipulate, the unrest in Ter Chadain might come to an end."

"How does having me on the throne benefit King Englewood," Teah complained.

"We need not get into that now," Grinwald said abruptly "We need to get back into Treebridge without running into anymore trouble."

"Why are we going back?" Logan pressed.

"We need to retrieve some items to help make your transformation into the protector complete. Get some sleep." The Viri

Magus lay down, rolling his back to the two siblings.

Logan lay with his head next to Teah's.

"I don't like going back there," Teah whispered anxiously.

"Neither do I, but he isn't giving us much choice," Logan said.

"No, he is not," Grinwald said his back still to them. "Now get some sleep."

Teah and Logan looked at each other, the anguish evident on their faces even in the darkness. The memories from the farmstead, still very fresh, weighed heavily on their minds. Tears formed in Teah's eyes and she turned her head away. Unaware, Logan wrapped himself tighter in his bedroll and closed his eyes.

Logan lay listening to the frogs calling to one another as he let his muscles slowly relax. He fell into the vision as soon as sleep took him. He was Falcone on a sprawling battle field. He stood on some kind of platform, directing troops in silver and red against enemy troops in gold and maroon.

First the red side pushed the advantage, and then the gold side gained ground. Falcone's voice shouted out moves and countermoves to the enemy positions.

The Battle of Crandberg unfolded.

Three men in different military attire ran up next to Falcone. These were Falcone's generals, and their faces were grim with welts and blood.

We are losing ground at all fronts, Protector, one general shouted over the din of battle.

Without a word, Falcone jumped from the platform onto his mount. He charged into the battle. His blades shot out taking off an arm, then a leg. Cutting down anything in gold and maroon as cries of horror rose up around him. The enemy ranks began to break as soldiers scrambled for their lives, slipping uncontrollably as blood from the fallen soaked into the earth creating a muddy, bloody, nightmare.

Once that front moved in Ter Chadain's favor, Falcone raced to the next, decapitating the first soldier who dared step in his path of death and slaughter, then taking a hand off still holding a sword that ventured too close. He was a one man regiment dealing out brutal annihilation before him as appendages fell severed all around.

Waves of cheers rose as the enemy began to retreat as a whole. The battle field fell eerily silent, and then a rush of arrows came to Logan's ear. He tracked one of the arrows as it arched smoothly. It came down and drove deep in his right knee.

Logan cried out in pain and came awake.

"Logan, are you all right?" Grinwald was beside him, one hand on his shoulder and a glowing ball floating above his other.

"I dreamt about a battle and was shot with an arrow."

He grabbed his right knee and looked from the Viri Magus to his sister who now knelt by his side. When he held his hands up in front of his face, they were covered in his blood.

"What's happening to me?" he yelled.

Grinwald felt around his leg vigorously, regardless of Logan's sharp moans. "You are reliving the other protector's lives in your dreams. The magic of the protectors is causing real physical damage to you. You need to block your dreams if you are to survive this part of the transformation. If you keep living the events of past protectors, you will eventually come to the event which killed the last protector. That may prove fatal."

"How can I control my dreams? Are you going to teach me?" Logan shouted as his hands raked through his hair and his eyes opened wide, giving him an insane look in the soft light of the glowing ball.

"I don't have the knowledge to teach you, but I think I know someone who does. After we get what we need from Treebridge, we will go see this person. But first we need to heal your knee if we are going to make good time." Grinwald bent down to inspect the injury, and then recoiled.

"What's wrong?" Logan asked.

"There's no injury to your leg." The Viri Magus said, holding the light orb closer to the boy's knee. Sure enough, there was blood on his pant leg, but the knee underneath was not injured and showed no signs of ever being so.

"How can that be?" Teah asked, biting her lip.

"It must be the magic of the protector," the Viri Magus surmised. "He must be able to heal himself."

"What do you mean *he must be*? Don't you know?"

"No, child, I don't know. No one alive knows much about the protectors except what they have read."

"Then get the book out and let's find out." Teah pressed.

"Then I don't need to worry about reliving the death of the last protector." Logan added with a sigh.

"I can't be sure that is the case. If you can heal yourself after you are injured, you may not have the opportunity to heal if you are dead. As far as I have read, you are still as vulnerable to being killed as the last protector was."

Logan ran a hand through his hair and Teah bit her bottom lip as they turned to each other. Teah gripped his shoulder tightly as he placed his hand upon hers, giving it a squeeze.

"Since Logan is going to be fine, I suggest we all get some rest before dawn so we can be on our way at day break." He moved over to his bedroll. Teah did the same and Grinwald closed his fist on the light to extinguish it.

Logan lay staring at their figures in the darkness as Teah turned to him.

"Do you suppose I will have the same thing happen to me?" she whispered.

"I don't know. Do you have the tattoo?"

"Yes."

"Did you see visions?"

"No."

"Do you hear the voices of the past protectors in your head?"

"No. You have voices in your head?" She blew out her breath. "That's how you knew about Stalwart. He told you, didn't he?"

"Quiet. I don't want Grinwald to think I'm losing my mind. All of the protectors are in my head."

"You mean they can talk to you?"

"Yeah, it's really annoying. These visions just happen while I sleep, but they can talk to me anytime. I've asked them to keep it to a minimum so I can concentrate on what's going on around me."

"Why don't I have the visions or the voices?"

Because she is the first female protector, Galvin answered. *There are no spirits to aid her in her journey. She must endure this alone, while you have us to guide you.*

I never heard voices since I was the first, Bastion agreed.

"Galvin and Bastion say since you are the first female protector, you don't have them to guide you as I do." Logan sighed. "I don't know which is worse."

Logan grimaced as all four protectors shouted their protests in unison.

Quiet, Logan thought. The voices went silent.

"Just get some sleep," he said.

Teah rolled over without a word and went back to sleep.

Logan lay awake staring at the sky, finally dozing off as the faint light of dawn began to glow in the distant horizon.

He woke to his sister gently shaking him. The sun was just creeping over the tall grass. He rubbed his eyes and stretched. Grinwald was already putting his pack on his back.

Logan sat up and rolled his bedding.

"Let's get going children. I'm afraid soldiers aren't the only thing the King has sent after us."

"What do you mean? Who else would be after us?" Logan got to his feet and pulled on his pack.

"Bounty hunters, mercenaries, anyone who can be bought to murder innocent children," the Viri Magus said, turning his back to them and heading into the sunrise.

Teah and Logan stared at each other and headed out after the old man.

The two Lassains remained alert all morning, busily scanning for anything that didn't belong in the grass blowing softly in the light breeze flowing across the prairie. They walked most of the morning until the trees of the forest loomed in the distance. Grinwald stopped, taking out some bread and dried meat and passing it to the siblings.

Logan dropped his pack to the ground and flopped down on it with a sigh. Closing his eyes, he inhaled deeply and stretched his arms over his head.

Teah slid her pack from her back, letting it fall heavily to the ground and began lowering herself on top of it. A scream escaped her lips bringing Logan's eyes open with a snap.

A large man in a gray cloak barreled between them. He snatched up Teah and kept running.

"Teah," Logan cried out.

Logan jumped to his feet. Out of nowhere, a second and third man hurtled into him and Grinwald.

"Logan!" Grinwald shouted, as the man collided with him.

The Viri Magus went down in a heap. Logan nimbly rolled, pushing the much larger adversary off of him with his legs. Logan leapt to his feet and rushed over to pull the attacker off Grinwald. The old man recovered quickly. He advanced on the fallen man, hands raised, but Logan threw the assailant he was grappling with into the other sending them tumbling.

The two men got to their feet, shoulder to shoulder. Grinwald hurled a ball of fire large enough to envelop them both.

The flames swallowed them and then flashed out.

They began laughing, one of them saying, "We expected that much from you Viri Magus and so did the King. We cannot be hurt by your magic."

Logan wasted no time.

Stalwart's memory of a similar battle came to him and instantly Logan knew what to do.

Logan dove into the two men, wrapping his arms around one man's neck and his legs around the second man's neck. Then he spun.

Two loud cracking sounds echoed across the field. The three fell to the ground, the men dead before they landed in a jumbled heap in the tall grass.

Rolling, Logan came to his feet and raced after his sister.

Necessity drove Logan faster. The landscape began to blur. Before he knew what had happened, he stood on a path as the man came running towards him, Teah struggling in his arms.

The man slowed, throwing Teah off to one side as he came within a few feet of Logan.

Teah landed in a heap. She had some sort of binding pinning her arms to her sides, glowing with a soft white light. She moaned and raised her head. Her face shone with hope as she saw Logan.

"Well, well, well. If it isn't brother here to save the day," the man sneered.

"Who sent you?" Logan growled.

"Caldora knew you would be in this area. She felt you would try and return to your home even though it would be dangerous, she said you couldn't resist going back."

"I want you to give a message to King Englewood and Caldora from me," Logan said softly, his body visibly shaking.

"And what would that be?"

"I will kill them," the boy said calmly.

"How are you going to kill them when I kill you first?" The man scowled.

"I'm going to break both your arms and send you to deliver the message. Then I will free my sister and we will be on our way," Logan told him.

Before Logan finished his promise, the man lunged.

Logan smoothly grabbed the man's large arms, one in each

hand. He bent at the waist and spun. The subsequent snapping sounds caused Teah to yelp, turning away when cries of pain erupted.

Logan released his hold and the man fell to the ground.

Logan moved to Teah, taking the glowing cord in his hands, he broke it with little effort.

Teah leapt to her bother's arms. They turned, walking arm in arm to where the injured man lay.

The man was crying in pain and didn't see them until they stood over him. His pain-stricken eyes focused on them and he struggled to get away, dragging his injured arms along the ground. Realizing his attempt to escape was futile, he laid his head back, gasping for air.

"What do you want from me?" The man screamed.

"You know what I want. What is your name?"

"Rongren," the man cried.

"Rongren, you will return to the King and inform him I will kill him. If you fail to do this, you will suffer the same fate as he." Logan's voice was void of emotion and his gaze was level and steady.

Rongren's eyes showed no doubt he knew the boy was deadly serious.

"Now get up and get moving."

"How am I supposed to survive out here with two broken arms?" the man pleaded.

"You should have thought about that before you took this mission. Now get going." Logan reached down taking hold of the man's shirt collar, lifting him up Logan tossed him down the trail in the direction he fled with Teah.

The man caught his balance without breaking stride and began running, both arms awkwardly dangling at his sides, bouncing uselessly with every step.

Logan watched until the early morning fog enveloped him. Then he turned to his sister. She watched the veil of fog.

"Who were those men?" She asked.

"They must have been the mercenaries Grinwald warned us about." Logan started. "Grinwald! We have to hurry and get back to him in case there are more men around," Logan said, taking his sister's hand.

They ran. Logan smiled as he pushed faster and faster, finding Teah kept pace. A wide smile spread across both of their faces, sharing something that no one else would understand.

It took much longer getting back to the camp than it had taken Logan to intercept Teah by himself, but they finally reached the campsite. The Viri Magus sat in front of a small fire. When the two youths slowed, Grinwald looked up, giving them a slight smile.

"It is good to see you unharmed," he said, turning away to concentrate on the small rabbit cooking on a spit.

Logan looked to the bodies of the two men he killed laying over to one side of the clearing. Their corpses contorted in ways humans should not bend. The boy ran into the high grass vomiting. His insides heaved again, emptying whatever remained in him into the grass. He stood there for a moment taking deep breaths.

It was either you or them, Bastion spoke up.

It is okay to feel this way, Logan. You should never take lightly the lives you must end. You are less likely to kill without cause that way, Galiven countered.

He needs to kill without remorse, else he becomes too trusting, Bastion countered.

Stop it, he shouted. The protectors went silent.

Turning back to the clearing, he walked slowly to the fire where his sister sat beside Grinwald in silence.

"How could I do that?" he motioned to the bodies.

"If you hadn't, we would be dead," Grinwald pointed out.

"But we both could have overpowered them without killing them. They didn't even have any weapons. Surely you could have done something to render them harmless," Logan argued.

"You saw what happened when I tried to use magic on them. They had a counter spell woven upon them so my attack had no effect. I think you need to look a little closer at those men and see what they are holding." The Viri Magus instructed.

Logan went and looked down at them but saw nothing.

Then he noticed something dark in the hand of one of the dead men. Kneeling, Logan peered closely and then checked the other man's hands as well. Each digit had a thin strip of brown leather on it.

He looked back at Grinwald with a questioning stare.

"Turn their hands over."

The boy did as he was told and his eyes shot open wide. The back of each man's clammy hand bore three long blades attached by the brown leather straps.

"They were going to kill you and me. If you hadn't killed them first, they would have succeeded. They were trained for this. Their entire life is built around killing people. They are known as Shankan Warriors. Taken from their families at a very young age and trained to be merciless killers, they would not have stopped until either we killed them or they killed us."

"The man who took me didn't have those on his hands," Teah stated.

"Then he was not a Shankan. He must have been sent specifically to capture you, Teah. The King may fear sending only Shankan would make it difficult to guarantee you'd be taken to him alive," Grinwald explained.

"The man said Caldora sent him, not the King," Logan replied.

"Caldora's every move is made with the King's authority. It was as if Englewood gave the command himself," Grinwald said.

Logan smiled in spite of himself.

"What?" Grinwald asked.

"I told the man to tell Englewood and Caldora I was going to kill them. I have every intention of keeping my word."

"I doubt it not," Grinwald agreed. He took the rabbit off the spit, divided it three ways and handed it to the others.

Logan put his hand up to decline, but when the meat's smell drifted to his nose, he accepted his portion of the meat, devouring it without hesitation.

After eating, the travelers put out the fire, gathered their discarded belongings, and set off for Treebridge Forest. They walked silently all morning, each deep in their own thoughts. Logan was the first to notice the birds circling an area up ahead.

He pointed them out to the others. "They're circling what was once our homestead."

They approached with caution. As the woods parted, charred timbers reached for the sky and the smell of manure mingled with the odor of burnt flesh and wood.

"I can't do this," Teah cried out, dropping to her knees, the tears streaming down her cheeks. She looked up at Logan as he came beside her, sobs contorting her mouth. Logan's face was like stone, but the tears defied his resolve, a few escaping his watering eyes as he turned away so she wouldn't see.

The Viri Magus kept on task without waiting for the youths to follow, but walking into what once was the barn.

Logan and Teah stared at each other, panic across their faces. "I can't go in there," Teah gasped. "I can picture Senia against the well bleeding to death."

"Don't worry. I'll stay here with you." Logan's voice cracked. The arrows still stuck out of what remained of the pillar, both pillar and arrows charred by the scorching fire.

Grinwald soon emerged from the barn, carrying a small bundle that he began placing in his pack.

"What is that?" Logan called out as Teah sat cradling her head in her hands.

"What is needed to continue our journey," Grinwald said, placing his pack on his back and walking around the homestead.

"Did you see any bodies?" Teah asked as she bit her bottom lip.

"None are there as far as I can see my child," Grinwald told her as he continued moving away.

Teah and Logan exchanged confused glances. Logan helped his sister to her feet and they hurried after the old man. "Doesn't that seem odd to you? Do Ter Chadain soldiers usually bury their victims?" Logan pressed.

"Not usually, but I guess they could have. Maybe they just threw them in the fire and let them burn, but that's not like them at all. The only bones I could see were from your animals," Grinwald shrugged.

"We need to check where our father was," Logan said as they caught up with the Viri Magus.

Grinwald nodded his agreement and Logan took the lead. They walked along the edge of the forest for a short distance, and then turned sharply into Treebridge. Shadows engulfed them immediately and they paused briefly, letting their eyes adjust to the sudden lack of light.

Logan continued until arrows protruding out of trees appeared. They walked a little further. Then, after a few hundred feet, noticeable mounds of earth rose off the forest floor. Dark, rich, freshly turned soil marked them, contrasting with dried leaves and cracked twigs scattered across the forest floor. There were three mounds, with small pieces of wood at the end of each. On the wood were burned the same five words: "Let your souls be free."

"That definitely isn't something the King's soldiers would do. Those words are from a people long removed from Ter Chadain," Grinwald spat. "Someone is toying with us.""

"What do you mean?" Logan asked.

"That was a death blessing from a people who have been banished from this land for centuries. The Betra, the betrayers of the protector," the Viri Magus explained. "What would they be doing here? They are exiled from Ter Chadain."

"The betrayers?" Teah asked.

"The Betra, as they were labeled by your ancestor, Queen Jennavia. They were responsible for the death of her brother, Protector Galiven."

"The only protector to be murdered," Logan said.

It was his own doing, Bastion shot.

If he wasn't so naïve, he could have foreseen it, Falcone added.

Enough, Logan cut them off and they fell silent. Logan thought he could feel sadness from Galiven.

"That's the one. He was betrayed by these people, who were then exiled by the Queen to the Forbidden. There they live feeling the loss of the protector, just as the Queen felt the loss of her dear brother."

"What do you mean they <u>feel</u> the loss?" Teah questioned.

"It is said that the entire Betra people, generation to generation, feel a pang over the loss of Galiven. It is their burden to carry forever."

The three fell silent.

The two youths knelt next to the graves their family. Senia, the sister who was just years older than them, Mother, who was always supportive and loving as well as their teacher, and Father, who was a kind man and faithful subject of Ter Chadain. The loss of them held no less pain now than the night they had first been murdered.

Logan's face turned bright red as he fought to control the images of past protectors killing men who had wronged them.

Go kill Englewood, the voices screamed inside his head. *Take your vengeance now.*

His body shook as he clenched his teeth and flexed his fists. He could see nothing but the visions of the protectors in front of him. He fought to keep from leaping to his feet and running to the castle in Cordlain to tear the King apart with his bare hands.

He finally lifted his face to the sky and cried out, "No!"

Teah and Grinwald jumped.

Logan breathed in a ragged breath. "There is nothing left for us here, where to now?"

Grinwald nodded and headed away from the homestead, deeper into Treebridge.

Logan and Teah got to their feet and the girl brushed up gently against her twin, sharing a brief moment as Logan's body began to relax.

They turned and followed the Viri Magus without a glance back.

As they walked, Logan lifted his head, and his stride gained new strength. Even Teah began to look up from her plodding steps as they walked. Her gait matched her brother's.

"We have something to accomplish now," Logan said.

Teah nodded. "We must be sure all of our loved ones did not die in vain."

"We must do all we can to hold the one person responsible for their deaths accountable."

"And all who did his bidding as well." When no response came, Teah looked over her shoulder.

Logan walked with mouth agape.

"It is time I start to think as a queen would think. Caldora and all who helped King Englewood will pay for their murderous ways. This I pledge."

"I too, as the Protector of Ter Chadain, swear to continue to fight until I am either dead, or all who have had a part in the murders of all our parents and Senia have perished."

Teah looked over her shoulder at him again and shivered. "I would hold you to that, brother, but I can see I will not have to."

Now you are seeing things the way a protector sees things, Bastion said in the ringing silence.

Chapter 7

They traveled into the forest all day, stopping only to rest momentarily and to take nourishment. They continued on into the night, the Viri Magus illuminating the darkness with magic he conjured over his extended palm.

They finally paused long after midnight. Grinwald held his magic shining in the darkness before them. "Take some rest now and we will continue on at first light."

"Grinwald, have you ever been on the Magical Council?" Teah asked.

Grinwald sent her a questioning glance. "What do you know of politics?"

"Mother explained the three councils in Ter Chadain. The Noble Council, with either the duke or duchess representing their duchy; The Defense Council, which has a head general from each duchy; and then finally the Magical Council, where the Magical Advisor of each duchy has a seat. Did you ever serve on the Magical Council?"

"Your adoptive mother did a fine job educating the both of you on the political order of Ter Chadain. Yes, my dear." Grinwald puffed up. "I was on the Magical Council as the Magical Advisor to your mother, Queen Gianna."

"Is it true what Mother told us, that the councils often fight over the laws and decisions for Ter Chadain?"

"It is a fact. There are often political battles fought through the councils that rage on for years without resolution. The entire functioning of Ter Chadain can come to a halt when the councils won't agree," the Viri Magus explained. "The king or queen then decides the outcome. That is why the person ruling Ter Chadain is so vital to its wellbeing. Their final decisions effect everyone."

"Mother always said both the Zele Magus and the Viri Magus tried to do what was best for Ter Chadain, but were often at odds; not always agreeing," Teah pressed.

"It is too late to discuss that now. Maybe we can talk about the differing views another time?" Grinwald asked.

"Very well, good night," Teah replied turning and getting into her bedroll.

Logan sat, watching and listening, as Teah and Grinwald spoke of politics.

Beware of any politics that one speaks of, Stalwart warned.

The Zele Magus are no better, Falcone added.

They are all in it for their own reasons, Bastion agreed.

But without them, your journey will be very short and very disastrous, Galiven said sadly.

With all the plotting and secrecy the magicals have done throughout Ter Chadain history, it confuses me to think that any of you would want anything to do with either of the Magus, Logan told them.

Confusion often foreshadows enlightenment, my boy, Bastion comforted. *Be patient. All will make sense in time.*

Logan closed his eyes and fell asleep. The vision came quickly and this time it was peaceful. He walked in a tranquil valley of Galiven's memory. Logan looked to a woman with long dark hair, olive colored skin, and deep brown eyes that shone up at him with love. She smiled widely as he leaned down to kiss her and her giggle sent waves of happiness through the boy. They walked to a secluded spot under a large tree which overlooked a river and lay down together.

He woke with a start as Galiven's anger pounded inside his head.

That is not for your eyes, boy, Galiven shouted.

I'm sorry, I wasn't trying. It just came to me while I slept, Logan explained. He waited, but there was no reply from any of the protectors.

The sun was coming up as Logan sat up in his bedroll. Teah lay looking at him, but Grinwald was sleeping soundly.

"What is it?" Teah asked.

"Another vision," Logan whispered.

"What about?"

"I'd rather not say."

"Come on, I don't get them in my head, so maybe by sharing them with me, I will be able to understand being a protector better," Teah persisted.

"This one won't help you," Logan assured her.

"Please," Teah begged.

"It was a moment between Protector Galiven and," Logan hesitated for a moment. "And his true love, Sadalin." Logan looked confused to Teah. "I don't know how I knew her name, but it came to me."

"Tell me more," Teah urged.

"I can't. Galiven wasn't happy that I saw that memory of his and I don't think it would be right for me to tell you about it."

Teah cocked her head to one side, sucking on her bottom lip absently. "Maybe you're right; it wouldn't be nice to tell secrets that weren't meant for you."

"Yeah, I think that would be best," Logan agreed.

Thank you Logan, and thank your sister as well, Galiven said.

"Galiven said thank you for understanding," Logan smiled.

Teah looked shocked, smiled broadly, and then nodded.

Grinwald stirred, cutting any further conversation short as he hurried them to gather their things. He handed them some dried meat and bread for breakfast as they headed out of camp. They walked all day until early evening when they came to a large cliff face looming high above them.

"We will stop here and make camp," Grinwald instructed, dropping his pack on the hard ground. "Logan, gather some firewood. Teah, take these water skins and go to the stream we just passed and fill them please," Grinwald said handing Teah the skins.

By the time they returned, Grinwald had a small fire burning from a few sticks gathered quickly from around the campsite. He placed Logan's wood on the fire and the orange flames warmed their aching limbs. They ate without speaking and then moved to their bedrolls for the night.

"I will explain why we are here in the morning when our minds are fresh. Get a good night sleep; you have much to learn tomorrow."

Logan looked to Teah, rolling his eyes. "That won't make getting to sleep any easier. What do you suppose he meant by that?"

"I have no idea," she admitted.

She spread her bedding out and crawled into it. "Goodnight, Logan." She rolled over.

"Good night, Teah."

Logan tossed and turned, then lay staring up at the stars. His mind still raced with the encounters of the day and everything the past protectors had told him. He feared falling asleep, unsure of what might be waiting for him in his dreams, but wanted to erase the day's events from his mind even just for the few hours of sleep he could claim.

Closing his eyes and clearing his mind, his exhaustion finally overwhelmed him and he succumbed to sleep.

The dreams came once again, but this time he stood in a large building before a beautiful woman sitting on a throne. She smiled warmly at him but scowled as her eyes focused next to him. He turned. Saladin stood at his right, smiling lovingly at him. Turning back to the woman on the throne, he started. Her scowl was now rage. She opened her mouth, rising from the throne. The scream that began ripped through his mind, echoing on and on and on.

The smell of something cooking woke him. The name Queen Jennavia stuck in his thoughts.

Jennavia didn't like you being in love with Saladin, did she Galiven? Logan asked.

No, Logan, she felt Saladin was below my station and forbid me to see her again.

But he did anyway, Bastion interrupted.

Stay out of this Bastion, Logan reprimanded. ***Each of you has a right to voice defense of your life choices to me, but not to condemn the choices made by others.***

You are right, Logan, Bastion admitted sheepishly. *I apologize, Galiven, and will try to refrain from doing so in the future. But I make no promises.*

I tried my best*,* Logan sighed.

I do appreciate that, Logan, and it was a gallant effort, Galiven chuckled.

Grinwald fed them juicy grouse for breakfast and Logan was soon sitting around the small fire, picking his teeth with a bone from the breast of the wild bird.

Teah watched the Viri Magus expectantly, leaning towards him in anticipation. The old man busily heated some kind of herbal tea, stirring the tea and mumbling softly.

"Are you putting a spell on the tea?" Logan asked.

"Why would you say that?" Grinwald looked up, his eyes wide.

"You're mumbling to yourself like you did when you killed those soldiers."

"I was getting my thoughts together about our conversation this morning."

"What are you going to tell us this morning?" Teah asked.

"All in good time," the Viri Magus said, pouring each a cup of tea and handing them the steaming mug. "You and your brother have been isolated your entire lives. Thankfully your mother, your foster mother, has taken the time to educate you to the extent of her knowledge, but now you need to know more of the world you're being thrown into. Things have changed over the past thirteen years and you must have an understanding of what came before in order to know the severity of the situation we now face."

Logan frowned, tossing the small bone into the fire. "What's going to happen today that makes this information so important?"

"I don't know if anything is going to happen today, but if something does happen, I want the two of you to be aware of your destiny and the importance of you fulfilling that destiny."

"Tell us," Teah demanded suddenly. She covered her mouth in surprise.

Grinwald stiffened. "Very well, where should I begin?" the Viri Magus thought out loud. "Let's start with a little history about Ter Chadain. Ter Chadain was once a great country, a continent as well, as it is entirely surrounded by water. In this great country are nine duchies stewarded by dukes and duchesses. The king and queen of Ter Chadain ruled over the entire continent, but lived in what was known as Ter Chadain proper or just Ter Chadain. Outside of those borders, the dukes and duchesses were allowed to run things as they saw fit under the laws of Ter Chadain. The lords and ladies of the duchies were loyal to the king and queen without question, and peace flowed over all of Ter Chadain."

Grinwald studied them. "I'm assuming you know the duchies?"

Straightening in frustration, Logan ran a hand through his hair. "They are Los Clostern, Cranberg, Brandermain, Stalosten, Fareband, Mellastock, Granstel, Ackerton, and Pasten."

"Very good," the Viri Magus smiled. "They all traded and cooperated with each other to offer a better life for the entire country, no matter the wealth of each duchy. We now sit in the duchy of Granstel, on the southeastern side of Ter Chadain. The country was at peace with benevolent rulers keeping everything in harmony. From time to time there would be invaders from across the sea known as Caltorians. They would try and take over one of the smaller coastal duchies, but the king and queen's army would defend the duchy, driving the attackers back to where they had come. That is the past history when your family ruled. Now let us move forward to thirteen years ago."

"You mean when King Englewood killed our real parents?" Logan growled.

"That's right," Grinwald said. The sympathy was present both in his voice and in his eyes. "King Englewood tried killing the entire Lassain bloodline to ensure he could rule without the fear of being overthrown by his enemy's heirs. That would have happened if your mother hadn't sensed the evil coming. She sent me away with the two of you as the attack began."

"She must have trusted you very much," Teah noted softly.

Grinwald didn't respond, except to nod ever so slightly before continuing. "Since Granstel is one of the least developed duchies, I thought it would be a perfect place to disappear. Once I found the most isolated settlement in Granstel, I sent for the Saoltos and helped them build the farmstead on the edge of the Treebridge Forest and then left them to their mission. They knew exactly what was expected and were proud to help keep the Lassain bloodline alive for our future."

Grinwald paused to take a sip of his tea.

Logan stared at the flames of the fire, his brow furrowed. "How could you put them in such danger? They were innocent to all of this."

"They were well aware of the danger they could be in if you were found out. You knew how they were," Grinwald pointed out. "They were proud to put their lives on the line to assure Ter Chadain had a chance at peace again."

Though the scowl did not leave Logan's face, he nodded.

Grinwald set his cup back on the ground. "King Englewood did not realize having a queen with Lassain blood kept us safe from the invasion of the Caltorians. Soon they were on his doorstep and would not be turned away. Knowing they couldn't be defeated, he made a pact with them. If Englewood was allowed to remain in power, he would assist them in taking what they wanted from the rest of the country. This worked for a while, but only for as long as the dukes and duchesses remained under the impression the king would protect them from such dangers. But soon enough it was clear. The king would not stand in the way of these invaders. That is where it stands now. Each duchy is fending for itself, trusting no one else. It is only a matter of time before the Caltorians, posing as our army from Ter Chadain, overpower every duchy's army, taking control of each duchy one by one."

"That's where Teah and I come in," Logan stated. Grinwald looked up from the fire to see the young man's chiseled chin set with determination.

"That is where you and your sister come in," he agreed. "The two of you must regain the throne for the Lassain line, driving out the invaders while uniting the splintered Ter Chadain."

"You make it sound so easy," Logan protested. "The country has no reason to believe us or follow us and if they don't follow us, we will never have a chance of defeating the Caltorians."

"This will have to convince them," Grinwald said, placing his hand over his heart.

"Their heart will know the truth?" Teah asked uncertainly.

"Not exactly, <u>that</u> will convince them," he said, pointing to Logan's chest.

The boy pulled his tunic open to expose the shinny symbol of two swords crossing over a crown.

"You are the only one who can be the protector and they must realize you are truly him."

As if in sympathy, Teah touched her own breast as Logan touched his. Breathing in deeply, Teah remained silent.

"How can I convince anyone when I'm not sure myself?" Logan complained. "I don't know what's happening to me. How can I be certain I can do what you say?"

"Because a true protector can do it, and I believe you are him," the Viri Magus smiled.

"I do, too," Teah added.

"As do I," another's voice proclaimed.

The three around the fire scrambled to their feet.

A tall slender figure strode forcefully into camp, robed in black from head to toe, only the eyes were exposed—the orbs so dark brown, they shone near black. The figure strode right up to Logan.

Before anyone could react, the figure dropped to a knee, bowing its head.

"You are the savior come to set my people free, and I am sworn to protect you with my life. Welcome home. Your people are ready for you to lead."

"My p-p-people," Logan stammered. He glanced at Teah. "Who are my people?"

"The Betra, my Master."

"No," exclaimed Grinwald.

The Viri Magus lunged between them. Logan tumbled backward as the Viri Magus pushed him aside and whirled upon the Betra with glowing hands.

"The Betra are a banished people by the Queen of Ter Chadain herself. You will not harm another protector as you did the last."

The figure stood to its full height, at least a hand taller than Logan, towering over Grinwald as his palms radiated light.

"This is the sworn vow of our people since the time of our exile, Viri Magus. When the Queen cast out my people, she cursed us with the pain of loss she herself suffered over the loss of her brother. That pain is passed down through the generations and would not diminish until the protector returned. The pain disappeared over four days ago and I set out on my journey at once. The boy must have become a man four days ago and our calling has come."

Logan lay stunned, sprawled by the fire, staring up at Grinwald and the figure. The voices of the protectors shouted inside Logan's head.

Kill him, cried Bastion.

Run for your life, shouted Falcone.

Rip his heart out, Stalwart insisted.

Only Galiven remained silent.

Logan pushed to his feet, brushing the dirt off his clothes. "I thought the Betra were dead."

Teah stood in shock, staring wide-eyed at the cloaked figure.

Grinwald whirled to face Logan. "They betrayed the last protector, your predecessor, who lived over five hundred years ago when times were peaceful."

"Please. I mean you no harm. Let me explain." The figure stepped forward, arms and hands extended. "I am here to offer allegiance and loyalty, not to threaten you."

"The Queen exiled the entire village to 'The Forbidden'," Grinwald spat, "a desolate land outside the borders of Ter Chadain, never to return."

"I cannot deny what he says, but we are not the people we

once were. In becoming outcasts, our people vowed to prepare every generation for your return. We have vowed no harm will come to the new protector until all our people have lost their lives in his service. We have learned to fight with the sword."

Without warning, the figure drew a long curved sword identical to the images on Logan's chest. Teah gasped and backed away as the glow from Grinwald's hands intensified.

"And the men," the warrior continued, "have learned to fight with the arrow and staff."

"The men?" Logan, Teah and Grinwald said at once.

In a flourish of black fabric, the stranger threw back the cloak, revealing a woman with long black hair tied in a tail. Her neck, midriff, and legs below the knee were bare. Tight fabric covered her chest and from her waist to her knees.

"I am Sasha, a defender of the Protector."

May the gods help us, cried Falcone. *They have sent a temptress to beguile us. And she is a beauty to be sure.*

Quiet, Falcone, every woman was a temptress to you. She is as evil as all the Betra, Bastion chided.

Grinwald, Logan, and Teah stared with mouths agape. The woman stood before them, every muscle chiseled to perfection, but not missing any of her more feminine curves. Her face was beautiful from her high cheek bones to the curve of her jaw. She was a magnificent sight.

"Do you think there is something familiar about her?" Logan whispered to Teah.

Teah shook her head in agreement and then shrugged in answer to his raised eyebrow.

Grinwald, meanwhile, absently nodded his agreement to Logan's whisper. The two young ones were the direct descendents of a royal and magical bloodline. But where did this woman claim her breeding from? Surely not just from the Betra?

*****

The suddenness of it all left everyone in camp silent for an uncomfortably long moment. Sasha used the silence to kneel before Logan again. Logan shifted uncomfortably.

She held her blade over her bowed head in open palms. "I pledge my sword to your life. Do you accept my pledge?"

Logan stared at the top of the woman's head and then at Grinwald. The Viri Magus nodded to accept the pledge.

The boy nervously cleared his throat. "I accept your pledge

of loyalty, Sasha, and thank you for it."

The Betra got to her feet and then bowed deeply. "Your words are too kind for the likes of me Master, but they are welcomed. We did not know how you would receive us when you came again. Know my pledge is a pledge not only for me, but for my entire people still waiting in 'The Forbidden' for news of your acceptance."

Grinwald stepped towards the woman. "How many Betra are there?" he asked.

She turned to him confidently. "When we were exiled some five hundred years ago, there were fifty thousand of us," she replied reverently.

"And now?" the Viri Magus urged.

"Now the Betra have over ten times that many," she said proudly, "not counting those who are not combat ready."

The three companions exchange looks of awe. "Five hundred thousand troops," Grinwald stammered. "And all of these Betra will follow and protect Logan?"

Sasha turned to Logan as Grinwald addressed him by name. She answered the Viri Magus while still staring into the young man's eyes. "Every one of them will give their life before the Protector is ever harmed." She bowed as she finished.

"It is our destiny to see the Protector will die of old age and never in battle. It is the cost of our salvation. Due to our betrayal of the last protector, this is the only way we can redeem our people for years to come. I am honored it is in my lifetime you have chosen to come again."

Kill her, Bastion, Stalwart, and Falcone cried in unison.

Show her mercy, Galiven pleaded.

Logan was shocked by Galiven.

The smile on her face was so radiant, Logan smiled as well. "At last something is going in our favor," Logan said confidently. "The King wouldn't try to kill us again now the Betra have vowed their protection."

"The King has an army which counts in the millions, maybe more since he has joined forces with the Caltorians. The Betra are surely welcome, but our work is not done yet. We have to gather more support for putting Teah on the throne of Ter Chadain."

As Grinwald said this, Sasha moved before Teah, sheathed her sword, and bowed. "Your Majesty, I pledge my people to help you regain your throne as long as your path and the path of the Protector is one."

Teah, a faint smile growing on her lip, bowed back to Sasha. The woman yelped. She drew her sword and dropped back into a defensive stance. Teah looked to Grinwald for help, but the Viri Magus's eyebrows rose in surprise.

Logan moved between the Betra and his sister, putting his hands up to calm them. "We don't want anyone to get hurt here, Sasha. Why don't you tell me why you have drawn your sword on my sister and see if we can work this out."

"No queen bows to the Betra. We are not worthy of such actions. Is she trying to shame me? Is she mocking me?" A mix of fear, outrage, and shock fluctuated across her face.

"Teah didn't mean any disrespect, Sasha. She realized she was a queen a few days ago, the same time I found out I was a protector. She still has to learn the correct way to deal with different customs and situations. Please be patient with both of us as we try to get comfortable in these new skins we have been given."

"You needn't ask for my patience, Master," She dropped the sword's point to the earth. "I regret drawing on Her Highness. It is I who now asks for your forgiveness." She knelt before him once more, head bowed.

Logan sighed, reached down to the woman, and helped her to her feet. "Let's all sit down around the fire and see if we can get some more information out of Grinwald. He seems to be in an informative mood today and I would like to take advantage of that."

Grinwald chuckled and moved to sit beside the fire. The others did the same with Sasha sitting between Logan and the Viri Magus. They all settled down and turned to the old magician.

"Galiven searched for a town in which to settle down. He found one, and then grew to love its people. He soon felt comfortable enough with them to fall in love with one of their own."

"Salabin," Logan whispered.

Grinwald nodded. "Protectors have certain defenses they retain throughout their lives, but his love convinced him to let his down. One night while Protector Galiven and his love slept, the brother of his betrothed snuck into their dwelling with some others after a night at the local tavern. Their intention was to hold the holy blades of the protector in their hands, but when Galiven awoke, startling them, they killed him. That woman, Salabin, had betrayed him by telling her brother where the blades were kept, thus allowing them access and eventually causing the death of Protector Galiven."

Logan grew pale. His hands clenched, then rose to rub his neck. Salabin—Galiven's beautiful Salabin—had done this? He trembled.

"Why are we here exactly, Grinwald? And what did you get from our homestead when we were there?" Teah asked after looking worriedly at Logan trembling.

Before Grinwald could answer, Sasha leaned closer. "That was your destroyed homestead?" Teah nodded. "And the people killed there were your friends?"

"They were our family." Logan frowned, then his eyebrows shot up and his mouth dropped open. "Did you bury those people when you found them?"

"Yes, Master. I hope that doesn't displease you. The Betra do not leave the slain to be eaten by wild creatures. It is a shameful end. I couldn't see those people as shameful so I gave them the traditional Betra burial."

Tears came to Logan's eyes. His eyes darted to his sister's, wherein the same wetness glittered. "Thank you, Sasha, for honoring our family with your thoughtfulness."

"I'm honored to know you approve Master," she nodded.

Logan paused a moment, staring at the fire.

"Now," Logan said, turning back to the Viri Magus, "why are we here?"

"The reason we are here is just over the next hill. In that valley, the Protector's Fortress lies. That is where you will claim special artifacts of the protector to aid you in your fight for Ter Chadain. Remember, you are the weapon that is the protector, but these items will help you accomplish your goals as protector."

He reached in his back pack as he spoke, pulling out the dirty cloth retrieved from the old homestead. "This is what I have recovered from your home."

He let the item unwrap, dropping into his free hand. Holding it for them to see, he displayed a golden medallion with the same images covering Logan's left breast.

"This key will allow us access to the Fortress. There would be no possibility of entering the great castle of the protector without it. We are going there to collect the artifacts within those walls, allowing us to continue our quest to reclaim Ter Chadain. There is an ancient society of warriors guarding the castle and none but the protector or magically trained, such as myself, would be able to access it without this key."

"Then why can't you just get us into the castle without it?" Logan reasoned.

"They would allow me entry, but not the two of you. That is why we needed the medallion. It is more proof you are who you claim to be and will allow you access to the items inside. Only you will be able to retrieve them," Grinwald explained.

"And then what?" Teah asked, breaking her silence.

"That should be obvious, my dear. We gather the support of the people of Ter Chadain to put you on the throne where you rightfully belong."

Chapter 8

The sun was high in the afternoon sky as the party prepared for the last leg of the journey.

Grinwald pulled Logan aside to have a quick word. When Logan gave the Viri Magus a questioning look, the old man placed a reassuring hand on his shoulder. "Keep an eye on Sasha. These people are exiled for a reason and I'm not sure they can be trusted. Don't let your guard down."

Logan began to object, but the Viri Magus gave his shoulder a slight squeeze. "Just trust me on this. One person's reason for doing something might be totally different from what they tell you."

Logan looked eye to eye with the old man, nodding. "Then why did you encourage me to accept their help?"

"Allies, even those you cannot trust completely, are often better than no allies at all," Grinwald answered and then walked away.

That is why you shouldn't trust the Viri Magus either, lad, Stalwart said, and fell quiet.

Their party, now four, headed up the cliff face. Grinwald was surprisingly agile for a man of his stature and years. The Viri Magus meticulously picked a path using the crevices and outcroppings created by years of rain runoff from the land above.

Teah followed after Grinwald slowly, keeping pace, easily pulling herself after him.

Sasha waited patiently behind, bracing or pushing Teah's foot with her hand, helping steady the girl as she went.

Patchy bushes dotted the cliff face and Logan mistakenly took hold of one for balance, causing the light roots spread across the barren rock to let go and leave him dangling by one hand precariously above the floor far below.

Teah screamed as she looked down, her face contorted with fear.

"Hold on Logan," Grinwald cried as he balanced above.

Sasha moved quickly, sliding down the few feet separating them, showering him with loose rock. She took hold of a rock outcropping and bent down to extend her hand to him.

Logan threw his hand up, slapping it into her strong grip with a grunt and was hoisted back up upon the rocks with a long exhale, staring back at the long fall that would have awaited him.

"Thank you Sasha," he gasped.

She gave a slight nod, turning and continuing after Teah.

After reaching the top and catching their breath, they began to descend into the valley home to the Fortress of the Protector. They followed an overgrown path meandering down the valley wall leading into a lush overgrowth of vegetation. Eventually the growth rose to block out the sun, plunging them into the unnerving shadows of the valley.

"I know the way to the fortress," Sasha announced. "I have visited it many times to be sure I could find it when you returned."

Upon hearing this, the others stepped to the edge of the path for her to take the lead. Logan followed directly behind the Betra, with Teah after him and Grinwald bringing up the rear.

They came upon a great gate appearing out of nowhere. Creeping vines covered the doors and high fortress walls loomed in either direction until they disappeared into the shadows of the canopy. Logan walked up to the gates and pushed the leaves aside. The deep brown of the wood under the plants was barely visible even then. The exposed wood changed color, blending into its surroundings. He dropped his hand as if burned.

Grinwald strode to the gates, running his hand along the wood for a while, and then smiled with relief. Reaching into his pack, he brought forth the amulet.

The others gathered around, peering at an uncovered indentation in the wood. The Viri Magus brought the amulet close. It looked to be a perfect fit.

Just as he was about to put it in place, Logan grasped his wrist. Grinwald turned angrily.

The boy's eyes and face were set.

"What are you doing, Logan?" the Viri Magus scolded.

"I need to do that. If you do, something bad will happen to you."

The Protector spoke with such conviction, the Viri Magus didn't argue. Handing the amulet to Logan, Grinwald backed away. The others followed the Viri Magus's lead backing up several paces from the door.

Logan slowly set the edges of the amulet into the socket,

carefully sliding the artifact into place. With lightning quickness, he flipped backwards and rolled to his right. He righted himself and looked back at his companions.

Shock infused their features.

Logan turned back to the door and understood why.

A dozen large spikes protruded from the ground where he was standing a moment earlier and another dozen spears jutted out from the door itself.

"I'm glad you didn't let me do that," Grinwald said softly. "There would now be one less Viri Magus in Ter Chadain."

Moving around the spears in the ground, Logan reached through the spears on the door and gently gave the amulet a turn. The gates rumbled and the spears retracted with a loud grinding noise as the enormous doors slid apart.

Logan pulled the amulet out of the door, tucking it into his shirt. Then, head held high, he strode forward.

The splendor of the Protector's Fortress rushed over the party. Gold and silver shimmered everywhere, the light refracting from a large fountain in the center of the courtyard. A golden maid poured water from a pot into the basin of the fountain, which fed into streams coursing beneath silver statues adorning the garden. As the light danced over them, the statues appeared to move.

Teah held her fingers over her mouth.

Sasha's face became grim and her eyes filled with tears.

Logan walked slowly into the courtyard followed by the others, all gawking at the riches surrounding them.

The sound from the forest enveloping the fortress disappeared and their footsteps echoed against the white marble floors and walls. Goosebumps rose on Logan's neck and Teah rubbed them on her arms.

As Sasha entered further, four large men in full body armor surrounded her. They leveled swords at her throat. Their golden armor displayed two large silver swords emblazoned on their breastplates, matching the symbol on Logan's chest minus the crown.

Two other men now strode forward, kneeling before Logan, their right fists over their hearts, and heads bowed.

"Welcome Protector, we are at your service. We are here to protect you and the contents of your fortress with our lives," one said.

The men were enormous, at least two heads taller than Logan and almost twice as wide. Before Logan could speak, the man spoke once more, "Why do you put yourself in peril by allowing a 'Forbidden' to travel with you?"

Logan turned. Sasha still stood motionless as the four swords pointed at her neck. "She has come to pledge her people's allegiance to me as you have just done. She has vowed to be my defender."

"We are sorry, Master, but she cannot be allowed inside the fortress. If you wish it, we will spare her life on your word, but she must leave here at once or my men will spill her traitorous blood."

Have them kill her now, Stalwart commanded.

My fortress is no place for the likes of her. Kill her and be done with this nonsense, Bastion ordered.

"Escort her out of the gates and see no harm comes to her as she waits for us outside," he told the man.

The man turned, nodding to the four guards around Sasha. They brought their swords down from her neck but did not sheath them. They motioned for her to move ahead of them.

Sasha looked to Logan beseechingly.

Logan motioned with his head for her to go. The group moved out the gate. Logan tightened his lips looking to Teah, her eyes watering.

Grinwald moved from statue to statue, examining the artifacts, oblivious to what had transpired.

Two guards marched back into the courtyard, saluting and taking positions behind their superior.

"Two of my men will stay outside the gates with her as you wish. This will ensure she remains outside and also keep her from harm," the guard said, coming to his feet.

"Welcome to your home, Master Protector. We are the Bantrees, sworn defenders of the Protector's Fortress. Our people have guarded this place since it was built almost two thousand years ago by the first protector, Bastion Lassain. It is our duty to make sure each protector has the ancient tools meant for only him. Can we show you inside?"

Logan looked to Grinwald and his sister. They stood in a stupor. Turning to the guard, Logan nodded and followed him. They walked up white marble stairs leading to two large doors of gold with intricate silver figures set within.

That is me in the battle of Divergent Pass, Bastion said proudly. *We lost three thousand men that day, but the enemy lost over fifty thousand. What a glorious victory over the Caltorians. I remember when they charged...*

Two guards opened the enormous doors and the party entered the main hall of the fortress. The hall did not disappoint. Sparkling white marble patterned in gold lined the floors and walls. Carved statues of animals and people were everywhere.

Logan glanced up at a statue of a beautiful woman with long hair flowing to her waist and penetrating eyes, Bastion stirred inside of him.

Isn't she the most beautiful queen? Bastion said reverently. Even though she was only made of stone, Logan could feel the intensity of her gaze and see black hair and blue eyes as if she were real. She seemed to be looking directly at him, arms extended from her side, hands turning towards him as if she beckoned him to come and embrace her.

I must disagree with you my friend, Falcone cut in. *Queen Caldera was not only my queen, but also my wife. She is the most beautiful queen of Ter Chadain.*

The protector's spirit directed Logan's eyes to another statue a little ways off with shoulder length hair, green eyes, and a very seductive dress barely covering her shapely figure. Logan blushed.

The guard noticed Logan's hesitation in front of the statues. He bent toward Logan and spoke quietly. "She was the first Queen of Ter Chadain. Queen Tera was said to have been the one who created the magic of the protector when her throne was seized over two thousand years ago. She worked with her cousin Bastion," the guard motioned to another statue next to Tera, "to create the magic of the protector. He was the very first protector and he built this fortress."

Logan walked over to Bastion's statue and stared for a moment. He was a muscular man with short cut hair and light facial hair. Even as a statue, his eyes were penetrating, causing Logan to shiver.

Hello, boy, Bastion greeted him, and was silent.

A movement on the grand staircase off to the side brought Logan out of his thoughts.

All heads turned. A woman moved gracefully down the stairs, her brilliant blue gown flowing out behind her, touching the floor ever so slightly as she went. Her blond hair fell to her waist and a deep blue gem adorned her forehead, held by a golden chain.

Together, all watched as she took the last steps and crossed the entry. The woman went down on one knee before him.

He took her by the arm, helping her to her feet. The shock on her face was a mix of disbelief and confusion. He quickly addressed her.

"I'm quite tired of all this kneeling. If you wish to show me loyalty, just bowing slightly will be enough. Does everyone understand?" he said, raising his voice at the end, looking from side to side.

The Bantrees in the great hall acknowledged their understanding. Logan turned back to the woman whose face was a deep crimson. "I am Logan Lassain," he introduced himself; "This is my sister Teah and the great Viri Magus Grinwald. We have come to claim the artifacts of the protector and gather support to reclaim the throne of Ter Chadain for my sister."

A cheer went up echoing through the great hall. Logan twirled around.

Where only a few men once were now hundreds filled and continued to funnel into the great hall through every doorway.

The woman did not cheer, but looked directly into Logan's face, waiting patiently for the cheers to subside. When he peered down at her, she finally spoke.

"I am Zele Magus Galena and have been waiting for your arrival. We are the female society of the Magus world. I have foreseen your arrival and the arrival of the new Zele Magus Queen of Ter Chadain as well. I have come to accompany her to the Zele Citadel in Ceait to begin her formal training to become Zele Magus and queen." She looked around Logan's broad shoulders to Teah as she finished her greeting.

Teah went pale. "I'm going to the Zele Citadel for training?" She protested, "What about Logan?"

"In order for you to be the true Queen of Ter Chadain," Galena said calmly, "you have to be trained as a Zele Magus, and that means going to the Citadel. All training for the past two thousand years has happened in those halls. You haven't developed your powers yet and may never do so without the special training you will need to get there. Your brother's path lies elsewhere."

She then turned to Grinwald, smiling. "And you—it is good to see you alive."

Grinwald came forward, taking her hand in his, bringing it to his mouth for a soft kiss. "It is a great pleasure to see you again, Galena. I see the years have blessed you, leaving you unaffected by their passing."

The Zele Magus gave the Viri Magus a small nod. "You have done well, Grinwald, and it is always my pleasure to be in your esteemed presence."

Logan stormed between the two Magus, facing Grinwald. "Why didn't you tell us that Teah was to go to the Citadel to be trained?" he shouted.

I told you not to trust him, Stalwart chided.

Him? How about her treachery? Announcing immediately she has come to take the girl, Falcone argued. *The Zele Magus only want to control men and training the girl would give her power over Logan.*

"Silence," Logan exclaimed. But he hadn't said this in his mind. He said it out loud.

The entire room was deathly quiet; everyone stared at him. The two Magus's faces were crimson as they glowered at Logan. "What else have you been keeping from us?" he accused.

Teah stood as motionless as Grinwald; Galena, and Logan exchanged glares. Her face was pale white, her lips turning blue. Her eyes began to roll in her head.

Logan leapt behind her, catching her before she fainted.

"It will be ok," he assured his sister, holding her tight.

"How can I go to the Citadel without...?" she began, but the words trailed off.

"My sister needs a place to..."

Before he finished his sentence, a slender woman with short, dark hair in a plain brown dress appeared and began to kneel, but hesitated, bowing her head reverently. Logan appraised the servant, lips drawn tight together. Gently, however, he addressed the bent head.

"I would like an adjoining room to my sister and have dinner brought up to my room for both of us. We will dine alone," he added, looking at the Viri and Zele Magus. He turned his gaze back to the servant. "Could you take her to her chambers and stay with her until I join you in a moment?"

The woman nodded and proceeded to place a supportive arm gently around Teah's quivering shoulders.

Teah looked up uncertainly to Logan as she moved past him.

"It will be all right," he whispered. "I'll be right there."

Teah and the woman walked slowly up the stairs. Logan didn't move or take his eyes from them until they were out of sight.

Grinwald began to question Logan before Teah was gone, but Logan stayed his questions with a raised hand.

When Teah was out of sight, Logan turned calmly to the Zele and Viri Magus, their displeasure evident.

"How dare you speak to us in that manner," Galena shouted. "You may be the Protector, but don't you ever forget the power that Grinwald and I command. Do you understand me?" A vein on the side of Galena's neck bulged.

"You may command respect in Ter Chadain, Zele Magus," Logan began, "but when the two of you keep valuable information from Teah and me, I feel that you are using us as puppets for your own goals. That I will not allow as long as I have a breath inside this body."

He spun on Grinwald.

"Why didn't you tell Teah she was to be trained at the Zele Citadel?" His voice was low and controlled, but it was now more of a hiss than a whisper.

Grinwald took two steps back, the shocked look on his face mixed with sadness. "I felt she had enough to endure without giving her more to deal with. How would that knowledge have changed anything we did?"

"It would reassure us that you are worthy of our trust."

"How could you question my motives?" Grinwald said, his voice wavering. "I have done nothing but care for you and protect you since we've met." He spun on his heels and stormed out of the hall.

Logan didn't wait, but turned his attention immediately on Galena. "How is it possible you can be inside the fortress without setting off the trap we encountered outside?"

"That is easily answered," Galena said condescendingly, moving over to him. "There is an entire village attached to the fortress, serving as the base for the Bantrees. Only they know the way into the fortress from their village and they will not tell a soul0. I found the entrance as only one with my abilities could and therefore entered the fortress. If someone with intentions of doing you harm, or of stealing the ancient artifacts stored here had entered the fortress, all the Bantrees would have died in the effort to defeat them."

Logan looked at the guard nearest him. The man nodded.

"Since they knew I was of no threat," Galena finished, "they allowed me to stay and wait for you."

That sounded reasonable to Logan, plus there were too many other things to think about and he was exhausted. "I am tired and hungry from our journey. Would someone please show me to our rooms for the night and bring some dinner?"

He took a few steps to the stairs and then stopped. "Also see that a fire is made outside the gate for Sasha and food brought to her."

"But, Master," the guard who had escorted them inside began to protest.

A raised hand by Galena stopped him.

"It is true then," she began, "there is a 'forbidden' traveling with you?" She looked at Logan, waiting for an answer.

"She came proclaiming the loyalty of herself and her people in my service to the death. Grinwald told me to be wary of her, but I allowed her to accompany to the fortress. I feel she is an ally."

"This is not possible," the Zele Magus protested. "She is not worthy to serve the Protector. She must be sent away before others arrive to aid in her scheme."

"Scheme, what scheme?" Logan stepped forward. "She vowed loyalty. I will not turn away the aid of over five hundred thousand warriors offered me."

"Dear spirits of our ancestors, they number that many now?" The Zele Magus exclaimed. "They are the 'Forbidden' for a reason, Logan. They could overwhelm the fortress with that many. We must not let her get word to the rest of them. Guards, take her to the dungeon."

"Hold that command," Logan shouted. "She will not be taken prisoner, and she will not be detained if she wishes to leave, which I believe she does not. Do as I asked and I will think on this matter until the morning."

His command overruled the Zele Magus. By the looks on everyone's faces, they were as surprised as she. Logan turned away from Galena's crimson face as the voices of the protectors argued either to keep or kill Sasha. Logan pushed them back into his thoughts and their voices quieted, but didn't stop.

A young boy approached Logan hesitantly. "I will show you to your chambers, Master Protector. Please follow me."

Weary of today's revelations, Logan followed the boy, hoping to leave the stress and confusion behind.

At the top of the stairs, a long hallway led deep into the fortress, a parade of large rooms forming on either side. The first two rooms didn't have doors and a number of guards were at different stages of either getting their armor on or off. None looked up as Logan passed.

The boy stopped in front of a large door which was adorned with Logan's image. Logan looked away and then turned back quickly to gawk. He wore a dark cape over a white shirt with brown pants and calf-high leather boots. Two handles projected over his shoulders, pushing out of the cape and exposing clear spheres on the pommels with the image of the swords and crown in them.

"This is your room, Master Protector, and the Queen has the room next door. There is a door allowing you to pass from the outer chamber in your room to the outer chamber in her room. Where would you like the food?" The boy waited patiently, head bowed slightly, for his answer.

"My room will be fine. I need to see my sister in her room and assure she is fine, if you would please take me there now."

The boy bowed then took several paces down the hall to a door with the emblem of a crown on it. Knocking lightly, a voice from inside admitted them entrance. The boy opened the door and stepped aside. After Logan entered, the boy quietly closed the door behind him.

Logan's mouth fell open in surprise at the beautiful fabrics and tapestries all about him. The outer chamber was decorated in lush furnishings of every color imaginable. Couches and chairs were upholstered in exquisite velvet and leather. Paintings of people long dead lined the walls.

He turned to Teah who sat staring around the room as well. Her escort stood silently in the corner with her head bowed.

"That will be all," Logan told her. "Thank you for staying with her. We will take our supper in my room."

The woman stared up at Logan for a moment and then left the room silently.

"I can't believe this. This is incredible." Teah said. "It all feels like a dream." She hesitated for a moment, looking around the room and then back up at him, the fear evident on her face.

"Do you think I handle going to the Citadel without...?" Her voice trailed off.

"Me?" Logan finished.

She nodded.

"I don't know, Teah. A week ago I would have told you that we weren't strong enough to go separate ways, but after all we've been through, it could be we are. You are Teah Lassain, the next queen to sit on the throne of Ter Chadain. If I must be the protector, then maybe it is our destiny to travel different paths."

"But Logan," she protested. "I don't feel any different. I don't feel as if I have magical powers," she hesitated as she made that statement. She felt the tattoo on her breast. "Except for seeing the colors when Grinwald fought the guards...and this..."

She pulled down her collar just enough to expose the tattoo.

Logan glanced at it casually and looked away, then spun back to stare at it again in disbelief.

"You weren't kidding, that looks exactly like mine."

"I got it the same night you got yours. It's the mark of the protector."

"Do you have all the same powers I have?" Logan asked. "You're fast, but are you as strong as I am?"

"I haven't checked, but I think since you're stronger than me anyway, you're probably stronger than me now." She bit her lip. "How could I become a protector, too?"

"Maybe it has something to do with us being twins," Logan reasoned. "I haven't heard anyone mention anything about protectors and queens of Ter Chadain being twins. We could be the first twins in this situation. It is possibly the reason you also became the protector."

"Possibly." She nodded.

"We need to ask Grinwald," he began.

"No." Teah gripped his forearm. "Not Grinwald, not anyone. If they didn't expect this to happen, then maybe it's bad it happened. I don't trust them, and until I do, we need to keep this between us."

Logan furrowed his brow, but nodded.

"Now they tell me I'm to be trained at the Citadel and Grinwald knew that was the plan all along. It makes it very hard to trust him or anyone else for that matter. Why don't I feel magical?"

"If Grinwald is right, you haven't gotten your powers yet or maybe you just don't know how to access them. We've been accepting everyone else's ideas and opinions lately, but haven't had time to figure them out ourselves. We have to stick together and talk everything out if we can. I know you wouldn't lie to me and you can count on the same. We need to meet every night and discuss what has happened. Together we can decide what to do, in private—away from other people's input. That is the only way we can be sure we are seeing things right. Agreed?"

Teah sighed heavily. "Agreed, but I'm scared."

"So am I," he nodded, "so am I."

They moved into the bed chamber to make sure everything was alright. Again, the lights were all lit, and as in the outer room, a fire crackled softly in the fireplace. After checking to assure that no one hid in Teah's room, they walked through the door connecting the two outer chambers.

As they moved into the Protector's chambers, awe arrested them. Large leather furniture and animal skins adorned a room with dark granite floors and dark wood paneling. Paintings displayed violent battles in which hundreds of soldiers bore down on a solitary figure.

After looking at the images for a moment, Logan realized the figure must be the protector. A closer examination of the painting caused him to run a hand through his hair. The face of the protector in each picture looked exactly like him. He stared for the longest time until his thoughts were disturbed by a light knock on the door. He looked at Teah who returned a questioning glance.

"Enter," he called.

The woman who escorted Teah to her rooms opened the door, giving a small nod and motioning several other people dressed in similar non-distinct clothing inside. Each brought a covered tray to the large table in the center of the room, arranging them neatly.

Grinwald stuck his head into the room with a curious smile on his face. "Is everything okay in here?" he asked quietly. "You left so quickly I didn't have a chance to speak with you about the day's events. Everything developed too rapidly for me to prepare you for it and I hope you will come to accept it."

"We're fine," Logan replied flatly.

"Good, good," Grinwald smiled, rubbing his hands together nervously. "I'll speak with you in the morning." Then he was gone.

The servers uncovered the food and carried the covers out of the room silently.

"If there is anything else you need, please tell the guards outside your room and we will see to it promptly." The woman bowed and exited the room, closing the door behind her.

The guards, Logan thought. *Are they to protect us or keep us from going anywhere?*

They are trained to do as you wish. Your word is law here, Logan, don't doubt the Bantrees. They are the most loyal subjects you could ever have, Bastion assured.

The thought slipped away as the warm smells of the food caressed his nostrils. Teah already dug into some roasted meat and he took the seat beside her, helping himself to some chicken and potatoes. Logan poured each of them a glass of sweet wine and began eating ravenously.

After they could eat no more, they sat back staring at all the food that was left and turned to each other with guilty looks .

"We never had food like this at home," Teah said.

"Yeah, it was always enough, but never this amount," Logan agreed. A smile curled his lips and Teah met his gaze as her eyes twinkled.

I know what your thinking, Logan, but that isn't done, Bastion warned. *They are peasants. They shouldn't have what we have.*

Logan stood and began to gather the uneaten food onto a platter. Teah did the same. Once they had all they could carry, he led the way to the door. Balancing his tray on one hand, he threw the door open.

The guards snapped to attention, eyes forward and motionless.

"Are either of you hungry?" he asked.

The two exchanged glances over Teah and Logan's heads, the turned once more into motionless as statues.

"If you're hungry, we are happy to share what is left," Logan pressed.

"It is not that we are not honored," one guard spoke, "but it is not allowed on duty."

Logan frowned for a moment and then smiled again. "What if you're off-duty?"

"Even if we're off-duty," the other guard said, "we're not allowed to eat the Protector's food."

"Says who?" Teah said, causing all three men to jump with a start.

"It is not done my Queen," the guard replied with a slight bow.

"Who has authority over the Queen of Ter Chadain?" she asked.

"No one except the Protector in this Fortress," the guard answered hesitantly.

"I guess if my sister wants the guards to have the remaining food, that is what will be done in the Protector's Fortress," Logan told them. "Please send for someone to help carry the other trays," he told one guard, "and you, grab a tray and follow us," he ordered the other.

The two men didn't hesitate. Soon Logan, Teah, and the guard carried trays of food into one of the rooms at the end of the hall. As they entered, all the guards came to attention.

"What is the meaning of this?" a man began. He was the man who addressed them when they first entered the Fortress. Upon seeing Logan and Teah, confusion filled his face and he looked to the trailing guard.

"They insisted on bringing this to the guards, Captain," the man explained with a shrug.

"This is not done, Master Protector," the captain said.

"The Queen wishes the guards have the food remaining from our dinner and I happen to agree with her. Are you telling us our wishes mean nothing here?" Logan said calmly.

"No, Master Protector."

"My sister and I grew up on a farm where food like this is very rare. We will not see it go to waste when there are hungry men who can enjoy it as we have. If anyone wishes to argue this point, inform them to come and see me. I will deal with it. I am the master of this fortress, am I not?"

All the men in the room nodded.

"She is the mistress of this fortress is she not?" he said, pointing to his sister as he set his tray down.

All nodded she was.

"Then this matter is settled. Distribute the food between the guards who are off-duty, being sure to save some for those who are currently on duty."

Logan took the tray from Teah and set it down on the table as the guard carrying the tray did the same. He turned to leave as the woman who had brought the food to his quarters entered.

"The remaining food from my quarters is to be distributed among the guards and then the rest of the fortress staff. That goes for all food served to my sister, myself, and anyone else here who is getting food different from the rest of the fortress. Is that understood?"

The woman nodded and Logan moved past her into the hallway, directing the staff who had arrived with her back to his quarters. There Teah and he watched as every last tray was taken to the guards.

"This is highly unusual," the woman said with eyes lowered. "Traditionally, food good enough for royalty does not touch any other lips. Instead, it is given to the livestock."

"I feel the guards and your staff are more worthy of it than the livestock," Logan stated. "Don't you agree?"

"Yes, Master Protector," she replied, eyes still lowered.

Logan reached out, gently taking her chin and lifting her face until her eyes met his. "What is your name?"

"Magda, Master Protector."

"Magda, I wish you to call me Logan."

"I could do no such thing, Master Protector," she said in horror, trying to pull away from him.

"I was raised to believe all people are fundamentally the same everywhere. Our differences come from our decisions and the circumstances of our lives, not always by choice. I did not choose to be the protector and you, I would guess, did not choose to be born Bantree. Am I correct?"

She nodded. "But you are the Protector no matter if you wanted it or not. It is your birthright."

"Again I point out, not by choice. I will do my duty as protector, putting my sister on the throne for the good of Ter Chadain. You will do your duty to see to our needs running this fortress's daily schedule. I respect your desire to do your best and thus respect you as a person. I see you as a servant who provides a necessary service to me in seeing to my needs while I am here. I want you to think about that and remember I am a person like you. Unlike you, I'm expected to use my abilities to reclaim a throne. Those abilities allow me the opportunity to fulfill my duty, just as your abilities allow you to do your duty. We are both people. Only our duty is different. Both are vital to the fulfillment of our destiny."

Logan looked down at the woman whose chin he still held. Tears streamed down her face through his fingers. Logan looked to Teah for help. Her eyes also welled with tears.

Can't you just leave well enough alone, complained Bastion? *Are you going to dismantle all the traditions that have been upheld for over two thousand years?*

Only the ones that make no sense and treat people disrespectfully, Logan replied.

Good for you. I never had the courage or foresight to do what you have. I feel ashamed that I didn't, Galiven cheered.

Humph, Bastion added and went silent.

"Master Protector," the woman said meekly, "I am honored to serve you and will use all my abilities to see to your needs. There has been speculation as to a new kind of protector who will enter our world and now I know that to be true. You have wisdom beyond your years and a generous heart, which cannot be rivaled. I can't call you by your first name alone, but I will see it as a privilege to use the title of Master along with your name. I hope it pleases you?"

"Yes, Magda, that will please me." He gently kissed her forehead as she bowed. The woman's face stretched into a beaming smile.

"Will there be anything else, Master Logan?"

"Let the kitchen staff know the meal was wonderful and have a good night."

"I will," she smiled again, closing the door behind her.

Logan turned from the door. Teah stared at him as if she was seeing him for the first time.

"What?" he asked.

"My brother is now a man." She went to the door and then turned back, "The future of Ter Chadain is in good hands." She smiled and shut the door behind her.

Chapter 9

King Englewood sat in his dining hall enjoying a roasted boar dinner and fine wine. He leaned back, letting the wine wash the last remnants of the boar down his throat, and smiled with satisfaction.

The door to the hall burst open and a large bald man entered.

Englewood shuddered.

The man's thick black beard partially hid a long purple scar running down the right side of his face. It puckered the skin from his temple to his eye, and then under his chin. That eye stared emptily at nothing, while the other scanned the hall.

"Englewood, we need to talk," the man scowled, moving next to the King, pulling a chair from the table. He dropped heavily into it and lifted his boots to the table. Mud dropped onto the nearby platter of boar.

"General Cecil, what can I do for you this evening?" Englewood glowered.

"News has reached me that you have your witch running around Ter Chadain chasing children. What have you up your sleeve?"

"What makes you think I have something up my sleeve? Caldora often handles minor security issues for me. There is nothing out of the ordinary. She is able to move between the northern duchies and southern duchies unseen. I wouldn't want those unhappy with my reign to know how I plan to deal with them before I am ready."

"So you don't know anything about her heading out of Cordlain with a murder of Shankan or about the regiment of men following after her a few days later?"

"No, Cecil, I can't say that I do," Englewood shrugged.

"Then I guess you would have no idea about a man named Rongren leaving a few days before your witch with two Shankan Warriors? He returned last night with two broken arms and a message for you."

Englewood's eyes grew wide and he licked his lips nervously. "No, I don't know anything about that."

"Bring him in," the general shouted.

The doors to the hall flew open, banging against the walls. Two guards dragged a man between them. The man was beaten and battered and his arms hung uselessly by his sides. The man's head slumped, listing to one side.

"Rongren, deliver the message to King Englewood so we all can hear what has happened to you and the two Shankans who accompanied you," the general ordered.

One of the guards took the man by the hair and lifted his head up to face the table.

"Go on, Rongren, you need to have those arms set, if there is any point to that, and you need to get some food in you. Just deliver the message to the King that you refused to tell me."

The man hesitated. At a nod from the general, the other guard twisted Rongren's broken arm. Rongren cried out in pain, whimpering as the man released him.

"All right, all right, I'll tell ya." He looked for mercy from King Englewood, but the King sat staring at him without emotion. "The Protector told me to tell you and Caldora that he will be coming to kill you and any who have aided you."

Englewood started. The general smirked. At a sign, the guards dropped Rongren to his knees and left. Rongren broke down crying.

"So, that legendary hero from Ter Chadain history has returned," Cecil said sarcastically. "I bet your scared out of your mind, eh, Englewood. Don't you worry, the big bad Protector will not harm you as long as you do what the Empress wants. If you decide to try anything funny and have a change of heart about staying loyal to her majesty, I'll throw you to this protector and then cut his head off myself after he has taken care of you. Then I will send your precious Caldora over to Caltoria to be the slave of the Empress herself."

The general stood. "Understand?" He leaned down to stare into the King's red, watery eyes.

Englewood nodded.

"Good." The general slid the tray of boar into the King's lap, then turned and walked out laughing.

King Englewood sat staring at the broken body of Rongren crying on the floor. The King stood, sending the tray and boar crashing to the floor, and walked slowly over to the man. Reaching inside his robes, Englewood drew a dagger.

Rongren screamed. Englewood took the man's hair in one

hand, pulling his head up. He slit the man's throat and walked away as the man gurgled his last breath.

"Clean up that mess," he said to the stunned guard at the door as he passed.

Chapter 10

Logan's sleep was restless. Again he moved in one of Falcone's battles. They raced down a ravine towards a line of men holding back a flow of soldiers.

The Battle of Gallatin's Pass.

They dove into the fray, barreling into the line, and shoring up the weakening areas. The tide was turning in their favor when a shout came up.

"Archers on the hill."

Falcone's head swung up to the side of the ravine. A line of archers loosed a barrage of arrows into the pass.

"Shields!"

Falcone's arm reached up, cutting a number of arrows apart in midflight, but one stuck under his left arm and imbedded in his chest.

Logan arched in pain, screaming as he woke, gasping for air. Teah rushed to his side as two guards burst into the bed chamber.

"Get Grinwald," she ordered, trying to keep Logan from sitting up.

Blood flowed through the white night shirt, the crimson spreading out across his chest.

In a moment the Viri Magus was at Logan's bedside, along with Galena. The old man's hands passed over the boy's body, the magic filling the room. Galena followed his movements with her hands, though her actions seemed more precautionary.

Teah studied the magic moving over and into her brother. She shook her head; hazy lines of energy flowed around and across Logan's flesh. They changed colors and shapes as Grinwald worked. Suddenly, yellow lines became fists and then plunged into Logan.

Logan's body arched then went limp.

Galena placed her hands directly on the Protector. "How long has this been going on?" she asked, keeping her focus on Logan.

"Just a few days ago he had the first incident."

"A few days!" Galena spun on the old man. "Why haven't you trained him to guard his mind against the dreams?"

"I don't have that knowledge. I have never dealt with a protector before. I knew it was a danger, but not a pressing one. How do you know such things?"

"Zele Magus's have to always guard their minds against the unwanted thoughts escaping them. Don't Viri Magus practice mind control?"

"Of course we do, but we don't let our thoughts control our magic. We never dream. Do you?"

"That is why we need to train our minds to keep our magic at bay while we sleep." She turned back to the motionless boy, putting her hands to his forehead. Closing her eyes, she stood perfectly still for a while and then, as if with great effort, pulled away.

Teah, watched, trying not to shake.

Galena's face was weary and exhausted as she smiled at Teah. "He will be fine. I put a temporary block in his mind until he can learn to do it himself. I will begin training with him this very morning." She turned, walking slowly out of the room with Grinwald close behind.

Teah glanced at the two guards standing just inside the door. They nodded and shut the door quietly behind them as they exited, leaving the two siblings alone.

The girl sat on the edge of the bed, gently taking Logan's clammy hand. "I know I'm a Zele Magus now. I could see what Grinwald was doing to you and even understood it a little. You are the Protector and I am the Zele Magus Queen. Our destiny is carrying us forward like a raging river. I hope we don't drown before we learn how to swim."

*****

Logan woke later that morning, still aware of the vision in his sleep. His shirt bore the only traces of the night's events. Lifting his bed clothes, he gingerly tested the dried bloodstain. A small scar was visible, showing up as a light pink line on his chest, but there was no other sign of damage from the arrow.

He slowly got up, moving over to the dresser to wash. Removing his bed shirt, he stood naked, splashing water from a basin on his face with his hands. He glanced at himself in the mirror; his brown hair was always long, but now hung past his shoulders. A dark shadow was visible on his face, his facial hair growing in earnest.

He paused for a moment. The voices ever present in his mind

since he became protector were now noticeably silent. No, not silent. If he listened intently, they were still there, but muffled, as if speaking through a wall or door.

"That's odd," he said to his image in the mirror. He couldn't make out their words, but they were shouting just the same. He thought the word "witch" came through and then was muffled again.

Touching his tattoo, he traced the shapes as he looked absently into the mirror. There came a light tap at the door and Magda leaned her head into the room.

Logan shook his head to clear his thoughts.

"The Viri Magus Grinwald would like to see you when you are dressed. There are clothes in the wardrobe that should fit you."

She pointed to the large armoire opposite the bed and then closed the door, red faced.

Logan smiled sheepishly as he hunted through the wardrobe. Dark pants and a white shirt fit him perfectly. He even found some stockings and shoes to fit as well.

He ran his fingers through his hair after wetting it down and used a lace from another pair of shoes to tie back his hair into a tail. Somehow he knew how to tie the lace to keep the tail good and tight. Looking in the mirror, his image gave him pause. He studied himself from all angles, giving a nod to his reflection in the mirror and a smile of approval.

Logan emerged from the bed chamber to a waiting Grinwald sitting and eating some fruit off a small plate he had prepared from larger platters on the table.

"Good morning, my boy," the old man greeted. "I hope you are feeling better. That last vision you had gave us all a start. Galena has promised to help you with some training so, hopefully, we won't have to deal with them again. Get something to eat. We have things to accomplish today of the utmost importance."

Logan selected some roasted meat, fresh fruit, poured himself a glass of sweet wine, and then sat down.

"What do we have to do today?"

"Why, my boy, we get to claim the gifts of the protector for you today. I have already said too much, I don't want to ruin the surprise. Hurry and eat. You shall see soon enough." The two finished their meal, Logan wolfing down his plate of food and hurriedly following the Viri Magus to the door.

"Where do we go?" the young man mumbled with a mouth full of food.

"Follow me." Grinwald smiled, proceeding down the hall in the opposite direction of the main stairs. At the end, they found spiral stairs cut into the floor. Down and down they circled until they stood in another long hallway, torches lining the walls every several feet.

Condensation dripped down the dark stone block walls. Logan touched one, pulling his hand quickly away at the coldness. He moved closer to the Viri Magus, keeping pace until they came to a large door. Grinwald reached out to push it open.

Two large guards seemingly materialized out of the blocks.

They wore black armor from head to toe and blended in perfectly with the black walls. Their spears fell in front of the doors.

"Now men..." Grinwald began cordially.

"No one is allowed into the sacred chamber until the Protector has given the password," one guard said stoically.

The old man turned to Logan expectantly. Logan shrugged and stared back at the Viri Magus.

A flash of light passed before Logan's eyes and he smiled. Leaning close to the guard, Logan whispered.

The guard nodded to his companion and they snapped to attention, once more fading away.

Grinwald smiled excitedly. "What was the password?" he asked.

"If I told you, I would have to kill you. Only the guards of the sacred chamber and the Protector will know."

The Viri Magus scrambled back as Logan's eyes glistened threateningly.

"Shall we?" Logan asked, stepping forward to the door leading to the chamber. A socket stood ready for the amulet in this door, as in the fortress's front gate. Producing the amulet from inside his shirt, Logan inserted the artifact.

As the latch clicked, a chorus of thundering voices echoed down the hall.

"Long live, the Protector!"

Logan and Grinwald jumped and turned around.

Lining the hall from one end to the other, guards in black armor kneeled with their heads bowed.

"Strength and health to the faithful guards of the sacred

room," Logan shouted.

The guards stood and cheered.

Grinwald looked stunned at the boy.

Logan turned, removed the amulet, placing it back within his shirt, and then pushed open the door.

They took in a wondrous sight. White marble radiated light. There were no torches and yet the room was as bright as a summer day. The perfectly round room had three stone pillars placed in the center which rose to Logan's waist.

Logan strode confidently forward.

On one pillar lay a long shirt of shimmering silver mail. With Grinwald by his side, he lifted the mail, laughing. "It feels as light as a linen shirt." Holding it before him, the emblem of the crossed swords over a crown shimmered in the light.

"Put it on," Grinwald urged.

Logan, jolted from his thoughts, began to put the mail on over his shirt, but he paused, removing his shirt first, and then pulling the mail over his head. A warm smile spread across his face. "The metal isn't cold, but warm and soothing. It was heavy at first but now I can hardly tell I have it on." Glancing over at Grinwald, Logan found his features those of shock.

"What?"

"Look." The old man whispered as he pointed at Logan's chest.

Logan glanced down and then jumped back. Where there should have been the mail shirt, was nothing but his own skin and the tattoo of the two crossed swords and crown.

He looked to the Viri Magus in distress, but Grinwald shook his head in amazement.

"What's going on?" Logan shouted, his voice bouncing off the round walls. He touched his arms and chest in a panic and then stopped. He closed his eyes, concentrating, grabbing where the mail shirt once was, and instantly he pulled the shirt away from his body, the entire shirt now visible.

He again looked at the Viri Magus who stood with his mouth agape. Logan let the shirt touch his body again, watching the mail blend seamlessly into his skin.

Grinwald clapped his hands and began dancing around. "Don't you see?" he asked after seeing Logan's continued look of confusion. "The mail becomes one with you to help keep you protected. If I'm right, it will not allow you to become injured as long as you have it on. Plus it becomes one with you so you are able to still move fluidly."

Grinwald made to touch Logan, but drew back his hand of his own accord. His eyes glistened with wonder. "This is extremely magical. I haven't witnessed anything like this in my lifetime. This magic is very old. I would never have the knowledge or the magical power to create something like this." He finally took his eyes off Logan's chest, peering into his face. "I can't even tell you have it on. Can you tell?"

"Only when I concentrate and pull it away from my skin," Logan smiled. "Do I need to take it off every night?"

Grinwald shook his head vigorously. "It is a continuous form of defense. Keep it on. Obviously there has been a great deal of thought put into it. Be grateful these types of tools are available to you. This should aid you greatly."

"If this was worn by the last protector, how was he killed?"

Logan didn't look for Grinwald to answer, instead waiting for the protectors in his mind to respond. But all he heard was muffled voices.

"When Galiven was in the village of the Betra, he was given a false sense of security," Grinwald explained. "It is said that his lover asked him to remove the shirt of mail. He did as she requested and was therefore vulnerable to the attack which occurred that fateful night."

Logan moved to the second pillar, staring down at it, his eyes wide and mouth open.

Two large, sheathed swords shined up at him. The sheaths were midnight black, glimmering with perfection, placed crossing each other. The grips were black as well, with golden wire winding around them, flowing along to form the guard. Black crystal shaped into a ball formed the pommels. Suspended within the crystals was the emblem etched onto his chest.

Carefully Logan drew one of the curved blades free. A metallic ring filled the chamber. As he did, the grip formed to his palm and the guard molded to the back of his hand.

Grinwald backed away.

Logan stood holding one sword before him, the polished steel shining brilliantly, the swords and crown engraved upon the blade.

"Careful with those blades…"

Logan burst into a flurry of slashes and spinning steel. The

Viri Magus stumbled back.

Logan turned back to the pillar, drawing the other blade. He began spinning the blades in unison. Instantly, he created a continuous field of metal, showing no space of air discernable to the human eye. Stopping suddenly, he sheathed the swords in their scabbards with one fluid motion.

Looking to Grinwald, he smiled sheepishly. "It just came to me," he said, answering the questioning gaze of the Viri Magus.

"That seems to be happening a lot lately." The Viri Magus smiled.

"What makes these blades different than any other weapons we have seen so far?" Logan asked, still staring at the swords resting in their scabbards.

"They were created by the combined magic of a Viri Magus and a Zele Magus. That combination of magic is very powerful and very unpredictable. There have been many a Viri Magus and Zele Magus killed when this kind of magic has been duplicated. It has been forbidden, in fact, for the past thousand years, it is so dangerous." Cautiously, Grinwald moved close to the pillar.

"It is said that they pass on to the protector, the abilities needed to be a master swordsman. It is the combination of your physical strengths as the protector and the magic in the blades that give you the power to excel with the swords as you do."

"It seemed completely natural to me when they were in my hands. It is as if they were made for only me," Logan said with a muted smile.

"They will not behave that way for anyone but the protector. That is what makes them so unique. If someone were to take them from you, they would not gain their magical advantage."

Logan nodded.

"I know. When the swords were in my hands, they were an extension of me. The movements of the blades flowed so effortlessly, I couldn't tell if I was moving them or if the weapons were doing it on their own.

Logan walked to the final stand. Grinwald followed, stopping a couple of feet behind. The object looked like a knife in a sheath at first. Logan frowned and bent closer. Now it appeared to be a rod of solid silver the size of a large dagger. It had a black sheath with the same protector's emblem on it and Logan lifted it into his hand to take a closer look.

Grinwald leaned over and stared curiously at the item.

"What is it?" Logan asked, turning to the Viri Magus.

"I don't know. Take it out so we can have a closer look."

Logan took the cold silver rod, its thickness slightly bigger than his thumb, and turned it between his fingers. He gripped it tightly in his fist. The rod burst to nearly Logan's height.

It happened so quickly, Logan dropped it, the rod clattering to the chamber floor.

"What was that?" he shouted, backing away as it shrank to its original size.

Muffled voices resounded in his head, but nothing discernable came to him.

"It was definitely magic, but its purpose is still unknown to me," Grinwald said as he strode over, gingerly picking the small rod up. He tentatively gripped it as Logan had, turning his head away and pressing his eyes shut, expecting some dramatic event. They waited, but nothing happened. Grinwald looked at it once more then tossed it to Logan.

"Try that again so we can see what it does."

Logan caught the rod in his hand, holding it at arms length in a tight fist.

The rod shot out to full length again. This time he didn't drop it, but stared at it curiously. It was entirely uniform from top to bottom, with smoothly cut ends, except for a nearly indiscernible line running the entire length of the shaft.

Logan touched the line and it became a silver strand in his hand. He slowly pulled the strand back to his cheek, the feeling of an archer coming as naturally to him as when he stood in the Treebridge Forest with a buck in his sights. He held his breath, not wanting to give himself away to the creature, and slowly exhaled, releasing the string.

A solid thud echoed as he came back to his current surroundings in the chamber. Grinwald was staring, his mouth open wide with amazement. Logan followed the Viri Magus's gaze to see something protruding from the chamber wall.

He walked over, discovering a silver arrow thrust deep into the stone. "Where did that come from?" Logan asked, not looking at Grinwald, but still staring at the arrow. The silver shaft and fletching of the arrow matched the bow.

He pulled upon the arrow until it came free, and as it did, it disappeared.

Looking down at his empty hand, he turned to Grinwald, shocked.

"It is another rare artifact for use in your quest," Grinwald said in a whisper. "The arrow simply appeared when you drew the string back. This kind of magic is unheard of in our time. The creation of matter out of a magical bow is one of the most incredible things I have ever witnessed."

Logan picked up the small sheath. As he concentrated, the bow shrunk down in his hands and was once again the silver rod.

Logan thought of the bow and the rod expanded to become the bow once more.

He giggled as he changed the silver rod back and forth between the two forms in his hand.

Grinwald crossed his arms and frowned with disapproval. Logan quickly turned it back to a small rod and placed it into its sheath. He tied the thin leather strap around his waist and turned sheepishly back to the Viri Magus.

"Let's take them upstairs and find your sister and Galena."

He handed Logan his shirt and waited for him to button it up. Then he handed him the swords, one at a time, watching as Logan strapped the baldric across his chest. The swords rested on his back with each handle sticking up above his shoulders.

Once they were secure, Logan quickly drew the swords smoothly. Only a metal ringing gave indication of his movement. He stood poised with the swords crossed before him, like the image on his chest.

A short display of spinning steel followed, and then they once again rested in their scabbards on his back.

Grinwald shook his head in disbelief as he backed out of the door into the hall. There was no sign of the contingent of guards who once lined the hall.

"There is no need for them to be down here now that the artifacts have been claimed by a protector," Logan said.

Grinwald smiled as they walked to the stairs. This young man was now the most terrible weapon to walk in Ter Chadain in the past five hundred years. He pitied those who dared defy him.

"Maybe you should keep your new tools a secret for now," the Viri Magus suggested.

"Why would you say that?" Logan asked, his shoulders dropping.

"They will see them soon enough, but it may be wise keeping

them under wraps until you need to present them. It has been over five hundred years since anyone has possessed them, but the legend is still strong and may bring unwanted attention to you. Just hold off on showing them openly for now."

Logan nodded with a sigh.

After leaving the swords and bow in Logan's bed chamber and instructing the guards stationed outside to admit only them, they found Teah and Galena in the queen's outer chambers. The two were in deep conversation.

"We have accomplished what we came for," Grinwald announced. "We should make plans to begin our gathering of support to put Teah on the throne where she belongs."

"Logan and I need time to train him to control the visions," Galena insisted. "That can take awhile, depending on how quickly he masters the technique."

"What's the hurry, Grinwald?" Teah asked. "With the help of the Bantrees, we should be able to gather a small army with little effort."

"The Bantrees will not go with you," Galena explained. "Their duty is to protect the fortress. They cannot become part of the army that is needed to put you on the throne. Logan must gather support from the duchies where those loyal to the Lassain line reside."

"Don't you think Logan and I need to gather support from the duchies?" Teah corrected.

"No Teah, you will accompany me to begin your training as a Zele Magus at the Citadel of Sisterhood in the town of Ceait in Ackerton Duchy. But first we will accompany Grinwald and Logan to Wilderton, in Ackerton Duchy, where your faithful members of the Queen's Guard wait for your return. We will convince them to join with Logan and gather the others who remain loyal to Ter Chadain and the Lassains."

Anguish spread across Teah's face. "I don't want to be away from you," she said, looking at Logan. He wrapped his arms around her. "I know I need training to be a Zele Magus, but can't Galena do it as we travel around to the duchies?"

"I couldn't train you in the manner required," the Zele Magus said compassionately. "The Magus Matris would not allow it and she is in charge of the Citadel." The siblings looked over at her. "I was sent to retrieve you for training and nothing short of that will be acceptable."

"Don't worry," Grinwald said, putting a comforting arm around both youths. "The Brotherhood of Magic is also in Ceait and I have some friends there who will keep an eye on Teah. Not that she needs to be watched when the sisters are involved," he added, seeing anger spread across Galena's face. "I know the Magus Patris personally and will get his word that the castle will give the citadel added security when Teah is there, if it pleases you, Galena?"

The Zele Magus nodded her acceptance and turned back to the distressed brother and sister. "That is days away and you shouldn't concern yourselves about it until you have to. Besides, we have much to do before then.

"Come Logan, we need to go somewhere quiet to concentrate on training you to control your visions." She ushered Logan out of the room, leaving Grinwald to comfort the girl.

Galena led Logan down the grand staircase to her chambers on the other side of the great hall. Her room was also extravagantly adorned in art and expensive furnishings. She instructed him to sit in one of the four chairs in front of the fireplace. A warm fire crackled in the hearth and the orange flame gave a soft glow to the room as the sun set outside.

The Zele Magus sat down in the chair opposite him.

Taking his hands in hers, she looked into his eyes. "All people dream except accomplished Viri Magus such as Grinwald. When people dream, their sleeping mind takes control of their thoughts and many things can happen. This is not a problem to one who is not gifted with magic, but it could be catastrophic to those who allow their magic to escape them during their unconscious sleep. You have a similar problem, but even more dangerous since your dreams are actual visions of past protector's lives. Most protectors died of old age, but as we know, the last protector was murdered by the Betra. As these visions continue to come to you unchecked, the odds increase that the vision you will have is the last moments of the most recent protector. If that happens, you will die as he did."

Logan listened intently to Galena's musical voice as she explained how to gain control of his mind at sleep.

Even as he concentrated on Galena, however, the muted voices of the past protectors screamed out warnings. The muffled words "Witch, witch!" were barely discernable and strong fear penetrated him. He pushed the voices further back into his mind until their cries became a dull drone. The fear, however, remained.

"First you must consciously place a barrier around your thoughts before you sleep. To do this, you need to envision your thoughts as energy in your mind. Seize this energy and wrap a very strong, good memory around it. Almost as if you are wrapping a present to give someone. It must be an extremely powerful memory, something which fills you with joy at the mere mention of it. Can you think of such a memory?"

Logan nodded. He remembered finding his twin sister, Teah, safe in the hay loft.

"I will put you into a sleep and then probe your mind to see if I can penetrate your memory. It will not hurt and I promise not to probe too hard. I will gradually increase the strength of my probing until I am satisfied you can contain the visions of the past protectors. Now take your memory and encircle your consciousness."

Logan closed his eyes and did as he was instructed, wrapping the happy memory of finding Teah around the rest of his thoughts. He felt himself getting sleepy, only slightly cognizant of the cries from the protectors.

Suddenly Logan came awake, the protectors shouting through his mind.

Keep that witch out of your mind, Falcone ordered. *They are evil vile beings who manipulate and use men. Oh, they say they do it for their love of Ter Chadain, but they do it because they hate men.*

Falcone was betrayed by a Zele Magus, Stalwart said softly. *She wove a spell on him to forget his love and marriage to Caderal. He was popular with the ladies before he met Caderal, but never strayed after they were together. Except for the time that Zele Magus wove a spell, erasing his memory. The Zele Magus kept Falcone to use as her own protector and withheld him from his beloved Caderal for almost a year.*

In that time, he was with many women, never able to satisfy his urges that only Caderal could fulfill, Bastion added.

Why didn't you and Stalwart tell him about Caderal? Logan wondered.

She closed us off from his mind as well. We could not reach him, Stalwart explained. *Galena must not be allowed here.*

Logan looked around the room. The fire was nothing more

than embers in the hearth. He rose from his chair and searched until he discovered Galena.

The Zele Magus lay on the floor, her chair tipped to one side. He moved over to her, relieved to find her breathing. Logan gently lifted her up, placing her into the chair as he set it upright. She came around as he sat in his chair, leaning close to her.

"Are you all right?" he asked as she rubbed her face with her hands.

"I think so," she replied, opening her eyes wide.

"What happened?" he pressed.

"You fell asleep and I began to probe your mind to see if I could gain access to your thoughts. I was amazed at how solid your defense was as I probed, so I pressed harder and harder, trying to get in. I know I promised to go easy on you, but your defense was so solid I just kept pushing. When I finally thought I was using enough magic to break into anyone's mind, even those trained magically, a force burst from your thoughts, expelling me. The force raged like several voices screaming at me all at once. It must have pushed me over, knocking me unconscious."

"I'm sorry, Zele Galena, I didn't know what I was doing," Logan apologized.

Were you trying to kill her? Logan asked.

No, but we weren't going to allow her to touch us, Stalwart explained.

Never again, Falcone shouted.

"It was amazing," the Zele Magus said breathlessly. "In all my years as a Zele Magus and teacher at the Citadel, I have never encountered such a defense mechanism. I truly believe you are ready to secure your mind against the visions of the protectors."

"So soon, are you sure I'm ready?" Logan asked in disbelief.

"You are more than ready."

They sat in silence for a while, both staring at the embers.

I thought you were blocked from me by her magic? Logan asked.

We were, Galiven told him. *But her probing of your memory actually released that spell and allowed us out.*

So I still don't have any control over the visions? Logan lamented.

Over the visions, yes, Stalwart replied, *but not over us. You see, we are a part of the protector's magic that was designed to aid you in your journey. We are not meant to cause you anguish, but act as guides along your journey.*

Logan looked at Galena expectantly.

"I'm ready to take you back to your room," she finally said. They stood and walked back to Logan's room where they found Grinwald waiting with Teah.

"How did the lesson go?" the Viri Magus asked.

"His first has become his last," Galena said, mustering a smile. "He mastered the technique and should have little trouble controlling his visions now."

"That is something," the old man grinned, putting a thoughtful hand to his chin.

"You should both get some rest now," Galena said to the siblings. "We will need to get all the details of our journey decided tomorrow. Good night."

Logan and Teah bid the two good night and went to their separate bed chambers, leaving the Viri Magus and Zele Magus alone in the outer chambers.

*****

"What happened?" Grinwald asked. "No one catches on to that kind of mind control so quickly, especially one so young."

"As I was probing his mind, thoughts surfaced much different than the first thoughts I touched. Logan thought of his sisters and his parents, but then there were thoughts that seemed completely out of place."

Galena moved next to the fireplace, gazing silently at the flickering flames creating shadows on the walls and ceiling.

"I believe the boy is not only the Protector, but also a Viri Magus," the Zele Magus whispered not taking her eyes from the flames.

Grinwald's eyes shot wide. He moved beside her as he struggled to speak. "That means he will be more powerful than any being in this world. He will be able to command the magical and physical domains. Do you realize what you are saying?"

Galena turned away. Lightly, Grinwald touched her shoulder and she turned to look at him. The tears running down her cheeks said it all.

"The unimaginable horror of such a powerful human scares me. For a protector with the powers of a Viri Magus has been warned of in ancient prophesy," Galena whispered.

Grinwald walked over to his pack resting in a chair off to one side. He pulled The Protector's Prophecy out of his things.

Opening the ancient tome, he read:

"The One shall come to this world with the warrior skills of a protector plus the magical skills of the strongest Viri Magus and nothing can withstand his might. The world as known will end and the magic of the ages will be changed forever. He is at once the savior and the destroyer."

"What can we do?" Galena sobbed.

"We must keep this to ourselves above all else. No one must know of this and we must assure Logan gets no training for his magical potential."

"You can't be certain that will be enough. He may develop his magic naturally, by himself, and that could prove even more dangerous. Having such power without guidance is too risky. You must assist him as each stage of his development takes place to assure he does not lose control."

"I will not tell him he is a Viri Magus and neither will you," pressed the old man.

"And what if he finds out we have kept this knowledge from him?"

"Then the heavens help us both," the Viri Magus said grimly, "for nothing will be able to save us or the world from him if he loses control." They sat down in front of the fire and stared silently at the flames for a time.

"When do we need to leave for Wilderton?" the Zele Magus asked softly.

"As soon as we can make preparations for the trip. What shall we do with the Betra?" he turned to her.

"He needs an army and they have the largest in the land. If we accept their help, what is the worst that can happen?"

"They can betray him again," the Viri Magus pointed out.

"That may be exactly what we need when the time is right," Galena conceded.

"I have spent the last thirteen years preparing for the return of the protector and a new Zele Magus Queen. It is for the greater good we keep the truth from both of them. Without Teah on the throne, the Caltorians will continue to take what is ours." Galena's face grew outraged as she addressed Grinwald. "Have you heard they take untrained Viri and Zele Students before we have a chance to find them and bring them to Ceait?"

Grinwald's expression turned to match hers. "Why would they be so blatantly taking what is rightfully the property of the societies in Ceait?"

"Because King Englewood cannot control the Caltorians anymore. They are taking every resource from Ter Chadain back to Caltoria." Galena seethed. "Even though we need Teah on the throne to stop them, Logan may turn out to be a problem we have to contain once that is accomplished. I will not save Ter Chadain from the invaders only to have Logan destroy it if his power eludes his control."

Grinwald stared at her long and hard, but she did not look away. It was a troubling concept.

"Very well, I will encourage him to accept Sasha's offer and we will gather the Betra after we deliver you and Teah to Ceait. You realize she is our only hope all of this will work out."

"I do. I will not inform anyone at the Citadel of her true identity except the Magus Matris. She alone knew of my mission and we will keep it that way in order to protect the girl. As far as the occupants of the Citadel are concerned, Teah is just another recruit I have gathered on my travels. Her identity as the Queen of Ter Chadain will not be revealed. I'm sure King Englewood has many spies and we can't be certain he doesn't have one within the walls of the Citadel."

"Maybe I should try putting a power-binding spell on Logan?"

"Even if Logan's current powers as protector would allow you to do such a thing, the spell may inhibit his protector power as well as his Viri Magus Power," Galena warned.

"That could prove fatal to the youth. My only way of keeping Logan from developing as a Viri Magus is keeping him from realizing he is indeed, a Viri Magus. I hate the idea of such unscrupulousness, but like you, I realize desperate times call for such measures."

For a long time they looked into the fire, studying the flames as if for guidance.

"I will not be able to sleep tonight," he finally said to the Zele Magus. "I will begin making plans for our departure."

"I agree, the sooner we leave, the sooner Teah will be within the protective walls of the Citadel and on her road to becoming the Queen of Ter Chadain."

They stood and left the room.

Chapter 11

As the door closed to the chambers of the Protector, a small figure emerged from behind a tall cabinet across from the fireplace. She had every right to be in the room. Master Logan ordered her to bring any uneaten food to the guards and staff and she came to do just that. When Magda entered to find the two magicals sitting in the Protector's chamber instead of their own, she decided to find out why.

It was the way they talked—hunched over, cautious—which caused her pause. So the Protector was also a Viri Magus? She had never heard of such a thing. And now the two magicals were planning to keep this from him because they were afraid of him?

As she hurried to enter Logan's bedchamber, Galena burst into the room as if she'd forgotten something. Upon seeing Magda, she jumped. Comprehension grew.

Magda let out a soft cry. Then the binding weave hit her and she fell stiff to the floor. She couldn't move, and when she opened her mouth to speak, nothing came out.

"I am sorry, Magda, but you have heard things not meant for your ears. Now we must make sure you don't tell anyone of what you have heard. You know what they say, 'wrong place and wrong time'." The smile on Galena's face was terrifying.

Magda made one last effort to cry out and then everything before her eyes went black.

*****

It seemed like forever waiting for Grinwald and Galena to leave the outer chambers. Logan listened to their murmured conversation and at one time thought they had left.

After waiting a while longer to be sure, he started to enter, only to hear Galena's voice again. He listened carefully long after the outer chamber door closed.

Now carrying his precious bundle in his arms, he moved through the outer chamber to his sister's bedchamber and tapped lightly on the door.

It flew open before he could knock a second time, Teah pulling him into the chamber so quickly he stumbled, falling onto his hands and knees. His bundle tumbled onto the floor.

"What took you so long?" She closed the door behind him, her hair swirling as she turned.

"I had to wait until they left. Grinwald didn't want me telling you about what we discovered so I couldn't do it while he was around." He gathered the fabric rolled in a long bundle. He moved over to her bed, unrolling the cloth and exposing the two swords with their scabbards and baldrics, as well as the small silver rod in its sheath.

Teah gasped. Taking a sword, Logan drew it from the scabbard. The ring of steel filled the room, soon joined by a second ring.

Teah held the other sword like a trained warrior. Logan smiled and then started to spin his sword in front of him. Teah narrowed her eyes, studying the movement, and then she duplicated the maneuver. They continued the sword display—Logan showing, her replicating—until they finally gasped from the exertion.

"That was incredible," Teah smiled. "I thought the protector had two swords, why is there only one for each of us if we are both protectors?"

"This was all there was," Logan tried to explain.

"Where did you get them from?" Teah pressed.

"In a room down in the bottom of the fortress," Logan told her.

"Let's go and take another look. There should be weapons for me as well since I am also a protector."

"I know I wouldn't have missed that." Teah stared at him stoically. "All right, we can go down and check again," he sighed.

Teah giggled and jumped into his arms. "Thank you, Logan," she said sweetly.

Logan rolled his eyes and led her to the door of her chambers. Two guards stood outside at attention. Taking a deep breath, he strode out confidently with a firm hold of Teah's arm, pulling her after him.

"Master Logan." One of the guards snapped to full attention and then began to follow them as Logan and Teah walked towards the end of the hall.

"We won't need your escort where we are going. Stay here and make sure no one enters the chambers until we return." Logan pointed to the door. "We shouldn't be long."

"Yes, Master Logan," both guards said, taking position.

The guards outside Logan's chambers, concentrating on protecting the entrance to the Protector's chambers, never moved or looked their way as the two passed.

Teah and Logan proceeded down the spiral staircase as it wound down and down into the depths of the fortress. When they reached the long dark corridor, Logan took one of the torches and walked down the deserted hall.

"This was lined with special guards whose sole purpose was to protect the swords and the other possessions of the protectors. There is no need for them to be here now that the chamber is empty."

They walked to the open door and looked into the now dark room. "You should have seen it when the weapons were in here. It glowed with magic," Logan told her, leaning in and holding up the torch so she could see the clear crystal blocks comprising the walls.

Teah squeezed past Logan. As she set foot into the chamber, the blocks illuminated with light once more.

Teah turned with excitement.

Logan shrugged.

"Do you think this means?"

Logan strode to one of the three pedestals, his hands coming up to cover his mouth. "No, it can't be."

"What?" Teah walked up beside him.

On the pedestal sat two swords in their black scabbards and golden wrapped handles, the crystal balls with the emblem floating within.

Logan moved over to the next stand and the rod sat neatly in its sheath. He ran over to the last pedestal. A shirt of mail was folded neatly upon it.

"I didn't see the shirt before," Teah said. "Do you have one of those?"

Logan laughed and then held up one finger. Pulling his shirt over his head, he grinned at his sister. "Watch." His expression turned to concentration as he took his first two fingers on his right hand, pressing them against his left shoulder. A silver shirt of mail appeared where there was only his skin a moment before.

"Where did that come from?"

"It was on me the whole time, it kind of 'melds' into me for protection."

"Turn around, I want to put mine on," she said excitedly.

Logan turned around and waited. Teah tapped him on the shoulder. She was back in her night gown. "Well?" he asked.

Teah frowned with concentration as she put her thumb and index finger to her bare arm and the shirt appeared between her fingers, around her neck, and on her other arm as well. She smiled brightly. Letting go, the shirt disappeared once more.

Logan also let go of his shirt and it united with his skin again. He then walked over to the metal rod sitting in the sheath.

"Oh, my," Teah sighed. "It was so cold and heavy at first, but now is warm and light."

"What is that?" she asked, pointing to the sheath.

"You aren't going to believe this." Logan furrowed his brow and the rod extended to its full size. Teah, as expected, gasped with delight.

Taking hold of the strand, he pulled back as the silver arrow appeared, and then he carefully let the string relax once more without firing. The arrow disappeared. The bow contracted.

He handed Teah the rod. "What do I do now?" she asked.

"Think of a bow."

As the words were still leaving his mouth, the rod sprung to its full length. The girl nearly dropped it in surprise. She took the fine wire between her fingers.

"I've never fired a bow." She said turning to Logan. "But I think I know how to do it. How is that possible?"

"Grinwald told me the swords transfer the knowledge of the past protector's sword skills to the new protector. Maybe the bow does so as well."

As she drew the string back, the rod bent into a bow and a silver arrow appeared notched on the string. She carefully let the string relax once more and the arrow disappeared. The bent ends of the rod straightened as the string touched the bow again. Holding the metal rod extended from her body, it neatly contracted once more. She placed the rod back in the sheath and moved over to look at the swords.

"They are identical to the ones you have." Eyes wide, she drew the weapon. The ring of metal filled the room.

"It seems that way. Let's get them back to your room and we can talk more there," he told her.

She nodded her agreement, sheathed the swords, and scooped

up the swords in her arms, refusing Logan's offer to help her. "If I am a protector and these are my weapons, then I need to get used to carrying them."

They climbed the spiral stairs back to the hall. The guards stood looking straight ahead. Logan placed a hand on Teah to stop her and motioned for her to wait. He walked up and the guards snapped to a stiffer attention.

"I need both of you to close your eyes until we get back into the room," he told them. They instantly closed their eyes tightly and Logan motioned for Teah. She scurried from the stairs into the room.

"All right, you can open them now and carry on."

The men opened their eyes and stared straight ahead. Logan gave a nod and closed the door.

Teah had laid the weapons out on the bed next to Logan's identical set by the time he entered the room. He smiled softly.

"When do you think I should tell someone?" she asked.

"When you have no other option. You can only tell when keeping it a secret will let down the people who trust us."

"And who are those people?"

"I don't know right now, but you will know when the time comes."

"I think we can trust Grinwald," she insisted.

"He didn't tell you about having to go the Zele Citadel or let you read what the book said about the dangers of a certain type of protector," Logan argued.

"He may not be telling us everything he knows, but he isn't lying to us either. Has there been anything he has actually lied about?"

"No, but sometimes keeping the truth is no different than telling a lie," Logan pointed out.

They looked at each other for a moment.

"Ok," she nodded, "until the time is right."

He nodded back. "Until then."

They sat in front of the fire, going over the day's events and what they needed to do in order to keep their secret. Talking through the night, Logan finally slipped back to his room early the next morning. He did what Galena had instructed, blocking off his thoughts before he went to sleep. It was as if he just laid his head on his pillow when Teah was waking him up.

In the outer chambers Galena and Grinwald already waited.

Logan and Teah had expected to find food instead.

"Hasn't Magda brought breakfast this morning?" he asked the two Magus.

"No, we haven't seen her," Grinwald replied.

"I will go to the kitchen and find out why you have no food yet this morning," Galena said as she walked from the room.

"We will be leaving for Wilderton as soon as you two are ready," Grinwald informed them. "The sooner we get there and gather the men from the Queen's Guard to support us, the sooner we can get Teah and Galena to the Citadel."

The siblings looked at each other apprehensively.

Galena entered the room, followed by two serving girls carrying trays of fruits and breads.

"You didn't find Magda?" Logan asked.

"She hasn't been seen since last evening when she went to retrieve the food from dinner. She was planning on distributing it to the guards and staff," Galena told them.

Logan stopped one of the girls as she set her tray on the table.

"Is that like Magda? Does she usually not complete her duties or not tell anyone if she were to go somewhere?"

The girl fidgeted, looking at the floor, but he placed his hand gently on her shoulder and her eyes lifted to his.

"It is very strange, Master Logan," the girl said timidly. "Magda takes great pride in her work and duty. She would always complete her tasks, but last evening she did not return from your chamber with the remaining food. We gathered the food this morning."

"I think it is strange also," he smiled softly down at her. "I would like you to get me the captain of the guards, what is his name?"

"Captain Stanton, Master Logan."

"Have Captain Stanton come and see me in the library at once. We will discover why Magda is not about this morning."

He waited for the girls to leave and then turned to the remaining occupants of the room. Confusion and anger mixed in his eyes. "I want the two of you," he instructed the Viri Magus and Zele Magus, "to do everything in your power to find Magda. If we don't find her today, we will stay until we find her."

"We are not your servants to be ordered around." Anger simmered beneath Galena's quiet words.

"Logan, mind your tongue. We are Viri Magus and Zele Magus of the highest order. You mustn't forget your place," Grinwald cautioned.

"She is a trusted servant and friend." Logan cut them off. "Teah and I will not let her whereabouts go undetermined. I will not leave here until she is found and it is final. Teah and I will wait for you in the library. We have some studying to do this morning."

Teah, after flashing him a surprised look, followed him out of the room.

"Very well," Grinwald finally conceded, grabbing Galena's arm.

*****

"Why do I get a feeling you had something to do with this?" he asked once they reached the end of the hall.

Galena looked flatly at him and gave a devious smile.

"Where is she?" he asked.

"She is hidden in the wardrobe in my bedchambers."

"What were you ....?"

"She overheard our conversation last night. She was in the outer chambers with us and I discovered her when I returned for some parchment I had left there. It was obvious she was on her way to tell Logan about our conversation. I couldn't let her tell him what we feared."

"You're right," the Viri Magus agreed. "But why do you still have her?"

"I was going to see that they would find her when we were gone. It is going to complicate things for her to appear without her memory, but at least the boy will leave if he sees her."

"What do you think our options are now?" Grinwald pressed. "You can't think of letting them see her."

"What choice do we have?" the Zele Magus pointed out. "I have wiped her memory of last night. The only problem is memory cleansing is not precise. I had to remove a chunk of her memory to make sure she had no recollection of our encounter, but I may have wiped out other things, too."

"We have no options left. Let's allow her to wander until she is discovered."

"You better keep your boy on a shorter leash," she told Grinwald. "I may have to put him in line, even though he is the protector, if he continues to overstep his bounds."

"I can only do what I can do. Why do you think it's been

said that controlling the protector is a tenuous ordeal at best?"

"If he insists on speaking to me like a serving girl, I may have to teach him some manners the hard way."

"We all do what we must," Grinwald smiled, ushering her down the hall toward the other side of the fortress. They passed the serving girl with Captain Stanton in tow, but continued on their mission without pausing.

*****

"I will do as you direct, Master," the captain nodded. "We will search everywhere to find Magda. And when we find her, we will bring her to you here in the library."

"Good, Captain." Turning back to a stack of books, Logan felt, more than saw, the captain's nod.

"You honor us with your concern for one of the Bantrees." The man bowed.

"You all honor my sister and me with your service and loyalty."

"I am deeply humbled," Stanton said, dropping to one knee and bowing his head.

"No more kneeling, I thought we went over that. Now please find Magda."

Stanton moved quickly out the door to get the search underway.

Logan and Teah looked down at the book open on the large table. "It seems that Bastion, the first protector," Logan read, "was known for his bravery, never backing down from a battle no matter what the odds."

There was never a battle I could not win.

"And here they tell of Stalwart and how he was forced into being the protector due to the coup by the Viri Magus and the killing of all other Lassain men," Teah said.

Those filthy Viri Magus took my life from me and stuck me with Bastion in my head for the rest of my days. She would understand if she had to listen to his incessant boasting all the time.

"Here they say that Falcone was a favorite of the ladies, having many women admirers until he first saw Queen Caldera who he then married and was faithful to until his death, except when he was under a Zele Magus's spell," Logan told Teah.

Women are like wine. Until you give them a taste, how do you know which one you were meant to be with until the end of time, oh my Caldera, Falcone pined, then added, *filthy Zele Magus.*

"And finally, the last protector, Galiven, brother of Queen Jennavia, the only protector to not die of old age," Teah said sadly.

But I would do it all again to have the happiness I beheld when I was with my true love. Surely, Falcone you can agree with me on this. True love is worth dying for. Falcone remained silent. *My only regret is that my death caused Jennavia to curse those good people for all these years. Logan, free them of this curse I have caused to be put upon them.*

Logan didn't respond.

Galena and Grinwald appeared shortly after the captain left to begin laying out the plans for the trip to Wilderton. They pulled some maps out and traced the path they would take. The fortress had stables to supply them with horses for the journey, but Grinwald argued another method.

"Our path lies through deeply forested terrain that does not allow horses to traverse it. It would mean several more days taking the horses and following the road back towards Treebridge, then back to the east and Wilderton. We are better served going by foot and buying horses in the village. It would take us only two days if we stop during the night."

They all agreed that shortening the time spent traveling would be advantageous even if it meant going by foot.

"What about Duke Kensitram? Will he support us if we seek council and shelter in Wilderton?" Grinwald asked Galena.

"I believe he is supportive to our cause. Zele Elnora is his advisor in Wilderton and understands the importance of such matters. I would prefer to enlist the Queen's Guard before we approach the duke, however. I feel it is best to get Teah to the citadel and relative safety before any of this is exposed too openly to anyone outside these walls."

Logan looked up suddenly, "What about Sasha? She's been outside the gates since we arrived. Have her needs been seen to?"

Grinwald patted the boy on the shoulder. "They have been treating her very well. She has ample wood for fires and fresh food for every meal. Magda has seen to it. Sasha only complains a little, but she will be happy to know we are ready to depart the fortress."

There came a knock on the door. Captain Stanton entered with a very confused looking Magda following.

"Magda." Teah ran to the woman, hugging her.

Logan was close behind and fell into the group hug.

Magda stepped back, horrified.

Teah looked concerned to Logan, then back to Magda. Teah could see a blue light glowing around the woman.

"What is it, Magda? You act as if you have never seen us before," Logan asked.

"I know who you are, Master Protector," the woman replied stoically.

"Don't you mean Master Logan?" he pressed.

"Of course I don't. That would not be proper," she said sternly.

Logan glanced at his sister.

"That will be all, Magda. I'm very pleased we found you in good health."

"Thank you, Master Protector." She bowed and left the room.

Logan looked as if he would be sick. "Thank you, Captain Stanton," he said. "Where did you find her?"

"She was wandering out by the stables. It was like she didn't know what she should do next."

"Again, thank you, Captain. That will be all." The man nodded to Logan and left the room.

Teah was by his side, pulling at the sleeve of his shirt.

"Teah and I will meet you back at our chambers," he said to Grinwald and Galena.

They walked out.

"What is it?"

"I don't know for sure, but I think I can see magic around Magda."

"What do you mean you can see magic around her?"

"Back at the village when Grinwald destroyed those soldiers. When you were having your vision and were hurt, and Grinwald and Galena used magic to help you. I could see the magic as colors. That is when I realized I was truly a Zele Magus. I can see the same kind of magical glow around Magda which wasn't there before."

"What do you think it means?"

"I think someone used magic to make Magda forget our conversation with her the night we arrived."

"Why would anyone go to such trouble getting rid of that memory? It didn't hurt anyone."

"Maybe it wasn't <u>that</u> memory they wanted to get rid of," the girl reasoned.

"She was fine last night before we went to bed."

"Grinwald and Galena were still in the outer chamber when we retired last night. She could have heard something they didn't want us to know."

"Then why didn't they erase that memory and let her wake up to do her normal duties? That way no one would have had to look for her and everything would be routine. Unless they were afraid that when we spoke to Magda, we would figure it out," he said, spinning to his sister. "I forced their hand when I insisted on staying until she was found."

Teah bit her lip.

"We now know they are keeping something from us, but also how far they are willing to go to keep it secret. Let's hope Sasha ends up being more trustworthy or else it's going to be a long trip to Wilderton."

Teah nodded.

"Go gather your things and be sure you don't forget the special pack you need to bring."

"Like I would forget that? Make sure you bring yours as well, brother."

Chapter 12

They quickly gathered their supplies and met in the main hall. Teah carried an extra bedroll.

The two siblings wore light green shirts with dark green pants. A dark green cloak with blotches of different browns and greens covered them from shoulders to just below the knee. Logan slid the handles of his swords down low so they would be easily concealed on his back.

The Viri Magus and Zele Magus waited for them; Grinwald wore a grey robe and Galena wore a modestly plain green dress with a brown cloak wrapped around her. They turned to greet the two youths, but Teah and Logan walked past them to Captain Stanton without a word.

"I will return when I can," Logan told him. "I expect you will be ever diligent now that war will surely begin."

"Yes, Master Logan," the Bantrees nodded.

"I do have one request," Logan said, glancing over his shoulder. Taking the captain by the arm, he moved further away from the Viri and Zele Magus with Teah following. "If the Viri Magus or the Zele Magus should return without either Teah or me, you are not to allow them entrance. Do you understand?"

The captain began to protest, but Logan stopped him with a raised hand. "Yes, Master Logan."

"Good. I have my reasons and someday when I return, maybe we could discuss them over a mug of ale. For now, you must trust me."

"Yes, Master Logan. What you say will be done."

Logan gestured to Teah. They walked side by side out the gates of the Protector's Fortress. Two guards stood near the gate, bowing as Logan and Teah passed. Logan gave them a slight nod but kept walking to the campsite down the path.

Sasha stood as they approached and started to bow. Logan raised his hand. "If you are to come with us and act as my personal guard, you must adhere to my wishes. First, you will no longer bow to me."

Sasha began to protest, but Logan stopped her with a raised finger. "Second, you will call me by my rightful name of Logan, or Master if you cannot call me just Logan."

Again she began to object and he stopped her. "Finally, you are to always tell me the truth when I ask it of you. That includes when I ask you to give me your opinion on matters of importance. These three things you must do without question or you can leave me now, returning to your Betra and proclaiming your vow to safeguard the Protector has been refused. Do you understand?"

Sasha stared for a long moment, measuring him up. A smile crossed her lips and she gave a slight nod.

"Very well, now we can begin our journey to Wilderton. Is that all right with you?" He smiled at the woman.

"I was hoping you would accompany me to The Forbidden and the city of Courage to gather your troops first."

"It would appear Galena and Grinwald would like us to gather the Queen's Guard at Wilderton first, and then accompany them to Ceait where Teah will begin her training as a Zele Magus." Logan paused as the Viri Magus and Zele Magus walked up.

"This is Zele Galena. Zele Galena, this is my personal guard Sasha," he introduced.

The two exchanged glances, but didn't acknowledge each other further.

"What did you tell Sasha?" Grinwald asked.

"That we were headed for Wilderton."

"Before that, before we came over here?" the Viri Magus pressed.

"Some things will remain between Sasha and me." Logan said flatly. "Shall we get started?"

Grinwald stood dazed.

"Well?" Logan sighed.

After pausing a moment, Grinwald turned, heading off to the Northeast towards Wilderton. Galena followed after, then Teah, Logan, and Sasha bringing up the end.

As Logan moved past Sasha, she leaned in, whispering, "It is good to see the Swords of Salvation are once again worn by a protector."

Logan stumbled. He reached for the pummels, but they were still covered.

Sasha also had her sword hidden under a black cloak, and as he turned to look at her, she pulled her hood up, drawing her cowl around her face, revealing only her eyes.

Watch that one, Falcone warned, *she is more than she seems.*

At first, there was no path to follow and Grinwald used magic to clear away the brush. They traveled this way for most of the morning, finally stopping at the edge of the Treebridge Forest for a rest.

Grinwald addressed the group as they sat chewing on some dried meat Magda had provided for their journey. "There should be a road not far from here that will take us to Wilderton. It connects Overby in Granel Duchy to Wilderton in Ackerton Duchy. If we continue at our current pace, we should arrive in Wilderton by late tonight or early tomorrow morning if we stop for the night. My only concern is we might be discovered by one of the king's groups of assassins."

"Would they be looking for us this far from our homestead?" Logan asked.

"Not likely," Grinwald conceded, "but if they have any idea where the Protector Fortress is located, they may come looking for us."

"In that case, I suggest we proceed with caution and haste through the night so we arrive in the relative safety of Wilderton as soon as possible," Sasha said. The group looked back and forth to each other a moment, then nodded their agreement. Gathering their supplies, they started off again.

"You might consider keeping those swords ready," Grinwald said as he walked by Logan. "We might need them."

Logan pushed his cloak off his shoulders. The black scabbards reflected the sun and the golden inlay shone brilliantly. The pommels looked as if they were large black jewels with silver images of crossed swords suspended within.

"Do you have any idea how to use them?" Galena asked with doubt.

Logan wavered. "It seems to come naturally when I draw them."

The air filled with the ring of metal as the glistening silver blades cleared their scabbards. The guards and pommel magically formed to his hands as he began spinning the blades in front of him.

The ring of another blade caught the party's attention. Sasha spun her own sword effortlessly in front of her. Her black cloak fell back, revealing tight-fitting black garments.

"What are you doing?" Grinwald shouted.

"I think we should be sure the Protector is able to defend himself. He only obtained his blades recently. Did he have time to practice with them?"

"You don't intend to test him here and now?" Galena protested.

"There is no time like the present," she proclaimed, pivoting to Logan and unleashing a slash at his head.

Logan's blades shot up, trapping the Betra's blade between them.

Sasha pulled, but could not remove the blade.

Logan let his blades drop and the warrior took the opening to come back at him with a series of combinations. He easily deflected them.

Sasha stepped back to regroup, but Logan advanced so quickly, he was a blur of green. Her sword tumbled harmlessly to the ground.

Sasha's expression of shock mirrored that of the others. She dove into a tight roll, coming up with her sword. A slight nod and her weapon easily slid back into its scabbard.

Logan fluidly sheathed his blades and gave a hint of a bow. "Is my personal guard satisfied?"

"For now, but I reserve the right to test you in the future without notice." She smiled broadly.

Everyone stared at the Betra. Logan spread his arms wide, slightly bowing his head. "As you wish."

Sighs of relief echoed through the group.

Then the forest erupted with the crash of Shankan.

Chapter 13

Logan and Sasha leaped to Teah, unsheathing their swords.

Galena and Grinwald began showering the attackers with bursts of red energy. Magic like Teah had never seen before advanced on the men. Twenty Shankan poured out of the shadows.

Teah crouched behind her brother and the Betra. She reached for her bedroll, but then drew back her hand and turned her attention to the battle. Sasha and her brother fared well as a pair, their blades tearing at the attackers, leaving them writhing on the ground in pain as more assassins advanced.

Teah then made out a figure further in the shadows not joining in the fray. Teah began to shake uncontrollably.

"Caldora," Teah's voice quivered.

Logan looked at Teah, then to the figure. His eyes narrowed to a glare.

With the initial rush countered effectively, Caldora walked calmly forward, stopping out of reach of Logan and Sasha. Grinwald and Galena strode forward, their crimson magic pouring out of them and into her.

Caldora laughed. With a sweep of a hand, the woman propelled the two Magus across the path. Teah saw the wall of red smash into Galena and Grinwald as they hurtled backward. They fell motionless in a heap.

Sasha turned to attack, but Logan stretched an arm in front of her. The Betra fought his restraint at first, but then held her ground as she was instructed.

"So the Protector is not an unthinking fool. He can see when he is outmatched. I will be taking your sister now, unless you think you can stop me?" Caldora had not made a move towards the three, but they all bristled at the words. "You believe you can stop me from taking what I want?"

"I <u>know</u> I can stop you from taking my sister," Logan said softly, his voice neither threatening nor timid. His confidence gave the Zele Magus pause.

"You may be stronger in magic than Galena and Grinwald," Logan admitted, "but neither was prepared for your powers. The element of surprise is no longer yours. We are now aware you are an adversary to be wary of. That does not mean I am willing to concede the fate of my sister without a fight."

"How does one so young have such courage?" Caldora hissed. "Are you just too naïve to understand the danger you are in? I was instructed to kill you and everyone with you except your sister. Her, I am returning to King Englewood alive so he can have use of her magic."

"I have heard all of this before from others who would slay me and take my sister. What makes you any different from the others I have killed?"

Caldora stepped one pace forward, drawing back the hood of her cloak. Long golden hair flowed on a strange breeze that did not reach Logan or the others. Her soft beautiful features marked her as not much older than Sasha. "Because I am the Zele Magus Caldora, personal magical advisor to King Englewood himself, and there is no power in Ter Chadain as great as mine. If you allow me to proceed without a fight, I will make your end as quick and painless as possible. I will also treat your sister with the respect she deserves. I give you my word on this."

"What makes you believe you can just take Teah if I choose to stop you?"

The woman let out a loud laugh, tilting her head back. "I wish I didn't have to kill you. Your innocence is invigorating." She snapped her fingers.

Pain erupted in his head, dropping him to a knee.

Sasha, too, fell beside him, gripping her head. Gathering his senses, Logan pushed the pain from his mind, standing slowly bringing his swords up defensively before him. His eyes watered with pain, but he managed to raise them, meeting the gaze of the Zele Magus. For a split second, he caught a shimmer of doubt within the deep blue orbs.

"You are a persistent one, aren't you?"

She swept her arm towards him, but instead of being cast aside like Grinwald and Galena, Sasha was the only one who flew off the path into the forest.

"What...?" the Zele Magus began, but Logan was already moving.

His speed hurtled him into Caldora in an instant, the collision sending her flailing into the shadows. Logan grabbed his sister's hand and raced forward. Passing where the Viri Magus and Zele Magus were lying, he abruptly stopped.

Kneeling by Grinwald he checked for any sign of life. The Viri Magus stirred, opening his eyes.

That was when something struck Logan from behind, sending him sprawling. He tucked and neatly rolled to his feet, spinning. Caldora bore down on him, arms extended in attack. He hesitated as he saw bits of light come from her fingertips, pulse after pulse of magic hurtling towards him.

Instinctively, Logan swept each burst away with his swords. The Zele Magus's attack only intensified and his defensive movements quickened to deflect the bombardment.

Two pulses of magic impacted Caldora from behind him. She was propelled backwards down the trail. Grinwald and Galena stood with their hands smoking before them, not taking their eyes from where Caldora had vanished into the shadows.

Teah and Sasha stood behind the Viri Magus and Zele Magus.

"You must go now," Grinwald shouted. "We'll hold her off and catch up with you. Follow this path until you reach the main road that will take you to Wilderton. Wait there for us. Now go."

No one stopped to argue. The three ran up the trail towards the village.

Then Logan hesitated. "I can't leave them alone. Go ahead; I'll catch up with you."

"No. You must come with us. Who is to protect your sister if the magicals fail? I have nothing to counter her magic. You must come now." Sasha grabbed Logan and pulled him behind her and Teah.

They raced along the path for what seemed hours. The Betra and Logan took turns dropping back to assure they were not being pursued while the other would run slightly ahead of Teah. When finally stopping to catch their breath, they sat in silence. Logan crouched, brooding off a distance, watching his sister.

Teah was visibly shaken, but didn't cry.

He went to her. "So that was Caldora?" he asked softly. Teah nodded without looking at him.

"She was the one at the farmstead that day?" Again she nodded.

"She will die for what she has done," he said and walked away in silence.

Sasha moved closer to the siblings and looked to Logan. He nodded and the party once more set off.

"Didn't Grinwald say we should be coming to a road somewhere around here that will take us to Wilderton?" Logan asked. The others nodded and they continued moving in the same direction. It grew dark now, the full moon their only light. Finally, the path they followed intersected a more traveled roadway up ahead.

The night was cool and even though sweat ran down their faces from the exertion of running earlier, they now shivered from the cold. Pulling their cloaks closer around them, they steeled themselves against the night air.

Logan led the way with Teah and then Sasha guarding the rear. They didn't meet anyone along the road, yet constantly listened for any sounds. None came.

That was bitter sweet. Fearing Caldora had killed Grinwald and Galena weighed heavily on them all.

They were resting beside the roadway when Teah finally broke the stoic silence. "How are we to know the Queen's Guard? And how do we convince them once we find them that I'm the Queen?"

The three exchanged bewildered looks.

"Traveling with a Viri Magus and Zele Magus might have been enough proof of my identity. Now, without them with us, how do we go about finding the guards and convincing them we are who we claim?"

"I don't know," Logan said, "we will hopefully think of something by the time we reach Wilderton." He began moving down the road once more.

Sasha turned to Teah, "Your brother will surely think of something." They got to their feet.

Keeping a slower, but quick pace, they moved into more hilly terrain and in a short time the three stood on a rise overlooking a town spread out before them. The lights from homes twinkled through the trees and street lights shone brightly.

"I hope you thought quickly," Teah said. "Welcome to Wilderton."

"I think we should find an inn and get a room for the night,"

Logan said, raking a hand through his hair.

The two women nodded.

"We'll search for the guards in the morning. Let me do the talking. We're travelers with business in another town and just passing through. I'm Josiah and you can be Calindra," he told his sister who scrunched her nose up.

"No one is looking for you, so you don't need to pretend," he told the Betra. She agreed and headed down the road into Wilderton.

Logan gave a faint smile to Teah. "Here we go." He said letting her walk ahead of him into the town as he pulled his cloak up over his swords.

They came upon an inn almost immediately. "Dusty Road Inn," the sign read, set over the door of a three-level building with a flat roof. Noise burst through the door as a man stumbled—or was thrown—out.

The man fell directly into Sasha's arms, looking up at her in surprise. He gave a large, but crooked smile void of many teeth, then his eyes rolled into his head and he went limp.

Sasha stepped back, dropping him on the road in a cloud of dust.

The three stepped over him, entering the inn. They squinted; the lanterns glowed brightly and a warm fire roared in a fireplace on the far side of the room. A long, crowded bar greeted them and the large open room with tables and chairs was filled with people.

A heavyset, bald man stepped to the side of the bar, shouting his welcome over the noise. "Come in, come in. Welcome to the 'Dusty Road.' I'm Silan, the proprietor. Make yourselves at home. What can I do for the three of you?"

Logan hesitated for a moment then took an awkward step forward, catching his balance on the bar. "We would like a room for the night. A hot meal as well, if we can?"

"No problem, if you get a room, meals and light ales come with it. The question is how many rooms would you be needin?"

"Just one," Logan stammered.

"We don't take to any funny business," Silan said with distaste. "A man and woman cannot be sharing a room unless they are promised to each other, and a man is not allowed to sleep in the same room as two women for that matter."

Logan stood dumbfounded.

"My fiancée is not use to our engagement yet, but we are traveling with my sister to our home to be married. There is nothing indecent here," Sasha said, grabbing Teah's hand. Logan turned to her in surprise.

Silan nodded and collected a key from a shelf behind him. "That will be a silver for the room for the night."

Logan paused again. Sasha tapped him on the shoulder and handed him a small pouch. Leaning her head close to his ear, she whispered, "I only have silver in this so take one out and hand it to him. Tell him there is another in it for him if the food can be brought up to the room."

Logan did as she had instructed.

Silan seemed elated to make another silver just for bringing the food to their room. "I will send the serving girl right up," he smiled, motioning them to the stairs at the back of the room.

The rough wood creaked under their weight as they climbed the stairs. The hallway was dimly lit, but enough light outlined the inn keeper as he stopped at a door at the far end. As the three reached Silan, he went in before them to light some candles.

"I hope this will suit you," he said. Without waiting for their response he quickly exited, closing the door behind him.

"I guess we have little choice," Sasha said sarcastically.

Logan took in the small room. A dark, cold fireplace sat on one wall, a table and two chairs before it. A bed rested against the opposite wall, another under the window. There were no curtains on the windows and the moonlight shone in, giving much needed light to the dark space.

A knock came at the door and Sasha opened it slightly.

A young woman in a plain brown dress rushed into the room with a platter of food. She set it on the table and left as swiftly as she came.

The Betra shut the door behind her. Logan and Teah dug into some mutton and bread. Soon they were all licking the juices off their fingers and smacking their lips in satisfaction. Logan and Teah sampled the mead the serving girl left, but Sasha declined when he offered her some.

"I do not drink such things. Only pure wine and water enter this body," she said proudly.

Logan, sleepy and sated, took off his cloak. He then dropped to a knee and felt the rough hewn wood on the floor. He turned to the women as Sasha helped Teah check the bed for insects.

"I will take the floor. You two can have the beds."

Sasha turned on him, a hurt expression across her face. "You cannot sleep on the floor. It is I who guards you. Not the other way around. Besides, I will not be sleeping much this night. There is something about Silan I don't trust. If the Shankan and the Zele Magus found us on the trail, maybe they were here and have spread the word of their search for us. I will sleep in this chair." She pulled the rickety wooden chair closer to the door. "So I may hear anyone approaching." She sat down abruptly, wrapping her cloak tightly around her.

Logan gave a sigh and looked to Teah who shrugged. They removed their cloaks, Logan taking off his swords and Teah tucking her pack under the edge of her bed, and crawled into bed.

Chapter 14

Sleep came quickly to the two youths and soon Sasha had extinguished the candles and started a small fire out of the limited supply of wood beside the hearth. The crackling fire was soothing, but she remained alert; sure Silan had something planned for them.

She didn't have to wait long before the wood groaned at the top of the staircase and soft footfalls could be heard moving down the hall to stop outside their door. The honed Betra senses first heard, then saw, the latch rise ever so slowly and the door begin to open.

Sasha seized her chance, pulling the door open abruptly, her sword already drawn. Two figures tumbled into the room.

Sasha's sword was already moving down into the pair before they stopped falling.

A sudden flash of steel followed by the clash of blades and bursts of sparks lit up the dim room as the Betra crossed swords with the Protector himself.

"What are you doing?" she shouted. "They were coming to kill or capture you. Why did you stop me?"

"Because we are not who you think we are," came the familiar voice of Grinwald.

*****

Teah lit candles quickly and the light shimmered off of the crossed blades over the fallen Galena and Grinwald.

"How did you know who they were?" Teah asked Logan, placing a hand on his sword arm. The touch brought Logan out of a trance. He straightened and sheathed his sword as Sasha did the same.

"I don't know. I think I felt them coming down the hall. It was as if I knew who they were and what Sasha intended to do, so I reached for my blade and the rest just happened."

"Thank goodness for that," Galena sighed, glaring at the Betra. "She would have killed us both if you hadn't 'felt' us coming."

"Then it's a good thing he did," Grinwald smiled, smacking the boy on the back. "Nice work, Logan."

"What happened with Caldora?" Teah asked.

"We managed to drive her back and then retreated," Grinwald explained. "We have seen no signs of her since, and believe me, we looked for any sign that would tell us she was following. We're all tired, let's get some rest and discuss matters in the morning. We should be safe enough here for a while."

"Silan will let us know if anyone comes looking for us," Galena reassured them.

When they looked at her inquisitively, she shrugged. "We've been friends for many years. I pass through here quite often on my travels away from the citadel."

"What's wrong with the Protector and the Queen?" Sasha asked.

Logan staggered, reaching out to place a stabilizing hand upon the bed frame. Teah swayed, looking around disoriented as she stumbled forward slightly.

Grinwald and Galena turned as the two youths fell to the floor. Teah was out cold, but Logan was on one knee, struggling to stay conscious.

"The mead," he said softly and then slumped to the floor.

Sasha rushed to the window as the sounds of horses echoed into Wilderton. "King's soldiers, what are they doing so far into this duchy?"

"Damn, Silan," Galena cursed. "I will make him wish his mother had never conceived him. He must have given us up."

"Later," Grinwald shouted as he hurried to Teah, hoisting her over his feeble shoulder. "Sasha, grab Logan and follow me."

Before the Betra could move, Silan stormed into the room. "You need to get out of here quickly."

Sasha jumped over Logan, grabbing the man's shirt.

"We wouldn't have to if you hadn't betrayed us," Galena accused.

"It wasn't me. I think it was the new serving girl. She brought up the food. Are we going to argue amongst ourselves or are we going to get the Protector and the Queen out of here?"

Sasha released his shirt with a shove. He slammed against the far wall of the corridor. Sasha scooped Logan up in her arms, following the innkeeper away from the noise of the soldiers climbing the stairs. Grinwald followed closely behind with Teah. Galena entered the hall and paused, moving her feet apart and beginning her spell.

Silan went to a dead end in the hallway and tapped the wall. The wall swung open, revealing stairs leading down. "This leads to the stables. Take what horses you need and get a head start. I will do everything I can to delay them."

Sasha reached into Logan's purse, finding a gold piece and tossing it to a stunned Silan. She fled down the stairs.

"Thank you," Grinwald said, short of breath as he moved after Sasha. The Viri Magus had just reached the stable when his feet flew out from under him as the inn shook. The Zele Magus unleashed her spell upon the soldiers.

Galena sped past him, carrying the protector's swords and Teah's bedroll. She rushed over and began helping Sasha saddle the horses and secure their belongings.

"What are you doing lying down?" she said, glancing down at him. "That was just a shock wave spell to throw them down the stairs to give us time."

They laid Teah and Logan over the horses in front of Grinwald and Sasha. They sped out of the stables at a full gallop, leading extra horses the two could later ride. Soldiers shot a few wayward arrows in their direction.

The small party sped out of Wilderton into the night.

The sound of pursuit was immediate. Shouts and clamor of armor along with the thundering of hooves echoed off the trees lining the road.

Grinwald looked back, making out the glow of torches. "Hurry, they're getting closer," he shouted.

The moon outlined the road against the overgrown forest. The horse Sasha led stumbled, nearly bringing down the Betra and Logan.

Galena pushed her mount to the front of the party, lifting her arm upward, producing a ball of light floating over her raised palm. The magical light shone brightly in all directions, illuminating the terrain.

Sasha moved closer to Galena, "We must leave the road."

"Where?" the Zele Magus cried back to her.

"Follow me," the Betra replied, taking the lead. She took such a sudden right the others had to pull up hard on the reins to make the turn in time.

They found themselves on a narrow path leading through the deep forest.

"Douse that light and follow this." Sasha reached into her

pocket pulling out a small item and shaking it violently. It began to glow an intense green instantly. "Just keep your eyes on this," she said attaching it to the back of her saddle. Sasha quickly took out another, repeating the hand gestures and tossed it to the Zele Magus.

Galena released her magic, sending it out behind her back down the main road and caught the item, attaching it to the rear of her saddle as Sasha had.

"Follow me," she shouted to Grinwald and kept riding.

The old Viri Magus could barely make out Galena's words, but nodded as her light orb shot past him back to the road. Kicking his mount to move closer to the others, Grinwald leaned over, sheltering Teah while avoiding any low lying branches.

They rode into the night until all signs and sounds of pursuit disappeared.

When Sasha finally pulled up, she was soaking with sweat. Her mount was steaming in the cool night air. They were in a small clearing on the side of the trail, the moon shining high in the clear night sky.

She dismounted. "We need to get a fire going and try reviving the queen and protector. Can you mask our campfire?"

"I think I can handle that," Grinwald said weakly. He wearily climbed down from his horse and helped Galena gently lower Teah to the ground. "Keep an eye on her while I put a perimeter weave to mask our presence." He wandered off around the camp, mumbling to himself and waving his arms.

Sasha made short work of getting the fire going and soon had Logan lying by it wrapped in a blanket. She helped Galena move Teah next, covering her as well.

Walking over, Grinwald knelt beside Teah. "Logan mentioned the mead," the Viri Magus said, looking up at Sasha.

"I consumed everything the Protector and the Queen did except for the mead. He must be correct, it was the mead that contained the poison," Sasha agreed.

Placing a hand to Teah's head, Grinwald closed his eyes and let his magic flow into her, probing for the cause of unconsciousness.

He sat back with a sigh. "She will be fine. It was a potion to render her unconscious, but nothing more. The effects should wear off in a few hours."

He moved over beside Logan, glancing at Sasha. The concern was evident on her face. The Viri Magus again sent his magic reaching out and into Logan. He recoiled.

"What is it, what's wrong with the Protector?" Sasha cried coming to her feet.

"He is in a much deeper state of unconsciousness. How can that be?" Grinwald puzzled.

"It's a gender-specific potion."

Galena stood over them. "What did you say?" the Viri Magus asked.

"It's a simple enough potion. When you don't want a female harmed, but wish the male she is with to die, you can create a potion which will only hurt the male. We must work together and act quickly. I only hope we're not too late. Come over here and take my hand."

Grinwald stared at the Zele Magus's extended hand, trying to digest what she said. "Logan is in dire trouble and only a melding of our powers will have any chance of saving him." Galena said sternly.

"Melding between Viri Magus and Viri Magus or Zele Magus and Zele Magus is common enough, but the cross melding of powers between Viri Magus and Zele Magus is highly risky and usually discouraged," Grinwald argued. "The mixing of the Viri and Zele powers could destroy us all."

"Take my hand." Galena shouted. "We don't have time for this nonsense. The Zele Magus and Viri Magus have been working on the melding of powers for the last ten years. We can't control it for very long, but we can do something as simple as extracting a poison from a boy. Now take my hand and weave a healing web while I do the rest."

Grinwald roughly took her hand and began chanting softly as Galena joined in. The boy's back arched off the ground and his mouth opened in a silent scream of agony.

"Stop it, you're going to kill him," Sasha protested, drawing her sword. "I'm warning you, if you don't stop this at once, your last breath will come before his."

A bright flash of light burst from Logan, propelling Sasha, Grinwald and Galena across the clearing to land in a jumbled mass of arms and legs.

Logan slowly opened his eyes. Grinwald, Galena, and Sasha pushed off the ground twenty feet away from where he lay.

Sasha stood and sheathed her sword. Logan raised an eyebrow looking questioningly from her to Galena and Grinwald.

"Desperate measures are sometimes required in desperate times," Grinwald said, brushing the dirt from his robes. He glanced warily towards the Betra.

"Sit up and I will explain what has happened since you lost consciousness at the inn." Galena told him moving over to sit next to him as he sat up.

"What about Teah?" Logan asked looking over at his sister sleeping soundly.

"She will be fine. We made sure of that before we helped you."

It took some time, but finally the Zele Magus concluded her accounting of their situation.

Logan sat quietly listening to Galena's recounting of the night's events. No one spoke for some time after she went silent, the four companions staring into the small fire. He glanced over to his sister sleeping, giving a sigh of relief. He turned back to the fire and gazed into the flames for a long while.

"How did you escape Caldora?" he asked without taking his eyes from the burning embers.

"Galena and I were able to overpower her by using our magic in unison. I don't know if we killed her, but we shouldn't have to worry about her for a while."

"How long will it be before Teah wakes up?" Logan asked.

"It is hard to say, but we can use the rest this night as well. We shall take turns keeping watch," Grinwald said.

"I will take first watch," Sasha volunteered, walking to the rock behind which she had collected the wood for the fire. She climbed on top of the boulder and crossed her legs as she settled in.

The others crawled into their bedrolls and were soon fast asleep.

All except Logan, that is. The protectors were all discussing who they could trust and who they couldn't trust. Logan lost patience.

It is the Viri Magus of the time who were to blame, not the entire society of Viri Magus for all time, Logan sighed. *Now can I get some rest?*

When no reply came, he closed his eyes, gathered his happy memory and blocked off the rest of his mind with it. He was soon asleep.

The next morning Logan woke only to see his sister still sleeping peacefully. Grinwald and Galena sat on the other side of the fire, having a discussion in hushed tones.

"Glad to see you awake, Master," Sasha said standing over him.

Logan jumped. "Goo... Good Morning," he stammered.

"How are you feeling this morning?"

"I'm fine."

"No lingering effects from the poison?"

"None that I can tell."

"Good to hear. I have some meat over the fire if you are hungry and here is some fresh water from the stream down a ways from here," she said, handing him a water skin.

"Thank you. How long have they been like that?" he said, motioning to the two magicals and then taking a drink.

"All morning. They woke early and began to speak privately. What about, I couldn't tell you." The Betra shrugged.

Logan took some meat from the spit and juggled the hot meat from one hand to the other, taking bites in between. He ate the last and wiped the juice from his chin with the back of his sleeve.

"How long are we going to have to wait here?" He raised his voice to get the attention of the preoccupied magicals.

"Logan, you're awake," Grinwald smiled.

Sasha shrugged and moved off to her position as watch.

"As soon as your sister wakes up, we shall depart. That may not be until dark. It will be safer anyways under the cover of darkness." Galena said.

The Viri Magus and the Zele Magus turned back to their whispers.

Logan stood and stretched. He strapped on his swords and fastened the rod to his belt once more. Then he went over to Sasha.

The Betra looked up as he came over, "Not interested in talking to you either?" she smirked.

"No," he shrugged. "I was wondering if you would do some sword play with me to see what I can do with these things."

"I'd be happy to, Master." She laughed as she slid down from the rock.

The ring of drawn steel filled the small clearing. Logan's mouth dropped open as Sasha pulled the black cloak back, exposing her tight undergarments that left little to the imagination.

"What's the matter," Sasha laughed. "Haven't you seen this before?"

"I haven't really taken a close look before," he blushed.

"Not to worry, there is nothing here that you cannot see if you wish," she smiled and attacked.

They attacked and parried over and over again. Sasha would push Logan until he disarmed her for fear of her cutting him, or restrained her with his arms wrapped around her. They would then regroup and go at it again. Over and over again Sasha pushed him with a different attack, and every time, he would come out victorious. They trained all day into the early evening as the light was fading.

"Are you sure you have never been trained with the swords before?" she asked, panting.

"No, never. The first swords I have touched are these."

"Amazing. What is that on your side?" she asked, pointing to his contracted bow. Logan sheathed his swords and Sasha did the same.

He took the metal rod from the sheath and it sprang to its full length. Taking the wire between his first two fingers and thumb, he drew back. The silver arrow appeared. Turning to the large rock, he loosed the arrow and it stuck into the stone.

"That is truly amazing," Sasha said, shaking her hands in front of her.

Logan walked to the stone and pulled on the arrow, grunting several times before it came free. As it cleared the stone, the arrow vanished.

Sasha's eyes widened with shock. "Such powerful magic must be rare."

"Yes it is," Grinwald said sternly as the pair turned. Grinwald was frowning with his arms crossed on his chest and Galena had her hands on her hips, tapping her foot.

"Those are not toys," Galena scolded.

"How is he going to learn to use them correctly if he doesn't practice with them?" Sasha defended.

"I will say this only once to you, Betra," Galena hissed. "You are here only because Logan has insisted upon it. It is my feeling that you and your people are as traitorous today as you have always been. So don't address me unless I address you first."

"That is no way to treat Sasha," Logan protested. "She has

fought Caldora by our side. She has proven her loyalty."

"To you maybe, but not to me," Galena argued. "You had better watch the tone you take with me boy, or you will learn respect the hard way."

"What do you mean by that?" Logan shot back, his hand sliding the now retracted bow back into its sheath.

Galena murmured something under her breath, flexed her fingers and pointed at him.

Logan opened his mouth to protest, but nothing came out. He gripped his throat with his hands, moving his mouth without a sound escaping his lips.

I told you those women always like to have the last word, Falcone shouted. *Now we know she doesn't like the way you speak to her. Do something.*

Like what?

Draw your sword, Stalwart suggested.

No. Calm down and bow your head to her, Bastion said.

Do what? Falcone cried.

She is asking for more respect from you, Bastion explained. *Show her some.*

Logan took a deep breath and moved over in front of Galena. He looked her in the eye and then bowed his head slightly.

"There, that is much better," she smiled victoriously. A wave of her hand and Logan could hear himself clear his throat.

"Thank you, Zele Galena," Logan replied.

"Is that how you are going to let her treat you?" Sasha said indignantly.

Logan gave a quick, harsh look, and the Betra bowed her head and moved behind him.

"It is not bad to practice with your weapons, Logan." Grinwald put an arm around the boy. "But within reason."

"I need to be prepared the next time we meet Caldora."

"Don't worry, we won't be seeing Caldora anytime soon," Grinwald assured.

"I wouldn't be so sure about that Viri Magus," a terrifyingly recognizable voice spoke from the darkness.

Chapter 15

They jumped, spinning around.

Caldora stood tall with confidence, a slight smile of satisfaction on her face.

"Thank you for sending us a clear signal as to your whereabouts. I knew that only the melding of your two powers would be enough to break the weave. The magical burst of energy needed to save the Protector was a beacon in the darkness last night. We found it very easy to locate you after that."

Caldora extended her arms gesturing to a large number of soldiers on either side of her.

Logan and Sasha reached for their swords, but Caldora's stopped them short.

"Don't be stupid. These are not mercenaries, but soldiers loyal to King Englewood. They will not be so easily discouraged. I have archers out of sight training arrows on you. Your weapons will not clear their scabbards before you are cut down."

Don't do it. You can't believe her, Falcone warned.

"You want me dead anyway," Logan shot back. "What would I have to gain by going down without a fight?"

"I will offer you respectful imprisonment for your sister. Do you know how military men love girls of pureness? I will also guarantee quick and painless executions for the four of you. I assure you, we have the means to draw out your deaths for days, even weeks."

Without warning, Grinwald unleashed a blast of energy.

Instead of impacting them, it just hung before Caldora and the troops, glowing with a soft golden color.

Caldora screamed.

"I can hold them for only a short time," he shouted over the cries of Caldora and the soldiers as they tried breaking through the barrier to get them. "Run."

Caldora unleashed blasts of energy into the barrier over and over again, frantically trying to get at her prey.

"We can't leave you here to face them alone," Logan protested.

"You and your sister must get to Ceait and the safety of the Zele Citadel. That is the most important thing here. I'll join you there. There is no time to argue this, boy, now go."

A new blast of energy ricocheted off his barrier and into the two lines of soldiers. Men flew in all directions, propelled by the blast.

Sasha tossed Teah over her shoulder and hurried away. Galena ran off behind her. Logan drew his swords.

"I won't let you face this alone," he cried.

"I'm sorry, but you don't have a choice." Grinwald raised a hand to Logan's chest, catapulting him in a heap at Galena's and Sasha's feet.

Logan jumped to his feet starting to go back. Grinwald erected another barrier, blocking him. Then he flipped the barrier holding off Caldora and her troops, engulfing them and preventing their pursuit of his companions, but trapping him within.

"No," Logan cried.

"I've tied off the weave," the Viri Magus shouted. "Flee while you can. Save my beloved Ter Chadain from Englewood and the Caltorians"

Grinwald spun just in time to see the blast of magic leave Caldora's hands. It hit him square in the chest. His gaze turned to Logan as he dropped to his knees, his vision already becoming hazy. He never saw the second burst, but felt his body hurtle through the air.

A sudden impact with the ground, and Lucias Grinwald, High Viri Magus of Ter Chadain, saw his world go black.

"No," Logan cried, trying to break through the barrier, but hands on each arm restrained him.

"It's too late to help him now," Galena said solemnly. "He's gone. We must flee so his sacrifice will not be in vain."

She pulled him. He followed in a shocked stupor. They mounted their horses as Sasha threw Teah across one and leapt into the saddle, kicking the horse into motion. The others followed her lead, kicking their horses into a dead run.

Chapter 16

I must admit, that one had some courage, Bastion said.

Do you think it was some kind of ploy to control events? Stalwart asked suspiciously.

He let himself be killed so he could manipulate Logan? Falcone jeered.

A noble Viri Magus who sacrificed himself to allow Teah and Logan to escape, giving Ter Chadain a fighting chance, Galiven added.

Logan didn't respond but rode on silently.

They rode hard the rest of the night and into the mid morning. They stopped only when Sasha's horse faltered.

The Betra gathered Teah in her arms and slid to the ground before the mount tumbled into a lifeless heap.

They made camp and Galena took the time to check on Teah's condition. A little probing and soon the girl stirred.

She opened her eyes to the three gathered around her, looks of worry across their faces.

"What's the matter? Have I overslept?"

"You might say that," Galena replied without emotion.

"What's the matter with all of you? Where's Grinwald?" Her eyes searched for the Viri Magus.

"We lost Grinwald," Logan replied solemnly.

"Lost? What do you mean lost? How do you lose a Viri Magus?" She asked.

"You abandon him to Caldora and her troops instead of helping him," Logan said, getting to his feet and moving a few paces away, his shoulders hunched and his head hanging low.

"And what would you have had us do?" Galena shot back. "If we stayed to fight, Teah would be in the hands of Caldora and we all would be dead."

Teah gasped, burying her face against the Zele Magus's dress. "Is it true? Is Grinwald dead?"

"I'm afraid it is true," Galena said calmly. "He sacrificed himself to allow us to get free. If your bull-headed brother would have had his way, we would be executed and you would be on your way to meet King Englewood. I do not like the choice we were forced to make, but remember, the Viri Magus chose his course and he died for something he truly believed in. Trying to stay and help would have been a disaster, making Grinwald's sacrifice a waste and his death for nothing."

"I don't believe in sacrificing his life to save me," Logan shouted back.

"Is that what this is all about?" Galena said sternly, gently moving Teah away and coming to her feet. She walked up to Logan until they were nearly touching, the Protector towering over the petite Zele Magus.

"You think Grinwald sacrificed his life to save yours and now you don't think your life was worth his. Boy, you're so naïve. He didn't die to save Logan the boy, but to save the Protector and the Queen of Ter Chadain. He has lived these past years waiting for you and your sister to come of age. He hid his magic and pretended to be a simple healer until you came to him. He had a true vision of what life would be like if you once again ruled Ter Chadain, which drove him to sacrifice his life to save yours. In doing so, he believed he was saving his beloved Ter Chadain from an eternity of pain and suffering. Don't think him so foolish as to die to save two people. He died to save thousands, maybe millions, and generations to come."

Outrage radiated from her pores. Her eyes locked onto Logan's and their fire caused him to turn away.

Galena spun on her heels, walked over to her horse, and mounted. Looking at the three of them frozen in place, she asked, "Are you going to just stand there waiting for Caldora to catch up with us, or are we going to get to Ceait?"

The others jumped at her command, climbing on their horses. Teah doubled up behind Logan and Sasha took the one brought for the girl.

Galena hardly waited for them to become seated before she started out at a brisk gallop. Kicking their horses into motion, Logan and Sasha followed.

They rode for a long time, keeping a moderate, but steady pace. Logan's stomach was rumbling so hard Teah began to giggle at the sound.

Galena pulled up at the top of a rise in the road.

"Below is my home," she said reverently, "the Citadel of the Zele Magus. And the large building directly across the river from the citadel is the Viri Magus's Castle."

The witch's den, Falcone hissed.
The traitor's lair, Stalwart added.

The three traveling with the Zele Magus stared at the wonder. The river wound down the ridge on which they now stood. As it reached the valley, it grew into a great river some hundred yards across. Built on opposite sides of the river, but attached by a large bridge, stood the two houses that trained the future wielders of magic in the land. Towns had grown around each and high walls surrounded the settlements. The river not only flowed to divide the two towns, but also surrounded them, thus giving the two great houses of magic and their towns the appearance of islands. Stone walls encircled the castle and the citadel, adding another level of protection once the town walls were breached.

The citadel shone a glorious white in the fading sunlight with brilliant blue roofs on each tower and hall. The castle was a contrasting deep brown with black roofs jutting skyward with many ramparts. Boat traffic moved between the towns and people on foot streamed back and forth across the bridge.

"We shall all be safe here and Teah can finally begin her training. I don't want any of you to speak your true names unless I give you my permission and I am in your presence. Only the Magus Matris will be aware of your true identities. Logan, please make sure you keep those swords hidden and by no means let anyone see you without your shirt on. Sasha will be another Zele Magus in training until I decide what you and Logan will do now Grinwald is gone." She paused momentarily after mentioning Grinwald.

"It is not uncommon for relatives of Zele Magus' in training to accompany them to Ceait at the beginning and we will claim that is your purpose here. Do we all understand?" They all nodded they did.

"Sasha, we need to get a change of clothing for you before we enter the citadel. The Forbidden are not welcome here and we must disguise you the best we can. It is only because the Protector wishes your company that I am allowing this. I could be expelled from the sisterhood if you are found out. Wait here, I shall return momentarily."

She turned and proceeded into the settlement. A short while later she returned carrying something light green across the front of her saddle. Galena tossed the green dress to Sasha.

"Put this on and be quick about it, we need to get inside the citadel before Caldora catches up."

Sasha went behind some trees and soon reappeared wearing the dress. It was a simple cut with a square neckline and the bottom dropping just below the Betra's knees. A simple green silken ribbon acted as a belt, tied in the back with a bow.

Sasha mounted her horse, hiking her dress up to straddle the beast, exposing a good portion of a shapely thigh.

Logan cleared his throat and shifted in his saddle.

The boy has good taste, Falcone noted.

"When can we speak without your permission?" Logan asked.

"I will leave that up to the Magus Matris. Until you are told otherwise, it is best we not divulge your true identities. I must insist upon this for now," Galena stressed.

Nodding, they followed her down the road toward the Citadel of the Zele Magus, riding at an easy canter.

The smells of food being prepared for evening meals wafted over them and Logan's stomach complained loudly. He groaned, getting a stern look from Galena, a smirk from Sasha, and a giggle from Teah. Soon enough, the citadel loomed ahead of them and they paused before black metal gates, two guards stepping forward. Their bronze helmets and breastplates reflected the world around them.

"Welcome home, Mistress Galena," one guard greeted, bowing his head as he spoke her name. "I assume you are taking responsibility for your guests to enter?"

"That is correct, Captain Balik. I have gathered two new charges and this young lad rides along with us to protect his sister from any harm during our journey."

The captain smirked. Logan's hand crept towards the hilt of his sword, but Sasha gripped his wrist. Logan inhaled deeply, letting it exhale slowly, until his body relaxed, and Sasha slowly released her grip on his arm.

Control, Logan, Galiven urged.

"You may precede, Mistress. The Magus Matris has sent word you are to meet her in her chambers with your guests as soon as possible." They stepped aside, allowing the party to enter the courtyard.

There were soldiers moving about the yard, but none paid them any interest. The party moved over to the stables where a boy took away their mounts.

Logan, Sasha, and Teah followed Galena in silence, moving up the front steps to the main entrance of the citadel. Once inside, Galena quickened her pace, giving the others little time to take in the splendor surrounding them. High arching columns lined the corridors and chandeliers glowed with candles every ten feet to light the way. Artwork adorned the walls in the form of tapestries, paintings and metalwork. They tried taking in as much as they could, but soon they stood in an outer room to a grand chamber.

"Stay here until I summon you. We will get something to eat as soon as we are done here," she added, glaring at Logan and then down at his stomach as it groaned in response. She disappeared behind a large wooden door.

The outer room was larger than Logan's entire set of chambers at the Protector Fortress. Dark wood panels lined windowless walls. Portraits of women hung in rows, hundreds of them. A large desk polished to perfection stretched across much of the room, a high-backed chair upholstered in a plush crimson fabric sitting empty behind it.

They waited for a long while until Galena opened the door, motioning them in. She put a hand to Sasha's chest as the Betra attempted to follow. "I have already taken great liberty with our laws letting you enter the citadel. You must remain here and trust I will allow no harm to come to Logan."

The two women exchanged stares for a moment before Sasha finally nodded her acceptance. Teah and Logan followed Galena into the chamber.

The room was entirely dark except for a small corner of its great expanse. A petite table held a single candle, making it difficult see the path through the shadows. Logan bumped into some furnishings several times before finally reaching the table.

Two chairs were set on one side and Galena motioned for them to sit down. She moved over to the other side of the table to stand next to an empty chair. As soon as Galena stilled, a woman appeared out of nowhere.

She wore a soft blue satin dress with pearl buttons all the way up to her neck. A white lace collar was tucked neatly under her thin chin. Short black hair framed her pale face and hollow cheeks.

Logan made eye contact with her and realized she was taking him in as well. Her light blue, almost white, eyes stared at him eerily, making him give a visible shiver.

The leader of the witches, Falcone hissed. *The worst of them all.*

"Do my eyes bother you, my son?" She asked in a soft, but authoritative voice. When he didn't reply, she continued, "My eyes don't see the way they use to. I must use magic now to see the world around me. I can see much clearer the makeup of a person this way, but I sometimes miss the subtleness of an expression from time to time. I am the Magus Matris of this house of training. My close friends still call me Jelisia. I would be honored if you two called me that in private. Of course, if others besides Galena are present, we must keep up appearances, mustn't we?"

The youths nodded stoically.

"Good, Galena has informed me of our loss of Grinwald and I share your sorrow. I had known the great Viri Magus for most of my life. He will be missed in the struggle for Ter Chadain."

"We must go on, however. He would have wanted us to continue the fight. I'm afraid none of us can accompany you in gathering support for your war against King Englewood," she told Logan. "You will have to rely on the Betra to give you the aid you need. Your sister will remain here training so she may one day sit on the throne of Ter Chadain and bring peace back to the land."

She looked to Teah smiling softly. "You cannot be Teah Lassain while you are here. Even inside these walls, you are not completely safe from harm. There are those here who may decide it is prudent to prevent your rise to power. While you are at the Citadel, you will be referred to as Teah Glasson. It is an old name in Ter Chadain and no one will think it out of the ordinary."

Teah smiled uneasily. She looked to Logan who still watched Jelisia closely. He had a strange look on his face.

"You say you have known Grinwald your entire life?" He asked.

Good, Logan. Make sure she tells you the truth, Falcone urged.

"That's right," Jelisia smiled.

"Have you ever had a meal with him?" Logan pressed.

"Many, why do you ask?" the Magus Matris puzzled.

"Then you can tell me what his favorite meal was?" The boy

prodded.

"What are you doing, Logan?" Galena chastised. "Who do you think you are, questioning the Magus Matris like this?"

Careful, boy, don't press them too hard, Stalwart cautioned.

Jelisia raised her hand to the Zele Magus. "It is all right, Galena, the boy, or should I say the Protector, is just doing what he does best, protecting his sister and Queen."

She leaned across the table until she was only inches from Logan and whispered softly to him as their eyes locked in a stare: "Rabbit stew."

She sat back with a smile across her face, not taking her eyes from his.

Logan didn't break eye contact for a long moment. Then he sat back in his chair with a sigh, "She is right."

"Of course she is right, she is the Magus Matris. How dare you question her? You should have taken my word, if nothing else, she was who she claims to be," Galena scolded.

Logan looked up at Galena calmly. "I am the Protector of Ter Chadain and the protector of my sister. I must be sure of whom I leave her with and I must have confidence she will remain safe. It is my skills as protector that will assure her safety and rise to power, not the powers of a Zele Magus. So I will ask what I feel is needed in order to protect the Queen of Ter Chadain."

He stood, bowing deeply. "I'm grateful for your word to keep my sister from harm, but if you should fail in that capacity, remember, you will not escape my retribution. Now if you will excuse me, I must find some nourishment and get some rest. I will be on my way at daybreak. I do have a war to begin."

Leaning close to Teah, Logan whispered, "I will see you before I leave," and he walked out of the room.

Is it wise to threaten such powerful allies like that? It could make them powerful enemies if you're not careful, Bastion cautioned.

He needed to let them know he isn't afraid of them, Falcone said.

It appears to have worked, Galiven pointed out.

Galena started to follow Logan, but Jelisia put a restraining hand on her arm. They waited in silence until the door closed.

"Why did you stop me?" Galena protested. "He threatened you. How can you let him get away with that?"

"Because, my dear Galena, if I fail in this mission to protect his sister, there will be nothing any of us can do to stop him from seeking his vengeance upon us. Don't ever think that young man can be stopped when he has a cause. Don't ever be fooled you are controlling him. You can control him no more than you can control a raging cyclone."

The calm certainty in the Magus Matris's voice sent a chill down Galena's back. She did not speak, but stood with her mouth agape and her eyes wide.

She whispered so Teah wouldn't hear. "Does Logan have that kind of power that he could have snuffed out my life at will all this while?"

The Magus Matris looked blankly up at Galena. "What do you think?"

Galena shivered involuntarily and looked to the door in terror.

The two women turned to Teah and smiled, Galena's was clearly forced. "Your brother is quite a man," Jelisia told her.

"Yes, he is. He is the only one in this world I trust completely without question."

"As well you should. Your faith is well placed. Please show her to her quarters and get her some food," she told Galena. "Also make sure the others are well taken care of."

Galena nodded.

"Rest up, my dear, tomorrow you will begin your journey towards becoming a Zele Magus."

"Good night, Magus Matris," Teah said as she stood and bowed. She followed Galena from the chambers and out into the empty hall. She looked around, then her head dropped and her shoulders slumped.

"Pick your chin up, Teah," Galena spoke up. "Your paths lead you in different directions for now, but they must come together again if we are to be victorious."

They moved down the ornate hallway further into the recesses of the citadel, descending a staircase until coming to a hallway and a small wooden door.

Galena opened the door, lighting the candles with a flick of her wrist. Teah could see the red flows of magic as they caressed the wicks and flames erupted.

"This is an ordinary novice room. We mustn't let on you are anything more than a charge found with the ability to become a

Zele Magus. I am sorry it is not very elaborate," Galena apologized.

"I understand. How long do you think I need to study before I can help Logan gather troops against Englewood?" The girl asked.

"Most women take several years to reach the pinnacle of their power. If we are lucky, you will be able to rejoin your brother in two years."

"Two years?" she whispered. Tears welled up in her eyes and she turned away.

Galena reached over and took Teah's chin in her hand, forcing her to look up. "You are the only one who can determine how long it will truly take to reach your pinnacle. Don't worry, if you are half as driven as your brother, you could be out of here in half that time. Be strong, my child, the future of a country depends on it."

Wiping the tears from her eyes, Teah forced a smile. "I will do my best."

"That is all we ask. I will send some food to your room. Try and get some sleep. The initial classes tomorrow will be draining and you will need all your strength." Galena gave her a gentle smile and closed the door quietly.

Teah glanced down at a bundle sitting on the edge of her bed. It was the pack she had brought with her from the Protector's Fortress. She sat next to it, unrolling the cloth and pulling out the items she had placed there for safe keeping. The two swords took up much of the space and she set these under her bed.

From inside her rolled up stockings, she carefully drew out a small, circular golden locket with a crown on it attached to a chain. She opened the locket, staring at the initials in the gold.

"I thought it was an 'S' but after everything that's gone on..." She held the jewelry closer to her eyes peering at the letters. The letters 'GL' appeared clearly. Her eyes went wide. "Gianna Lassain, the Queen of Ter Chadain." She clutched the locket to her chest squeezing her eyes tight. "Mother, please help me be strong enough to do what I must."

There came a light tap at the door and Teah went over, expecting to find a servant with her food. Instead, her brother held a platter full of bread, meat, and cheese. He smiled wide.

"Aren't you going to ask me in?" he chided.

She stepped aside as he walked in.

Logan looked around. A small bed sat on one side, a tiny fireplace on the opposite wall; on the other side of the room, a narrow table with a couple debilitated chairs. Striding over to the table, he placed the tray down, pulling a bottle of ale and two mugs from a pocket of his travel cloak. Pouring the drink, he motioned for her to come and eat.

Teah hesitated.

"Don't worry," Logan said. "I took this from the keg myself while many others were drinking from it. Even Sasha assured me it was safe."

Teah took the mug and drank deeply. The ale tasted light and refreshing on her tongue and she turned her attention to the food. She began to eat, growing ever more ravenous as she did so. She took another drink from her mug, washing down a large mouthful.

"Easy, easy, you're going to make yourself choke," he laughed. "I do know what you're feeling, though, I ate like that after I left the Magus Matris's chambers. I found Sasha and we went down to the kitchen. The cook was right pleased with herself to feed two malnourished travelers such as us. I think she started worrying we were going to eat all of her supper for the entire citadel, though."

Smiling broadly, he walked over to her cot, picking up the locket. "I thought you lost this," he said, holding it up.

"I would never lose that," she mumbled with her mouth full of food. "Mother gave that to me." She waited, looking at him expectantly.

When he just shook his head in agreement, she walked over, opened the locket, and handed it to him.

Looking at the engraving, his eyes opened wide and he turned back at her in amazement.

"Mother gave that to me," she repeated slowly.

"Gianna Lassain," he said in a nearly inaudible whisper. "Do you think there is anything special about it? Other than being from her," he added when he saw the accusing glare.

That locket use to belong to Queen Tera and has been handed down from generation to generation, Bastion told him. *The crown is the symbol of the Zele Magus.*

"She was a Zele Magus. Anything is possible I guess. We'll have to wait and see," she shrugged.

"You'll have to see," he said matter-of-factly. "I'm leaving in the morning to gather supporters to put you on the throne."

"How long do you think you'll be gone?"

"I'm guessing four to six months, maybe longer. It all depends on how well I can convince people I'm who I claim to be."

"Everyone we've met since leaving Treebridge has believed you. Why do you think people won't believe you?"

"I've had Grinwald with me to help convince them. Now it is just me and Sasha. How many people are going to join up with a boy and traitor to Ter Chadain?"

"Sasha is not a traitor."

"But her people have been exiled as traitors for over five hundred years. She carries that with her and some people know what a Betra looks like."

Their conversation was interrupted by a knock at the door. Galena glanced in without waiting. "Both of you come with me. We have a problem outside the citadel."

"What kind of problem," Logan began, but the Zele Magus cut him short with a raised hand.

"Just come with me."

Chapter 17

They followed her through the corridors and out the main entrance where Sasha stood leaning against the wall, watching the events. Filling the courtyard, the entire garrison stood, weapons at the ready, holding back a sea of men all wearing grey cloaks with hoods pulled tightly around their faces.

One man shouted at Captain Balik. "If we aren't allowed in at once, we will take the citadel." The man was very tall and broad, towering over everyone by at least two heads. His grey traveling cloak flowed nearly to the ground and his hood covered most of his face except for a salt and peppered beard trimmed short.

As the three of them pushed through the garrison, they slowly stopped in front of the men. Teah and Logan gazed at the mob in grey, then at each other, Logan with a raised eyebrow and Teah biting uncertainly at her bottom lip.

The man spotted Teah and spun to face her as she walked up. "My Queen," the man said loudly, dropping to a knee as his words were echoed through the mass and the entire mob followed his lead. Soon a sea of grey cloaks and hooded heads bowed before Teah, Logan and Galena.

"Quiet, you fool," Galena spat. "Are you trying to get her killed?"

"On the contrary," the man argued.

The man stood, throwing off his cloak. His silver breastplate reflected the blazing sun. Teah lifted her hand to her face and squinted. His breastplate displayed the emblem of one large star circled by six smaller stars.

"We are here to protect her," the man said, eyes locked on his queen.

One by one, each man tossed their cloaks aside, dropping to a knee and creating a wave of grey cloaks turning to silver breastplates.

Galena stepped forward, raising her hands. "Not here, you are putting her in grave danger by exposing her like this. Get to the wooded area around the side of the citadel and we will talk there."

Gathering up their cloaks, the men strode back through gates.

Logan and Teah followed after them, but Galena addressed Captain Balik. "Not a word of this to anyone. All of your men shall be sworn to silence, and if they betray that silence, they will be silenced for good. Is that understood?"

The look in the Zele Magus's eyes left the captain no room for argument. He nodded, bringing his men together as Galena stormed after the others.

After gathering in the wooded area, the men once again knelt before Teah.

Logan and Sasha exchanged wondering looks as the men stayed motionless before them. "I think they are waiting for you to tell them to rise," Logan suggested.

Teah looked dumbfounded at Logan and then the men.

"You may rise," she said softly.

All the men, in unison, rose to attention.

Galena stormed through the unit.

"What is the meaning of this," she berated the man who had spoken at the gate. Before the man could respond, she continued. "Don't you realize a stunt like that could get the girl killed? Don't you realize how many would love to know this is the Queen of Ter Chadain and try to kill her? Now tell me who you are and what is your business?"

The man stood stoically looking forward, never showing any signs of emotion on his face except for the slightest tensing of his jaw muscles. "I am Talesaur, Captain of the Queen's Guard of Ter Chadain. We have been waiting these thirteen years for a sign our queen has returned to us and a sign came at the inn in Wilderton. Once our spies had determined your identities, we quickly followed you to the citadel."

Logan, Teah, and Sasha exchanged glances.

Captain Talesaur moved over in front of Teah, dropping to a knee and bowing his head. "I give you our loyalty to the death, my Queen. No harm will come to you as long as a single man of our company of one hundred is still able to lift a sword in your defense."

Standing, he returned to the front of the formation.

"That is all well and good, captain," began Galena, "but now you must disappear so Teah will be able to keep her secret while she studies at the citadel for her preparation to take back the throne."

Talesaur's lips thinned. "We have come to protect her. We will set up a perimeter and escort her throughout the citadel. It is our duty to keep her from harm."

"Do you think you will be able to keep her from harm if a Zele Magus weaves a spell on her and she dies from jumping out her window because her mind tells her she is jumping into a swimming hole for a cool summer swim? Only secrecy and cunning will keep her from harm within the walls of the citadel. Her identity will not be known to any but the Magus Matris and me. That is why you must now go and let her be just another student at the citadel."

"We will not leave Ceait, Zele Magus, but will remain within the city, keeping close watch over the Queen from there."

"I was hoping you would accompany me to the other duchies, helping me gather support to overthrow Englewood," Logan said.

Talesaur turned to Logan and his eyes widened. He dropped to a knee and bowed deeply. "I am sorry I did not recognize you at first, Great Protector, but finding the Queen was such a driving force for us, we had no idea you were with her."

"That is quite all right, Captain, what about it, do you think some of you could help me gather support?"

"I'm sorry Protector, our duty lies with the Queen. We are not able to accompany you."

Logan started to object, but a hand on his shoulder drew his attention. Sasha, empathy evident on her face, shook her head, and then turned away.

Logan nodded. "This I must do myself."

"Not alone, Master, but with me," Sasha assured him.

"This has taken too long, we must disband before someone sees us and suspects something," warned Galena. "Disperse, soldiers, for we must get back inside."

"We will be ever watchful, our queen," the captain assured Teah, and then the men were gone.

Logan and Sasha followed as Galena led Teah back around to the gates of the citadel. There she turned to the boy and his personal guard. "It would be best if you did not reenter the citadel. The quicker Teah gets into the routine of the teachings here, the less suspicion there will be."

Teah ran into her brother's arms. Her face buried in his

chest, she cried openly. "I don't want you to go, but I know we can't be selfish about this. Both of us need to prepare in our own way."

Hands gentle on her shoulders, he brought her away from his chest so he could see her face. Tears streaked down her cheeks and he wiped them away with the back of his hand.

"When did my sister become so grown up?" He smiled down at her. "We both know what needs to be done. It doesn't mean it is any easier leaving you. If you ever need me, just think of me and I will be there." She smiled up at him, nodding.

"I'll work hard and join you as soon as I can," she said confidently.

"As will I," he assured her.

They embraced once more, leaned back, and locked eyes with each other. With a nod Logan turned and walked with Sasha towards town and Galena followed Teah into the citadel.

Chapter 18

Logan and Sasha found an inn in Ceait to stay for the night. The Ruddy Traveler's sign depicted a red-faced, red-haired man inviting entrance. The common room was empty this time of day, but the innkeeper didn't ask any questions and showed the two to their room.

Once inside, Logan sat heavily on one of the cots.

"What troubles you, Master?"

"I have no idea where to start. If Grinwald were here, he would know, but now he's gone." Logan paused, a lump caught in his throat.

"May I suggest The Forbidden?"

Logan spun on Sasha. She lost her footing, falling heavily to the floor. "That's it. With you along, I shouldn't have any problem convincing them to follow me. How many troops do you have?"

Sasha picked herself off the floor, sitting down on the cot. "Every adult is trained for battle, Master. That is around five hundred thousand ready soldiers. We have prepared many years for the time you call us into service. We will follow you without question."

"That many troops may be enough for some wars, but Grinwald said Englewood has a continent full of support from across the sea." Logan gave a forlorn whistle, shaking his head. "We need to bring the full might of Ter Chadain against the King. If we are to reunite Ter Chadain, we will require troops from every duchy in the country. If they don't support the war, they won't have anything invested in the effort and may falter if the war draws out. We need to gather support from each duchy to insure cohesiveness."

Logan paced the room. Then, expression heavy, he dropped back down beside her.

"We will go for your troops after I have gathered troops from the other duchies. We can count on your troops supporting the effort, but we need to gather the others first."

"That is wise Master," she said nodding. "We know our warriors will be there, but the others might not want us there."

He nodded. She was perceptive. "How well do you know Ter Chadain?" he asked.

"I have only ventured into this country in preparation of finding you. I don't know Ter Chadain well enough to be of help."

"I only know the little mother taught us. We need to find someone who knows this country well enough to guide us. The problem will be finding someone whom I can trust. We should sit in the commons room tonight and listen for anything that might point us in the direction of a guide."

"That is a very uncertain way to find a guide, Master."

"I agree, but I don't think we have much of a choice," he nodded. "But it is at least a place to start."

Sasha changed back into her traveling clothing and they waited until just before the meal hour to go downstairs.

They managed to find seats on the far side of the room across from the entrance with their backs to the wall. It was a large common room. There was a bar next to the door and a fireplace beside them. Tables and chairs filled the space between where they sat and the bar.

Their table was small with four chairs crowded around it. They took two chairs, positioning them so each had a clear view of the remaining room. The stairs rose up behind them giving them a safe place to discuss their options and not be overheard.

The room completely filled in a very short time. The owner, a man names Joshua, smiled broadly through his bushy black mustache as men and a few women entered with a wave. He was tall and skinny to the point Sasha questioned the quality of his food. "I have never seen a thin innkeeper."

It was soon obvious he kept thin by serving his customers mainly himself. Darting to and fro carrying trays of food and drink, he moved at a mind numbing rate. Occasionally, a small woman would appear from the kitchen with a large tray of food, leaving it on the end of the bar for the innkeeper. Logan couldn't get a good look at the woman, except she was also thin with dark hair and a dark completion.

He and Sasha ordered some roast pork and mead. Before he could get the money out of the pouch, the inn keep was back with steaming plates of food and frothy mugs. He wondered at the two's smooth routine and the speed of it all.

While they ate, Sasha said, "Remember to listen to as many

conversations as possible. I don't want to have to sit exposed more than one night."

Logan nodded, turning his attention to eavesdropping after putting a large piece of pork in his mouth. The juices ran down his chin and he wiped them away with his sleeve. He was taking a drink of mead when the word 'guide' wafted to his ears. Trying to hold back his excitement, he turned his eyes slowly.

A table away from Logan and Sasha sat a party of three; all still wore their hoods, and shadows hid most of their facial features. Two were clearly men by their build and a small amount of facial hair jutting out from the base of the hoods. The dark grey cloaks expanded over wide shoulders and hairy forearms.

The third person held a different air, wearing a dark green cloak more suited to the woods. The slender figure moved gracefully as it picked up a mug and drank deeply.

As the green clad figure sat the mug on the table, it turned its head to the other two. "As I have just stated gentlemen, I'm not interested in being your guide."

One of the grey cloaked figures reached across the table, grabbing the green cloak in his hand. "Are you saying you're too good for us?" he growled.

"I'm saying nothing of the sort. I'm simply leaving my options open for other endeavors that may come my way that would preclude you from my future."

The man glanced to the other who shrugged. He released the green cloak and sat back. "As long as you're not saying you're too good for us."

The slender figure rose.

"Where are you off to? Let us buy you a drink and convince you it would be a good business decision to guide us," said the other man.

"I would," the person said softly, "but my next client is waiting for me." The figure took two steps, sitting agilely down at Logan and Sasha's table.

Both men shot to their feet. "You mean you're going to guide these two misfits instead of us?" One of the men shouted. The entire room went quiet and still with anticipation.

Sasha began to stand, her hand moving to her sword, but the green cloaked figure placed a firm hand on the Betra's arm.

"This is mine to deal with," the figure said. The green cloak billowed as the figure spun, the ring of steel being drawn filled the room. The two men stumbled over their chairs as they tried to back away and draw their weapons.

They didn't have time as two short swords were held tightly against their necks.

"Now gentlemen," the figure said softly, "you are at a very dangerous junction in your lives. You can choose to turn and walk out the door and live, or you can choose to try and save face using your size and strength to overpower me, but I assure you that will only result in your own death. Now, what will it be, life or death?"

No one moved in the room. The two men looked to each other and lifted their hands away from their swords. They edged away until their necks were clear of the swords. Without hesitation, they ran from the inn.

The entire room took a collective sigh. The figure sheathed the swords, sitting down at the table again, taking a long drink.

Logan and Sasha stared at the figure, then at each other.

"I think you have found yourself a guide," the hooded figure said, peering at them. Brilliant green eyes shone out from beneath the hood.

"I guess we have," Logan said, turning to Sasha. She nodded her agreement.

"Agreed then," the figure said, reaching up to pull back the hood. Long red hair tumbled forth and a deeply tanned face of a young woman not much older than Logan stared at them.

"Saliday Talis at your service," she smiled widely, extending a hand.

Logan grasped it firmly, still in shock.

"What's the matter, darling? Haven't you ever seen a Tarken before?"

Logan shook his head that he hadn't, having to think to close his gaping mouth.

"My people are the best trackers and guides in all of Ter Chadain. You are lucky I could tell you were in the need of a guide, otherwise you might have ended up with some no good conman who would take you around in circles until he had all your money, then leave you to wander around in the wilderness."

"How did you know I needed a guide?" Logan asked.

"Tarken know these things instinctually. Besides, I figure if you are in the company of a Betra, you probably didn't know the lay of the land of Ter Chadain."

Sasha went for her sword, but Logan caught her hand. Their eyes locked and he left no room for argument. Her muscles relaxed and he released her. "I suppose your instincts told you she was a Betra as well?" Logan asked.

"I've been to one of their villages before and would recognize one by sight anywhere. Once you see a Betra, you know their characteristics enough to pick them out of a crowd. At least I can. The question I have is why you are with one of the Forbidden?"

Logan looked to Sasha who shot him a warning look. "That is not part of the deal. I'm not ready to tell you that yet. If you prove to be as valuable a guide as you claim, I'll consider trusting you."

"Fair enough, boy, but why do you talk for the Betra?"

"Ma--," Sasha began, but hesitated when Logan nudged her under the table. "He is better with words. I'm better with actions."

Saliday shrugged at the answer. "You going to finish that?" she asked, pointing to the meat.

"Help yourself. I think I've had enough for tonight. We'll meet you down here at sunrise." Sasha and Logan stood.

Shouts erupted at the doorway. Pushing their way through the crowd at the bar the two grey-cloaked men led two dozen more men dressed the same.

The leader of the pack pointed to the Tarken, heading for her.

Logan began reaching for the swords concealed beneath his cloak, but Sasha took his hand, pulling him close to her. "You must not expose yourself. If they see the swords, they'll know you're the Protector."

Their eyes met, an understanding passing between them in an instant. Sasha tossed him her sword and drew two long daggers. She jumped ahead of him, taking the first attacker in the throat before he could bring up his sword to defend himself.

Logan leapt to her side, moving so quickly his sword was a blur of metal. The grey-cloaked attackers went down as fast as their numbers flooded through the door.

Before they knew it, a pile of bodies lay on the floor before them. Saliday had just joined them when the remaining assailants turned and fled.

The entire room was deathly silent as all eyes trained on Logan and Sasha. The innkeeper rushed over. "You must leave at once, the authorities will be here shortly and it matters not that we all saw it was self-defense, it won't keep you out of their dungeon this night. Hurry, out the back door to the stables, I have already alerted the stable boy to have your mounts ready."

Sasha ran up the stairs, gathering their packs while Logan paid the innkeeper for the damages and food. The Betra rushed down the stairs and they headed out the back door.

The Tarken came running as they secured their packs and mounted the horses. "My mount as well," she shouted to the stable hand who had brought the other horses.

The boy ran off, bringing back a painted pony. He threw the saddle on it and Saliday quickly secured it along with her pack.

"You're not bound to us," Logan told her. "Now we're fugitives, I will understand if you don't wish to be our guide."

"Are you crazy," she smiled broadly. "You and the Betra saved my life back there. Those men were after me, not you. Besides, I've always wanted to guide the Protector."

The last comment caused Logan and Sasha to spin in their saddles.

White teeth shone as Saliday pulled her hood over her head. "As I told you, Tarkens can sense these things." She kicked her mount into motion, disappearing into the darkness at the edge of the stable lights.

Exchanging glances, the Protector and Betra sped after their guide into the night.

Chapter 19

Teah sat quietly on her bed. She sat alone in her room the rest of the day. When a knock came on the door, only the food was there when she had answered.

At dinner time she was summoned to the Magus Matris's quarters by a young serving girl. Following silently behind the girl who never looked back at her, Teah arrived at Jelisia's outer chambers.

"You are to wait here until you are called," the girl said and walked away.

Sitting down, she noticed two men standing on either side of the door leading to the inner chambers. They wore off-white robes, standing as still as statues with their dark hair cut short and their arms folded over coarse rope belts. On each of their robes by their collars was a pin depicting two swords crossed. Teah touched her tattoo reflexively.

As she sat, her mind wandered, wondering what was happening inside the inner chambers. Closing her eyes, Teah tried remembering the inner chamber from her visit earlier in the day.

For an instant, images of people began taking shape in her mind and then vanished. Looking around the room, she found the other occupants paying her no mind.

She closed her eyes and tried to envision the interior of the Magus Matris's room again. This time the images clarified and she heard voices. Then they were gone. Again she looked to the men, but they were whispering quietly back and forth.

She closed her eyes once more and pressed hard to remember the inner chamber. Suddenly, the images burst into vivid clarity and the voices were clear and loud.

There was Magus Matris, Galena, and a man dressed in a black robe with long blonde hair flowing down to nearly his waist. His beard was trimmed neat and his face was old with wisdom, but youthful with energy and spirit. His arms flailed irritably and he spoke in a loud voice.

"Why wasn't I informed one with the power for Viri Magus

was here in the citadel?" he questioned.

"We don't know who you speak of?" Magus Matris replied calmly.

The man strode closer to the desk aggressively.

"I was told Zele Magus Galena had brought in a brother and sister to the citadel. The boy had the powers of the Viri Magus. The 'calling stone' indicated his presence. As soon as we read the signs, we came only to find you had sent him away. How could you be so irresponsible disregarding our treaty in such a manner?"

"I never knew the boy had the power," Galena protested. The Magus Matris raised her hand to silence Galena.

"We are not responsible for screening possible Viri Magus Candidates," the Magus Matris replied smoothly. "Our mission is finding female candidates. It's not our fault you acted too slowly. Maybe your readers of the 'calling stone' should be reprimanded for not being more diligent. If it wasn't for their slow response, you may very well have the boy at the Viri Magus's Castle as we speak and be screening him."

The Viri Magus paced, fuming over the Magus Matris's response. He paused for a moment longer. After taking a deep breath and slowly exhaling, he bowed to the two Zele Magus.

"I apologize for the misunderstanding and will take your advice about our readers. I'm sure the Magus Patris will be speaking with you," he said. "We are thankful Zele Galena has returned safely, but saddened by the news of Viri Magus Lucias Grinwald. He was an honored member of our society. We will miss him greatly. Have a good evening." He bowed again then moved to the door.

Hesitating, he turned to them as his hand touched the door latch. "The stones said the boy had more power than any since the beginning of the Viri Magus. We will be searching for him." He nodded and left the room.

Teah came out of her daydream as the Viri Magus strode past her. The two waiting men snapped to attention and followed. Without warning, the man paused, taking in Teah. His gaze made her fidget in her seat, and then he turned was gone.

She waited for a moment, deep in her thoughts. Logan was a Viri Magus and the Protector? That was what the Viri Magus had said—"The strongest since the beginning of the Viri Magus." She thought hard about Logan. *Do you know you have the*

power of a Viri Magus, my brother?
*****

Somewhere outside Ceait riding hard, a thought came to Logan in the form of three words: *Viri Magus Protector.* Logan swore he had heard Teah's voice.

What was that? Galiven asked.

Was it any of you? Bastion questioned.

No, not us, Stalwart and Falcone denied.

It sounded like a woman's voice, Galiven said.

It sounded like Teah, Logan told them.

That can't be. She is not a dead protector, Stalwart pointed out.

You must be right. Logan shook the thought from his mind riding on into the night.

They stopped at dawn in a small clearing thirty paces or so off the main road.

Saliday lead the way all night. She dismounted first, gathering her things as Sasha and Logan brought their mounts to a halt. The horses were steaming in the early morning air as sweat glistened over their bodies.

Logan took a brush out of his pack, starting to rub his mount down after removing the saddle. He tossed the brush to Sasha and she also tended to her horse.

Saliday was already starting a small fire and spreading out her bedroll when the other two joined her.

"You should tend to your horse," Sasha said as Saliday looked up.

"He can wait until I get some rest," she replied flatly.

"He will develop saddle sores before then, you need to tend to him now." She tossed the brush at Saliday's feet.

The Tarken tossed the brush aside, rolling over. "Do it yourself if it bothers you, but I'm getting some rest first."

Logan bent down, retrieving the brush without a word, and went over to the painted gelding.

Seething, Sasha stormed over, spinning him to face her. "Why are you doing this? She should be tending to your horse. This is not right. I should teach her a lesson on how to respect the Protector."

"I don't think she is certain I am the Protector and I prefer it that way. Maybe she was guessing when she said it back at the inn and she changed her mind during the ride. Now get some sleep and I'll stand watch."

Sasha began to protest, but his look left little room for argument. She spread out her bedroll on the opposite side of the fire from the Tarken and was asleep in an instant.

Logan assured himself the two women were asleep and then took off his cloak. The two sword handles jutted out from his back just slightly above his shoulders. He loosened the baldric, dropping the double sheaths with their swords to the ground.

"So what have we here?" a whisper came from behind him. He spun. The red headed Saliday stood staring at him in disbelief. "You do have the protector's swords. So you must be the Protector, or else a thief."

"I'm not a thief," Logan protested.

"Then you're the Protector?" she said, raising an eyebrow.

"Some say that I am," he admitted sitting down heavily next to the weapons. "I'm still trying to decide."

"You are a Lassain?"

"Yes." As he spoke the words, he grimaced. He moved his hand cautiously toward his swords.

Come on boy, you must learn to keep that mouth of yours shut, Bastion chided.

"Your Highness," Saliday said, dropping to a knee and bowing her head.

"I'm not a king, Saliday. Please get up."

"But you are royalty. Do you have a sister somewhere?" she asked, sitting down crossing her legs before her.

"Why do you ask?" he hesitated as his hand touched a pommel.

"If you have a sister, you will be aiding her to regain the throne and bring peace back to Ter Chadain. That is what the prophecy has foretold. The way you're acting, I assume that means yes. She must be with the Zele Magus at the citadel. It makes sense, she needs to be trained to control her powers, and who better, but other Zele Magus?" she added, seeing his amazed look.

"You got all that information from my expression?"

"You can learn much by observing reactions to subtle questions. It is the same as reading the signs of the trail. That is what makes a good guide," she smiled broadly, pleased with herself.

"You're kind of young for a protector. How old are you,

fourteen or fifteen?"

"Sixteen," he shot back.

"Easy, I could see you're young. I expected you to be older. I didn't mean anything by it."

"You aren't much older. How old are you?"

"I'm twenty. But I've been out on my own since I was fifteen—and a guide since I was thirteen. Tarken's don't judge you by your age, but by your abilities as a guide and scout. I learned quickly and have been allowed to be on my own since a young age."

"It sounds kind of lonely to me."

"It is in my blood. I'm a pure blooded Tarken and the 'sense' has been in me since birth."

"The 'sense'?" Logan asked.

"True Tarkens have this sixth sense of direction helping them find what they are looking for. We can feel where we need to be and move toward our goal. That is how I found you last night. I was drawn to the inn and to that table. I could sense I was needed there."

Logan sat staring at the girl. "You're serious. You were in the inn's common room last night because I had a need for your services?"

"That's right," she said, sitting taller.

"Who were those men in the cloaks?"

"Monks of the Mist. They are a violent sect of monks who search out people with the power and try turning them to their cause. If the Zele Magus or the Viri Magus had known that many were in Ceait, there would have been a major confrontation. The only reason there wasn't was most of them were hiding in the woods outside the city until the first two gathered them. They would have forced me to be their guide if it weren't for you and the Betra. You two were amazing. Did you realize you killed nearly twenty monks in less than a minute? That was incredible."

Logan looked at her in shock. He rolled away from her. His last meal emptied onto the ground.

She placed a comforting hand on his shoulder. "You <u>are</u> new to this. It's not your fault. It would have taken many dead monks for them to stop no matter who killed them. If any of the men in the room would have tried to help me, there would have been plenty of innocent men dead as well."

He took deep breaths, trying to calm his convulsing stomach.

Her voice turned soft. "You and the Betra saved me from a life of servitude to the will of the monks. It is a good thing, I promise."

Rolling over onto his back, Logan stared up at the early morning sky. Then he closed his eyes tight, trying to remove so many images flashing before him.

"It will be all right. What is your name? I can't go around calling you Protector."

"Logan," he replied, opening his eyes to see her face only inches from his.

For an instant something stirred inside of him he could not explain. Looking into those beautiful green eyes filled with wonder, he felt both excitement and embarrassment as a warm sensation rushed to his cheeks.

Saliday quickly backed away from him as he sat up, her cheeks red as well.

"I'm pleased to be your guide, Logan. I need some sleep and so do you. Wake the Betra in an hour or so and get some rest. We have a long night ahead of us. It will be safer to travel in the dark."

"Where are we headed? I don't even know where to start?"

"Leave that to me. I told you I'm drawn in the direction of need. You need to gather support for overthrowing King Englewood. I will know which way to go when we head out."

Logan watched Saliday as she stood, walked over to her bedroll, climbed in, and turned her back to him. He smiled to himself as he scanned the surroundings for any signs of intrusion. His cheeks remaining flushed as his mind raced with thoughts of Saliday Talis.

Concentrate on what you're doing, reminded Bastion.

I am, I am, Logan assured him.

Sasha woke in less than an hour and he didn't argue when she pushed him towards his bedroll. He wrapped up in the bedding and was asleep instantly.

His sleep was filled with dreams of the past few week's events: his family murdered, Grinwald killed, and Logan himself becoming a cold blooded killer as the monks fell at his feet.

When Sasha finally woke him, he was even more exhausted than before.

"You look like the dead walking," the Betra said, concern in her voice.

"I dreamt the whole time. I can't get death out of my head. It seems to replay over and over."

"It should get easier in time," Saliday said as she sat beside the fire. "At least it has for me."

"When did you have your first kill?" Logan asked.

"I was fourteen when some Caltorians came upon me on the road. They said I needed to come with them, but I refused. There were two of them and they thought this little girl would be an easy mark for them to take as a slave, but my short sword between the ribs of one and a dagger across the throat of the other ended that. I didn't sleep afterwards for weeks. But when the next time arose to defend myself, I slept like a baby that night. It will get easier when you realize it is either you or them. It is always better when it is them."

"Have you decided where we will be heading?" Logan changed the subject.

"Longstand in Fareband Duchy, the further we are from Cordlain and the King in Ter Chadain Duchy, the better. We will be able to gather more support before Englewood gets word of our efforts. Hopefully he will react too late to do any good."

"You seem to have given this much thought," Sasha smiled. "We must have made a good decision to have you guide us."

"We will know soon enough," Logan said. "Let's get going." Sasha and Logan packed up their supplies and loaded their horses as Saliday kicked dirt over the fire. They mounted up and were soon on their way to gather the support they needed.

It is going to be a long journey before I see you again Teah, Logan thought as he rode along. *Watch after yourself.*

You watch yourself as well, brother, Teah's voice echoed in his head.

Logan stiffened and Sasha turned at his sudden movement.

"Are you all right?" She asked.

"Yeah, I'm fine," he nodded.

That definitely was a woman's voice, Falcone said. *I, by far, have had the most experience with women and that was a woman's voice.*

We all know what we heard, Falcone, Stalwart sighed.

Hesitating, Logan breathed a sigh of relief. *At least I'm not losing my mind all by myself. The four of you are losing your minds as well.* The protectors had no response for that.

The three rode out of Ackerton Duchy into the Duchy of Fareband.

Chapter 20

A serving girl ushered Teah in for supper.

She walked in and sat across from the Magus Matris and next to Galena. The steaming hot food filled the room with the rich aroma of the savory dishes.

Looking awkwardly to the Magus Matris, Teah asked, "Who was the Viri Magus in here?"

"It is not a first year student's business what happens within these chambers," Galena scolded.

The Magus Matris raised a hand, stopping Galena. "He was the Ambassador to the Citadel from the Viri Castle. Why do you ask, my dear?"

"Were they looking for Logan?" she asked, biting her lip.

"That is no concern of a Magus Student," the old woman said flatly. "Now enjoy your dinner."

"You will begin your classes in the morning. Are you excited?" Galena broke the silence.

"I guess," Teah said flatly.

"Most girls are thrilled to have the opportunity to develop the inborn talents that you are being given," Galena said sternly.

"I suppose you're right. I just miss Logan and worry about him. He is the only family I have left in this world."

"We are your family now, dear child. The Zele sisterhood is now the most important thing in your world and we will help you obtain the throne once more," the Magus Matris corrected.

"Logan has his own path to follow. You can't waste your time and energy worrying about him. He and Sasha will be fine. You will see. Concentrate on the task you have at hand," Galena counseled.

"How long will it take before I'm ready to take the throne?"

"Every student advances at their own pace. You can't rush magic," Galena explained.

"How long does it take most girls to elevate to Zele Magus?"

"Three to five years," The Magus Matris replied.

Teah dropped her fork and bit her lip as she began to shake. "I can't leave Logan that long to wage the war without me. I have to be ready when he needs me to take the throne of Ter Chadain."

"It will take as long as it takes," Magus Matris sighed. "It does not matter what anyone feels the need is. It is said that the time required to train a Lassain queen is not typical. From what I have read about your various predecessors, Lassain women can have extraordinary abilities innate to only them."

"What kind of abilities?" Teah pressed.

"Some were gifted at healing with very little training while others had the innate ability to weave intricately with little instruction."

"This is uncharted territory for all of us," Galena added. "Only your mother, Gianna Lassain, came to the citadel for training in any of the current Zele Magus's time. She was capable at most aspects of our schooling, but she didn't have any unique abilities which stood out."

"How long did it take my mother to become Zele Magus?" Teah asked hopefully.

"Your mother and I went through training together. Both of us took about three years to reach the Zele Magus level," Galena said. "Now don't think that is written in stone," she replied after seeing Teah's shoulders drop and her head bow. "There is no telling how quickly you will develop."

"It really depends upon you," the Magus Matris said drawing their attention. "As the Queen of Ter Chadain, you are required to rule the land with the poise and dignity that befits a Zele Magus. You must learn to control your fears and reason with a level head at all times. There are many who would like to manipulate you to their agendas. You need to be prepared to see through their control and choose what is best for Ter Chadain."

"There have been many instances in the past where a queen has been lead astray from her basic teachings at the citadel," Galena nodded her agreement. "You must learn to read people's intentions if you are to hold true to your beliefs."

"How do I do that?" Teah asked.

"One way is to use your magic to tell if someone speaks the truth," Magus Matris told her. "Try this simple lesson. I am going to tell you something that we all know to be false. Concentrate on my face and look for anything that is new to you."

Teah sat up straight in her chair and leaned closer to the Magus Matris, staring intently at her face.

"Your real mother and father were the Saoltos and they gave birth to you in their home on the edge of the Treebridge Forest." Jelisia said the words without emotion and never displayed any facial indications one way or another as to her deception.

As Teah watched the woman and listened to the words, a soft white glow appeared around her face that grew brighter as she spoke, then went out as her words stopped. Teah sat with her mouth open in shock.

"What did you see?" Galena asked intently.

"There was light around her that got brighter as she spoke," Teah told them. "Didn't you see it?"

"That is a magic that is said to be reserved for the Lassain line alone. No other Zele Magus has ever been able to duplicate it," Galena told her.

"Why did the light grow brighter?"

"It is written that the greater the deception of the statement, the stronger the magic's reaction. The first statement that the Saoltos were your real parents was only partly a lie since they were the ones who raised you. The fact you were born in Treebridge was a complete lie, so the magic responded stronger," Magus Matris told her.

"Why haven't I seen the magic before now?" Teah asked.

"You need to call upon it in order for it to work. Galena and I could sense you using magic, so you need to be aware that those with the ability can also sense you are using your magic. That may put you in danger if you don't use caution."

"Why would using magic put me in danger?"

"It is hard to determine how liars will react when they are exposed. I would advise against using this magic on any Zele Magus and suggest caution in using it against Viri Magus. I am not sure they have the ability to sense its use," Jelisia told her.

"Why are you so distrusting of the Viri Magus?" Teah asked.

"It is not distrust, my dear. It is lessons learned through the years that have made us very cautious when dealing with the Viri Magus. They have their own agendas and that is something you should never forget.

"It is getting late and the food is getting cold. Finish your meal."

They fell silent, eating the remaining meal in silence until the Magus Matris spoke, "Go get some rest now, my dear. Tomorrow is a very big day for you."

Teah rose and was escorted back to her room by a girl waiting outside the chambers. She crawled into bed and tears rolled down her cheeks.

The next morning Galena woke her with a gentle shake. "It is time to start your journey to becoming a Zele Magus." The woman smiled warmly, but Teah looked stoically back.

"The sooner I start this, the sooner I'll finish."

"Don't be in too much of a hurry, Teah," Galena warned. "If you're to master the skills of a Zele Magus, you must take it slowly. No one can become a Zele Magus by rushing into it."

Teah smiled a crooked smile. "Have any students come here with their abilities already developed to a level?"

"Only the slightest amount and that is very rare," Galena assured her. "Just be happy if you can understand the basics in your classes today. Don't expect too much right away. I would hate to see you disappointed." She moved away from the bed. "There is a basin of water next to the mirror for you to freshen up before breakfast. Today you will be joining the other students in the dining hall."

Teah raised an eyebrow at the news. "I get to eat with the other students?"

"Yes, it will be too obvious for you to be isolated from the student body. It would create too many questions. We have to have you blend in."

Teah wished she could stay hidden until Logan returned. She moved over to the wash basin and splashed her face with the cold water making her shudder.

"I'm sorry, my dear. I forgot you don't know how to warm your morning water. Allow me." Galena waved her hand and a weave of blue moved over to the basin, then disappeared into the water.

The girl dipped her hand into the water and smiled pleasantly. She splashed the warmed water on her cheeks and ran wet fingers through her curly blonde hair. She pulled the brush through all the tangles, grunting as they tugged at her scalp.

Once she had finished, she turned to find a light grey dress with long sleeves and high collar laid out on her bed by Galena. An attached belt cinched the waist and the length would come to mid-calf.

"This is the attire of all the students. You want you to fit in, don't you, Teah Glasson?"

Galena let herself out and waited until Teah opened the door, wearing the dress. Galena fidgeted nervously.

"What's wrong?" Teah asked.

"It appears it will be difficult for you to blend in no matter how we dress you." Galena sighed.

"How do you mean?"

"Nothing, you look fine."

"Shall we go?" the girl asked. Galena nodded and they proceeded down the hallway to the dinning chamber.

The chamber was a large room with rows of wooden tables and benches. Most of the benches were filled with girls wearing the same attire as Teah, but on the dais at the front of the room, older girls sat at a long table in golden dresses, radiating power and beauty.

Teah stopped and stared at the nearly twenty women.

"They are the chosen, the students who will soon become full Zele Magus. If they ask you to do something, you must treat them as if it were a command from a Zele Magus. Do you understand, Teah Glasson?" Galena emphasized her name.

Teah nodded staring at the front table.

Galena moved to a table in the back of the room and stood waiting for Teah to follow. The young queen moved to an open seat on the bench between two girls. Galena motioned for her to sit and left the room.

Teah sat without looking at the girls around her, and began to dish up some eggs and bread. Eyes down, she began eating. She ate steadily until she noticed no one around her moved. Teah cautiously looked up. The entire table stared at her. The eyes were of various shapes and colors, all with accusations.

She turned to the girl on her right. The long brown hair framed a round, freckled face with deep brown eyes filled with uncertainty.

Turning to her left Teah found a girl with light blonde hair and bright green eyes. The smooth light skin showed rosy cheeks as she fidgeted nervously.

"My name is Lizzy Bridon," she said softly. "What's yours?"

"Teah Glasson."

"My name is Rachel Cradick," said the girl to her right. "You must be real special if the Mistress found you and brought you herself."

"Mistress?" Teah asked.

"Zele Magus Galena is the Mistress of Power," Rachel whispered. "That is what everyone calls her behind her back. She is the most powerful Zele Magus alive and no one, not even the Magus Matris, is stronger. She usually doesn't go out recruiting students."

Lizzy nodded, as did all the girls at the table.

"Maybe she just came across me when she was traveling to someplace else for another reason."

"Maybe," Rachel said unconvinced. "I think she thinks you're important. Are you important?"

"Leave her alone, Rachel," Lizzy cut in. "Don't mind her, Teah. She's always that way. It's because she is the most advanced student at the citadel and will be the next raised to chosen."

"That's right, Lizzy, and don't you forget it. It will take you years to reach my level, Teah. Lizzy will take almost as long, even though she has been here for two years already. I have been here just a year and a half and the Zele say I am the brightest student in many years. Most of those chosen took at least five years to be elevated."

Teah stared at Rachel. Five years!

She turned to her meal, eating without saying another word, nodding and grunting as Lizzy and Rachel asked questions.

Once breakfast concluded, Teah followed the girls of her table to a large, circular room with tiered seating. Down at the bottom of the seats stood a woman in a bright red dress. The dress barely held in her massive body, her breasts nearly escaping the fabric. Her dark skin was as black as night and she wore a ruby on a chain across her forehead.

The woman examined each student as they took a seat.

Teah sat with Lizzy and Rachel. It appeared all the students sat in the same order as when at breakfast.

The woman raised her arms and the entire room went silent.

"Hello, my students," she said in a sing-song voice.

"Hello, Headmistress Zele Astoria," the entire room sang back.

A frown crossed the woman's face; she looked directly at Teah. "Now that our new student, Teah Glasson, knows my name, we will try once more. Hello, students," she sang again.

"Hello, Headmistress Zele Astoria," they sang back, Teah included this time. The woman smiled broadly, nodding her approval.

"Rachel and Lizzy, be sure to take Teah to her lessons with you and be nice to her, the Mistress has her eye on that one."

"Yes, Headmistress," the two girls said in unison, bowing their heads.

"There are no other announcements today students, be on your way, except for you, Teah. Lizzy and Rachel, would you please wait in the hall for her?" The girls got up and exited the chamber.

Teah walked down and stood patiently in front of the Headmistress. Once the door closed behind the last girl, Astoria leaned over, smiling broadly.

"I wanted to welcome you personally to our home. I do hope you will come to me if there is anything you need. I know how demanding Galena can be at times, but remember you are always welcome to visit me if you need someone to talk to. Do you understand?"

"Yes, Headmistress," Teah said nodding.

"Good. Just think of me as you would your mother, dear."

"My mother is dead," Teah said flatly.

"Then by all means think of me as you would your mother before she was murdered," Astoria said, smirking.

Teah looked back at her again, but there was no smirk, just a look as if she said too much. "How did you know my mother was murdered?"

"Zele Galena must have mentioned it to me, my dear. Now you better be off. You don't want to be late your first day." She shooed Teah with a wave of her hand and turned to something on her desk.

Teah took a few steps, and then paused, looking back at the Headmistress. Shaking her head, she frowned and strode out of the room.

"Just follow us, Teah," Rachel ordered, leading the way.

"Where are we going?" Teah asked Lizzy.

"Weave reading is first, then weaving, conjuring, and healing. We need to build all of these to master the four arts: healing, weaving, potions and defense."

They entered a room with rows of wooden benches and tables along each wall. A large empty area in the middle of the room separated the tables from a desk. Sitting behind the desk was a short, skinny woman in a brilliant green dress, her blonde hair up in a bun.

"Welcome class," the woman said smoothly.

Her voice cradled Teah, making her sigh.

"We will be working on reading various weaves that influence how a person feels. How did that feel, Teah?"

Teah's eyes opened wide.

"I didn't mean to startle you, my dear. I am Zele Hazeline. That was a hug weave. Was it unpleasant?" Hazeline frowned.

"No, it felt nice, but I didn't expect it."

"That is quite all right, child. You will learn to see the weaves forming before you can feel them. Then you will be able to ward off the weaves that may do you harm. Now let me try another on Lizzy. If you can see it, I will ask you to try telling me what kind of weave it is."

Teah bit her lip, concentrating.

"No first day student is expected to actually do it," Rachel whispered smugly.

Teah turned her attention to Zele Hazeline. Gradually, a soft green glow surrounded her and began taking shape as if an outline of a picture. It formed into a hand, which tugged the hair also forming in the air. Then, the image turned back into random lines moving wistfully to Lizzy and falling over her. The girl gave a little yelp sitting up straight.

Teah stared at Lizzy for a moment longer and then to Zele Hazeline.

"What kind of weave was that?" The teacher asked.

"It was a spanking weave," Rachel interjected.

Hazeline's calm face turned into a storm. "I was asking Teah, but you are wrong, Rachel. Perhaps it is too soon." She turned to another student who raised her hand.

"It was a hair pulling weave made up of green weaves."

The room went silent. All eyes turned to Teah who came to her feet as she answered.

"What did you say?" Hazeline asked in a cross between a whisper and a hiss.

"It was a hair pulling weave," Teah stammered.

"No, the other part," the teacher said staring at her hard.

"It was made up of green weaves, or whatever you call them; they were all green lines."

Hazeline's jaw dropped.

"Did I say something wrong?"

Lizzy tugged on Teah's dress and she sat down. Lizzy tilted her head to Teah's ear. "You saw colors along with shapes?"

Teah nodded. "Why?"

"Most Zele Magus cannot see colors of weaves. It is said the only one living who can is the Magus Matris."

Teah looked at Zele Hazeline, silent with shock. She finally shook herself out of her stupor.

"Try this one, my dear."

An image of a bee formed in yellow and floated to settle on Rachel. The girl yelped, jumping to her feet. Rachel began to speak, but Hazeline silenced her with a raised hand.

"What did you see?" she asked Teah.

Teah hesitated. "It was a bee made with weaves that were yellow, I believe due to the harm it caused. Green means it does not hurt much, yellow hurts a bit more. I would guess orange would do some serious damage and red would possibly kill a person?"

The entire class stared with open mouths and her teacher sat heavily in her chair.

"Lizzy? Would you please find Zele Galena for me and ask her to join us here? Tell her it is of great importance and is in reference to her new student."

Lizzy nodded and scurried out of the room.

The entire room erupted with whispers as Hazeline stared off at nothing.

The first thing Galena did upon entering the room was glare at Teah. *This is the way you blend in?* Galena and Hazeline then exchanged excited whispers. Teah slipped inside herself, immediately able to hear those whispers.

"You have found a prodigy," Hazeline said ecstatically.

"She just got lucky," Galena assured her. "She has some talent, but she just got lucky."

"She saw colors," Hazeline replied.

Galena went rigid and slowly straightened.

Teah shot back into her own head just as Galena turned to look at her.

Galena marched over in front of Teah. "Come with me."

They did not speak as they exited the room and soon were sitting in the inner chambers of the Magus Matris. Jelisia sat at her desk as Galena whispered in her ear. When Galena reached a point in the story, the Matris's cloudy blue eyes widened, looking at the girl as if for the first time. Magus Matris motioned for Galena to sit in the chair next to her desk. Both faced Teah.

"I understand you saw weaves as well as colors for the first time today. You have a rare gift for one so young, and an even rarer gift of seeing colors as well. We haven't seen the ability here since I have been Matris and that is many, many years."

"Actually Matris," Teah began as the woman leaned forward, "I saw Grinwald and Galena making weaves of many different colors over my brother when he was ill."

"Why didn't you tell me you saw the weaves?" Galena asked.

"I didn't know what they were until today in class."

"You saw Grinwald's weaves as well?"

Teah nodded she had.

"In the history of the Magus, no Zele Magus could see the weaves of a Viri Magus nor could a Viri Magus see the weaving of a Zele Magus. What did Grinwald's weaving look like?" Galena pressed.

"Like yours, I couldn't see any difference, but I didn't know what I was seeing so I wasn't paying close attention," Teah explained.

"Well, it seems talent is latent in you, waiting to come out. Let us have you attend all the other classes, but this time, try not to stand out so much. If you become aware of another gift, save that knowledge to tell Galena and me, do you understand?"

"Yes," Teah nodded.

A knock interrupted them and the three looked to each other in surprise.

"Go see who it is," the Magus Matris told Galena.

Galena opened the door a fraction, then stumbling backwards as Headmistress Astoria marched in and stopped in front of the Magus Matris's desk. "Why did you not summon me to this meeting?"

"It did not concern you," Galena said, coming up beside her.

"When has the wellbeing of a student stopped being the concern of the Headmistress?"

"That is not what she meant and you know it," Jelisia sighed.

"Then what did Zele Galena mean by it?" She glared at Galena.

"We handled the situation and you needn't worry about it," Jelisia said.

"I spoke with Zele Hazeline and she said that Teah saw colors and shapes. Is that true?"

"Yes, Astoria, that is true. But we discussed this with Teah and have found she may be mistaken about seeing colors along with shapes. We will work with her to assure she can develop her skills, if this is truly the case."

"I wish to take Teah and work with her on weave reading myself. She will be my personal student for weaving every day," Zele Astoria said.

"That's ridiculous," Galena scoffed.

"And why would that be ridiculous?" Astoria glared. "I was the weave reading teacher before I became Headmistress. It makes absolutely perfect sense that Teah receive private tutelage for her very special gift."

"I will be her teacher," Galena began.

"That is quite enough, both of you." Jelisia said. "She does have a point, Galena. She is the most qualified of the Zele Magus to train the girl in weave reading. She can start tomorrow."

"But Magus Matris," Galena protested.

"That is final. Is there anything else, Headmistress?" Jelisia turned to Astoria.

"Don't you think Teah should return to her class schedule? She will still need to develop the other skills of a Zele Magus with which she doesn't have a natural ability."

"I think that is a good idea," Jelisia said. "I will have Zele Galena escort Teah to her next class. Galena, I believe you know which one."

"Yes, Magus Matris, weaving class is next," Galena rolled her eyes.

"If that is all, Headmistress, I have something I need to discuss with Zele Galena. Would you two please wait in the waiting room until I am through?"

Teah nodded and walked to the waiting room, Zele Astoria behind her. As Teah took a chair, the Headmistress stood looking at the girl. Teah gazed up at her curiously.

"Do you have other abilities we should know about?" Zele Astoria asked.

"Like what?"

"I don't know exactly. I'm just very curious about you."

"And why is that?"

"Why would Caldora and King Englewood find you so interesting?"

Teah stiffened.

"There has been word from Cordlain that Caldora and the King are looking for a young girl who fits your description."

"I doubt that would be me." Teah replied.

The door to the inner chamber opened and Galena appeared in the outer chamber.

"We will discuss this further tomorrow during our weave reading class," the Headmistress smiled, and with a nod to Galena, walked out.

"What was that about?" Galena asked.

"Seems she feels I resemble a girl Caldora and the King are looking for," Teah replied.

"We already knew that. The news of the search for you reached us weeks ago. That is why we needed to be careful you weren't discovered. Did she know who you are?"

"She didn't come out and say it."

"Dear spirits, she suspects. This is what I was dreading. Come with me," she said taking her by the hand and pulling her into the inner chamber of the Magus Matris behind her.

They walked right up to stand in front of Jelisia's desk. She looked up, "Yes, what is it now?"

"Astoria suspects Teah is the girl Englewood is searching for," Galena told her.

"I think she has guessed it since Teah arrived with you. The interesting thing is she hasn't told anyone else at this point. It is unusual that news such as that has not been spread around. I am curious as to why she is keeping it to herself."

"Why did you allow her to be my teacher if you suspected she might realize my true identity?" Teah questioned.

"If I had refused, it was surely going to draw suspicion from the rest of the citadel."

"What do we do now?" Galena asked.

"You take Teah back to class as if none of this has happened. While you are in Astoria's private lessons, be careful not to divulge too much. Deny her claims if she accuses you of being the one they are searching for."

"Back to class," Galena told Teah and the two left the Magus Matris's chambers.

Galena led Teah to the weaving class room as the students filed in. They walked over to Lizzy and Rachel who stood just outside the doorway.

"Here you go," Galena said as she started back down the hall. "Try not to get into trouble this time."

Teah turned to the two girls and smiled sheepishly.

"Come on," Rachel said turning into the classroom.

The three moved over to a table. A short woman with short brown hair and a long grey dress stood at the front, watching the three girls take their seats. The woman's head tilted to one side. Her slender build and long nose gave her a hawk-like appearance.

"Good morning, students," the woman greeted.

"Good morning, Zele Cassandra," the students replied.

"Today we will take weaves and tie them off so we can proceed to other weaves. This allows you to do more than one thing with your magic at the same time without trying to concentrate on holding a weave.

"Shall we begin? Rachel, would you be so kind as to weave a flame in the air in front of you and then, while it is still there, weave another flame to light this candle on my desk?" She finished by pointing to a candle in front of her.

Rachel nodded and her face fixed in concentration. A small yellow flame appeared before her and then the candle on the teacher's desk lit.

Teah watched closely as a red weave formed in front of Rachel and the flame appeared. Another weave formed and moved over to the candle on the desk and touched the wick.

The class applauded politely.

"Very good, Rachel," Zele Cassandra smiled, blowing out the candle.

"Now, Teah, after you have seen Rachel do it, would you please do the same?"

The room fell quiet and all eyes flew to the newest Zele Magus student.

Teah furrowed her brow and a flame appeared before her at the exact same time as the candle lit.

Zele Cassandra's eyes shot open and flickered between her candle and the small flame in front of Teah. "You need to first weave the flame in front of you and tie it off, and then you light the candle. You seemed to have done it the other way around. Try it again." She blew out the candle.

Zele Cassandra looked up to find Lizzy's hand in the air. "Yes, Lizzy, what is it?"

"Uh, Zele Cassandra, I couldn't see Teah weave," Lizzy said uncertainly.

"You must have just missed it," she reasoned, but as she looked around, the other students shook their head.

"Really," she paused. "I will be certain to pay closer attention this time. I am sure she is weaving, the flames were created." Zele Cassandra turned back to Teah. "All right, please continue."

Teah concentrated once more, and again, the two flames appeared in the same instant. This time Zele Cassandra gasped with the entire room of students.

"Rachel, please get Zele Galena."

"Yes, Zele Cassandra," Rachel said, glaring at Teah before she left.

Teah let the flame in front of her go out, rolled her eyes, and slouched down in her seat as the whispers amongst the students began again.

Zele Cassandra dropped in her chair, staring right through Teah.

Galena stormed into the room, Rachel right behind her. Teah received yet another glare. This one, Teah neatly returned, squaring her shoulders.

As Galena bent over to whisper with Cassandra, Teah closed her eyes and let her mind drift to the women. "I tell you she is not weaving, but the flames still appeared," Cassandra said.

"How can that be?" Galena charged. "What are you saying?"

"Teah is not weaving. I believe she is casting the spell."

"There has been only one spell caster in the history of Ter Chadain," Galena argued.

"You don't have to tell me about our history, Galena," Cassandra shot back. "We all know that Queen Tera was the only spell caster in Ter Chadain History. The girl is not weaving. I am certain of that and the entire class witnessed it."

"Do it again," Galena insisted.

"I am telling you she is not weaving."

"Do, it, again," Galena said through clenched teeth.

Cassandra looked up and Teah's mind jumped back into her body. "Teah, would you please do the exercise again?"

"Of course, Zele Cassandra," Teah replied and instantly ignited the two flames.

The whispers started up as Teah let both flames wink out.

"You will come with me," Galena stated, storming past Teah.

Teah stood and followed the Zele Magus out to the room and through the halls, back into the Magus Matris's chambers.

"She is a caster," Galena proclaimed when Jelisia looked up.

Jelisia slumped back in the chair. A hint of a smile curved the lips. "My, my, this is an interesting development. We can't have any more revelations occurring in front of the rest of the students. You will take her as your personal student as well, Galena. I know you are worried about the talk, but she needs to get this kind of advanced attention with her skill. We don't even know what other abilities she has. We cannot risk finding out about any other talents as we did today."

Galena nodded her agreement.

"What about the Headmistress?" Teah asked.

"She will have to be satisfied with teaching you weave reading. Galena will work with you on everything else," Jelisia sighed heavily.

Chapter 21

Logan fell out of his saddle into Sasha's arms. His horse had barely stopped when the Betra caught him. The last thing Logan remembered was seeing her running.

When he woke, the stars shone brilliantly and a small fire crackled. He slowly sat up and looked around. Their camp was in a small clearing guarded by tall pines. The horses grazed off to the side of the site, but there was no sign of Saliday and Sasha.

He searched the edge of the camp where the pines stood so close to each other they blocked the rest of the landscape. A sound floated in on a light breeze. He couldn't discern what it was, but it was strangely familiar.

Pushing past the boughs, he followed the echoes. The full moon lit a small path weaving its way through the tall grass beyond their camp site. The path slowly descended until Logan stood on the banks of a large body of water, its surface glassy. Off to his left came splashing, then the same sound that echoed through the forest.

Laughter. Sasha and Saliday were playing. Eyes narrowed, he caught their silhouettes as they plunged beneath the surface of the water.

His face began to warm.

"What are you doing sneaking up on us?" Saliday scolded with just her head above the water.

"I thought I heard laughing. What are you two doing down here?"

"Unlike you, we are not comfortable stinking for the entire trip and decided to take the opportunity to bathe while you slept," she lectured.

"Where is Sasha?"

The Betra surfaced next to Saliday, sputtering.

"What are you doing?"

"Just washing up, Master," she replied, wiping the water from her eyes.

Logan glanced around. Two bundles of clothes sat neatly on a log. His eyes grew wide as he turned back to the women, this time his face a bright crimson. "You don't have any clothes on?"

"We will remedy that if you could move away and turn around," Saliday said.

Logan awkwardly moved beyond their clothes and turned his back. Splashing came from the lake, then a long silence.

Finally he felt a tap on his shoulder. He found himself face to face with Saliday, her hair hanging wet about her shoulders, her eyes glistening in the moonlight. Sasha moved off silently towards the camp.

"You should take a dip as well," she said, her scowl softening a bit. "You smell like a barn."

She turned and followed Sasha, leaving him beside the lake. Watching her leave made him blush again. He began removing his clothing. As he raised his arm over his head, he gave it a quick smell. He grimaced. Once he was naked, he touched the water with his foot and jumped back.

"Don't be such a baby, it's not that cold," Saliday said from behind him.

He froze in place, looking over his shoulder at her, shivering.

"Men are always more sensitive to external conditions than we are," Sasha said walking up beside Saliday. The moon shone on their smiles of satisfaction.

"You saw us; this is just to keep things fair," Saliday said as her smile broadened. "Very nice, wouldn't you say?"

"We should not make comments about the Protector," the Betra cautioned.

Logan turned further at the waist, looking at the two women. The moonlight caught the metallic emblem over his left breast.

"Is that the protector's mark?" Saliday said. "Can I have a closer look?"

"Enough of the show," Logan frowned, then ran into the lake and dove in. He came up with a gasp. "Sasha, take her back to the camp and tie her up if she tries to come back down here. I'm not going to parade around for either of you anymore tonight."

Sasha took Saliday by her arm, the Tarken's mouth still hanging open, leading her away from the lake.

Logan reached under the water, taking the sand in his hands and rubbing it over his body. After rubbing his entire body down, he raised his arms over his head, smelling beneath them.

Nodding in satisfaction, he walked out of the lake to his

clothes. He started putting his shirt over his head then stopped. Raising the shirt to his nose, he cringed.

He moved over to the edge of the lake and rinsed out his clothes. As he laid them out, he touched his chest where the swords crossed each other.

Cold like steel, he thought. He concentrated on the mail shirt he wore and touched his stomach, gripping the mail between his fingers. Looking down, he made out the shirt in its entirety. He released it and it disappeared.

I wish Grinwald was here.

There are many casualties in war, Logan, Stalwart said. *We never did know what he was keeping from you.*

No, but like he said, sometimes any ally is better than no ally, Galiven added.

Anger swelled.

Imagine the damage to Englewood's cause if you remove his most powerful weapon from play? Bastion agreed.

We should go now and kill Caldora, Falcone concluded.

Logan gathered his wet clothing and walked to the camp. He laid the clothing out on the rocks by the fire to dry.

She is an evil and vile being, but we have greater things to accomplish, Stalwart reasoned.

How about that Tarken, Falcone purred.

That's enough, Logan cried.

The two women sat next to the fire, stunned. Logan stood naked, laying his clothes out to dry. He turned to them, his mind elsewhere.

"I think you forgot something," Sasha told him.

"What?" Logan said, glancing down in shock. He crouched, covering himself with his hands. "Turn away until my clothes are dry. Turn away," he said again more firmly.

The protector's voices laughed uproariously inside Logan's mind.

The women giggled, but did as he asked and in a short time he told them they could turn around.

Once he was eating by the fire, he sat staring across the flames at the two women. "Saliday, where are your people? Would any consider joining our cause?"

"I'm positive they would, but it is not likely."

"Why is that?"

"They are the prisoners of the Caltorians. At least those who survived the raid on our village are. You see, the Tarken are a very old race. We were here before Queen Tera arrived to unite the duchies some two thousand years ago. We are born with this magic of need and direction and it has served our people well. Queen Tera appreciated our gift and she made a treaty allowing us to remain free in Brandermain and answer only to the throne. My people remained true to that treaty, as did the Lassains over the years.

"Through the years, many of my people chose to leave and start families in other duchies, but many stayed to learn the old and valued ways of the Tarken. It was in that last Tarken village I lived with my family. That was until the Caltorians decided they needed our tracking abilities to track down magicals in Caltoria. They tried to persuade us to go voluntarily, but we had no stomach for hunting magicals."

"Hunting magicals?" Logan asked furrowing his brow.

"Yes, hunting magicals," Saliday turned with a frown. "You honestly don't know?" Her eyes went wide when his expression didn't change. "Logan, Caltorians use magicals as slaves in Caltoria. They are possessions of the royalty, nobles, and anyone wealthy enough to afford them. You honestly didn't know, did you?"

Logan stared at her in shock. He nodded his head slowly. "Did you know?" he asked Sasha. She shook her head.

"Maybe most people here don't know, but we were told that is what they wanted us to do for them. When we refused, they took everyone captive and killed all those who they couldn't beat into submission." She paused taking a shaky breath. "My father died that day; my sister and mother were taken. I managed to escape, but I did not see anyone else get away. There may be some, but I could be the last Tarken in Ter Chadain."

Logan opened his mouth to offer his sympathy, but Saliday jumped to her feet, kicking dirt on the fire. "We should get moving. I don't want to waste a night sitting still. Now that you're awake and clean, we can be on our way." She threw her saddle on her mount.

The protectors were eerily silent as Logan packed up.

Magicals as slaves, Bastion said bitterly. *That was why we left Caltoria in the first place.*

What do you mean by that? Logan asked, but Bastion was silent as were the rest of the protectors.

The three rode out of the ring of pines and back onto the trail. Following the path lit by the full moon overhead, the three travelers kept their horses at a brisk walk. Saliday led the way with Logan following and Sasha guarding their back. A few hours later, Saliday slowed her horse enough to move in beside Logan as she leaned into him.

"Have you ever met a duke or duchess before?" she asked.

He admitted he hadn't.

"How do you expect any of them to listen to you?"

Logan shrugged.

"You better think on it quickly. We only have a few hours before you will try and convince your first."

Kicking her horse, she took the lead once more.

She's right, he thought. All four protectors began to give him advice at once and he closed them off to a dull murmur. He rode on, deep in concentration.

He still struggled with his ideas when his horse stopped and he looked up.

A city lay sprawled out before him, lights twinkling in the valley below the ridge. The lights glistened off dark wooden logs stacked neatly for the building's walls. The roofs shone a dull copper in the glow of lanterns on long poles lining the streets. The streets formed uniform lines in a reddish brown color.

Before they could start down the road to Longstand, a mass of armed men surrounded them, each man leveling a long pike at the travelers.

Sasha reached for her sword, but Logan stopped her with a look. He raised his hands slowly, showing he held no weapon.

The men had bronze breastplates with the emblem of a great tree pounded into them. Bronze helms with one long white feather sat atop each man's head. "State your business in Longstand at this hour," one of the men ordered.

Logan hesitated for a moment.

"We have business with Duke Banderkin," Saliday said confidently.

"The duke does not receive visitors at this hour. Is he expecting you?"

"He has been expecting me for thirteen years."

Everyone present turned their attention to Logan as he removed his cloak revealing the protector swords on his back.

Sasha and Saliday stared, but the guards all spoke to each other at once.

"We do not expect to see the duke at this hour but would like to be treated with respect and escorted to an inn where we could rest," Logan told them.

"How do we know you didn't steal those?" The guard nodded towards the swords.

"That will be up to your duke to decide for himself. You can set guards at the inn where we are staying to assure he has the chance."

The men nodded, lowering their pikes.

"Follow me."

Saliday and Sasha rode on either side of Logan, guards in front and behind. Saliday leaned in, whispering, "Where did all that come from?"

"I decided how I was going to convince the duke of who I am."

"I guess you did. I'm glad it worked," she smiled.

"So am I," he admitted.

The group halted before a large building with a sign showing an image of a man sleeping under a large tree. The Shading Inn.

"Wait here." The head guard scurried inside. He soon reappeared with a small woman.

"This is Madam Comfry, the owner of The Shading Inn. She has consented to lodging you for the night. You will remain in the room until the duke has summoned you. Do you understand?"

The travelers all nodded. The petite woman grunted for them to follow, her dark eyes taking them in without a hint of emotion. Her black hair brushed her shoulders as she walked with a noticeable limp ahead of them. Together, they entered a large common room filled with people. All eyes fell upon them and the room went quiet. Logan furrowed his brow until he remembered the polished handles of the protector swords were still visible.

"Why are the blades so recognizable?" he whispered to Saliday.

"Maybe it's the black pommels or the crystal balls on each with the emblem of the protector in them. What do you think? Is there anything about those swords that doesn't scream Protector Blades?"

"Enough talking, follow me to your room so they can get back to spending their money," Madame Comfry ordered.

They only went a few paces when a very large man stepped in front of them so suddenly that Logan ran into the man's chest.

Sasha rushed to Logan's defense, but another man moved to impede her way.

Saliday started to draw one of her knives, but a firm hand on her wrist pulled her up short. The Tarken turned to see Madame Comfry holding a dagger against her stomach.

"Let the boy figure this out himself. If he is truly the owner of those blades, he will be able to handle this."

"He may handle it by cutting everyone into pieces," Saliday warned.

"Not if he is truly here to lead us back to a unified Ter Chadain. He will not harm true believers," the innkeeper said confidently.

Logan stood staring up at the man towering over him. He stunk of sweat and ale, and dirt covered his greasy face.

"You should give those to me, son, and let a real man lead us back to our former glory," the man scowled.

A smile crossed Logan's face. "A man is defined by what is inside of him and by the blood pulsing through his veins. Size and age have nothing to do with this, so maybe you need to sit down with your friends and have another drink on me," Logan finished, tossing him a gold coin.

The man snatched the coin out of the air with a laugh. "I will do that, lad, and I thank you for it, but it still doesn't resolve you having those swords instead of me."

He reached for one of the blades, but his hand never touched the pommel as Logan struck him firmly in the stomach with a blow, driving the wind from the man's lungs.

Dropping to a knee, the man growled, his head snapping up.

Logan placed a firm hand on the man's shoulder, applying pressure to keep him on his knees.

"That was your only warning, friend. The next may take your life, which I do not wish to do if uniting Ter Chadain is truly your desire. I will need every man of your mindset to do the job."

The man stopped struggling and looked into the boy's eyes.

As Logan stared back, a man from the rear of the room drew his sword and charged. "Death to the Protector, long live Englewood," he cried.

Several men jumped to halt his advance, but the man hewed them down. Logan quickly pushed the man in front of him away and drew the blades with ringing smoothness. He caught the man's blade before it cut into a nearby serving girl.

The man spun to free his sword and swept around. People were packed too close within the crowded room and were hit. Screams filled the room.

Logan dove into the crowd and drove the hilt his swords into the man's belly. The man doubled over as Logan twisted his sword, pulling the blade from the man's hand.

The crowd was upon the man instantly, restraining him.

"I'll kill ya," the man cried. "I won't let you and the witches gain power in Ter Chadain again."

There was a cry from the crowd as two more men drew their weapons, causing the people to part quickly. The group of men holding the first attacker was startled, and the man broke free and retrieved his sword.

The three men stepped forward together.

"I don't want to do this," Logan pleaded.

"You don't have much of a choice, boy," one of them replied. "We will not allow you to put magic back on the throne. Englewood is our rightful king."

"But he is letting the Caltorians bleed us slowly," a bystander cried.

"Better that than have these freaks in control of us," the man argued.

"So there is no way I can convince you to stand down and let us be?" Logan asked.

The man lunged forward with a high strike for Logan's head.

Logan easily deflected the blow and spun away from the blade. He spun back to deflect a blow from the other side.

The other two men jumped in as Logan deflected blow after blow, alternating from side to side. He moved so quickly that his blades became a blur to all in the room.

Saliday turned to Madam Comfry and pleaded, "Let me help him."

"I'd say he has it under control," Madam Comfry nodded.

Saliday looked up just in time to see Logan turn his defense into offense.

Logan dropped to a knee, avoiding another strike at his head.

He reached out with his left hand, sweeping across the men knee high, as he deflected another strike at his head with his right.

The Sword of Salvation never slowed as it went through the last man's leg with the same velocity it had the first. The three adversaries were lying on the floor, screaming as they looked down at legs missing everything below the knee.

Blood gushed everywhere.

Madam Comfry withdrew her blade from against Saliday's belly and the Tarken drew her dagger and walked to each man, slitting his throat.

"Even misguided men deserve a quick death when it is their time," she said as she walked past Logan to stand by the innkeeper again.

The people were seeing to the others injured in the battle and the man who had first confronted Logan stepped up to him again.

Placing a hand on Logan's shoulder, he looked down at the boy.

"All hail the Protector of Ter Chadain," he shouted. The entire room dropped to a knee, repeating the man's refrain.

Saliday looked around. Even Madame Comfry was on a knee.

It took some time, but eventually everyone stopped cheering and kneeling so Madam Comfry could lead them to her best room in the inn. They knew this since she repeated the point all the way to the doorway.

She was right; the room was adorned elaborately with paintings and rugs. Plush chairs sat in front of a fireplace already lit, and off the main room, two bedrooms sported large feather beds and fireplaces.

Madam Comfry shut the door only after the serving girl Logan saved had placed a large platter of meat, cheese, and bread on a table along with a pitcher of ale.

Logan walked into a bedroom, flopping down on the bed. He felt the rage pushing at his self-control as the man tried touching the sword. The voices of past protectors shouted behind a muffling barrier. He fought them back with all his will. The rage wanted him to take the sword and kill everyone.

He fell asleep remembering his sister's face.

Chapter 22

By the time Teah had left the Magus Matris's offices it was lunch time. Galena had other things to speak with Jelisia about and instructed her to go to the dining hall, then to return to her room until the Zele Magus summoned her.

As she entered the hall, the room fell silent. All heads followed her as she joined the food line. Anyone she made eye contact with turned away instantly.

She proceeded to get her lunch. Then she became aware of two people standing beside her, one on either side. Glancing up cautiously, she found Lizzy smiling on her right. On her other side was Rachel with a more controlled look of interest on her face.

"You didn't think you were going to get away with showing everybody up today without making most of them mad, did you?" Rachel said.

"Most of them, you two aren't mad at me for showing off?"

"You weren't showing off, Teah," Lizzy frowned. "You're just the most gifted Zele Magus student ever to walk these halls and we're proud to be considered your friends. We are your friends, aren't we?"

"Of course you are, Lizzy. You and Rachel will always be my friends as long as you want to be."

"All of the chosen are angry you have skills superior to them. I was next in line for chosen, but I will understand if you are raised first. I have accepted that and will take your friendship in payment for you embarrassing me."

"It sounds like a fair trade, Rachel, thank you."

"You're welcome. Get some food and come sit down. The other girls want a chance to speak with you, even if they are afraid to come up here and show it."

They waited patiently until Teah gathered her food and then led her to the table where they'd sat for breakfast. None of the other girls spoke, but most stared. Teah looked away uncomfortably.

One of the chosen got up from the head table.

"Don't look now, but here comes Petenza," Rachel whispered to Teah.

"She is the 'Head Chosen,' the chosen that is the most advanced and next to be raised to Zele Magus," Lizzy explained.

"She must have heard about you today," Rachel said.

Petenza moved up behind Teah and stopped. "I guess you think you're something now?" she sneered. "Just remember, only chosen get to be Zele Magus. You haven't been here for a day yet. It will take you years."

As Teah looked over her shoulder, the yellow weave of a slapping hand approached her bottom. Teah thought of a pillow covering her bottom and the weave of the chosen disappeared, never reaching her.

The chosen growled with anger at the realization her weave didn't have the intended result and began weaving once again. This time Teah saw a red hand moving to strike her head.

Teah lashed out. The red weave vanished, the chosen tumbling back.

The woman's anger turned to fear. She gathered herself off the floor, running from the hall.

Strange expressions greeted Teah.

"What?" she asked.

"Did you do that to her?" Rachel asked in a loud whisper.

"I defended myself. I wasn't going to let her touch me with a red weave. It would have done some serious damage."

"Did you weave?" Lizzy asked.

"I don't know how to weave yet. I thought of what I wanted to do and it just happened. Is that weaving?"

"It doesn't work that way," Rachel told her. "Usually we concentrate on the intensity of the weave and then build it in our minds first. Then we release it. Just like you saw the Zele Magus in weaving class do it today."

"Did you see me weave?" Teah asked.

"I couldn't see a weave. Could you, Lizzy?"

"No," Lizzy nodded. "I didn't see any weaves except the ones the chosen created."

"Enough talking in here," Zele Galena scolded, coming up behind the three. "All of you to my chambers at once, and not another word out of any of you until I instruct it."

The girls hesitated for a moment and Galena clapped her hands, sending them into motion. They dropped their trays off at the kitchen window and ran to Galena's chambers.

They entered without a word, standing in front of the Zele Magus as she sat in an overstuffed black leather chair. The look on her face could have melted steel.

There was little time to take in the tapestries adorning the walls or the dark wood paneling, as Galena released her rage upon them. "What were you thinking, attacking a chosen?"

Teah began to respond, but the Zele Magus didn't allow her. "And the two of you discussing how she attacked a chosen in front of the entire citadel, you should know better. Since you have decided to befriend Teah and already have discovered her special talents, you will now be joining her in her private studies with me."

The disbelief was evident on the two girl's faces. Galena motioned in front of herself with her hands and then stopped. "You will report here every morning for lessons and none of you will speak of what goes on in these chambers to anyone. I have placed a weave upon you that will not allow you to do so. Do you understand?"

The girls nodded. "What did she do back there?" Lizzy asked. Three heads spun on her.

"Teah is not a weaver like the rest of us," Galena said surprisingly calm. "She is a spell caster, the first spell caster in over two thousand years. And since she has this gift, she also has the ability to teach this gift, to a certain extent, to anyone with the Zele Magus ability. That will be part of her lessons, teaching Rachel and you. Congratulations, girls," she turned to the stunned youths. "You are going to be part of something bigger than all of us."

Rachel turned to Teah. "Who are you?"

"Since you are forbidden to speak of what is spoken in this chamber, I guess there is no harm in telling you the truth. Remember, if you try to speak of this, you will be unable to do so. You and Lizzy are now the attendants of the Queen of Ter Chadain, Teah Lassain."

Lizzy dropped to a knee, but Rachel stared at Teah with amazement. "What have we gotten ourselves into?" she said with her mouth agape.

"Yes, indeed," Galena agreed. "Yes, indeed."

Very awkwardly, Rachel fumbled into a deep bow. "What are we to do now?"

"You are to return to your classes as planned and return here tomorrow morning to begin your lessons with Teah. Teah, you are to report to the Headmistress's chambers to start your weave reading training."

"I thought I was to start that in the morning."

"Zele Astoria has decided to begin early since she has heard of your weaving class as well. You must remember not to expose too much of your abilities except what she already knows about. Is that understood?"

"Yes, Zele Galena," Teah sighed.

"The two of you may bring Teah to the Headmistress's chambers on your way to your next class," Galena told them.

"Yes, Zele Galena," the girls replied.

"Then get a move on. And Teah, remember to be cautious," Galena warned.

"I will," Teah said as they exited Galena's chambers. The walked silently down a long hallway and up some stairs. They climbed and climbed and climbed until they reached the top of the highest rampart in the citadel.

"Here you go," Rachel said gasping. "Why doesn't Galena trust Astoria?"

"Zele Astoria knows who I am and thinks I should go to Cordlain and serve King Englewood. Only Zele Galena and the Magus Matris are keeping her from sending me there herself."

Before any of the girls could reply, Zele Astoria's chamber door swung open and the woman stood before them with hands on ample hips. She frowned at the three, but then quickly changed the frown to a large smile. "Welcome, welcome. Come in, come in," she said with flourishing hand gestures.

As Teah passed, Zele Astoria placed a hand on Rachel's chest. "That will be all, girls, back to class for you." She smiled sweetly and closed the door in their faces.

Teah stood in the middle of the room, looking at all the deep mahogany wood and brilliant chromed fixtures. There were several overstuffed furniture pieces, including two large, high-backed arm chairs sitting in front of a fireplace. A small fire burned quietly and it imparted a soft yellow glow to the room.

Astoria took Teah by the shoulders and gently, but firmly, led her to one of the chairs. She moved over to the chair opposite and leaned back to relax into the soft fabric. Her red dress and her ruby shone in the dull light as if they illuminated by themselves. Her dark skin contrasted the fabric in the chair and made the dress stand out all the more. She leaned forward.

"I am so pleased you were able to come today instead of tomorrow. The sooner we start, the sooner we can develop all of your special talents. We wouldn't want anymore to just pop out of you again, now would we?" she smiled.

"Why do you tell me to hurry and learn my abilities while Galena and the Magus Matris tell me I need to be patient?" Teah said, her eyes narrowing.

"It is imperative that we all work to reach our potential and better Ter Chadain. That is the goal for every Zele Magus. Don't you want to help Ter Chadain?"

"I would do anything for Ter Chadain."

"You don't sound like some country girl, as Galena suggests." Astoria smiled again.

"Why would you think that? Shouldn't we all care what happens to Ter Chadain?" Teah asked.

"There is just something about you that seems different. I mean, other than your special abilities. I feel you could be hiding something."

"If I were this girl that the king is seeking, then why am I still here?" Teah pressed.

"It is the Magus Matris who makes those decisions. It does not matter what I think. She insists you aren't the girl King Englewood seeks." She threw her hands up and leaned further back into her chair.

"So what would happen to me if I was this girl?"

"Oh, there is no need to worry. King Englewood would not be so foolish to take you with force or against the wishes of the Magus Matris. The political ramifications of that might cause a severe backlash throughout the Magic Council and Ter Chadain. It is better for all of us if you are not this girl. It would greatly complicate life here at the citadel."

"From what I've heard of King Englewood, he would be foolish enough."

Astoria reached over and slapped Teah hard on her face. Teah's head jerked to one side and she turned her head back slowly, the woman's handprint becoming redder by the second across her cheek.

"I will not have you speak treason in my quarters. Do you understand me?" Astoria said slow and deliberate.

"Yes, Headmistress," Teah said softly, but her eyes shot daggers at the woman.

"Good, let us begin our lessons. I will weave a spell to strike your bottom and you will identify the color of that spell each and every time. When you get it correct twenty times in a row, we will then move on to another lesson. Do you understand?"

"Yes, Headmistress," Teah replied. Even as she responded, a red weave was forming over Astoria's moving hands. It took the shape of a hand striking a butt. It lifted away from the Zele Magus and settled on Teah.

Teah gritted her teeth as the slap struck her and she flinched. "It was a red weave, Headmistress," Teah told her.

"Oh, my dear, I think you misunderstood. You need to tell me the color before I set the spell on you. That one will not count, try again, and twenty in a row now."

An orange spell wove in front of the Zele Magus and Teah shouted out, "orange weave", then it changed quickly to red and settled over the girl once more. This time Teah let out a soft squeak when her bottom was slapped.

"No, I am sorry, but it was also a red weave. Again, that one did not count. Twenty more to go," Astoria smiled coldly.

Teah glared at the woman, but she didn't seem to notice as she smiled sweetly back and began to weave again. It started as orange once more, but Teah waited calmly. Just as Teah was about to call out orange, she reached out with her thoughts and held the weave with her mind and called out "orange."

The orange weave settled over Teah and she felt a firm smack on her bottom.

"No, ah, my dear," Astoria hesitated. "Yes, I guess that was an orange weave. You only need nineteen more to go."

The lesson continued with the Headmistress weaving and Teah holding that weave one color until they finished the twenty correct identifications.

The Headmistress sat scratching her head, looking at Teah when they had finished. "That was very good, Teah. It seemed so natural."

"Thank you, Headmistress," Teah replied meekly. She reached down and rubbed her sore bottom gingerly.

"I think that is enough for today. Now let this be a lesson to you in the future. Do not question my beliefs in my chambers. Your lessons will be severe if you do."

"Yes, Headmistress," Teah sighed.

"That will be all, you may leave," Astoria motioned to the door.

Teah got up to leave, but hesitated by a small cage on the table near a window overlooking the courtyard. The cage held a number of insects, both large and small. "What are these for?" she asked.

"I find them fascinating. That will be all, you're dismissed." The woman waved a hand.

Teah closed the door behind her. She looked down the long flights of stairs as she rubbed her bottom. With a groan, she took the first step.

Chapter 23

"It is time," the guard said, leaning into the room.

Logan, Sasha, and Saliday looked up from the bedroom table where they took their noon meal. None spoke, but began gathering their things, Logan strapping on the swords and draping his cape over them.

"What is the point of that?" asked Sasha. "Everyone in town will have a description of us by now. Hiding those won't make any difference." She pulled the cloak off the two blades, exposing the handles over each shoulder.

Logan began to protest, but Saliday cut him short.

"She's right. The events in the common room last evening will have spread throughout the city. You are exposed and there is no way to conceal your identity now. You might as well go with it."

She followed the guard out the door with Sasha and Logan close behind, Logan fastening the compressed bow upon his belt.

The common room was packed and everyone stood as they descended the stairs. Logan nodded as he passed while the others ignored it all, exiting the inn ahead of him.

The street was filled with soldiers sitting astride their mounts. The traveler's horses were saddled and waiting for them in the middle of the armed men. Logan and his companions mounted and soon the entourage was moving through the city. More people and soldiers lined the streets.

They arrived in front of a large mansion stretching many stories above them and sprawling out in all directions. The gate was made of black steel, but the walls were made of the same dark wood from which the rest of the city was constructed.

They silently followed the guard through the gates and into the mansion, climbing up the stone stairway into a grand entry. Turning down a hallway to the left, they entered a large audience room filled with people, many of them wearing some sort of uniform. The people began to murmur amongst themselves as the three travelers entered.

Three chairs were placed before a raised dais where a large

throne sat with smaller ornate chairs to either side.

Logan looked to his companions as the doors closed behind them. Saliday shrugged, taking a chair. Sasha followed suit, leaving the middle chair for the boy.

They didn't have to wait long as a number of guards marched in before a large man with short grey hair. Everyone in the chamber rose and Saliday, Sasha, and Logan followed their lead.

The man strode to the throne where he stood for a moment, taking in his visitors. His deep green, silk shirt and light brown pants were tailored to fit his blocky body. He was nearly as tall as Logan but much broader with an obvious muscular build, the tight fitted shirt showing cut muscles underneath. He was clean-shaven, revealing a scar across his left cheek. This man knew battle, and his green eyes shone brightly at the youths, an amused smirk crossing his lips.

He motioned and the entire audience took their seats.

People now occupied the chairs to either side of the duke. To the duke's right sat a woman with light grey hair tied up in a bun. Her velvet green dress was cut low in the front, exposing the top of her round breasts. She wore a signet on her head with a single green jewel in silver. She looked at Logan suspiciously.

Sitting to the duke's left was a young woman also all in green, wearing not a dress, but trousers and a shirt matching the duke's. Her brown hair was tied back in a tail and her clothing was as tight as the duke's. A scowl twisted her full lips. Logan pulled his reluctant eyes from the young woman.

"I'm told you are the one I have been waiting for," the duke said, his deep voice echoing through the large chamber. "I will tell you up front, I'm not convinced you are the Protector merely because you carry the sacred blades. I'm not even certain those are the protector blades. May I have a closer look at them?"

Nodding his acceptance, Logan moved closer to the throne drawing one sword from its scabbard. The ring of steel reverberated off the walls in the hall. The guards drew their weapons before Logan's blade cleared the scabbard. Logan deftly spun the sword so the handle faced the duke, holding the blade gently in his palm.

Don't let him take the blade, Stalwart said.

Never let anyone, take the blade, Bastion agreed.

It is a hard lesson Galiven learned, Falcone pointed out. Galiven was silent.

The duke went to take the weapon, but Logan pulled it back lightly. "I can't allow you to take the blade, duke," he said calmly. "You may touch it and examine it while I remain in possession of it, but you must not try grasping the handle."

The duke nodded his understanding, gently caressing the black handle and the pommel with the crystal ball on the end. He traced the gold hand guard's intricate shapes and slowly slid back in his seat.

The woman to the duke's right did not show any interest in the sword, but the young woman leaned in close.

Logan turned to her so she could touch the sword without reaching, but she quickly pulled away, sitting back in her seat once more.

Logan glanced up at her, but her eyes stared vacantly into the distance.

He withdrew, and when he was a few steps back from the dais, spun the sword, fluidly sheathing it over his shoulder.

'Ahs' erupted from the audience.

He bowed deeply, and then returned to his seat, never turning his back, but facing the three.

Once Logan was seated, the duke spoke. "I will admit to you the swords do appear genuine, but I'm confused as to how you came by them."

"I went to the Protector's Fortress and claimed them as is my right as Logan Lassain, Protector of Ter Chadain," he bowed his head slightly.

The crowd began to whisper again.

"The Lassain family was assassinated nearly thirteen years ago. Besides, you are the fourth person in the last week to come to me claiming to be the Protector. Why should I believe you over them? They may not have the swords as you do, but they appeared more likely candidates for becoming the Protector."

"I did not claim this, it is my birthright as a Lassain," Logan replied. "I would not have chosen this if I could avoid it, but I have been told by a very wise man I need to embrace this calling in order to unite Ter Chadain once more and drive King Englewood and the Caltorians from across the sea out of our country forever."

The duke's right eyebrow rose. The two women at either side joined the audience in gasping.

"It is not wise to speak openly of treason, young man. I could have you hanged for those words under the King's law." The duke crossed his arms over his chest, staring stoically at the boy.

"Then I have chosen wrongly. I was led to believe that you, above all others, wish the country to be one once more. We will be on our way and leave you and your duchy in peace."

Logan stood and bowed, motioning for Sasha and Saliday to come. The crowd exploded with outbursts.

"I'm sorry, but that will not be possible," the duke said, clapping his hands twice. The doors to the room burst open and soon the entire chamber was filled with armed guards.

Logan looked to the men surrounding them with swords drawn, then to the duke.

"I do not wish to harm these men. I believe you want what I'm offering, but you are reluctant to believe in me. We will need every man here to take up arms for our cause, and I don't want to lose even one of them in this misunderstanding."

The duke tilted his head back, laughter erupting from him. "That is quite noble of you, lad. Just hand over your blades and they will escort the three of you down to the dungeon to join the other false protectors."

The duke nodded to a guard; the man moved over to confiscate Logan's weapons.

Logan raised his hand to halt the man.

The guard stopped, looking back over his shoulder to the duke. The duke motioned for him to continue. The guard reached. Logan took hold of the man's wrist and twisted his body, throwing the guard over his shoulder into the stunned onlooking guards.

Before anyone could react, the ring of steel filled the hall and Logan stood with both swords drawn crossed before him.

Saliday and Sasha drew their weapons, standing at the ready.

Saliday deftly stepped over to Logan, his eyes catching hers for just a moment as she raised a dagger and cut away Logan's shirt in the front. The fabric fell, exposing his chest.

The three royals inhaled in shock.

Those in the crowd closest to Logan began shouting: "He has the sign, he has the sign."

The torch light in the hall glistened off the silver tattoo on Logan's chest.

Logan didn't flinch as Saliday continued to cut his shirt open. Upon seeing his tattoo and the two swords he held before him, most of the guards dropped to a knee.

"Is this proof enough?" Saliday shouted over the noise.

"It is more proof, but we need time to think on this," the duke replied hesitantly. He glanced to the women on either side, then to the men in the uniform for assistance, but found none.

"You may keep your swords, but we need to discuss this in private." He stood to leave and then stopped. "Stand down men and wait outside until you are summoned."

The men sheathed their weapons and filed out of the room, some helping the man who had tried to take Logan's swords. The duke then led the women out of the room, the youngest one pausing a last time to consider Logan. The men wearing uniforms in the audience filed past Logan and his companions to follow the duke.

Saliday dropped into her chair heavily. "That was close," she exhaled, glancing back at the crowd.

"It isn't over yet," Sasha pointed out. "They still may wish us to be their house guests in the dungeon like the imposters."

"Why would anyone pretend to be the Protector?" Logan asked, fiddling with the flap of fabric from his shirt, trying to find a way to fasten it once more.

"To make it less likely you will be believed," Saliday explained. "Englewood must have known you would be seeking help. He probably sent out several impersonators to cloud the duke's and duchess's judgment. You can bet if they are here, they are all over Ter Chadain."

"We need to speak to these imposters and interrogate them." Sasha rounded on them. "I will get the truth out of them."

The intensity in the Betra sent a shiver through Logan. Movement on the dais drew their attention, and they turned to see the duke standing with the young woman and the uniformed men behind them.

"My daughter, Dezare, would like to ask you a few questions."

Logan stepped forward, nodding.

"Have you been the Protector all of your life?" she asked emotionless.

"I was told I have been the Protector since birth, but I just received my powers on my last birthday."

"Have you had the tattoo your whole life?"

"That also appeared around my last birthday."

"They say the Protector will only appear as protection for the Queen of Ter Chadain and the defense of her seat on the throne. Is there also a new Queen of Ter Chadain?"

Logan paused. "I have a sister who will claim the throne of Ter Chadain when the time is right." He carefully chose his words.

The young woman nodded, biting her bottom lip in thought. She looked up at him once more, but this time she had a curious look in her eye.

"Can I touch your tattoo?"

All eyes shot to her in disbelief, including the duke's.

"It looks like metal and I was wondering if it felt like metal."

Logan smiled, the heat of embarrassment touching his cheeks. He gave her a slight nod and she descended the dais.

She was a head shorter than he and she reached up tentatively to the tattoo. He took her hand in his and gently guided it to the symbol.

She began to pull away in surprise as the swords felt cold to her fingers, but Logan's hand held her hand firmly to his chest. When he was satisfied she wasn't going to pull away, he released her and she began tracing the emblem. She stared dazedly up into his eyes as she traced the tattoo.

Logan didn't know how long they stood there, gazing at each other with her hand on his chest, but finally someone cleared their throat and they both blinked uncomfortably at each other.

She withdrew her hand, stepping back, the color evident on her face. She turned to the duke and gave a curt nod of satisfaction.

"My daughter believes you are the Protector. This means my generals and I believe you as well. You see, she has the ability to know if people are telling the truth. So, Protector of Ter Chadain, what do we do now?"

Logan gawked back at the duke and his generals.

"I don't know."

Chapter 24

Teah sat alone, staring down at the locket opened between her fingers, when there came a tap on her door. "Come in," she called.

The door opened tentatively. Lizzy pushed her head in.

"Lizzy, come in."

Rachel pushed past Lizzy, storming into the room and taking one of the rickety chairs. Lizzy closed the door and took the other chair.

The two girls stared at Teah for a long moment before Rachel talked. "Lizzy and I want to know if you're going to be a Zele Magus supporter or a Viri Magus supporter when you are queen."

Teah looked at them dumbfounded. "What?"

"Are you going to give favor to the Zele Magus, or are you going to award your advisory seat to the Viri Magus?" Rachel repeated.

"It is important to us," Lizzy added. "We have always believed in the Zele Magus and so has each of our families. That is why they sent us here."

"I didn't know I had a choice," Teah admitted.

"Of course you have a choice," Rachel squawked. "Where do think you are, Caltoria?"

"I really haven't been exposed to this before. My mother, foster mother, told us about court, but she never told me what side was better."

"We don't want to tell you what side to chose," Lizzy began.

"But Zele Magus is definitely better," Rachel interjected.

"Rachel. That is not true," Lizzy cried.

"Yes it is and you know it. Those Viri Magus are deceitful, and they have used every queen they have counseled to get what they wanted."

"There have been some very good Viri Magus advisors to the Queen," Lizzy defended. "I myself believe that a woman is better suited to look after a queen and what is best for Ter Chadain's people."

"What makes them different?" Teah asked.

"I'll answer that," Rachel said when Lizzy opened her mouth. "The fundamental principle of Zele Magus Beliefs is that everything is done for the betterment of all Ter Chadain, not just for the privileged. Zele Magus believe the Queen should give the support needed to keep the people healthy and happy and should keep any conflicts with the Caltorians to a minimum."

"Who would disagree with that?" Teah asked.

"The wealthy, mostly," Rachel continued. "The dukes and duchesses like to hold on tightly to their wealth and believe it is theirs by right. They do not want to allow the Queen in Ter Chadain to take taxes from them and supply support for the entire country. They feel they can take care of their own duchy by their own means."

"So all the dukes and duchesses support the Viri Magus?" Teah questioned.

"You would think so, wouldn't you?" Lizzy added.

"But you would be wrong," Rachel continued. "There are some that believe it is their duty to support the Queen in seeing to the overall welfare of the entire country. They are willing to make sacrifices for the greater good."

"That is noble of them," Teah replied.

"I wouldn't give all of them your praise yet," Rachel corrected. "Some may seem like they are out for the greater good, but if they work things correctly, they get the queen to give aid to their duchy, which, in effect, lessens their burden by spreading their responsibility to every duchy in the country. So by supporting the taxing and equalization of funding to all duchies, some come out better than if they just kept their taxes and took care of their own needs."

"Then what does the Viri Magus believe and who supports them?" Teah sighed.

"Let me tell her, Rachel," Lizzy blurted out.

"Okay, tell her." Rachel rolled her eyes.

"The Viri Magus principles are these: the state offers strong protection from the Caltorians, each duchy financially supports itself and also supports the Queen, and the duchies decide what it will provide for its people."

"That sounds simple enough," Teah decided.

"It may sound that way, but it is far from simple," Rachel ranted. "These Viri Magus see support for the Queen as men, money, and food to support efforts to defeat the Caltorians. The duchies that support the Viri Magus often have factories where the weapons and armor are being made, so their duchy becomes more influential and wealthy."

"How can anyone decide?" Teah gasped.

"You decide which is best for the country," Rachel said.

"Queens have changed from one advisor to another, depending on what events are taking place in the country. If we are at war, many queens would choose a Viri Magus advisor, and when times were peaceful, the Zele Magus would be chosen to provide an adviser. This sometimes causes whichever magus is not in power to plot a change by manipulating events," Rachel concluded.

"Like the overthrow of Lonavette," Lizzy added. "We were at peace and Lonavette was a Zele Magus supporter. The Viri Magus killed all the Lassain men and removed Lonavette in a coup."

"But they forgot about Stalwart Lassain, a cousin to the Queen, and he became the second protector," Teah said proudly.

"Exactly," both Lizzy and Rachel cried at once, startling each other.

All three girls laughed.

"Why do some people think they can control all the variables in the universe?" Teah said, catching her breath.

"What do you mean?" Lizzy asked as the smile left her face.

"Every plot in Ter Chadain history is based on the ignorant assumption that the people plotting can control or predict everyone's reaction to a chain of events that change randomly based upon those reactions. A hero will always step forward, eventually, to change or ruin the well made plans of such plotters."

"Or heroine," Rachel added.

Lizzy and Teah turned to her in confusion.

"There have been as many women as men in Ter Chadain history that made a stand against injustice. And you are the next one to take her rightful place in the history books. Do you realize that you will be the youngest queen of Ter Chadain when you take the throne?"

"That will depend on how long it takes me to become a Zele Magus and if Logan can gather support for our cause." Even as she spoke the words, Teah wished she could pull them back. She covered her mouth.

"Is that the new protector?" Lizzy asked.

Teah did not speak.

"You are a Lassain queen who is not rightfully upon the throne of Ter Chadain," Rachel told her. "It is apparent that you would have a protector aiding you. Is he a cousin or an uncle?"

Teah sighed. "He is my twin brother."

Both girls' mouths gaped.

"What is it?"

"There has never been a twin who has been a protector to the Queen," Rachel said.

"Why is that important? I thought we just had to both 'be' Lassains to have the magic work."

"That is true," Lizzy agreed, "but the closer the ties between the Queen and her protector, the stronger the magic. There is no closer connection than twins. Teah, you and…" She paused.

"Logan," Teah filled in.

"You and Logan may very well be the most powerful combination of queen and protector Ter Chadain has ever seen"

The three girls sat in awkward silence as they stared from one to the other.

"We are witnessing history in the making," Rachel whispered.

All three nodded.

The girls talked into the early hours of the morning before Lizzy and Rachel snuck back to their own rooms. Teah went to bed feeling as if she was no longer alone for the first time since Logan left, but an invisible weight of responsibility still pressed heavily upon her shoulders.

The next morning, the three girls found themselves in the Mistress of Power's chambers watching the Zele Magus gather her magic inside of her, then lash out at a large piece of marble in the center of the room. As Galena's weave entered the stone, the mass of rock exploded into tiny shards. Before the shards reached the stunned students, a glowing shield enveloped them and the projectiles dropped harmlessly to the floor.

"Well done," Galena smiled, watching the dust settle. "What did you see?"

Teah thought for a moment then raised her hand. Galena nodded. "I saw white weaves leave you and enter the stone. As the shards burst into the air, I thought of a barrier of air to protect us."

Lizzy and Rachel stared in disbelief.

"How did you create the shield?" Galena pressed.

"I just thought it."

Lizzy and Rachel shared another look. Galena examined Teah thoughtfully.

Teah concentrated on the remaining fragment of stone perched on the pedestal. She drove a pulse of energy into it. At the same time, she blocked the explosion with a shield around the rock. The projectiles from the stone dropped at its base.

Curiosity mixed with anger in Galena's tone. "Don't do any magic unless I specifically command you. Do you understand me?" She strode over, towering over Teah.

"Yes, Zele Magus," Teah curtsied, keeping her head bowed and not making eye contact with the magical. The tension was broken by a knock at the door.

Without looking away from Teah, Galena gave the command to enter. Another Zele Magus entered the room and paused, waiting for Galena to acknowledge her presence. Galena looked over.

"Your audience is requested in the Matris's chambers at once," the woman announced.

"I'm in the middle of my lessons. I'll be there shortly."

"I was told you must come with me at once."

"What is so urgent it cannot wait until I have concluded my session?"

"I don't know if I should say?"

"I will decide if you should or shouldn't say. Why is my audience needed?"

"Zele Magus Caldora has come, demanding we hand over the Zele student Teah to her for transport to King Englewood."

The girls gasped, but Galena didn't betray her feelings. "Clean up this mess, girls, then go to the dining hall and take your lunch. I will collect you there when I'm finished." She closed the door behind her.

Lizzy and Rachel hurriedly took a broom and dustpan and started sweeping up the marble shards and dust from the floor.

Teah, however, tossed herself on the coach.

"We need to get to the dining hall," Rachel warned, barely pausing with her cleaning.

"No. There is something else we need to do." Teah waved them over. When they hesitated, her mouth turned stern. "Come here."

They slowly put down the broom and dustpan walking over to sit on either side of Teah cautiously.

"I'm going to do something you mustn't tell anyone about. Promise me." She looked to each of them; though hesitating, each nodded.

Closing her eyes, Teah left her body, taking a moment to look back at herself sitting between Lizzy and Rachel as they stared at her anxiously.

She then floated out the door and down the hall until she reached the inner chambers of the Matris Magus. Galena must have just entered. She stood before the Matris while Caldora sat comfortably in one of the chairs before the leader of the Zele Magus. Galena bowed and seated herself in a chair next to Caldora. Teah moved over to a corner.

"What makes you think we have the future Queen of Ter Chadain?" The Matris asked calmly.

"I have followed Galena here."

"Galena?"

Galena shrugged. "I found a worthy student, as you know, Matris."

Silence weighed heavily between the three. "I'm not sure the girl you are seeking is with us, Caldora," the Matris finally said breaking the silence.

Caldora's eyes narrowed and Galena's lips thinned and pressed tightly together as their gazes met.

"I'm sorry, Matris, but I am charged by the King to search the citadel and deliver her to him upon her discovery."

"You have no authority here, Caldora." Galena came to her feet.

"The King has given me the authority, but I do not wish to have to exert it. I will take the girl and leave as soon as she is brought to me."

"Again, I don't think the girl you seek is here, but I will have all the students questioned."

"Thank you, Matris, I will look for the girl as well. I believe you were giving private lessons in you chambers," she said turning to Galena. "I will start my search there."

She stood and strode out of the room.

Teah was stunned. They were going to let Caldora take her.

The Matris stood and addressed Galena as she came to her

feet. "You must get to your chambers before Caldora discovers Teah."

"Not to worry, I sent the girls to the dining hall. We will leave at once."

"Where do you intend to go?"

"I'm not sure. Go west and try to find a duke who is sympathetic to our cause."

Galena hurried from the room. Teah's spirit was frozen in the corner.

The Matris turned her head towards Teah, seemingly seeing the girl's spirit with her white eyes. "Get back to your body and flee Galena's chambers, else our mission is lost."

Teah snapped from her stupor, rushing past people with a blur to jump forcibly into her empty body on the couch. She leapt to her feet between the stunned girls. "Run to the dining hall, now," she shouted at them and ran for the door.

The echoing of footsteps came down the hall. She ran with all her strength around the corner and stopped. The footsteps paused at the door of the chambers. Teah looked around the corner, her cheek pressed against the cold stone. She caught a wisp of Caldora's hair as she burst into the room. Teah spun around, running after Lizzy and Rachel for a few steps, and then stopped. Realization spread across her face. Turning around, she raced in the direction of her room.

Chapter 25

Logan, Sasha, and Saliday sat in a common room connecting separate bedrooms in the duke's mansion. The fire burned quietly in the hearth and they stared silently into the flames. A tap on the door broke their trance and Sasha strode to the door.

Two guards stood on either side of a young man about Logan's build with long black hair. A slight scar running down his right cheek gave him a fierce look, accentuating his green eyes.

"The last one," the guard informed them.

They had questioned the other two imposters, but neither had much information. Both said a strange and beautiful woman paid them a large sum of money to travel throughout the duchies, spreading word the Protector had returned and was there to unite Ter Chadain under King Englewood's rule.

This is getting us nowhere, Galiven complained.

Sasha took control of the prisoner, ushering the guards outside. She used a long established Betra practice involving small needles under the fingernails. The previous two "protectors" spilled all their information within seconds of the first needle's placement.

This boy sat down in the open chair on his own, looking flatly at them as they studied him. "What do you want?"

"Are you willing to talk without the Betra torturing you first?" Saliday asked from over by the fireplace.

"I have nothing to hide. I have come here to kill the Protector under orders of King Englewood."

"You admit openly you are here to kill the Protector?" Logan asked.

"It doesn't matter if you know or not. No one can stop me now that you brought me here. I will finish my task and be on my way."

Sasha and Saliday drew their weapons. Logan placed his hands on the hilts of his swords which lay across his lap.

"You are no match for me. I am Senji." He smiled smugly.

The women gasped.

A blur of movement passed before them. When they looked

back to the Senji, he now sat with a look of puzzled astonishment on his face. The two swords of the protector protruded from his chest as he listed to one side, his green eyes staring emptily.

"Do you realize what you've done?" Saliday whispered.

"I killed someone who announced he was here to assassinate me."

"You killed a member of the most feared assassin clan in Ter Chadain. They'll keep coming after you until you are dead or until there is none of their clan left."

"How many is that?"

"No one really knows, not even the Senji."

"Then Sasha will have to be even more diligent in safeguarding me."

Now you've done it Logan. The Senji are as old as Ter Chadain itself. They were here when I was alive. Even I didn't mess with the Senji, Bastion cried.

They are a nasty lot, the Senji, Stalwart added.

Even women are Senji and they will use their wiles to put you at ease and then put that crooked knife in your back. Nearly happened to me, Falcone cringed.

Some thought that was what happened to me, Galiven told him.

Logan drew the blades from the young man, wiping them clean on the deceased's clothes.

"Have the guards take him out of here."

Summoned, the guards lifted him off the chair, the holes in the fabric visible along with bloodstains. A jagged knife fell from either sleeve of the man.

Logan and Sasha each bent to retrieve a blade and inspected it. Short hilts with a thin crooked blade designed to inflict much pain. Logan handed his over to the Betra.

"It's time to discuss our next move," he said as the guards left the room. "See if you can find the duke and request an audience with him as soon as possible. We must gather more support than one duchy in order to defeat Englewood." Saliday nodded and left.

He quietly stared into the fire until Sasha spoke up.

"You should be very concerned about the Senji. They are a secretive society who could be anyone or anything, a serving girl to a store keeper. They are killers for hire and when they have a contract to kill someone, the entire society is bound to fulfill that contract. That is why it is very unlikely we have seen the last of them."

"What makes them any different from the Shankan?"

"The Shankan are created when orphans or bastards are handed over for training to the Shankan clan from Stalosten Duchy. They are constantly wandering, but train these children to kill without remorse or mercy. If you kill a Shankan, that is the end of that. There are no agreements that live on once a Shankan is eliminated. I have more sympathy for the Shankan because they never chose to be what they are turned into.

"A Senji has made the choice to become a member of their society and knows what is expected of them. They choose to kill for a price and are a member of the society until death. They come from all duchies and are everywhere. It is this network that makes the Senji such a dangerous foe."

"Then we need to be more diligent in keeping me alive until I can put Teah on the throne," Logan replied without emotion.

He turned back to gazing into the fire until Saliday returned with Duke Banderkin.

Logan motioned to the chair in which he had just dispatched his would-be assassin.

"I understand you have killed one of my prisoners," said the duke irritably, taking the seat while glowering at Logan. "I don't take kindly to you killing someone who is my responsibility."

Sasha stepped forward, placing one of the Senji daggers in his hands. The duke turned pale. Jaw hanging down, the duke looked at Logan in astonishment. "You killed a Senji?"

"It was either him or me. I preferred it was him." There was no expression in his voice and his eyes were hollow of all feeling. "Is that a problem?"

"No, no, no problem. I've never seen a Senji blade before, but I have heard them described by those who found them buried in the body of one of their victims. You know what they say about the Senji?"

"That they'll keep coming after me until the assassination is accomplished? I suspect I will be dead by other means before they get around to me. We need to meet with the other dukes and duchesses who are not entirely happy with the way Englewood is running the country. Could you give a list of these to Saliday so we can be on our way? You are just the first of many stops along a lengthy road."

"I think I can do better than that. I will be traveling to a meeting of the southern council of Ter Chadain Duchies tomorrow where most of the nobles are very unhappy with the King. My generals have already left for the meeting. If you accompany me, we can gather a wealth of support for you in one fell swoop."

"You wouldn't be drawing us into a trap, would you, Duke?" Sasha said slowly, running a finger along the hilt of her sword.

"I wouldn't betray the Protector." Anger flared in his face.

"Glad to hear, Duke Banderkin," Logan said slowly. "I would hate to have to put more holes in that fine chair you are seated in." The duke leapt to his feet, spinning to find the blood and two holes in the back of his chair.

"I assure you, I will never betray you." The duke bowed awkwardly, fear seeping from every pore in his body. "We leave at first light. I'll see your mounts are prepared." He spun on his heels and rushed out the door.

"Do you think it is wise to threaten the one duke you have convinced to help you?" Saliday asked.

"He may have agreed I was the Protector, but I'm not sure he is going to help me."

"What makes you say that?"

"If the Senji was in his dungeon, why would he still have his weapons? The duke seemed pretty upset I had killed the assassin, maybe he expected the Senji to finish me. I'm tired, goodnight." He stood abruptly, retiring to the bedchamber off the sitting room.

"It seems we're not picking up on all the clues as he is," Sasha said when Saliday glanced at her. "His reasoning is sound. We need to be more diligent."

Saliday nodded her agreement, moving to the couch next to the window and stretching out. "I assume you will want first watch and the chair by the door?" she asked the Betra.

Sasha nodded and settled herself in the chair Logan had occupied when he dispatched the Senji.

Chapter 26

Teah burst into her room, nearly colliding Zele Astoria. The bedroll lay open, the swords and the sheathed metal rod exposed.

Astoria began to weave, but Teah released a rush of magic, sending the woman sprawling.

The Zele Magus got to her feet slowly, gathering her strength, and unleashed a weave that slammed Teah up over her bed. Teah hung suspended over her bed, pinned tightly against the cold stone wall.

"Caldora warned me about you, but I never envisioned you would have such use of magic or the possession of such weaponry. Only the Protector would possess swords such as these." She nodded to the swords on the bed. She absently slid her hand along the pommel of one of the swords, not giving much attention to Teah hanging.

Teah fought with all her might to get herself free, but her struggling produced no results and only drained her energy. Realizing the futility, she turned her attempts inward and magic surged through her. A flash of light burst from her, freeing her from her bonds.

The blast also sent Astoria tumbling near the door. The Headmistress immediately regained her feet and fled out the door.

Teah pulled the silver rod from its sheath and it instantly expanded to full size. She was already pulling the string back to her cheek as she stepped into the hall, Astoria in her sight just before the turn in the hallway.

Without a thought, Teah loosed the arrow. It drove into the woman with a thud, striking her in the back, pushing out between the Zele Magus's breasts in front. Astoria fell dead, colliding against the wall of the corridor.

Teah ran back into her room, sheathing the rod once more and fastened it to her thigh under her dress. Collecting her bedroll with the two swords and her locket, she ran.

The blades called for her to strap them on, to turn and fight Caldora, but she knew better. She and Logan were to keep her identity as a protector a secret, a secret that had nearly been discovered. A secret she had killed to protect. She would have been sick if there was time. She pushed the thought from her mind and ran with all her might.

Teah neared the dining hall when Caldora stepped out of a hallway. The girl collided with her. The bedroll slid across the floor, banging into the wall while the Zele Magus and Teah landed in a jumble of tangled arms and legs. The girl was on her feet, collecting the package and rushing away before Caldora knew what hit her.

Leaping to her feet, Caldora wove an attack.

Teah didn't hesitate as the noise of the spell exploded off the wall, but ran into the dining hall where Galena and the two girls waited at the far entrance. She raced through the hall, dodging the other girls rising and staring. Caldora entered, her face red with rage, and raised her hands over her head.

"Get down," Teah hollered to the girls as she ran past, but some were too confused to react and the next spell hit a group of them, sending them all sprawling, stunned and immobilized. Pushing hard, Teah finally reach Galena and the others.

"What took you so long?" Galena shouted, "Move." The three girls raced after Galena as she rushed down a set of stairs from the back of the hall, exiting into the courtyard and their waiting horses.

They quickly mounted and spun their horses to the back gate. As they rounded the corner of the Citadel, they brought their mounts to a sudden stop. In front of them were dozens of armed soldiers wearing Ter Chadain red and silver.

Teah, Lizzy, and Rachel cried out in surprise, but Galena sent a spell missing all the soldiers and impacting the door they guarded instead. As the door swung open, the Queen's Guard surged through, dispatching the soldiers barring their escape. The surprised soldiers didn't last long, and soon the women fled the walls of the Citadel, riding hard into the nearest forest with a hundred armed horsemen as an escort.

Teah caught the eye of Talesaur, Captain of the Queen's Guard, a broad smile nearly splitting his face in two. He moved his mount beside her when she gave him a smile, and they raced on, Talesaur leading the way.

Her arms and legs were cramping before they finally called for a halt. When Talesaur offered help to dismount, she tentatively placed her hand in his, sliding lightly into the captain's arms. Then he began taking the bedroll from her and she quickly pulled away.

"I'm sorry, my Queen." He fell to a knee, bowing his head. "I did not mean to overstep my authority. I was trying to relieve you of your burden and lighten your load."

"That's all right, Captain. I'm not over-burdened by this load. I must keep it with me at all times, but thank you for your thoughtfulness."

She moved off to one side as the men tended to the women's horses while others made camp and a small fire.

Galena bore down on her. "What in all that is good has gotten into you?" she shouted as she reached Teah. "When I tell you to get to the dining hall right now, you get to the dining hall right now. Your delay nearly cost us our lives and your freedom. It did cost some of your fellow students their lives from what I saw. Explain yourself."

"I had to get my things from my room. I'm sure those girls hit by Caldora's spell will be alright since she was only using a stunning spell."

Galena's anger went from outrage to disbelief. "Nothing is important enough to jeopardize your freedom."

"I went back for something personal that I would never leave behind," she said, pulling the locket from the pocket of her dress.

"A locket, you went back for a silly locket?"

"Not just any locket, but a locket given to me from the last Queen of Ter Chadain, Gianna Lassain. It is something I would never willingly leave." Teah slipped the locket back in her pocket.

"Teah, as a queen, you need to learn to make decisions less on feelings, but more on the greater good. If you would have been captured, our fight would be for nothing. All those who have offered up their lives to protect you would be for nothing. Grinwald's sacrifice would have been for nothing. You need to start acting like a queen before all the good men and women who are helping you lose their lives because you don't see the seriousness of failing."

Teah spun from Galena, tossed the bedroll to the ground, and stormed off into the woods.

"May the gods help us, the girl needs to grow up," Galena whispered.

Chapter 27

True to his word, Duke Banderkin had horses ready as they exited the mansion. The three mounts they rode into Longstand were saddled with bedrolls and tackle in place. The duke sat mounted, waiting for them as the sun crested the top of the estate's walls.

"It's time to leave. We must be out of Longstand before there are too many people about to see us," the duke said, motioning for them to mount up. The three companions climbed into their saddles, taking the reins and following the duke out of the estate gates.

Logan looked around at their party. "You don't ride with an escort or small security detail?" he asked.

"I feel with you at my side, there will be no need to have extra men along to draw undue attention to us. We'll only be traveling to the northern portion of my duchy to the mountain village of Brinstad. I have accommodations that will house the members of the council and their generals comfortably."

"How long has this council existed?" Saliday asked.

"Around ten years now. Ever since Englewood became a pawn of the invaders from across the sea and systematically stripped the resources from each duchy."

"Why don't you defy him directly? Why all the secrecy?" Logan asked.

"The invaders have taken over the Ter Chadain National Army. All of the key leadership roles are now under Caltorian control and their numbers have swelled the ranks of the forces. If just the southern duchies tried to stand against them, we would be annihilated."

Moving through the streets in the predawn light, only a few people were noticeably visible as they passed. It wouldn't be long before the city bustled with business of the day.

"What of the northern duchies?" Logan posed.

"We don't really know," the duke began. "Englewood has successfully divided the country along the borders of Brandermain and Stalosten, Mellastock and Ter Chadain,

Ackerton and Pasten. That leaves five southern duchies and five northern duchies. Englewood knew five duchies alone could not raise enough troops to pose a real threat."

"How are these duchies divided?" Saliday questioned.

"There are men stationed along each of the borders preventing passage to any who might pose a threat."

"You mean troops?" Saliday pressed.

"Any troops or dignitaries who may stir up problems for the king are detained and questioned. I have sent numerous emissaries to Brandermain, Pasten, Crandberg, and Los Clostern. None have returned or sent word back to me. These are very reliable men whom I now fear are either in the hands of Englewood or dead. I dare say which fate would be worse."

"Were all these men representing themselves as dignitaries?" Saliday asked.

It was if the Tarken had struck a nerve. The duke pulled his mount up, his face was awash with horror and shock.

"From your reaction, I would guess you sent them in full fanfare of their position. Did you send a herald along as well to let all who saw them know they were going to try and gather support from the other duchies?"

Shock turned to anger as the duke turned on the Tarken. "I sent those men to their death and will take full responsibility for that, but I will not take ridicule from the likes of you."

Logan and his companions nodded, not making eye contact with the duke. "We all need to avoid King Englewood's attention. He would love to have all of our heads on stakes outside his window," Logan reminded them.

They were out of Longstand and moving north on a well traveled road when the sun burst through the space between the treetops and the bank of heavy, dark clouds above. Minutes later, the once bright morning was no brighter than the predawn. Winds picked up and soon strong gusts with the scent of rain buffeted the four. Wrapping their traveling cloaks tighter around them, they dipped their heads. Their hoods came up just as the deluge began.

Sheets of rain drove into them. The firm road turned into mud and the horses gingerly placed each hoof down, unsure if it would be firm or not. More times than not, the step proved to be hazardous and the mount would slide a short distance until regaining its balance.

They didn't meet anyone on the road.

Most of the morning passed in this fashion and they were still far from their goal when the duke stopped them at an outcropping along a rocky cliff. The shelter was enough to keep dozens of riders out of the weather and a fire pit was placed far back from the road with stacks of wood lining the walls.

Before long, they were warming themselves at the fire and even getting their outer clothing dried by the flames. The duke supplied them with a nice meal of dried meats, fruits and bread he carried on his horse. They ate in silence, staring into the fire, the energy seemingly drained from each by the pounding rain and frigid wind.

"How much longer before we reach Brinstad?" Sasha asked.

"We should be there just after nightfall at this pace," Saliday surprisingly answered.

"I was hoping we'd be there just after midday, but with the weather..." The duke looked to Saliday puzzled. "She is correct. We will be there just after nightfall."

"I'm a Tarken, Duke Banderkin, I have the sense in my blood," She said.

"Would you have known to travel to Brinstad if I hadn't told you?"

A knowing smile filled the young woman's face.

"I suspect you would have." The duke left it at that as he continued staring at the Tarken.

The pause seemed to waken Logan. "Do all the dukes and duchesses feel the only way to overthrow the King is to place the true queen on the throne?"

"I can only speak for myself and recount what I have observed of the others, but seeing you here and believing you are the true Protector, I could only hope there would be a queen ready to take her place on the throne."

Logan noted the duke's questioning gaze. "What is it?"

"I believe I speak for all the nobles who are part of our council when I say we felt the protector would be..." The duke paused uncomfortably.

"Go on," Logan urged.

"Well, older. Not that you are not a great warrior with wisdom and abilities beyond your seemingly youthful exterior. But perhaps when we see the Queen, she is older than you, or at least looks older than you?" He leaned closer, hope lighting his eyes.

"Unfortunately my sister is not much older than me, but she is small of stature and her appearance does not belie her true age. For now, that is as much as I feel I should share about her."

At the word 'sister' the duke jumped up and down and clapped his hands lightly.

"Then it is truly a blessing to all of us. The strongest queen and protector are brother and sister. This is more than we could have hoped for. Praise the gods for hearing our cries for help."

The joy made Logan fidget. He turned away, numb to the world around him.

The vision came to him so unexpectedly that he was thrown upon his back.

He was Bastion surrounded by at least twenty men as they stood in an ornately decorated room in front of a large fireplace. These men didn't appear to be enemies, but allies. They were all laughing, smiling, and raising drinks to him. Bastion's voice added to the revelry.

Then everything went wrong.

One of the men stepped up to Bastion and plunged a blade into his midsection. The blade began to penetrate his clothing, but then broke in two and dropped harmlessly to the ground.

The other men stared in shock, and then wrestled the man down. He snarled at Bastion as he was raised to his feet by his captors.

"Why would you do this, brother?" Bastion cried.

"Because I am Senji and your death is my first step to becoming their leader."

Bastion slowly pulled one of the protector's swords from his back, paused to look into his brother's eyes, and then pushed the blade through his heart.

Bastion withdrew the sword and walked into the next room, closing the door behind him before dropping to his knees, the sword clattering to the floor and his tears running down his face.

Logan didn't even realize when Saliday and Sasha placed his outer traveling clothes back on him and moved him towards his mount.

He started and pulled away.

"Sure, now he comes out of it when all the work of dressing him is done," Sasha remarked over his head to Saliday as Logan slumped between them.

"It's typical of every man I've known. They try anything to

get out of work." She smiled back at the Betra.

Standing up quickly, Logan cut off their eye contact, but not their amusement as they continued to chuckle.

Why would I have a vision so suddenly like that after I haven't had one for days?" Logan asked the protectors in his head.

You must have been so overcome by emotions that you let your guard down, Falcone reasoned.

You must be more careful about keeping your thoughts in the present and not daydreaming in the slightest, Stalwart warned.

I wish none of you had seen that, Bastion said.

We all have times we are not proud of, Galiven comforted.

They joined the duke and mounted up. The duke was not privy to their conversation, looking blankly to them as the two women shared their humor and Logan mounted his horse in cloudy silence.

The duke shrugged his shoulders, beginning to lead the party out of the dry and warm rest stop, back into the pounding rain.

The rain covered any noise the arrow could have made, but the impact into Logan's chest sent him tumbling backwards off his horse. The horses reared and the others turned in all directions.

More arrows fell around them.

The duke bent low to his horse and rushed back into the relative safety of the cavern while Saliday and Sasha leapt from their mounts, slapping them to follow the duke's horse into the shelter. Rushing to Logan, they found him gasping for breath, a broken arrow lying next to him. The impact had pushed the air from his lungs, but had not penetrated his chest.

The women looked at him with disbelief as he struggled to get to his feet. Each grabbed an arm and drug Logan into the shelter as the arrows fell around them.

Laying Logan up against the back wall, the women ran their hands over him checking for an injury. He pushed their hands away and came to his feet.

The duke glanced over to the others as Logan pulled the silver rod from its sheath. Banderkin had tethered the horses along the wall and crouched behind a firewood pile eyeing the entrance.

"What happened?" the duke asked. "I thought you were hit?"

"It was a glancing blow," Logan answered. "Did anyone see who they are?"

"Shankan," Sasha announced, "I saw at least five against the far tree line beyond the path's far side."

"They have us pinned down," Saliday said, ducking behind the wood. "None of us are carrying bows. They can wait us out until we have to either make a break for it or starve."

"We could wait for help to come upon us." The duke said without any enthusiasm in his voice. "With this weather, that might be some time."

Logan crouched behind the wood pile holding the small silver rod in his hand. No one had noticed it until it expanded to its full length. The others jumped back.

Sasha cringed as an arrow struck the wall behind them. "Where are the arrows?"

Without saying a word, Logan stood, drawing the string back to his cheek and letting fly a shot at the first figure he saw.

A silver streak crossed the distance in an instant, hitting its mark and toppling the man over. Without pause, Logan let arrow after arrow loose even as numerous arrows bounced from his chest.

One arrow struck his leg. He stumbled slightly in pain, but the flight of that arrow exposed the last attacker to him, and Logan struck the man before his string had stopped strumming, dropping him from his hiding place in a tree.

It all happened so quickly, the others didn't realize it was over until Logan slumped to the ground, the arrow protruding from his thigh.

Sasha and Saliday gathered around him. Duke Banderkin drew his sword and went to investigate if their assailants were dead. Saliday rolled her cloak up, tucking it under Logan's head as Sasha cut away his pant around the arrow. It had gone in at such an angle that it missed the bone and came out the other side.

"You are lucky." Sasha said turning him over on his side to cut away his pant leg on the back. The head of the arrow had just cleared the skin and put a slight cut in his pants.

"I don't feel lucky, but I'll take your word for it," Logan said through gritted teeth as Sasha broke the broad head of the arrow off the shaft. She reached around and carefully pulled the arrow out.

Once the arrow was free, the blood began to flow rapidly.

Sasha tore several strips from her cloak, tying them tightly around his leg, covering his wound. Leaning forward, she made sure the blood flow had stopped, then sat back to catch her breath.

All this while, Saliday sat holding his hand in hers. Both looked down and awkwardly let go of each other.

"When did you get a bow?" she asked. "And where did you learn to use it like that?"

"It is a weapon of the protector," Logan explained, still holding the bow in his hand. The bow shrunk back to its smaller size and he placed it back in the sheath upon his belt.

"Where did the arrows come from?" Sasha pressed. "You have no quiver and you never had to nock an arrow once."

"The arrows appear as I draw back on the string. I have been using a bow since I was little, but I think the bow itself aids me in my marksmanship."

"And that marksmanship was deadly," Duke Banderkin said, walking up. "Not a single survivor. There were the five I saw on the ground and the final one in the tree was six. All heart shots, not a one lived to feel the ground."

Logan smiled sheepishly and laid his head back, closing his eyes. The voices in his head cheered him loudly, the first time they had all praised him since they entered his mind.

He began to get up and Saliday pushed him back down. "Where do you think you're going?"

"We need to keep moving; we don't know if there are others like those close at hand and we can't afford to get caught out here again." Logan pushed through her restraint and got to his feet. The pain in his leg was more like a dull throb and something he was willing to ignore to get out of here and closer to their goal. He hobbled over to the horses and untied his mount. Moving it clear of the others, he climbed up.

They watched with their mouths agape, then followed his example and were heading out of the shelter once more.

Within minutes, all semblances of dryness and warmth were gone with the cold chill seeping deep into their skin and eating away at their muscles and bones. It was only midday and they would be riding until after sunset. They had all agreed to riding until they arrived at Brinstad since stopping to dry out again had proven futile and somewhat depressing, not the least ending as an opportunity for an ambush.

Logan's leg throbbed incessantly, but he fought to keep the dull pain in the back of his thoughts. The relentless weather bowed their heads for most of the trip. Lifting their heads just enough, they kept an eye on the road that had become less muddy and more rocky as they went. The duke said Brinstad was a mountain village, and soon the trail climbed in elevation. Rising into the foothills of a mountain range, their spirits rose with the terrain.

They crested a hill and below them, in a valley between seven peaks of mountains standing diligent sentry over the village, Brinstad spread before them. They moved down the slope with a renewed strength. Not stopping or slowing as they passed the wooden gates, the duke led them through the streets of cobblestone with neatly kept clapboard, with wooden shingles, both single and two-story homes were painted in an array of colors. The clopping of their horses' feet echoed off the deserted streets, while the rain continued falling on the four travelers. Duke Banderkin led them to his home and the meeting place for the council of the southern duchies.

The residence was a peculiar structure the likes Logan had never laid eyes on before. For aside from the entrance of a large double door carved out of white oak inlaid with stained glass of every color imaginable, the dwelling was without corner or edge. The house was completely round. Logan looked down at the duke as he stood before them, smiling broadly at the amazed faces.

"Protector Logan, Tarken Saliday, and Betra Sasha, may I present the dream of my waking moments, the dwelling of my soul, and the inspiration of my visions. This is the Roundhouse of Brinstad and home of the Southern Council of Ter Chadain. May your words resound within these walls, bringing joy and hope to us as the house itself has brought hope to me over the years."

The three companions silently dismounted and Logan was soon chuckling under his breath, shaking his head.

Where else should he gather support for my sister and the throne of Ter Chadain?

It makes perfect sense to me, Galiven agreed. *The magic of the protector is without end and continues to ignite itself whenever there is a break in the true chain of rule. This heritage is ever circular and you are just one part of the never ending spin of it all.*

The pain of the loss of his family bubbled to the surface again. The sorrow from his losses filled his eyes as tears ran down his cheeks.

Teah, I wish you were here, he thought.

The throbbing of his leg caused him to grab his wound.

"Are you ready for this?" Saliday asked, looking up at him.

"I guess I have to be, everything I hold dear and will hold dear in years to come depends on it."

Chapter 28

Teah heard him inside her head.

I wish you were here.

She had walked off to be alone after her words with Galena. Sitting on a tree trunk with her elbows on her knees, her chin resting in her hands, Logan's thoughts came to her. She missed him terribly, wishing he would realize they could communicate this way.

The sound of someone approaching drew her out of her contemplation in time to see Rachel and Lizzy. She stood as they approached but kept her eyes down, embarrassed about storming off.

"Galena would like you to come back to camp, Teah," Lizzy said shyly.

"Is she angry with me?" Teah asked, already knowing the answer.

"No, why do you ask?" Rachel added.

"I left so abruptly, that's all. I expected her to be upset with me over leaving like that."

"Galena just sent us to come and get you," Lizzy repeated.

"You're right. It's time to be getting back." She motioned for them to proceed. As they walked slightly ahead of her, Teah noticed a strange blue glow around the girls. Teah tried to place where she had seen this glow before, but she couldn't remember.

When they returned to camp, the men were busy with their duties and Galena sat beside the fire with Talesaur. As they approached, Talesaur rose, placing a fist to his chest and bowing at the waist.

"I'm glad to see you back unharmed, my Queen. I had wished to send some guards after you, but Zele Galena assured me that would not be necessary."

"Zele Galena is generally right about things like that, Captain. As you can see, I'm just fine. If you wouldn't mind I would like a word alone with Zele Galena." The captain saluted again, moving off to take charge of other business.

Lizzy and Rachel hesitated, and then followed after him.

"Is there something you're not telling me, Teah?" Galena questioned.

"Why would you think that?"

"I find it hard to believe that you would be so foolish as to endanger yourself and others just to retrieve a locket, even one given to you by your mother."

"I am truly sorry that I put everyone in danger, but that locket is very important to me," Teah explained.

"I have come to a decision; one that I hope you will understand is for your own good." The woman's eyes gleamed menacingly, the anger just a fraction below the surface waiting to erupt.

"And what would that be?"

"Let me ask you this. When were you going to tell me that you were not only the Queen of Ter Chadain, but also a protector?"

Teah's voice cracked. "How did you…?"

"Lizzy and Rachel found the weapons in your bedroll when they were unpacking your things."

"So that was why they had a blue glow about them," Teah realized. "Is that the same spell you used to erase Magda's memory back at the Protector's Fortress?"

Galena's anger turned to surprise and she narrowed her eyes.

"That has nothing to do with what happened here today and don't try to change the subject. Magda is a servant who was in the wrong place at the wrong time. She heard things she shouldn't have. You, on the other hand, should have taken better care that your information wasn't discovered so easily. Haven't you paid attention to anything I've been trying to teach you? You must always exhibit control and that was a total lack of it. How long have you been a protector?"

"Now who's changing the subject? Did Magda overhear you and Grinwald speaking of Logan being a Viri Magus?"

Galena stood up abruptly. "How did you know about that?" the Zele Magus whispered.

"You've been deceitful to Logan and me from the beginning. What other secrets are you squirreling away like nuts for the winter?"

"You dare accuse me? I am the Mistress of Power. You are just a child who has yet to touch even a fraction of her potential. I'm the one asking the questions around here, not you." Galena's fingertips crackled with energy.

"I think I'm further along than you realize and you need to stop controlling me like a marionette on a string, but confide in me information which may play a role in mine and Logan's future."

Galena stopped her retort, suddenly glancing over to where she had placed the two swords.

"Grinwald and I were concerned. Having the powers of both the protector and the Viri Magus might be more than he can control. We were hoping to keep such knowledge from him so he wouldn't develop as a Viri Magus before you were placed on the throne."

"Then what were you planning on doing with him?" Teah pressed.

"We were not sure Ter Chadain could survive the powers he would be able to wield," Galena said cautiously.

"You were considering killing him?" Teah said in horror.

All the rage, all the fear, all the hatred rushed out of Teah. Magic flooded out and engulfed Galena, holding her fast. The golden glow around the Zele Magus almost blinded Teah when she looked at it.

Horrified at herself, she released the flow and the light winked out.

Instantly Teah was thrown backwards onto the ground. Her arms were smashed tightly to her sides, her mouth clamped shut. Galena moved over her, rage emanating from every pore of her body. The red magical light seemed to cut through her skin in ribbons as she leered down at Teah.

"How dare you use magic to make me tell you the truth? Who taught you that? I will now tell you what is going to happen and what you will do." Her voice was a mere whisper, but her anger drove it into Teah's brain to shout at a deafening volume.

"You will do as I say from here on. If you decide to use any magic against me, it will be deflected from me into pain for them," she motioned to Lizzy and Rachel. "Before I release you, I will weave a spell to take whatever magic you send to me, to go into them. It will not matter how your magic touches me, even if you are merely trying to use it to heal an injury I have been inflicted with. They will feel excruciating pain. Do you understand?"

Teah nodded. Moving off, Galena summoned Lizzy and Rachel. Teah could see the three of them talking as she lay immobilized and silent on the ground by the fire. A red magical glow surrounded the two girls, and then disappeared into them.

Galena moved back to the fire.

"You will keep your swords hidden at all times and you will tell no one of your powers as a protector. I am doing this for your own good. Lately your judgment has been lacking. In order for us to complete our mission and place you on the throne, you need to concentrate on doing what you are told. I hope you understand that this is for the greater good of Ter Chadain. We have no idea what will happen with Logan once you are on the throne. I want you to know that I will do everything in my powers to assure no harm comes to him, but if his powers become too great for him to control and he poses a danger for Ter Chadain, he will need to be dealt with. I'm going to release you and you will tell me how long you have had the protector powers."

The bonds released and Teah slowly got to her feet. "When Logan turned, I turned the same night. We are twins and we share everything."

"Does he know he is Viri Magus?" Galena asked.

"No, I suspected it after the way you and Grinwald were acting at the fortress. I didn't want to tell him until I was sure. I was sure when you told me tonight," Teah lied.

"You will not discuss any of this with anyone. Do you understand? It would be a serious mistake for your friends." A smile crossed Galena's lips. She motioned for Teah to sit on a log next to the fire and did the same.

"Now we need to plan out where to go and train you in safety. I know of one place within short travel. The Roundhouse of Brinstad is the headquarters of the Southern Duchy Alliance. It should be a fine location to prepare you for the throne."

Galena slapped her thigh. "Go get some food and some sleep, we start out at first light."

Chapter 29

Logan, Saliday, and Sasha were given a set of chambers on the main floor of the Roundhouse. Duke Banderkin had explained: the lower the level, the more influence the person had. He was in a set of rooms next to theirs and he excused himself after showing them to their quarters to get into dry clothing and have dressings sent for Logan's wound.

The three companions dug into their packs, pulling out some dry clothing and getting out of their drenched ones, shedding many pounds as the wet masses hit the floor. They showed no concern for their nakedness in front of each other as their attention was solely on getting into something warm and dry.

Before Logan could change into anything, he needed to remove the dressing. He sat on the edge of a chair.

Saliday, now dressed, came over to help. As they removed the bloody strips of Sasha's cloak, Saliday sat back on her heels in disbelief.

"You're completely healed?"

"Just another benefit of being the Protector," he grinned sheepishly.

"Everything about you is a mystery to me," Saliday said in awe.

Sasha came over to stare at the healed wound, shaking her head and smiling.

They all sat before a roaring fire when a knock came. The duke pushed his head into the room. "I see you are dry and warm now. How is your injury?"

"All healed with no need for any further treatment," Saliday replied.

The duke raised an eyebrow to Logan. "I am very pleased to hear it. May I speak with you about the gathering tomorrow?"

"Come and sit," Logan said, motioning to a vacant chair next to him.

The duke, looking particularly regal in a high-necked black coat with gold embroidery around the collar and his sleeves, sat in the tall-backed chair. His dark trousers had similar embroidery around the waist and cuffs. Crossing his legs comfortably, he looked to the Protector.

"Since we entered these chambers through the rear hallway, you didn't get a chance to see the gathering hall. On the other side of those doors," he pointed to a curtain partially hiding two large red oak doors, "the gathering hall is a large circular room with the emblem of the protector inlaid in the wooden floor. If you stand on that spot speaking in a normal voice, everyone in the chamber will be able to hear you easily. You will be able to hear anyone who speaks to you clearly as well. That is where you will make your case to unite us and place your sister on the throne. The rebellion is in your hands and in the persuasiveness of your words."

Logan quietly stared at the duke for a moment and then gazed at the fire. Looking back, he smiled slightly. "The future of Ter Chadain is in all of our hands, my good duke. If I fail, then we all fail. What kind of future would that leave you, a rebellious duke with an insufficient army? I pray you know the King will not allow your treason to go unchecked for long?"

Banderkin's shock was not lost to anyone in the room. "Then you mustn't fail."

Logan didn't change his blank expression. He glanced over to the doors leading into the main hall. Standing, he walked over, opening both of them wide. As they swung away from him, the massiveness of the enclosure swallowed him.

From the outside of the structure one would never guess such a large room resided within. The room was dimly lit by sconces on the walls displaying similar doorways to the one he now stood within. Balconies lined the upper levels as he counted four floors. There were more than twenty entrances leading to the hall from various chambers.

The walls were of white plaster that curved gracefully around the room. Logan walked to the center, the echoing of his steps resounding off the smooth walls back to him. Reaching the center of the room, he took in the silver emblem on the floor. Stepping onto the insignia Logan proclaimed in a soft but defiant voice, "I am the Protector of Ter Chadain and have come to gather your pledges of fealty." Turning to return to his quarters, Logan paused, noticing Duke Banderkin, Sasha, and Saliday standing in the doorway staring at him.

"Then we wait to hear you speak at more length in the morning before we decide."

The voice was female with a tone Logan knew must belong to a duchess. Tilting his head up to the second level, he found an unattractive older woman with a large mole on her cheek and many extra chins running down her neck. Her grey-and-red head was bowed over a brilliant blue, silken robe. The tiara in her hair sparkled with rubies and emeralds.

He spun around. Every balcony and doorway was now occupied with either a man or a woman, each dressed in equally elegant eveningwear. All with their heads bowed to him.

"We do ask you one thing yet this night." The angle of the duchess's head showed no sign of kindness or humility.

"And what would that be?" Logan asked, moving back to the inlaid emblem and extending his hands out away from his sides, giving a slight bow.

"We would like to see the sign of the protector upon your chest, unless you have something to hide from us." The accusation and doubt in her voice was not lost on the room.

He tore open his shirt, sending buttons scattering across the floor. Pulling it off, he tossed it to one side. The tattoo shone with an inner light as did the insignia on which he stood, illuminating him from the inside out.

"As I said, I am the Protector and have come to gather your loyalty to place the true Queen of Ter Chadain upon the throne." Raising his hands above his head, he turned in a circle, looking to every woman and man standing before him.

"I look forward to meeting each of you in private to receive your commitment to our cause."

He strode from the spot as silence filled the chamber.

Walking calmly back into the room past Sasha, Saliday and Duke Banderkin, Logan sat in the chair he had vacated only moments before.

The three closed the door as the nobles returned to their bed chambers. They took their seats, without a word. There was a long moment of silence before Duke Banderkin's voice came in a scratchy and uncertain tone. "That went better than we might have hoped. What do you have planned next?"

Logan made eye contact with Sasha and she nodded. "We travel to the Forbidden to gather my people," she said proudly.

"You must be joking," the duke scoffed. "Not a single noble will fight beside the banished ones, me included. I thought she was your token Betra, but to have an army of them would be out of the questions."

I agree, the Betra shouldn't be involved in this, Falcone said.

They are traitors to our cause and shouldn't be trusted, Bastion added.

They do have a large number of troops, waivered Stalwart.

They need the chance to prove themselves. To clear their name and remove the curse, Galiven pleaded.

Sasha began to protest, but Logan raised his hand.

"How many troops do the southern duchies command?" Logan asked calmly.

"Over three hundred thousand, maybe more, men and women are under our command," the duke puffed up arrogantly. "We don't need to rely on any traitors to join us in order to place the Queen on the throne."

"Since you only have three hundred thousands troops to their five hundred thousand troops, I would say it would be you who join them," Logan said, peering into the fire as he said the words, then glancing up to catch Banderkin's reaction.

The duke's eyes shot open wide.

"Did you s, s, say five hundred thou...?" He stammered.

"You heard me," Logan said. "The southern council doesn't have a choice. The Betra are the body of our forces and your nobles' forces will be their support. We need to make every noble aware of that when they meet with me to swear allegiance."

"The magicals will not join our fight openly," the duke told him, referring to the Zele and Viri Magus.

"I have every intention of changing that. The protector only comes along once in five hundred years. I will point out the honor of joining a quest that will go down in Ter Chadain history. Now I need some sleep. Please start bringing the first nobles in at sunrise," he requested, rising and walking to his bedchamber. "Good night," he said as he closed the door without looking back.

The others in the room looked to each other awkwardly. With a shrug, the two women lay down on the couches in the chamber and Duke Banderkin left for his own quarters.

Turning down the lamps, Sasha said to Saliday, "He seems to always rise to the task at hand and shine."

"It is almost as if he is much older than sixteen," Saliday agreed. She rolled over and fell asleep.

Logan lay awake in his bed, wondering how he could accomplish the huge feat of gaining the noble's support. Bastion, Stalwart, Falcone, and Galiven were singing his praises as he tried to silence their chatter. Using the technique Galena had taught him was the only way to quiet them when they acted in that manner. As he concentrated on partitioning his mind behind invisible barriers, he drifted off to sleep in the rare silence.

Chapter 30

It wasn't difficult to convince Talesaur that traveling to Brinstad was the right move. He was relieved to hear they were moving to safer surroundings that could be defended readily.

Galena knew Duke Banderkin met with the alliance. Some of the other dukes or duchesses would have an alternate location if the Roundhouse did not live up to her satisfaction.

They broke camp at first light. The sun rose over the tree tops below the cloud cover, giving the travelers an eerie glow as they moved silently toward what they hoped was a more stable setting to continue the Queen's training.

Teah rode amongst the group in silence, thinking of a way to eliminate the threat to her new friends' lives. They had become unknowing accomplices to her future path and she needed to get them out of harm's way as soon as possible.

They stopped and made camp that evening. The men made several small fires for themselves and one larger one for the women. After Galena retired, Rachel and Lizzy finally had a chance to speak with Teah alone.

"We overheard the men talking about your brother," Rachel said.

"Is it true that he is in the company of a Betra?" Lizzy blurted out, then covered her mouth when Rachel shot her a look.

"Yes, it's true," Teah smiled at Lizzy. "Logan and Sasha are gathering support for putting me on the throne."

"Aren't you worried that the Betra will take him prisoner, or worse, kill him?" Lizzy said incredulously.

"Why would she do that? He is the Protector and the only person who can lift the curse her people are under. She would do nothing to harm him. What gave you the idea that they would harm him?"

"Because I lost my sister to the Betra," Lizzy shouted, her face crimson.

"It's all right, Lizzy," Rachel comforted her, placing an arm around her shoulders.

"I had no idea the Betra were like that. I thought they kept to themselves in the Forbidden and rarely ventured out."

"That is usually the case," Rachel told her, "but on occasion they sneak into villages late at night and take what they want—livestock, supplies, and even people. It is said they enslave the villagers they take and work them until they die."

"Is that what happened to your sister?" Teah asked Lizzy, taking hold of her hands.

"When we went to bed that night, my sister Melandra gave me a kiss and tucked me in like usual. Then the alarms went up, and when the Betra had gone, she was gone as well. We never saw her again." The tears welled up in Lizzy's eyes.

"How long has it been?" Teah asked.

"Five years, when Melandra was nineteen. She was set to marry the Mayor of Dansberg's son. It was an arranged marriage and my family was very happy."

"I am so sorry Lizzy. How could Sasha be so loyal to Logan, but her people be so horrible? I hope nothing like that happens to Logan when he is in The Forbidden."

"Why would your brother go to The Forbidden?" Rachel spun on her.

"He is going to gather the Betra's support to defeat King Englewood."

"He mustn't go," Lizzy said grabbing the front of Teah's dress in her fist.

"Lizzy's right," Rachel nodded. "He can't trust the Betra after all the harm they have caused."

"I don't think he has much choice. Sasha said there are over five hundred thousand Betra ready to go to war for our cause. Even the Viri Magus Grinwald conceded we needed their support in order to win," Teah said biting her lip.

"I hope he never lets his guard down with them," Rachel said turning away as Lizzy nodded her agreement. "It would be a shame to have history repeat itself."

"It is getting late, we best get some rest." Teah stood, giving Lizzy a big hug. "I hope we find your sister once all this is over. I will be sure to ask Sasha to find out for you."

Lizzy's face filled with hope. "Thank you, Teah."

"Good night, Lizzy. Good night, Rachel."

"Good night, Teah," Rachel smiled.

The next morning, just as the sun stretched above the cloud cover, the rain came pouring down. It soaked the entire company immediately. The rain pushed them into their saddles, forcing them to slouch further down. The horses trudging along on the stone roadway didn't notice.

Teah felt as though the water passed completely through her body, the rain penetrated every pore of her. Glancing up to where Galena rode, Teah was could see the Zele Magus sitting elegantly straight in her saddle, the rain running off her as if the weather could not touch her. A glow of green light haloed her perfectly dry hair and every stitch of clothing moved freely as Galena road within her magical cocoon.

Teah thought for a second to try creating something of the kind, but she couldn't take a chance that an errant wisp of magic might contact Galena. The Queen of Ter Chadain bowed her head, riding on into the deluge.

It continued raining as they stopped for lunch under some trees and then poured even harder into the night without yielding. The fall rains always preceded the colder months. At least it was still barely warm enough to keep the rain from turning to snow.

She curled up in her damp bed roll when they stopped to make camp. It took some coaxing, but Talesaur finally convinced Galena to allow a small fire to take the chill out of the women. The men stayed clear of the fire and kept watch, not wanting to show any weakness.

Dread became reality early that morning as the rain turned to snow. Soon it covered the ground and created a layer of ice beneath it on the road. The horses could no longer gain any footing and the party walked their mounts in hopes of keeping the animals from breaking a leg and having to be put down.

The snow accumulated all day and soon they were not only fighting for footing, but also pushing through several feet of heavy wet snow. Teah was the shortest member of the group and the snow reached above her knees making her movements even more difficult than the others. Talesaur strode in ahead of her, motioning for her to follow in his path, easing her struggle. She returned his thoughtful smile.

They stopped for another night with little hope of drying out. Teah sat watching as the flakes fell into the flames with a sizzle, Galena beside her.

As Teah stared, Talesaur came rushing into the camp before her.

"Caldora and her forces are moving to get ahead of us. If we want to make it to the Roundhouse for a defensive stand, we need to move now."

Galena stood, addressing him and the entire camp. "That is not a good plan. We must change our course and seek another place to find safe haven."

"Where else could we find refuge and a defensible position like the Roundhouse?" Talesaur questioned.

"The Duchess Loistren of Stalosten has long been an ally to our cause. We must travel to her castle in Sharlet. She would not deny us her hospitality as long as we require it. Mount up, we ride at once."

"It is still hours before first light," warned the captain. "Travel would be much safer if we wait until dawn."

"There is no time. If Caldora realizes we haven't reached Brinstad ahead of them, she will send her entire force back and we will lose the precious head start we might need to outrun her. Get everyone ready in short order, Captain Talesaur, else it will be the last thing you do as Captain of the Queen's guard."

Talesaur scowled at this and his men grumbled behind him, but he snapped to attention, spinning on his heels and motioning his men to break camp. They ran off in every direction.

In a very short time they were all on their horses, once more heading west.

*****

It was still hours before dawn when Logan awoke to the voice of his sister. *Caldora is after us and on her way to a place called the Roundhouse.*

That is definitely a woman's voice and none of us did it, Stalwart said.

It sounds like, Teah, but it can't be her, Logan told them.

He tried to shake the voice from his mind, but then froze stiff as the word Roundhouse was uttered again. *We're headed west to Stalosten.*

He leapt from his bed, rushing into the outer chamber. Sasha came to her feet before he was more than a few steps into the room. Saliday slid from the chair against the chamber door.

"What is it?" Saliday asked.

"Has there been any word on the whereabouts of Caldora and the King's troops she was leading?"

"We haven't had any word of them since the night they killed

Grinwald," Sasha said, then grimaced. "Why do you ask?"

"Just a hunch," he said. "See if Duke Banderkin will send a scout out and look around. I just sense she may be closer than we think."

"Very well." Saliday put on her cloak, concealing her array of knives and the two short swords strapped to her torso.

When the door closed behind her, Logan sat heavily on a chair in front of the blazing hearth, the sadness showing on his face.

Sasha kneeled before him, looking up into his tormented eyes.

"I'm sorry I mentioned that night. It was a great loss for all of us, but much more to you than anyone else." Logan made eye contact for an extended moment, and then turned away. "You couldn't have saved him."

"I should have tried. You and Galena should have let me try."

"Why, so you both could be dead? What would have made that a better choice than the one we made? Grinwald sacrificed himself freely, allowing you to have the chance to fulfill your destiny. Don't let his selfless act be for nothing, but use it to fuel your determination to place your sister on the throne and exact revenge upon Englewood and Caldora."

Logan stared back at the Betra, taking in her watery eyes and the light tears making their way down her face. "I will remember his ultimate sacrifice always. Especially when I meet up with Caldora again, his death will be avenged."

The intensity of his expression caused her to back away as he wiped the lone tear from his cheek. He stood and moved back to his bed chamber.

As far as Viri Magus goes, he was an honorable one, Stalwart added.

That is a huge compliment coming from you, Galiven said.

Dressing quickly, he strapped his swords onto his back and threw his cloak over them, striding into the outer chamber once again. Sasha was speaking with Saliday and Duke Banderkin and they all stopped, turning.

"I don't know how you knew, but a large force of the King's soldiers is heading for the Roundhouse with Caldora at the lead," the duke said.

"It was a feeling I had. How long before she reaches us?"

"Maybe four hours, my scout was on patrol all night when he came across them. He just arrived with his report before Saliday came to me. I sent word to the other nobles, all will be gone within a couple hours to avoid detection."

"Did your scout see anyone else last night?"

Duke Banderkin spun on Logan, the surprise deepening the wrinkles of his brow. "Yes he did. He said there was a smaller party in route to Brinstad, but they were changing course in what appeared to be a move to avoid Caldora."

"West to Stalosten," Logan said softly.

"How could you know that? Yes, the scout said they were heading west toward Stalosten. Logan, how do you know this information?"

"It is just a hunch I had, nothing more. We must be leaving as well. We need to meet with the Betra and gather their support. Duke, would you please inform the nobles to come to my chambers for private meetings. I will meet with them in the order you prefer as to not cause any problems due to their status. I also wish to meet with all the generals after each noble has declared their loyalty to me and our cause."

No, ride out and kill the witch, Falcone cried. *Now is your chance to rid us of that vile woman.*

Not now, Logan told him.

Duke Banderkin nodded. "I will see to it at once. The first nobles will be lining up outside your door in ten minutes."

"Thank you, Duke. You are welcome to join me in each of the meetings if you would like."

"Thank you, Logan," he bowed. "I am honored."

Within five minutes, the first noble sat in front of Logan.

It was the woman from the balcony last night. Her fleshy chins were covered by extravagant diamonds; her dress shone of golden silk. Moles protruded from her neck, cheeks, and arms. By her side sat her commanding general. He was thin and drawn, his gray hair wisps covering a pale white scalp. His gray mustache hung over his top lip so far that it covered his bottom lip as well when his mouth was closed.

Egad, Falcone gasped. *She definitely wasn't considered when we referred to women as the fairer sex.* The other protectors laughed uproariously.

"Master Protector Logan Lassain, may I present to you the Duchess Elspeth Spelistan of Mellastock Duchy and her military counsel, General Darius Covrent." Logan nodded to each, a nod that they returned.

"And may I introduce my magical advisor," Elspeth's raspy voice grated as she pointed to a corner of the room where no one was standing a moment before.

A small woman with dark skin and even darker eyes, her black hair cut short to her head, moved smoothly beside the duchess. "Zele Althea is one of my most trusted advisors and she is very interested to meet you," Elspeth continued.

The woman's deep green dress hugged her shape.

Logan's gaze fell upon her for a moment and then turned hesitantly back to the duchess and general. "I am very pleased to make your acquaintance," he said. "I am very sorry to be so abrupt with meeting everyone, but as you know, time is of the essence now that Caldora is moving closer to the Roundhouse."

The three nodded their understanding as Logan continued. "I must ask you now, duchess, if you are ready to join in my cause."

Duchess Spelistan hesitated for a moment, and then motioned with her eyes for the general, then her advisor, to lean in close. The three whispered for a moment and then straightened up once more.

"We have seen your mark of the protector, but there is one more thing we would like to see," Elspeth hesitated.

"Yes, what is it?" Logan asked.

"The Swords of Salvation," General Covrent blurted out.

The slow grating of blades being pulled from their scabbards filled the room as the three guests pressed back. Logan sat with the two blades crossed comfortably on his lap. "Why are these so convincing for you?"

"Because, my boy," Zele Althea said, moving over closer to Logan and running a finger down the side of his face to his chin, then raising his face. "The protector's weapons are the only thing in Ter Chadain created by both the Zele Magus and the Viri Magus. They are the culmination of the most powerful magical forces to have existed in our world. Just seeing them, I can tell that they are genuine and so is the bow on your hip and the mail that you wear."

Logan's hand shot to his chest as he looked down. Relief spread across his face as the mail shirt was still hidden, melded with his body. He glared back at the woman.

"Not to worry, boy. I do not see your magical protection, but know it must be there if you are truly the Protector. I give you my word, Duchess Elspeth, this boy, or should I say man, is the true Protector of Ter Chadain."

The Zele Magus bowed deeply to Logan and backed away once more.

"Now that is settled, what are your plans for King Englewood and the Caltorians?" General Covrent asked.

"Cutting right to the chase, eh, Darius?" Duke Banderkin chuckled.

"You know me, Horatio," the general smiled. "Cut the small talk and get to it. Where are General Haveben and Viri Niles? You never travel without them."

"Cecily is speaking with your peers. She is trying to speed this up since we are under a time constraint. She has already seen Logan and is trying to give the other generals information that will make the meetings easier. Viri Niles does the same with the magicals."

"We feel honored that you have chosen us to meet Protector Logan first," Elspeth giggled, then regained her composure. "What are your plans now?" She turned to Logan.

"I will travel to the Forbidden to gather their support for our cause."

"That is preposterous," shouted Darius, leaping from his chair.

"We will not stand for it, even from you," cried Zele Althea. "They shall not be allowed into Ter Chadain. Your heritage should hold you firm to that."

Strangely Duchess Spelistan was silent, staring at Logan as his eyes were fixed on hers. "I don't think you two are going to have any luck at convincing him otherwise," she said calmly, never taking her eyes from his. "He has thought this through and has decided. In order for us to place the rightful Queen of Ter Chadain on the throne once more, we will need to accept the alliance with the Betra."

A gasp came from the others, but Elspeth sat smiling contently at Logan. "You are not afraid, boy? You know that King Englewood will do everything he can to kill you. He has even sent the Senji after you."

Logan denied his fear with a shake of his head and then confirmed with a nod the measures the King had already undertaken to remove Logan as a threat. "I know that I may not live to see my sister on the throne, but that is my goal, and I will not stop until the last breathe has left this body or she sits in her rightful place upon the throne of Ter Chadain."

"Then we will join you in your quest and we will accept the alliance with the Betra, because I cannot stand by any longer and watch as the Caltorians and Englewood ravage our country bit by bit."

Duchess Spelistan stood and moved to the door, then paused. "I am happy to hear that our next queen is your sister. That will make your bond to her that much more powerful. May the gods watch your back and speed you on your way. I will send Darius to speak with the other generals on your behalf and Althea will do the same with the magical advisors."

"I thank you for that, duchess." Logan said standing and sheathing his swords in one smooth motion.

"No, Logan Lassain, we all are in your debt for answering our prayers." She bowed slightly and left the room, leaving Darius and Althea standing there.

After a moment of shocked silence, Darius turned to Logan. "How many Betra are going to be joining us?"

"Around five hundred thousand," Logan replied.

The general's and Zele Magus's eyes shot wide. "When and where do we need to meet?" the general managed to get out.

"Hold on a moment," Logan turned. "Sasha, could you come here, please?"

Sasha entered the room. The visitor's eyes widened, then scowls took over their features.

"Your troops need to meet me and the Betra forces back here in…" Logan paused, looking to Sasha.

"Twelve days should be enough. Four to get there and another day or two to gather the required forces, and then six days to march here—twelve should be an obtainable goal."

Logan turned from Sasha as she finished and the general nodded his agreement.

"I will inform the generals to have their troops here twelve days from now."

"I thank you for that, but I would like to meet the others if you could take care of the troop preparations."

"That is all well and good," Zele Althea interrupted. "But what do you intend to do once you have the troops here?"

"That is simple," Logan smiled a smile that made the others back away. "I plan on marching on the castle in Cordlain and to kill King Englewood and any who stand in my way."

"That will be all," Duke Banderkin told them as they bowed and left. "I will bring the other dukes, duchesses, generals, and magical advisors in so we can have introduction after they have met with Duchess Spelistan, Zele Althea, and General Covrent. In the meantime, I will have food sent in while you wait."

After a meal and the impatient wait for the others to arrive, there came a knock at the doors of the Great Hall. When Saliday answered, Duke Banderkin stood in the doorway. "The others are gathered within for introductions and some questions."

Saliday looked to Logan, who strode over to the door as Saliday backed away.

As Logan entered the hall, he drew the Swords of Salvation, causing their ring to echo. Standing with blades crossed, the Protector of Ter Chadain now asked for the loyalty of the nobility, generals, and magical advisors of the southern duchies of Ter Chadain.

"I, Logan Lassain, Protector of Ter Chadain, humbly ask for your loyalty, your friendship, your honesty but most of all, your love for Ter Chadain. Join me in my mission to place the true queen on the throne of Ter Chadain. She is the rightful heir being a direct descendent of Tera Lassain herself. I ask that you understand that the Betra have been punished for their crime against the last protector of Ter Chadain for over five hundred years. They, as a people, have prepared for this opportunity to come to the aid of the new protector of Ter Chadain. I feel they have earned the chance to fight and die for the right of reclaiming their honor.

"I now ask as a servant to the throne of Ter Chadain, are you with me?"

One by one, starting with Elspeth Spelistan, Duchess of Mellastock, the nobles came with their generals and magical advisors, dropping to one knee and swearing fealty to the Protector of Ter Chadain:

Duke Ezra Barnhold of Stalosten, with Viri Jarvis and General Cyrus Plestor.

Duke Hirum Kensitram with Zele Elnora and General Regina Aspet.

Duchess Isadora Victroine with Viri Silas and General Griffin

Corneld.

Then, finally, Duke Horatio Banderkin, with Viri Niles and General Cecily Haveben alongside, came forward. "I feel it is an extreme honor that you have chosen me to be the first noble to approach and ask to follow. I humbly offer you my loyalty and my friendship for life, because I now truly know that you are an honorable man and one I will follow until the end of my days."

A tear escaped Logan's eye. Looking out over the room filled with bowed heads, he smiled broadly. "Rise and be welcomed into the Protector's Revolution for Ter Chadain."

The entire room came to their feet. Cheering and chanting resounded against the walls: "Long live, the Protector."

"Until we meet again," Logan said, striding back to his chamber. Sasha and Saliday gathered their belongings while Logan waited patiently for them.

Closing his eyes, Logan thought of Teah. *I know we can hear each other, sister. I hope you reach Stalosten safely.*

He didn't have to wait long before a warm thought dropped him to his knees with the intensity and joy it carried. *At last you have learned to hear, brother. Just think of me with your mind and your thoughts will come to me.*

It was a strange feeling, but Teah was now with him and he was no longer alone with the crazed ramblings of the past protectors.

Hey, we can hear your thoughts, remember? Stalwart complained.

Sorry, Logan apologized.

Logan and his two companions left the Roundhouse quickly, heading northwest, avoiding Caldora and her troops. Time was of the essence as Caldora bore down on the Roundhouse and the fleeing southern alliance members. Others moved off in various directions to avoid the King's troops.

Snow fell steadily on the already whitened ground. Picking their way carefully, Logan, Saliday, and Sasha allowed their horses to go at their own pace to assure good footing. They couldn't afford to have a mount come up lame. Logan pulled his hood up, keeping the snow out of his face and off his head. When they were certain they had cleared Caldora, they would head due south to the Forbidden.

Logan had the desire to go hunt down Caldora, destroying her this day, but he knew his chance of success would be slim. The voices inside his head were screaming to go kill the wench, but one voice spoke calmly and clearly above the rest. Teah assured him he would have his day with Caldora, and today was not it. Keep on his path, she urged. We will prevail if we stick together. He closed his mind to the voices, not wanting to be distracted while he rode. If Caldora was this close, he didn't want to be daydreaming if he happened upon some of her troops.

Chapter 31

As they first set out, the Queen's Guard set a torrid pace and the Queen's mount almost fell several times. Talesaur wished to slow down to a safer rate, but Galena would hear nothing of it, pushing him to go even faster. Only when Rachel's horse fell, breaking a leg, did reason prevail.

The horse's screams of pain made Teah cringe. Galena put the animal out of its misery with a spell. The weave shone blood red, taking the form of a dagger, and pierced the horse's side. There was no blood since flesh actually wasn't being damaged, but the effect was the same as a real blade. A small shudder and the beast stilled. The men removed the saddle and the packs, taking them upon their own mounts, and Rachel mounted behind Lizzy. The party continued on.

Teah rode, looking around at her party. The men of the Queen's Guard were a finely tuned regiment, reacting to subtle hand gestures by Talesaur with precise movements. Talesaur scanned the surroundings continually, only pausing now and again to give a silent command.

He sat high in his saddle, proud and confident. His black and grey beard was trimmed neatly and his long salt and peppered hair was tied neatly in a tail. His chiseled cheek bones stood out nobly and his deep blue eyes saw everything. Even with is cloak on his muscles could be seen rippling underneath.

He was indeed quite handsome and striking as he moved around the party as they rode. He suddenly turned to Teah and their eyes met and held for a long moment. A slight smile crossed the captain's lips and his face turned a light crimson.

Teah's own face radiated heat. In looking away, she failed to see the snow-sodden tree looming before her.

The branch caught her across the chest. She pulled on the reins, but the slushy ground made the horse slip. Teah fell sharply off the saddle. She landed on her shoulder, a loud pop echoed through her head. She cried out, rolling to one side. Before she could attempt to sit up, Talesaur was beside her. So was Galena.

"Are you all right, my Queen?" the captain asked.

"I can't move my right arm," she gasped as her left hand clasped her right elbow.

"Let me take a look at it," Galena said, kneeling and touching the shoulder gently.

Teah shrunk away but Galena placed her hand a bit more firmly upon the shoulder and caught the girl's eye with her own. "I will not harm you, Teah. You must trust I only wish to heal you."

"Why would the Queen not trust you, Zele Magus?" the captain said the concern and warning evident in his voice. "Has she reason not to trust you?"

His hand went to the hilt of his sword.

"She has no reason to mistrust me. This I can assure you, Captain, and I would not do anything as foolish as drawing iron on a Zele Magus. Make sure your men are not foolish as well, for I will hold you personally responsible if I need to harm one of them."

"I guess you don't realize the connection between the Queen's Guard and the Queen of Ter Chadain as well as you should Zele Magus Galena," Talesaur replied. "Once the Queen's Guard has sworn fealty to a new queen, they are no longer in danger of being harmed by magic from any Zele Magus or Viri Magus. So I ask you once more, Zele Magus Galena, is there any reason Queen Teah should have fear of you?"

Teah saw a yellow weave hover over Galena in the shape of a human fist. Upon release Teah nearly cried out in warning to Talesaur, but before she could utter a word, a glow appeared around Talesaur and the spell broke apart a foot before reaching the man. It then winked out.

"Thank you for your concern, Captain, but Zele Galena does not mean me any harm. My reaction is from the tenderness of my shoulder."

The captain nodded, moving back from them and giving Galena room to work. Lizzy and Rachel were by her side, comforting her as Galena wove spells of healing. The pain intensified at first and Teah cried out, causing the men to take a few steps closer until she raised her left hand and stopped their advance. The pain then began to subside until it was a dull throbbing and she could move her shoulder with only a minor amount of stiffness.

"You need to stop daydreaming and concentrate on what

you're doing," Galena scolded her. "I cannot heal a broken neck."

"I'm fine. Thank you for healing my shoulder," she said rubbing it lightly. Turning to Talesaur, she asked, "How much longer before we can make camp to get dry and warm again?"

"I don't feel safe yet. If Caldora has learned of our change in course, she won't waste any time pursuing us. We should continue on as long as our mounts allow."

Teah frowned, rubbing her shoulder and lower back, shivering uncontrollably. She nodded, but her teeth chattered and her hands had turned a deep shade of blue while she lay in the snow.

"Maybe we could stop and warm by a fire for a short time, Captain," Galena suggested. "Enough time to take the chill out of the girls is all we really need."

Talesaur motioned for his men to start a fire.

Soon a small fire was burning warmly and the young women were drying themselves off to some extent. Galena wove a spell concealing the smoke and the men placed more wood upon the fire, pushing the flames higher.

Teah drew her traveling cloak close around her as she mounted her horse. Everyone turned to her and she nodded slightly. "It is time to move on. I feel my destiny pulling at my being, drawing me towards the future. Let us ride."

The men quickly extinguished the fire, rushing to mount up. They were heading down the road within minutes and she allowed herself one distractive thought to Logan.

Leave a piece of Caldora and the King for me.

Teah studied the girls riding double, making out the soft red glow of the deadly weave Galena had tied to them. Gazing harder at the magic, a smile curled the edge of Teah's red lips. She had discovered the tie to the weave. She set to work with carefully directed magic, riding more closely to them, leaving the Zele Magus a safe distance ahead. The threat would soon be neutralized, and then neither Galena nor anyone else would have that kind of hold over her again, ever.

Chapter 32

Logan rode with his head down keeping the snow out of his face, only occasionally scanning the surrounding landscape. The rolling terrain was scattered with trees. Saliday and Sasha kept their hoods thrown back, actively searching from side to side, weighing every object as a risk.

Smiling to himself, he recalled meeting each of them. First, Sasha with her driven loyalty to him and her people. Grinwald had warned him of her, and Galena wanted to throw her in the dungeon, but she had become a loyal friend and companion like none he ever had ever known.

Then, Saliday with her arrogant air. And the moment at their first campsite where she pressed so close to him, he felt her breath on his lips. How he would have given anything to feel those lips touching his. Warmth burned his face as the thoughts of desire touched his cheeks.

Why were his thoughts always so infuriating to him lately? If it wasn't the past protectors crying for him to take action, it was his sister urging him to stay the course. Now he had flirtatious impulses pressing him to make a fool of himself.

Catching movement off to his left, Sasha was in motion before he could react, racing to intercept a party of six soldiers moving in their direction.

Saliday was rushing after the Betra, shouting over her shoulder back at him, "If they alert the rest of their party, we won't escape."

She's right, Bastion exclaimed. *Go after them.*

Logan kicked his horse into the deeper snow.

The soldiers hadn't seen them as they dipped their heads against the snow. Sasha flew from her saddle just as one looked up. He fell dead as the Betra slashed his chest.

She dispatched the second of the six by the time Saliday joined her, hitting one of the men in the forehead with a thrown dagger as she leapt from her horse.

The remaining three men turned on the dismounted women with a flurry. Saliday retreated behind Sasha, her knives and short swords futile against the men's longer weapons. Sasha danced gracefully between her adversaries, meeting every strike blow for blow.

Logan jumped from his horse drawing his swords in one

smooth motion. One man was caught off balance and a light strike deflected the man's sword. Before he could attack a second time, Logan dropped him in the now bloody snow.

Sasha turned, sword extended. Logan ducked. As she spun, Logan went under her arm and took the head off the man spinning to attack the Betra again. In an instant the threat was gone and the three stood looking around for the last man.

He was a few yards away and turned to run in a panic. Logan threw one of his swords. It arched high in the air, and then sailed down, impaling him with a thud. The soldier crashed into the packed snow. His arms and legs twitched for a second, and then the latest victim of the Protector lay still.

Logan moved to him, noticing his pale skin. He pulled the cloak back. "I haven't seen many people since I left the farmstead, but this man seems to be very different from those who I have come across. Why is that?" He looked at Saliday and Sasha as they walked up.

"He is not from Ter Chadain," Saliday said, staring down at the man. "He is an invading Caltorian. They have infiltrated the army, and now the Caltorians have vast numbers within our nation's troops."

Caltorians, Bastion hissed. *They are a vile race, enslaving innocent people only because they were born with magic.*

Logan drew his blade from the body, taking snow and cleaning the blade, then wiping it dry on his cloak. They collected their horses and returned to the main road, setting off once more to the south.

Logan brooded as Saliday came up beside him.

"We couldn't risk Caldora finding us out here alone. The scouting party would have brought her troops down upon us. Killing them was very necessary."

"I still hate all the violence," Logan said softly. "I know it was what we needed to do, but I'm afraid I will never be able to remove myself from it."

"Your destiny is intertwined with violence. I know you find ending someone's existence repulsive, but it is who you are now."

It is what you need to do, Galiven said. *It doesn't have to be who you are.*

They rode on silently the rest of the day and into the night. No one asked to stop or suggested a rest, so they rode into the next day as well. They didn't encounter any more troops or another human being.

Logan questioned Sasha and she assured him it was normal. "No one ventures too close to the Forbidden," was all she said.

On the second night out, they did stop. They ate dried meat and bread beside a small campfire in silence, drinking water from a skin canteen Saliday carried on her saddle.

"I'll take the first watch," Logan said.

"The Betra don't allow wanderers in the Forbidden. There is no need to watch what is already being watched," Sasha said. "I know the pathway that only a Betra would know. We are not in any danger this night."

Logan lay awake in his bedding listening for signs of intruders, but when none came, he slowly fell asleep, mindful to place his mental partitions up. When he woke, Sasha and Saliday had already broken camp and were saddling their mounts.

"When were you going to wake me?" he asked.

"Don't worry, we wouldn't leave you." Saliday smiled.

"You needed your rest and now was the time to regain your strength," Sasha assured him. "We have three more day's ride until we get to our main city of Courage. There you will meet with the elders and tell them of your wishes."

Logan groaned. "How long before we enter the Forbidden?"

"We are in the Forbidden now," Sasha told him.

Logan looked around. He turned to Saliday who merely shrugged.

The trees were sparse compared to the Treebridge Forest, but they were still plentiful compared to the Latrel Plains. The snow here was deeper than at the Roundhouse, but the path was well worn and even cleared to the stone road lying underneath.

"Why do they call this the Forbidden?" he asked confused by the title.

Doesn't seem so foreboding now that we're here does it? Falcone asked.

"When the Queen banished us, she said we were to live in a land where no other people were allowed to live and trade with. The people of Ter Chadain were 'forbidden' to interact with us, and thus the people outside called this place the Forbidden."

"Why wouldn't you name it something different," Logan asked.

"We didn't see a need to name a place we did not wish to

be."

"Just changing the name may have made the exile more bearable," Saliday suggested.

"It is the isolation that has been such a painful part of this banishment. If we redeem ourselves in the eyes of the Lassains, then we can give the Forbidden a new name that will instill pride in our people and our new duchy. When the Queen sent us here, there were no roads, waterways, or trade routes out this far, but now the other duchies have expanded to touch our borders. We yearn for the acceptance back into the fold of Ter Chadain and all the riches and trade goods that go with it."

As Sasha spoke, her eyes peered off at some unseen vision. She pulled her mind and eyes away from the sight and back to Logan and Saliday. "One day we will be a strong member of this country once more and all of Ter Chadain will praise the Betra and their loyalty to the Lassain line."

Sasha mounted her horse and began riding down the road, forcing Logan to quickly collect his possessions. Saliday waited for him to mount and then they kicked their horses into a light canter.

The three travelers rode without incident all day and into the night, not encountering another living soul. They saw plenty of wildlife: deer, squirrels, rabbits, and pheasants. They ate their meal of dried meat and bread as they rode, not wanting to stop and delay their return to the Roundhouse.

In the evening of their fourth day, they came to a campsite with others already present. A large fire burned brightly. Several deer hung butchered in trees and the smell of cooking meat made their stomachs rumble uncontrollably before they had come to a stop.

As they entered, there was a scramble to draw weapons. It took an instant for them to recognize Sasha, and soon the entire camp rushed to greet her as she dismounted. Everyone, men and women alike, dressed similar to Sasha with black cloaks from head to toe. The men had bows across their backs or close at hand, while the women had a single sword, like Sasha's, strapped to their backs.

Saliday and Logan fidgeted in their saddles, removed from the joyous reunion for a moment. They finally dismounted, waiting on the edge of the group until the greetings were completed. An awkward silence fell upon the camp.

Sasha, smiling broadly, strode over and placed an arm around Saliday. "This is my friend Saliday Talis of the Tarkens, the great trackers. I wish you welcome her to our fold."

There was no hesitation as the entire camp surrounded her. Logan was pressed further outside the circle.

When every Betra had greeted Saliday with an embrace, Sasha turned to Logan and moved before him. She dropped to her knee.

"This is Logan Lassain, Protector of Ter Chadain and Redeemer to the Betra."

There was a moment of hesitation, and even a chuckle or two, as the camp looked at this boy standing before them.

Logan rolled his eyes and began removing his cloak to uncover the swords and the tattoo, but Sasha stood, quickly placing a hand on his shoulder.

She turned back to her people, eyes burning. "I will say this only once more without recourse, this is the Redeemer, the Protector of Ter Chadain, and our salvation from the curse and exile we now endure. Bow down to him, giving your loyalty as was foretold from the elders of old."

No one hesitated. The people dropped to a knee, swearing their lives to him. They remained in that position after the words stopped echoing through the campsite. Sasha, too, dropped to her knee and bowed her head.

"I am truly sorry you needed to see that, Master. I assure you it is not your worthiness causing our hesitation, but our own unworthiness to serve you."

She raised her eyes to meet his. Suddenly, he realized. They all wept. Tears ran down every bowed head. He turned to Saliday; she, too, was on her knee, crying.

He raised an eyebrow and cocked his head. Had she sworn her fealty to him as well?

"Get them up," he told Sasha softly.

Standing, she turned to them with a whoop, and the entire camp broke into celebration.

Wine skins were opened and passed around, accompanied by a lot of backslapping. Some younger women gathered together, whispering and stealing glances in his direction.

"Looks like you have some admirers," Saliday smirked, elbowing him.

Her red hair blew around her silken face and Logan took in

those green, piercing eyes. Warmth touched his cheeks, but too quickly Sasha and a group of her peers surrounded him.

"Come," she urged, taking his arm leading him to the fire. "You need to eat and share your adventure with the camp."

He turned his head, trying to maintain eye contact with Saliday. She didn't break the connection, holding his gaze with a knowing smile on her face. He nearly tripped over a log around the fire. The others around him caught him. Roughly, he settled onto a log.

"Tell us your story, Redeemer," a man called out and the others joined in. "There will be plenty of meat, but first the story." Logan grinned as they cheered.

"It all began a hot fall day," he started, telling them of his loss and revelation of who he was.

As he told his story, he searched the eyes of the Betra, finding the need for him to be their salvation, to be an end to their isolation all these years. He reached the part where Sasha entered their camp just outside the valley of the Protector's Fortress.

"Sasha," he called to her. "Tell your people how you joined us and became an invaluable part of our party to allow us to be here today."

Sasha balked for a moment, but at a reassuring nod from him, she gave a short nod in return and stepped to the center of the group by the large fire.

Logan silently slipped to one side and waited patiently, hands clasped behind his back.

"I came upon them as they camped against the wall of a steep cliff," she began and proceeded to tell her side of their adventure.

Logan watched as pride beamed from every Betra's face as Sasha shared the role she played in their travels. The Betra smiled broadly and nodded at different parts of the tale, looking to each other with pride.

Logan then glanced to Saliday. He started. She was watching him. He blushed and looked away. Looking back, he found her still staring with a knowing smile.

"That is when we met Saliday Talis," Sasha said in her recounting of events, causing Saliday to tear her eyes away from Logan and look to the Betra. "Saliday, would you honor us with the story when you came to be part of our group?"

Saliday looked back to Logan hesitantly and then strode up

next to Sasha with a large smile. "These two were in a definite fix," she said loudly and continued.

Logan listened intently, making eye contact with Saliday every now and then, causing her to smile even wider if that were possible. When she had finished, the entire camp clapped merrily and stood to surround Saliday and Sasha, clapping them on the back in congratulations for getting the Protector to them.

Logan walked off by himself between the tents.

Saliday found him. "What are you doing? Are you all right?"

"Fine," he hesitated. "This is what I am fighting for. As I looked from face to face, each more enthralled by the story than the last, I now know I fight for the common people. Not so much the dukes and duchesses, even though they are worthy, but the common people who are suffering under the King's rule and the invader's oppression.

"This is who I kill for and who needs Teah on the throne. My destiny now has faces, real faces I can place in my mind. Not the dead spirits of my father and mother, but the living reality of the people before me. The Betra have been waiting all these years for me to come along and free them from exile. The Betra who have brought this curse upon them have been long dead. It is time they are freed from that debt. That is another reason I need to put Teah upon the throne. She needs to remove the curse from the Betra and return them to the Ter Chadain society where they belong."

He gently grabbed her arms.

Sasha came over after wading through the praising Betra. She looked inquisitively from Saliday to Logan.

"I need to rest," Logan told her.

"There is a tent you can use over there." She motioned to a tent made of furs that could accommodate several people easily, even allowing them to stand inside if they desired.

"Thank you all," he said, walking to the shelter as the Betra parted, allowing him through.

A torch lit the tent; a stack of steaming rocks warmed the interior. As he shut the large flap behind him, a pair of hands covered in furs pushed through a smaller flap nearby. They placed new stones on the stack, removing some near the bottom of the pile.

Logan slipped off his cloak and unfastened his baldrics, letting the swords and then the sheath holding his bow, drop to the tent floor.

He took his outer clothing off, wrapping up in some furs, and sat down cross-legged by the stone stack. Soon he opened the front of the furs to cool down a bit.

Logan saw the hands appear a few more times and then he moved over to the pile of furs off to one side and laid down for some much needed rest. When he woke it was completely dark except for the red glow of freshly added stones. It must have been the sound of them arriving that awakened him.

But then he realized there was someone sitting on the edge of his bed. He sat up slowly, measuring the level of danger he was in, looking to where the shadows of his swords sat against some pillows, too far to reach.

Logan began to make his move, but a soft whisper came to his ear. "Relax, I won't hurt you." He stopped, facing the figure.

Saliday leaned in and their lips met for the first time. He kissed her as if he had known those lips forever. Logan parted his lips slightly, jutting his tongue into her mouth. Saliday let out a soft gasp, and soon her tongue was touching his, pushing into his mouth. It sent ripples of pleasure through both of them.

She pulled slowly away catching her breath as Logan gently took her hands, drawing them to his chest.

"I want this as much as you do," he said breathlessly, "but until a new queen sits on the throne and I can assure you will not be hurt, I am afraid to get too close."

The silence pressed on them as they sat facing each other, and then she leaned in, kissing him gently. When she finished, she placed her head to his chest.

"I have never met anyone like you before," she said so softly he strained to hear her. "I will be waiting for the time you feel you can give that part of yourself to me. Until then, I will not assume anything more than what you are willing to give."

Logan looked questioningly at the top of her head. Saliday tilted her head up and her mouth brushed his ear gently, her breath sending shivers down his spine. "If you think I won't kick your back side if you need it, or tell you your head is full of fodder, you are totally wrong." She bit his earlobe so hard she drew blood.

He let out a small cry, and even in the darkness, he could see her white smile. She then pressed her head against his chest, wrapping her arms around him, giving him a rough squeeze.

When he just sat there, she repeated the squeeze even rougher. His arms wrapped around her hugged her back.

"Here," he said to her as he stood and drew back the cover of furs. "You need to get some sleep."

"What about you?"

"I will sleep over here on these pillows. There are plenty of furs for covers and you haven't slept in a proper bed since we left Ceait. You and Sasha always insisted I take the bed"

"I can't take your bed," she protested.

"It is not up for discussion. I will see you in the morning," he said, crawling under some furs and turning his back to her. He closed his eyes, but his thoughts raced as quickly as his heart. He was slowly drifting off to sleep when he realized he hadn't partitioned off his mind from the dreams. This time he took hold of a new memory to help him keep the protector's visions away. It had happened only moments before and it involved a kiss.

The next morning Logan opened his eyes slowly, looking around puzzled. "Did I dream that?" he whispered to himself. Saliday was not inside the tent.

He grabbed his clothes, only to find them washed, dried and folded neatly next to the hot rock pile. He put them on, strapped his swords across his back, tied the sheath to his belt, and then covered them with his cloak.

Outside, he squinted, taking in the camp. The only tent left was his. A handful of Betra remained around the fire, but they stood as soon as they saw him and began breaking down his tent.

Saliday, sitting at the fire, motioned him over, handing him breakfast. He looked at her, but she didn't betray any emotion. As he took a bite of the venison sandwich, she glanced up at him with a knowing smile. He smiled back with relief.

Sasha came walking up after giving instructions about tearing down the tent.

"I hope you two are ready?" She asked. "We have wasted hours of good travel time because your courtship rituals tired you out last night. You should have warned me you two are courting. I would have made arrangements to give you more time alone on our journey."

"We didn't know we were going to be courting until last night," Saliday smiled. "You must remember, people outside the

Forbidden don't betroth or court until they are at least Logan's age."

Sasha looked from one to the other, appalled.

"Betra are betrothed by our parents at an early age and wed after our training is complete, in our late teens. If you are not betrothed by sixteen, you will not likely become married."

Saliday and Logan shared curious stares. "Did you say that Betra are usually married by their late teens?" Logan asked.

"That is correct. Why is that so strange?"

"Not strange, but how old are you?" Logan asked gingerly.

"I am twenty years," she replied, then quickly continued when seeing the distressed faces before her. "I am not included in those statistics. I follow a different set of rules than the other Betra."

Her answer only deepened the looks of concern coming from Saliday and Logan.

"I mean that I took a vow when choosing to be the one sent to find you," she said to Logan.

"What kind of vow?" Saliday asked, causing Sasha to turn to her.

"I am sworn to marry only one man, when he chooses, if he chooses."

"Who is this man?" Logan asked.

Sasha turned slowly, her face showing the underlying sadness as she glanced back at Saliday. "That would be you, Protector Redeemer Logan. I am betrothed only to you."

Logan glanced around Sasha to Saliday. His shock was reflected in her face.

Logan could feel anxiety coming from the protectors, but they remained silent.

"It has been done this ways for almost five hundred years, Redeemer. It has worked well for us. The one given the responsibility to find the protector when he returns never marries. I am quite lucky; all the ones who preceded me never had the slightest chance of becoming married since the protector never came in their lifetime. At least there is a chance, even if very small, that you may choose to marry me, though I know that is not very likely now," she added, looking at Saliday.

Logan sat shaking his head as Saliday looked curiously at Sasha.

"Sasha, what is that name you call Logan now?"

"Redeemer?"

Saliday shook her head.

"Redeemer means the Protector Returned, or the One Who has come to save us."

"Why haven't you called him that before?"

"He was never truly returned to the Betra until last night."

"Wait a minute," Logan interrupted, frowning, "I'm still confused about this betrothing. The Betra expect me to marry you?"

"Only if you so choose. We would never force you into a marriage. If you don't find me desirable, then we need not wed."

"It isn't that you aren't desirable, Sasha," Logan said comforting. "I am not ready to marry anyone. Not yet at least. I have so much else to do that marrying is about the farthest thing from my mind."

"Maybe you should consider it," Sasha said, stone faced.

Logan looked at her in shock.

"Not for me, but for the Lassain lineage. If you were to fail in your mission and be killed, you would want an heir to carry on the possibility to reclaim the throne."

He couldn't argue that point, but he looked to Saliday uncertainly.

"We don't need to decide anything right now." Saliday said with a devious smile on her face that vanished when Logan turned to her. Saliday shrugged and looked back to Sasha.

Chapter 33

Teah blew the hair from her face in frustration. She worked on the magical weave around Lizzy and Rachel for nearly four days and had barely loosened the knot.

She pulled at the fastening with a thread of green magic, enveloping the red. Her patience was wearing thin and she needed to replace the weave with a spell of her own so Galena wouldn't be able to tell hers was gone.

She stopped her spell and trickled a new line to the threads. This line was red. Her red magic intertwined with Galena's magic, and Teah pulled hard. The threads sprang free and fell apart, vanishing into nothing. The unexpected result nearly caused her to fall from her horse.

With the weave gone, Teah cast another spell but with a twist. It was a dangerous spell, so it also bore the red woven magic of Galena's spell, but this time the spell was protective of the two girls, only harming those who sought to do them harm.

Securing the spell in place, Teah gave a deep sigh.

They rode on in silence, some men moving ahead and some bringing up the rear. The Queen's Guard was a well-trained unit, the men rotating turns of riding near the three girls. Talesaur would give a series of hand signals and a few men would branch off from the main road and ride into the woods to protect their sides.

The trees became more plentiful all the time and the snowfall lessened and then stopped. The temperature rose as well and soon the branches dripped with melting snow.

Teah glanced back at Galena, catching her attempts to send weaves at members of the guard. The weave would harmlessly fall apart and the man would radiate with the faint glow of the protective spell. The woman furrowed her brow in concentration and then began weaving again.

As the company crested a rise, the landscape changed vastly. The road winded through rolling hills dotted by little homesteads. Lights could bee seen in the windows and smoke curled out of the chimneys as the sun set before them.

Talesaur rode over to Teah, his arm gesturing wide. "Welcome to Stalosten, Queen Teah, home of my birth."

Teah showed surprise. "I thought you're from Ter Chadain Duchy?"

"Your guard comes from all across the country of Ter Chadain. Our loyalty to our own duchy is then put aside as we swear loyalty to only the true Queen of Ter Chadain." Talesaur bowed deeply.

"We will be sleeping indoors tomorrow night," Galena said. "There is an inn not far off and they will be overjoyed to have me in their company again." She rode past them without stopping and Rachel, with Lizzy behind her, passed them as well.

Teah watched them pass without response. She looked to Talesaur, smiling feebly. "I'm not sure I'll ever get use to being a queen, Talesaur."

"Some might say the best queens are the ones who are queens out of duty, not out of comfort," Talesaur smiled as a light shone in his eyes. He nodded his head, riding after Galena and the others while the men bringing up the rear of the company waited on her patiently.

Suddenly her cheeks blushed and her temperature rose. The sensations came from Logan.

She kicked her horse into motion, following the others into Stalosten. A second kick brought her mount to a canter and soon Teah rode next to Lizzy and Rachel.

They camped a short distance from the road that night and were back in the saddle early the next morning. The temperature seemed warmer in the valley and soon the snow gave way to green and golden fields filled with growing crops. The fields were in different stages of harvest with stacks of crops lining the sides of the road.

They rode all day and into the night, passing many homes. The people working outside stopped their farming and watched the parade. Those inside stared out the windows. The company continued on until coming to a large structure along the road with a number of out buildings housing livestock.

Galena dismounted. "Stay here. Captain, please send a group of four men to stay in a room next to us and a number of men to stay in the common room. The rest can make camp along the side of the inn and rotate at the entrances to assure nothing endangers the Queen."

"I'm well aware of my responsibilities, Zele Galena," he said with a stiff bow.

Galena didn't respond, but went inside the inn while the others dismounted, some men taking the horses to the stables.

Rachel, Lizzy, and Teah dismounted and stood off by themselves, a few of the men staying close. Teah held her precious cargo hidden in her bedroll in her arms.

"I can't wait to sleep in a bed again," Rachel said, stretching her arms over her head.

"Me, too," Lizzy nodded. "I wonder what a hot meal will taste like."

"And to think, we are on this adventure because we decided to befriend the new girl," Rachel quipped.

"You should feel privileged to be a friend to the Queen of Ter Chadain," Talesaur said, causing the girls to jump. None of them had seen him taking the post behind them. "Don't let her kindness delude your understanding of the power and authority she commands. She is still the Queen of all Ter Chadain no matter what duchy you call your home."

Rachel turned red, her mouth working without any words coming out. Only a slight gurgling sound emerged until she slammed it shut with a snap.

"I'm sure she didn't mean anything by it, Talesaur," Teah assured him.

"I do hope you are right, my Queen," he bowed and stepped back stiffening to attention.

"Wow, so they really are loyal only to you?" Lizzy asked.

"I guess so," Teah shrugged.

"That is so incredible," Lizzy giggled. "Isn't it, Rachel?" Rachel didn't answer, but stood looking at the ground.

"Rachel," Teah said, putting a hand on the girl's lowered chin and raising it gently until their eyes met. "I will never doubt your friendship, as I hope you will never question mine?"

Rachel didn't speak but shook her head without looking away. She lunged forward, embracing Teah. Teah's eyes widened and mouth dropped open, only thinking to return the hug after a moment. Lizzy joined in and the three had a group hug.

"Isn't that touching?" Galena said as she came out of the inn.

The girls awkwardly separated and faced the Zele Magus.

"I have gotten the three of you a room and I will be in the quarters next to you. You can send your men in to assure they are familiar with the layout," she added to the captain. He nodded and moved off to assure it was taken care of. Galena motioned for the girls to follow.

A large common room was cramped with chairs, benches, and tables filled with people. On one side of the room was a bar, and on the other side, a huge fireplace.

A woman stood singing on the raised hearth of the fireplace next to a seated man playing a stringed instrument. There was a very small bald man behind the bar, along with a huge woman who filled the space behind the wooden counter, nearly squeezing the little man into the corner.

Teah laughed, but then put her hands over her mouth. The little man dipped below the bar on one side of the woman, only to emerge on the other side an instant later.

But only the singer and minstrel seemed to take note of their presence at all. Their heads turned, following the group to the stairs. Teah watched them, too, climbing slowly, until they disappeared from view.

Midway down a shadowy hallway, they stopped at a doorway as a guard came out. He nodded to Talesaur; the room was clear. The three girls were motioned in.

Sconces were lit on the walls and a fire glowed in the hearth. Four cots lined the wall opposite the fire and a small table with four chairs sat in the middle of the room.

"Guards at every door at all times," Galena said to Talesaur. The captain nodded. "Good night, ladies, I will see you in the morning. There will be food brought up shortly." The Zele Magus turned and left the room ahead of Talesaur, who bowed, shutting the door.

The three girls each took a cot and began to undress. Teah slipped her bedroll under the edge of her bed. A knock came. They covered up and Rachel opened the door. Talesaur entered with a tray of food.

He turned to leave, and then hesitated as he glanced at the girls. "If you leave your clothing with the men outside the door, I will see to it they are cleaned and ready for you to wear tomorrow." He left without waiting for an answer.

The girls went to the tray of hot meat, potatoes and bread. The juices dripped down their chins and the room was silent except for the crunching and chewing of food. It was if they hadn't eaten in weeks.

After there were only scraps left, they took off their traveling garments and were about to pass them through the door to the guard when Teah stopped.

"I have a better idea," Teah explained. "Let's stay covered for a while longer and you will see."

Teah stuck her head out of the door for a moment, speaking to a guard. True to her word, a knock came a little while later. Six guards carried in three tubs. They pushed the table and chairs to one side of the room and stacked the cots so there was enough room to set the tubs by the fire.

The girls' eyes lit up. They grinned as more guards entered with water. A serving girl came in after the tubs were full to assist them, and then gathered their clothing.

As they relaxed in the steaming water, Teah sent a message to Logan. She was safe; she was near to her destination; she felt good.

Chapter 34

They rode on for another day, finally reaching Courage.

"I feel very exposed now that the swords are visible to everyone," Logan said looking around. The weather had grown increasingly warmer and the cloaks were packed away.

"There is no longer a need to hide who you are. The return of the Redeemer is a joyous occasion, and there is no one in the Forbidden who would want you harmed," Sasha reassured him.

News of their arrival preceded them. They passed several homes where people came out of the house, shouting to them. Thousands of people crowded to get a closer look at the Redeemer. Skepticism showed on many faces.

Looking at Saliday on his right, her smile fell on him, betraying all her feelings.

Blushing, Logan turned away.

Sasha grinned and Logan straightened uncomfortably.

Proceeding along the crowded stone streets in between white stone buildings, he looked up at people on the roofs as well. He caught the eye of a young boy; doubt was evident.

"We will meet the elders here later," Sasha said, stopping in front a large building. She dismounted. "One of the stable hands will show you to a room to clean up before we do. I will see you have clean clothing to change into." She strode into the building without looking back at them.

Logan and Saliday looked at each other. Several young boys came to collect their horses and one youth bowed deeply, motioning for them to follow him.

Passing through a doorway, they emerged into a large courtyard with many green plants and trees. Doors of various shapes and sizes lined the yard. The boy led them to a doorway with a pointed arch at the top. Painted a bright red, it hurt to look at it. The boy opened the door and bowed with an extended hand. They entered, the door closing behind them, leaving them alone in the massive room beyond.

Walls rose to nearly twenty feet high, curving smoothly to form the ceiling. The ceiling was painted with a beautiful landscape showing rolling hills and an enormous mountain range behind. To one side, the waves of a large body of water showed white on their tips.

The far side of the room, open arches led to a private courtyard. Couches, tables, and chairs were scattered throughout the room, spilling over onto the paved veranda with nearly a hundred pillows piled upon it. Every color known to Logan met his eyes—as well as many he had never seen. To one side of the room was a large overstuffed bed, its pillared legs reaching up to brush the ceiling. Sheets of see-through material in various colors intertwined with the pillars all the way down the wooden legs.

Logan gawked.

He smiled as Saliday wandered through the room, too overwhelmed to notice him.

There was a basin and a large changing screen on the opposite side of the room. Removing his shirt, Logan began to wash his face and upper body.

A warm and refreshing breeze flowed into the room, caressing his body, drying the moisture from his skin. He gave his head a shake to get the water from his hair. He turned. Saliday stared at him.

Her gaze was not upon his face but on his chest. He glanced down at his tattoo.

She came close, placing her head on his shoulder, taking her finger and tracing the symbol.

Breathing her scent in deeply, for a moment he forgot why they were in Courage.

"We have to get cleaned up before we meet the elders," he said in a cracking voice.

"Then I better wash up," she said as she pulled the screen between them.

Logan flushed red, quickly turning away. He stood frozen for a time, and then went over to the bed where clothing was laid out for the two of them. Looking around, there was no one in sight. Lifting up the shirt, he saw his emblem embroidered on the left breast.

Thinking of his chain mail, Logan touched his arm. The shimmering shirt appeared. Checking over his shoulder to see if Saliday had notice, he released the mail and quickly put on the shirt.

The grey shirt had black sleeves and collar. It fit perfectly across his muscular build. He took the pants holding the black material up for inspection and then slipped them on.

A thought came to Logan as he was standing there. *I am traveling to Sharlet in Stalosten Duchy,* Teah told him.

Safe travel, sister, Logan replied. **I am about to meet with the elders of the Betra. We will have an army to support you soon.**

There was a tap on his shoulder a short time later and he turned and smiled broadly.

Saliday had let down her red hair. It flowed past her shoulders but was pulled back away from her face and fastened with a hair comb adorned with emeralds. She wore a floor-length emerald dress with a long slit on one side nearly reaching up to her hip.

She sat down to fasten delicate string shoes with a moderate heel. Logan stared, mouth open, at her. She made to leave; pausing long enough to push closed his gaping mouth.

"I think it is time to meet these elders," she cooed.

Logan quickly pulled on the black leather boots supplied for him, and then followed her out of the room. They stood in the outer courtyard for a moment, not knowing where to go.

Sasha appeared out of nowhere. "It is time for the elders to see you now, Redeemer," she said with a bow, her traditional black cloak rippling with her motion.

She led them along the walkway in the courtyard. They entered a small vestibule with two enormous doors open onto a massive room lined with chairs on risers. People of every shape and size, and a considerable numbers of silver heads, sat within them.

They walked forward on a rug of red velvet lined with gold. Dark black stone formed the floor. The carpet brought Logan to five stately men standing on a raised dais. Beside each man sat a lady.

The voices started in his head and he muffled them behind his barrier. It took incredible concentration holding them there, but he needed a clear mind.

The oldest of the women was elevated above the rest. She bowed slightly and addressed him.

"We welcome the Redeemer to our city and are overjoyed at your return to the Betra. I speak for the elder's council and the entire race of the Betra when I say we accept you as the return of the protector to our world. Sasha has foretold of your authenticity and we accept the word of the chosen seeker of the protector."

Sasha bowed deeply to the council.

"We understand you have come to gather our forces for a war with the pretender King who now sits on the Ter Chadain throne. Will you lead the force directly or would you require some of our commanders to accompany you and assist in the operations?"

"I would be honored if your commanders would lend their assistance to me," he bowed his head slightly. "I would also like to keep Sasha with me as an advisor since she has proven herself to me many times over the past few weeks."

"That will be allowed," the elder said, turning to each side and receiving nods of agreement. "Now, what is your goal with our forces?"

"I intend to join with the forces of the southern duchies and march to Cordlain to kill King Englewood. We will secure the city, driving off the Caltorians who have infiltrated the country's forces in order to allow my sister to take her rightful place on the throne."

"Taking Cordlain may prove very debilitating for your forces. It is the most heavily fortified city in all of Ter Chadain. What would happen if you killed the King first, then marched upon the city?" the elder said, rubbing her chin absently in thought. "Do you think if you take the head off the beast the rest of the beast would fall?"

"I suppose it would. Only the King keeps the alliance with the Caltorians together. If he were gone, I believe the good people of Ter Chadain would rally to drive them out. If it were only that easy; we must lay siege to Cordlain and take it in order to reach the King."

"Perhaps not," the elder smiled, turning to the others. They smiled as well. "What if I said you could get into the castle in Cordlain without spilling any blood?"

"That would be incredible if it were possible," Logan started.

"It is possible, very possible," she said smiling, "If you were to use the Protector's Doorway."

The crowd let out a collective gasp. Sasha jolted. He looked with confusion at her, then at the faces confronting him.

"What is the Protector's Doorway?"

"It is a pathway for you to get inside of Cordlain. It is the way the protectors of old kept in touch with the Queen in Cordlain. It was thought to be lost, but we know its location. It is possibly your key to striking a deadly blow to the king and crippling the opposing army."

Logan released the protector's voices from his barrier.

I thought it was destroyed, Bastion murmured.

As did I, admitted Falcone, and then Stalwart.

It was then that all knew the responsibility lay with Galiven.

Logan inhaled. When he glanced to Saliday, her grin matched those of the elders on the dais.

"What are we waiting for? Let's go kill us a king."

Chapter 35

Teah sat by the window as the sun came up over the rise of a hill not far off. It was a very sleepless night for her; she couldn't get the images of the last time she had stayed in an inn out of her mind.

As she sat, she noticed a movement off to the south. At first she thought she was seeing things, but then the images became clearer.

She glanced down to the members of her guard standing watch. They couldn't see as far as her. She swung open the window with a bang. The men jumped.

"Caldora and her troops are coming from the east not more than two miles out," she shouted.

Chaos broke loose. She hurriedly woke Lizzy and Rachel. A gong sounded outside. Within seconds, Galena was through the door, hurrying them out of the room and down the stairs. Teah barely had time to finish fastening the sheath containing her bow or to grab her bed roll before scurrying down the staircase after them.

A few patrons eating an early breakfast stared at them as they raced through the common room.

Just before the exit, a man so large he dwarfed the door opening, stepped before them and blocked their way.

Teah ran into the backs of Lizzy and Rachel as they stopped abruptly.

Galena leaped ahead of Lizzy, but another man rushed forward, swinging a club. The Zele Magus flew into the bar, crumpling to the ground in a heap.

The girls screamed.

Two more men grabbed Rachel and Lizzy. The man with the club moved slowly towards Teah.

"We can do this the easy way or the hard way," he said through missing and crooked teeth, patting the club into his empty hand.

Teah cast a spell to hurtle the man backwards. Her magic parted around him harmlessly.

"Shankan," she hissed.

The realization struck her; she knew at once what she needed to do. Moving so fast she defied time and space, she drew the two protector swords from her bedroll and confronted him.

Shock spread on his face, then amusement. He straightened casually and towered over her. His laughter ignited the other men's humor, and soon, all laughed loudly.

"Little girl, you should never draw a blade on anyone unless you intend to kill them with it."

"What makes you so sure I'm not prepared to do that?" she said in a low, menacing voice.

She twirled the blades into a continuous barrier of sharp steel.

With a roar, the man lunged, club high, going for a knock out blow.

She raised her hands. The club was sliced into pieces. The man's right arm flew off. He fell to the floor, his blood arcing across the room.

The other men wasted no time but charged her. The two men holding the young girls flung them to the side. Three blades of steel shone bright in each hand.

Teah spun in a complete circle. She avoided the lunging blades and severed any appendage containing a weapon. The three men joined their comrade in a bloody pile.

The scene was ghastly

Teah sheathed her blades. Instead of hiding them, she strapped the baldrics across her chest and tossed the bed roll away. The time for concealment was now over.

Motioning for Lizzy and Rachel to pick up Galena, Teah drew her blades once more. The four women rushed out the door.

The guards battled a larger number of Caldora's troops in the muddy courtyard red with blood.

Teah spotted Talesaur battling three men. She rushed in.

Talesaur took the man he faced in the chest and turned to witness Teah in a deadly dance with the other two men. She gracefully moved one way and then, precisely, spun with swords held high to take one man's head off. As the decapitated body fell to the ground, she continued her rotation, dropping down on one knee then striking upward with both blades, impaling the last man through his chest. She pulled her blades free as he crumpled to the ground.

"My Queen," he gasped from exertion and horror. He stared at her swords. "You need to get yourself to safety while we guard your retreat."

"I will go nowhere without my guard," she smiled. "Gather your men and we will retreat to the north. Have you seen Caldora?"

"Not yet. I'm betting she's waiting for her men to clean us up before she comes and claims her prize. I doubt she knew how much teeth her prize possessed."

"I doubt she did," Teah chuckled. "Now go get the horses, we all ride out of here this morning."

Every man who saw her, friend or foe was caught up in astonishment as Teah unleashed her blades into the fray. She was the mistress of death that day and anyone who stood before her spinning and twirling blades fell mortally wounded. She moved from one battle to the next, removing limbs and ending lives in a blink of an eye. When it was over, she ran to the horses, pausing only to tear a cloak from a corpse and wipe the blades with it as she hurried to mount up, slipping the blades back into their sheaths.

Soon the guards, Lizzy, Rachel, and Teah were riding hard to the north with the battlefield behind them, the pursuing Caldora surely close at their heels.

Galena bounced unconscious across the front of Talesaur's saddle as the man pushed his horse harder.

They finally stopped. Galena's breathing was faint; Teah listened to her chest as Rachel and Lizzy hovered close by. Placing her hands on the woman's head, Teah trickled a small amount of healing magic into her, absorbing the pain herself. She cried out, falling into Talesaur's arms.

Teah took a moment to recover her strength and checked on the men with Lizzy and Rachel to assure none of their injuries were life threatening.

She came up to Lizzy as the girl mended a broken leg. "That's very good Lizzy," Teah smiled wearily.

Lizzy turned with a start when Teah spoke; disgust and fear contorted her features as she backed away.

"What's the matter with you?" Teah asked as she spread her arms to her side with open palms.

"What you did to those men back there," Lizzy began, but stopped suddenly, fear creeping through her features once more.

"I'm not going to hurt you Lizzy," Teah pleaded taking another step towards the girl.

"How long will that last?" Rachel said sharply, coming up next to Lizzy, placing a comforting arm across her shivering shoulders.

"You are my friends," Teah gasped. "I would never hurt you. You have to believe me."

"The brutality you showed today is nothing either of us has ever witnessed before, nor is it the kind of behavior we have ever heard of coming from a queen." Rachel glowered back at her, then her eyes dropped and she took an uneasy step back.

"What would you know of a queen's behavior?" Teah shouted, "Either of you?" Teah spun and rushed away. It took every ounce of self control she had not to run, but a queen didn't run. She moved around a clump of trees, leaning against them and looking up to the sky as she slid to a sitting position. The tears ran down her face as she fought for control, her breath coming in gasps.

"My Queen," Talesaur said coming around the trees.

Teah abruptly came to her feet, wiping the tears from her eyes with the sleeve of her dress. "What is it, Captain?"

"I didn't mean to interrupt," he stuttered. "Is there anything I can do for you?"

"I'm very tired. That's all," she said shaking her head.

Without another word, Talesaur walked up to her as she tilted her head to look at his face towering over her. Pain reflected in his eyes and he smiled softly down at her. He encircled her with his arms.

Teah's eyes shot wide as her cheek pressed against his chest. She could hear his heart racing almost as fast as hers did inside her chest.

"You saved us all today. Without your leadership and skills, Caldora would have had her way with us. Don't let a couple of girls' fear put doubt in your ability to be queen."

She leaned back and peered up at him. His confident face flushed and he began to release her from his embrace, but she pulled him roughly back to her.

"Talesaur, you would do anything that I asked, wouldn't you?" She leaned her cheek against his chest again.

"Of course."

"Do you think I'm evil, like Rachel and Lizzy?"

"They are foolish girls who forget their place by questioning the Queen's behavior.

Teah looked up once more as Talesaur bent, gently pressing his lips to her forehead. He held her tightly for a moment longer and drew her against his chest once more.

Silence surrounded them for a moment and then a call for Talesaur came from the other side of the trees.

"We must go," he said looking down at her, their eyes meeting and their understanding acknowledged.

They walked from behind the trees into the make-shift camp and Talesaur went one way as Teah went the other. Her soft smile was subtle as was his quickened step, but she watched after him as he strode away.

Teah moved to prepare her horse and get back on the road to Logan. She needed to reunite with him if she were going to survive.

They rode hard and she fought to keep her last meal down, the nausea pushing at her insides. The ownership of the title 'Protector' took on a new meaning. Killing was now a part of her, as it had become a part of Logan. She needed to find her brother, the one person who could assure her that she wasn't an evil person. One of the few people, she corrected, who knew she wasn't evil. She smiled as she watched the captain maneuver his men in formation, looking at him in a new light.

Chapter 36

Logan stared at the silver doorframe before him, the swords now strapped to his back and the bow fastened to his belt. It stood neatly against a block wall.

The elders gathered behind him, five women and five men. Saliday and Sasha stood by his side changed out of their formal attire back into their traveling clothes, also examining the glistening doorframe. Saliday shrugged.

Sasha touched the frame gingerly. Her hand snapped back. "It is ice cold," she whispered.

Logan touched the frame, immediately drawing back, too. He looked to the Seeker, and then extended his hand out again. He didn't touch the frame this time. Instead, he put his hand into the space within the frame. His hand brushed against the stone.

Then his hand passed through the rock.

Logan recoiled.

Saliday reached out to touch the same block as he. The stone held fast without change. Her eyebrow rose and she turned her face up to his, motioning for him to try it again.

Logan looked to the elders; none showing any emotion, but observed in stoic silence. The Protector placed his hand to the block once more, this time extending his entire arm into the block. It turned to liquid. He slowly pulled it free, looking at his arm as he turned it.

Sasha tried to duplicate his feat but met resistance like Saliday.

"Didn't we say it was the Protector's Doorway?" the elder explained as the three spun to her. "Only the Protector can use the doorway. It was a way for him to stay in constant contact with the Queen in Cordlain. When we were exiled here, we brought the doorway with us in the event it would prove useful to the new protector when he returned to us."

"This will take me to the palace in Cordlain?" Logan asked.

"If that is where the other doorway still resides," the elder smiled. "If they have moved it to another location as we have, then it will take you there. There is an easy way to find out."

Logan nodded. "If I go through the doorway, I will know if it is still in the palace at Cordlain."

He took a step closer, reaching his hands out carefully. As his hands touched the stones, they once again liquefied.

He stepped through.

There was no sensation to it. It was no different than walking through the doorway leading into the chamber where the silver frame stood, but he now stood in total darkness, except for a thin line of light a short distance off along the floor.

He crept towards the light with his hands out before him, feeling for obstacles until he touched a wooden door. Fumbling for the latch, he located the metal device, lifting slowly. When the latch would move no further, he pulled the door inward just enough to peer out.

The outer corridor appeared deserted with torches burning sparsely along its length. The stonework was very old and dampness seeped through the blocks. Deep within the room behind him, a silver frame identical to the one in Forbidden glistened darkly.

Waiting there for a long time without witnessing anyone pass, he left the door slightly open, moving back to the room where Sasha, Saliday and the elders waited.

"Is it still in the palace?" Saliday asked excitedly.

"I think so, but I have never been to the palace in Cordlain before. I saw very old stonework and the hallway seemed to be very long."

"That very well could be the palace, but further investigation is needed to be sure," the elder said. "You need to go back and continue your search for the King."

Logan knew he was right. If he could find the King and kill him, the entire conflict could be over in mere weeks. What if the King was surrounded by hundreds of men and Logan was killed? That would also end the rebellion in mere weeks. Uncertainty must have been evident on his face as Saliday wrapped her arms around him, worry in her deep brown eyes.

"You are the Protector, you will not fail. I would go with you if I could, but it seems I can't."

"Maybe we can," Sasha said, placing a reassuring hand on his shoulder. "Each of us tried to enter the doorway individually. Maybe if each of us took a hand, we all could pass through the portal."

"It is worth a try," Logan shrugged, hope returning to his features. "Are we ready?"

Saliday stepped to his right, taking his hand; Sasha did the same at his left.

They looked back at the elders. They smiled and nodded approval one by one. "May Redeemer return victorious to his people," the head elder said.

Logan looked at the door, then at Saliday and Sasha. After getting a nod of assurance from each, they strode forward together. Just like before, there was no sign they had passed through a magical portal, but they stood in the dimly lit room Logan had just left moments before.

The door still stood ajar, letting the light filter into the room in a thin stream.

Feeling more assured now they were with him, he slipped silently out of the room. Stopping for a moment to get his bearings, a swelling of confidence surged through him. The old protectors broke through his mind's barrier.

There are secret corridors and stairs throughout the palace, Falcone told him.

How would you know that? Bastion asked.

I had many female, uh, companions before I found my true love Caderal, Falcone admitted. *These passageways proved quite useful.*

Logan moved ahead.

Motioning the women to follow, he stepped quickly and with a purpose. Logan came to another room not far down the hallway and took a torch from the wall. Holding the door for the women to enter, he then closed it quietly behind them.

Just as the door was shutting, footsteps echoed.

Logan and the others stiffened. The footfalls came steadily closer. Then, they paused outside the door of the room. Logan leaned forcibly against the door. Someone tried opening it from the outside.

Suddenly three men pushed their way into the room. Logan slammed into the far wall.

Sasha and Saliday were upon the men. Sasha took a hit on her right leg as a man swung his sword downward. She thrust a dagger into his gut. He cried out and fell to the floor.

Saliday dodged the swinging sword of another man. She drew her knife. A flick of her wrist and the man fell with her dagger stuck in his throat.

Logan wrestled with the biggest man, someone much larger than he. Logan pushed him off with his legs. As the man fell to the floor, Sasha and Saliday attacked, the Betra plunging her sword into his chest and the Tarken slitting his throat.

The women rested leaning against the wall as Logan caught his breath bent over with his hands grasping his legs above the knees, panting.

"Thank you," he said in the dim light of the torch. "Are you all right?"

"Sasha is injured," Saliday told him.

"I'm fine. It is just a shallow cut," she said as she tore fabric from her cloak and tied it over the wound in her leg.

"Are you sure?" Logan asked. "I can take you back through the doorway."

"Don't be foolish," Sasha scolded. "I am here to protect you. I'll be fine, where to next?"

"I know where the King should be and I know how to get there. Behind this wall," he pointed to the stone block wall he rested on, "is a secret passage leading to the protector's chambers. Since there is no protector, I'm not sure who will be in them, but attached to these are the royal chambers where the King should be.

"I intend to enter the protector's chambers, subdue anyone present, and then proceed to the royal chambers. We must use extreme stealth, so quietly kill the occupants of the first chambers if need be. Do you understand?"

Both women nodded.

He placed a hand to one of the blocks. It moved slightly inward and the wall slid away, revealing a winding staircase. Carrying the torch, Logan led them up. The wall slid back into place behind them.

Only their soft footfalls echoed in their ears. After many stairs they came to a small landing before a wooden wall. Logan lifted a finger to his lips. He placed his ear against the wall. With a nod, he doused the torch and pushed. They burst into the room.

The ring of steel broke the silence. For the first time in over five hundred years, the protector's blades came alive in the palace.

A startled figure jolted up in a four-post bed. Saliday and

Sasha leapt upon the confused person while Logan crossed the room, pushing aside a heavy wooden door and springing through the opening.

He was at the side of the bed in two strides, one of the ancient blades to the neck of each of the bed's occupants.

A muffled sound came from the other chamber as Sasha and Saliday dragged in their prisoner. Saliday lit a lantern on a nearby table. A young man struggled against Sasha. The lantern revealed the hostages of the blades.

Logan smiled. A man in his fifties and a woman in her thirties lay motionless under the steel. Fear and tears welled up in the woman's eyes, but the man glared at Logan, hatred creeping through every pore of his being. There was no mistaking this man. This was the King of Ter Chadain.

Logan motioned to Sasha to move to the woman's side of the bed. Logan lifted the blade and Sasha restrained the woman, ripping off a tieback from the bed curtains and lacing up her wrists. Sasha stripped off the pillowcase and shoved it into the woman's mouth.

Logan placed both swords across the King's neck, the tips of the blades framing the man's head.

"So this is the new Protector of Ter Chadain," the King snarled, "sneaking around the palace like a common criminal to assassinate the ruler of his land."

"I will not get into any debate with you about assassination or sneaking around the palace," Logan said calmly. The Protector's voices were strangely silent.

"I have come to finish what you have started and you have no one to blame for your fate but yourself. I'm merely the justice which has been dealt you by destiny since your first act of treason upon the throne of Ter Chadain."

"Listen to the young whelp sounding all philosophical. The least you can do is to allow me to fight for my life and not die lying on my back in bed unarmed."

Logan stopped for a moment then stepped back, withdrawing the blades, causing them to ring anew. He turned to Sasha who immediately barricaded the exit.

"If you think you are up to the challenge of facing the Protector of Ter Chadain in a duel, you may try, but let me assure you, I have no intention of letting you live any longer than needed to give a dying man his last request."

Logan saw an ornate baldric hanging above a dressing table, a bejeweled pommel jutting from it. Reaching over with a sword, he unsheathed the weapon with a flick of his wrist, sending the blade hurtling to the King. The King caught it adeptly in one hand.

The King instantly lunged at Logan. Logan easily turned the attack to one side and deflected the continuing offensive to the other. The King spun and pressed the onslaught as quickly as he could, closing the distance between them.

He was as large as Logan, but much heavier, moving with deceptive speed and agility. He came at Logan again, swinging the weapon over his head. Logan stopped the blade's advance between his two swords, creating an instance of stillness. The King's blade quivered over Logan's head, inches from reaching its mark.

A slight twist of his wrist was all it took to shatter the King's sword into pieces. Gasps swept through the room. The two protector's blades came quickly down into the chest of the King.

The man's eyes stared at Logan in disbelief, then down at the steel penetrating his chest. He hadn't even had a chance to release the pommel of his broken sword or to lower his arms. He fell backwards, the blades pulling free from his body as he slumped to the floor, dead.

The two captives cried out through their gags and tears flooded their eyes. Logan looked from the woman to the young man, and then to Sasha and Saliday. The women seemed unaffected by the cries, elation filling their faces.

Chapter 37

Almost instantly, pounding came at the door. When they made no response, the cries from the hall increased and soon the door shook with the effort of men trying to break in.

"Take them into the next room and return here once they are secured," Logan told Sasha and Saliday. They did as he said. The door began to give.

"Take the barricade from the door and then come stand on either side of me," he said pulling a chair to where he stood. Taking his baldrics off, Logan cast them to the side, sitting down with the protector's blades crossing his lap, the blood of the dead king still dripping from the steel.

He held this pose. As soon as Sasha and Saliday took away the furniture, the door flung open. The first men stopped upon seeing them, but others pressed from behind, causing them to stumble forward a few paces before halting once more. The dead king was easily visible to any who looked into the chamber.

A loud commanding voice resounded in the hall. The men hastily parted. A large bearded man in an officer's uniform burst into the room. He froze in his tracks, the long purple scar along the side of his face quivering, upon seeing the deceased king.

With a cry of rage he drew his long sword and raced at Logan. Logan made no attempt to move. Just as the man lunged, he stopped short and his eyes grew wide. He stood motionless for what seemed an eternity, and then toppled face first onto the floor with a sword protruding from his back.

Complete silence engulfed the room for a moment, and then a cheer went up from the guards, echoing out the door and down the hallway. A man stepped timidly forward, retrieving his sword from the commander's back and wiping the blood from his blade.

He gave a slight bow and dropped to a knee, holding his sword in raised palms above his bowed head. Soon there many blades were drawn and held over bowed heads on bent knees.

"I proclaim fealty to the true Protector of Ter Chadain and the true queen he represents. May we aid in the reclaiming of Ter

Chadain from the false king and all his agents, including the Caltorians from across the great sea."

Once the man had finished his vow, a chorus of the same vow followed as hundreds swore loyalty to Logan and his sister.

Logan sat in that very spot with Sasha and Saliday by his side all day and night, and then into the next day, as person upon person in the palace came swearing loyalty to the Lassain lineage.

Guards removed the two captives, but the King's body remained on the floor, upon Logan's request, so all may see and be assured this king would not return to enslave them or their country again. Logan, Sasha, and Saliday did not take food nor drink during that time, attending to all who wished to come before the Protector. The next evening, the stream of people finally stopped, and the first guard who had knelt to him once again stood before Logan.

"I beg your pardon, Protector, but I have taken the liberty of having some nourishment prepared for you and your companions. Will you allow the servants to enter and set up for your meal?"

Logan nodded.

"Will you allow men to come and remove the King's body?"

Logan again nodded he would allow it.

Logan, Sasha, and Saliday had not spoken more than a few words during the entire time and as he turned to Saliday. Nothing came out as he placed his hand upon his throat.

Saliday took a pitcher and goblet from a tray, pouring him some wine and handing it to him. He drank without saying anything, but releasing a long sigh.

Looking at his swords covered in the dry blood, Logan felt no remorse. A young serving boy came before him with a wet towel, extending it to him. Logan took the cloth, wiping clean the ancient blades as the guards carried the body out of the room. The blades shone bright, erasing the last sign of Logan's wrath. The vengeance filling him the past few weeks washed out of him.

"No place of honor for that one," he said hoarsely. "A grave outside the city with a simple headstone showing nothing but his name of birth is all this traitor to the crown shall have."

Logan finished cleaning the blades then handed the rag to the boy.

"Please take these and throw them into a fire. I want no remnants of this man left in this city. Do the same with the rags being used to clean the floor," he added, pointing to the three women cleaning the blood off the wooden floors next to the bed. The linens had already been taken and the bedding lay in a bundle.

He stood stiffly with the help of Sasha and Saliday, and they sat down in exhaustion as he stretched. They'd stood beside him the entire time and he took this time to prepare plates of food for each of them.

He stood eating some bread when an older woman entered, standing quietly with bowed head. Logan cleared his throat and took another drink of wine. "What can I do for you, my lady?"

"I come to you to ask your mercy upon the queen and her son, the prince." She visibly cringed when speaking the titles, covering her mouth with her hands.

"If you are speaking of the woman and young man who we captured in these chambers, I have no qualm with them. I do ask you not address them in that manner ever again." He didn't raise his voice or change his tone, but there was no doubting the insistence behind the request.

"I'm sorry." She fell to the floor, prostrate. "I've been the boy's nanny since his birth and have never called them anything else."

"That is why I do not fault you for doing so this last time."

He looked to the guard standing by the door. "Bring them to me."

The man left. Shortly the two captives stood before him without bonds or gags. Their eyes were red from their sorrow.

He looked with no ill intent upon them. It was the King who had destroyed his life and set him upon this path. Certainly not this boy with head lowered. The slender youth was much smaller than Logan and only the small growth of red facial hair exposed his age.

The woman looked Logan in the eye. She held her head high and didn't hide her contempt for him.

"I hold you both as victims in the struggle for Ter Chadain," he began. "I wish you no further harm and will send you on your way as soon as the fighting within and around the city have quieted."

Both Saliday and Sasha rushed forward.

"Are you crazy?" Saliday whispered.

"I must agree with her, Redeemer," Sasha added. "If you let them leave, they will undoubtedly continue a revolution against you until they have succeeded or else have perished. You must remove them as a threat to the throne now."

Logan grimaced. "Kill these two innocent bystanders because they were connected to my enemy? I would be no better than Englewood if I were to start thinking in that manner. What lies beyond the Forbidden of the Betra?"

The question caught Sasha off guard, but she regained her composure. "Nothing, I mean, there is only wilderness. No settlements or civilizations are beyond our borders, but we do cover a large area."

"What is the southernmost city or settlement in the Forbidden?" Logan pressed.

"There is a very small village called Sacrifice. Only those who do not wish to deal with the obligations of the Betra retreat there and are left to their own means. There can't be more than twenty families there."

"Perfect." Logan turned to his captives. "You will be exiled to the land of the Betra in a village called Sacrifice. There you will be allowed to live out your days. If you try to leave Sacrifice or the Forbidden, the Betra will kill you on sight. Your needs will be met to assure your survival, but that is all. There will be no servants or guards to tend you."

"You might as well kill us now," screamed the woman. "You're giving us a death sentence."

"As your husband did to my family," Logan replied, his voice not changing in volume or pitch.

"Your family was an atrocity to Ter Chadain," the boy spoke, each word quivering with rage. "My father was trying to purge the filth of your kind from this land, and he would have, if you and your witch sister hadn't escaped. My only regret is I don't have a sword right now to finish what he could not."

Logan quickly took Sasha's sword from her scabbard, flinging in at the boy, the blade scraping across the floor to stop at his feet. It happened so rapidly everyone was caught off guard. But the boy instantly bent to retrieve it.

He brandished the blade, looking at Logan, the hate welling up in his eyes. Logan didn't move, but sat down with his blades in their scabbards and his hands resting lightly in his lap.

Sasha and Saliday began to move between Logan and the boy, but a raised hand from the Protector stopped them short.

The boy saw this and lunged at Logan, swinging the blade down with a powerful killing strike.

Logan reached up with both hands stopping the blade in mid-air a fraction from his face. Try as he might, the boy could not drive his sword any closer, nor could he withdraw the blade from between Logan's hands.

"I have given you the same chance your father had, which is much more than he has given my family."

He spoke to the woman who stood with a shocked expression across her face. "Take your son and live in peace in Sacrifice. If I ever see either of you again, it will be the last breaths you take. Is that understood?"

The woman shook her head, looking at her son still struggling to move the suspended sword.

Logan glanced at the boy, waiting for him to make eye contact with him. "Do you understand the conditions of your survival?"

The boy released the sword and it hung there ominously for a moment before Logan turned to Sasha. She took hold of the pommel and he released it.

She sheathed the sword smoothly and waited.

Logan looked toward the boy again. His head hung lower than when he had first entered.

"I will bring them to Courage through the doorway and the elders will see they get to Sacrifice," Logan explained to Sasha. "Make the arrangements and I will see to it later." She nodded her understanding, motioning for the guard to take the two away again.

Once they were gone, Logan looked at his hands. There was not a mark on them from the sword.

Saliday and Sasha were upon him instantly.

"How could you be so reckless?" Saliday said, flailing her arms.

"You cannot continually put yourself into dangerous situations and expect to come through unscathed," Sasha added.

He hardly heard a word they said when a thought came into his head.

I am coming north to find you, brother, Teah said. *Caldora is close behind.*

How did you know I was to the north? He asked.

I just knew, she replied.

I will send some soldiers to escort you to Cordlain safely. Where are you now?

There was a pause and then she told him. *We are in Stalosten, heading for Mellastock. I'm not sure if Caldora has support in both of those duchies.*

The King is dead and we have taken the throne. You need to get to us as soon as possible. He looked to Saliday, "Get me the commander of my army."

"I think that was him you met earlier with a sword in his back," she said.

"I mean the commander who is now in charge of the army loyal to me."

"I'll be right back," she said. A short while later she returned with a tall, dark skinned man at her side. His wide dark eyes showed fear.

"This is Commander Utherid," she said as the commander bowed deeply. "He was the commander under your mother and father and has been imprisoned the last five years when the Caltorians took over the troops and he protested."

"I'm proud to meet a man of integrity, commander," Logan smiled. "I need you to send two hundred men to meet my sister's party and escort them here safely. She is in the company of about a hundred Queen's Guard, but she could use your help as well."

"Talesaur is a good man, I'm sure he has things well in hand." The man smiled back.

"I doubt you not, but Caldora is chasing them and we need to assure her safety."

Upon hearing that name, Caldora, the smile left the Commander's face. "She is an evil and vile woman. I will send three hundred men."

"Very good, make it happen." Logan said, and the man turned away, striding from the room.

Logan sent the word to Teah.

Thank you, brother, she replied. *Talesaur said we should be able to stay ahead of them for three or more days, but Cordlain is almost a week off.*

Logan was glad to hear that. They should be able to stay ahead of Caldora long enough for the troops to reach them. *I*

will speak with you later, he told her, and then turned to the business of preparing for her arrival.

He made the trip to Courage and deposited his prisoners with the elders of the Betra to take to Sacrifice. The order was given that the woman and her son were to be left alone, but watched by the Betra to assure that they did not leave Sacrifice or try to stir up any trouble. A party of ten warriors was stationed in Sacrifice to see to Logan's orders and to report back to the elders on occasion. He then returned through the doorway and formed his plans for the Caltorians.

As the days passed, he spoke frequently with Teah. They were still ahead of Caldora when she said they spotted the three-hundred troops not far off. Talesaur was off scouting and most of the men were around the main camp, setting up to meet the incoming troops.

I can't wait to see you again, she sighed.

Me, too, he agreed.

He was working on some details in the throne room when her voice came to him excitedly. *The troops are here. I'm about to meet the Captain Ordestan and join you in a few days. I will see you then. Goodbye, brother.*

Later that day Commander Utherid came in to report on the troops as he did everyday.

"The troops from the Betra and the southern duchies have arrived in Brinstad and made camp around the Roundhouse," Captain Utherid told him. "They will begin their march to Cordlain in two days after they have all resupplied and rested. The duchy generals are not too happy about following Betra commands. I have ordered that armies shall follow my orders which I have given to each general. That way no one is ordering another's army except me by your command."

"Good," Logan smiled, looking up from the large map spread out on the table before him. "Have you any word on the Ter Chadian Army that is still under the control of the Caltorian generals?"

"They seem to be moving off to the west towards the coastline. We suspect they are headed for reinforcements being sent over from Caltoria. If we can get to them before more troops land, we have a chance to weaken their support and influence across all of Ter Chadain"

"We will corner them on the coast before they can fan out

and cause us greater problems. Have all the generals from the southern duchies and the commanders of the Betra troops report to me as soon as they arrive in Cordlain. Are you seeing any resistance from the northern duchies?"

"The dukes and duchesses appear to be taking a wait-and-see attitude. Some have substantial Caltorian presence in their duchies and they are not ready to choose a side until they can determine which side will win. Cowards," Utherid scowled. "They need to have something to believe in. That is why we must sweep across the duchies with our troops and scour the Caltorians from our lands."

"Oh, yes," Logan agreed. "By the way, the troops and Captain Ordestan have reached Teah. She will be here safely in no time."

The commander stood staring at Logan, his jaw working, but nothing coming out.

"What is it?"

The words exited his mouth in an almost indiscernible whisper. "We have no Captain Ordestan."

~*~*~

This Ends Book One of "The Protector of Ter Chadain" series.

Made in the USA
Charleston, SC
03 December 2012